THE RUTHLESS RICE

A PROVENCE COZY MYSTERY

JULIE CAVALLO INVESTIGATES

ANA T. DREW

CONTENTS

FREE BOOKS

ABOUT THE AUTHOR

Ana T. Drew is the evil mastermind behind a recent string of murders in the fictional French town of Beldoc. A first-place winner of the Chanticleer MYSTERY & MAYHEM Awards, her books have been released in several languages, both independently and through traditional houses, including HarperCollins France and Straarup & Co.

When she's not plotting mysteries, Ana can be found perfecting her low-carb cookie recipes or watching *The Rookie* to cope with the void left by *Castle*.

Ana lives in Paris with her husband and their dog, but her heart resides in Provence.

Website: ana-drew.com

amazon.com/author/ana-drew

x.com/AnaTDrew

facebook.com/AnaDrewAuthor

bookbub.com/authors/ana-t-drew

goodreads.com/anadrew

CHAPTER 1

I stand on tiptoe and crane my neck. "That's it, I'm getting a periscope for the next parade!"

Next to me, Gabriel is completely engrossed in the charming extravaganza. I pout, annoyed. Outdoor processions are so much more fun for someone like him because he's tall enough to see over people's heads! Don't get me wrong—I'm not complaining about my boyfriend being tall. I'm just stating a fact.

Gabriel points to my sneakers. "Next time, wear your platform shoes."

"They're uncomfortable."

"Climb on my shoulders?" He flashes a smile. "You'll see everything, and I'll get a workout. Win-win."

Though tempted, I shake my head, reluctant to draw attention. I prefer to lurk in the background and observe, thank you very much. My sisters are like me, even Flo. The only adult in the family who enjoys standing out in a crowd is my grandmother Rose. She lives to be noticed. That's fine for her current activities and even desirable as an elected queen of our town, Beldoc. But it might pose a problem the day she gets her license to become a PI.

"Julie, stand on my feet," Gabriel says.

I look at his sturdy shoes and take him up on the offer.

Ah, finally! I can see!

The Fête du Riz is winding its way down the Boulevard d'Émile Combes where we stand, surrounded by a compact crowd. The exuberant, joyously nostalgic procession displays every generation of Arlesians, all decked out in eighteenth-century costumes.

The men wear hats and formal suits with ties or bow ties. Almost all the women wear the iconic *Arlésienne* dress. It consists of a long skirt, lace breastplate, pretty shawl, choker with the Provençal cross, and, last but not least, a flirty mini headdress that sits high on the head.

Rose owns an Arlésienne and often wears it when on official duty as Queen of Beldoc.

The delicious smell of churros reaches my nose and overrides all other thoughts. I sniff the air around me. The scent must be coming from a food truck somewhere behind us. The moment I realize this, I know exactly what my boyfriend and I will do next. *Find that truck!* Because Julie Cavallo, the sophisticated pastry chef trained at the Cordon Bleu school in Paris, simply can't resist the olfactory call of deep-fried dough.

The rumbling of wheels and clanking of metal redirect my attention to the parade. Colorful floats glide onto the boulevard. Kids and grownups alike cheer with delight. Decorated with all things Provençal such as bees, lavender, rosemary, and olives, the floats celebrate the flavors of southern life.

A marching band follows, playing their *galoubets-tambourins*—Provençal flute-and-drum sets.

"Look, Julie, cowboys!" Gabriel exclaims.

I follow his gaze to the line of dashing Camargue cowboys, their horses neatly trotting. My head is far from the only one to turn in that direction. A hush falls over the boisterous crowd as a dozen of these mounted *gardians* make their entrance amid the pageantry of the parade. Dressed in their traditional attire of black hats, crisp white shirts, embroidered vests, and dark trousers tucked into tall leather boots with rounded toes, they ooze rugged charm and pride in their heritage.

Their white horses prance with a grace that matches that of their riders. From my elevated position atop Gabriel's feet, I listen to the rhythmic click-clack of hooves and gawk at the cowboys. Their hats are tipped at a uniquely debonair angle, casting shadows on their faces tanned by a life in the open air.

One of the riders is paler than the others. I take a closer look at him, and my heart skips a beat.

Can it be? Is this really the elusive man I've been trying to track down for years? Am I looking at the man responsible for my mother's death? *Yes, I think so.*

"It's him," I whisper to Gabriel, my voice trembling.

"Who?" he asks.

"The beach house contractor."

There's a brief pause. "Are you sure?"

"Positive."

He tilts his head toward mine. "Where? Point with your chin."

"The third *gardian* from our side," I say, already moving. "We have to follow him!"

We push our way through the throng, dodging small children and sidestepping enthusiastic festivalgoers. The crowd thickens, making it harder to keep the riders in sight.

I glance back at Gabriel, my blood boiling with urgency. "Keep up!"

"I'm right behind you!"

As we weave through the sea of people, I do my best to keep my eyes locked on the man who's now at the back of the group of cowboys. He turns his head and looks over his shoulder as if he senses our pursuit. My heart pounds in my chest.

I can't lose him. Not again!

The parade turns a corner, and the crowd surges, pushing us back. The riders slip out of sight for a moment. Sticky, nauseating panic flares in my stomach. I grab Gabriel's hand tightly and pull him forward with renewed urgency.

"There!" he gasps, spotting the horses again.

The boulevard narrows, funneling the parade and the crowd into a tighter space. We press on. My shoulders brush against strangers, my breath comes in strained gasps. Gabriel stays close. His eyes are fixed ahead, and his hand is clasping mine.

"Julie, watch out!" he warns.

We dodge two small kids.

The riders start to pick up speed. We accelerate, too, but the crowd around us continues to grow. As does my frustration. *What if he gets away?*

We reach a particularly dense cluster of people. Gabriel steps in front of me and tries to push through, but the mass of bodies blocking our path seems to solidify into an impenetrable wall. I frantically scan the area for an opening. There is none. When I turn back, my heart drops as I see the riders vanish one by one around the sharp bend.

"Nooo!" I yell in helpless rage.

Tears of frustration well up, and I slam a fist into my palm.

Gabriel puts a hand on my shoulder. "Julie, we'll find him."

I wipe away the tears. "I can't believe I lost him again. He was right there!"

"Let's try the side streets."

I nod, fighting defeatism with all I have. We turn away from the main boulevard and duck into a narrow alley that runs parallel to the parade route. The noise of the crowd fades, replaced by the echo of our footsteps against the cobblestones. A glimmer of hope returns.

Gabriel points to another alley that curves back toward the main route. "We can cut through here."

"Let's hurry!"

We streak down the alley flanked by nondescript buildings that loom over us on either side. As we approach its end, the distant sounds of the procession grow louder. My pulse quickens. *There's a chance we might catch up.*

We burst out onto the main street and find ourselves at the edge of the crowd. The parade is still underway, but the riders are nowhere to be seen. I squint, straining to find them as I catch my breath.

"Do you see him?" I ask Gabriel.

He shakes his head. "He's gone. All the gardians are gone."

I let out an angry curse.

He squeezes my hand. "We'll find him, Julie! We're getting closer. Next time, we won't let him slip away."

I want to believe him, to take comfort in his words. But after nineteen years of chasing a man as elusive as a ghost, it's hard to hold onto hope. The thought of another failed attempt fills me with trepidation.

Will I ever catch him?

Doubt consumes me, but I push it away. I'll never give up. I'll never stop looking.

And, maybe, just maybe, next time I won't let him get away.

CHAPTER 2

Eric boxes up the last of the éclairs, while I collect the payment. We watch the customer leave with a satisfied smile. She's shopped here before. Not quite a regular yet but getting there.

The thought brings a smile to my face, chasing the concerns.

My sous chef turns to me. "We're doing great so far today, Chef!"

"We are." I lean against the counter. "But it's not today that worries me."

Eric raises an eyebrow. "You're still having doubts about Ritzy Rice? Why? You're going to come out on top."

"It's not that simple."

"Yes, it is," he counters. "A prestigious culinary competition right here in our hometown was an opportunity not to be missed. So, you signed up—"

"No, you and Gabriel browbeat me into signing up," I correct him.

"And I'm not going to apologize for that. You'll thank us later."

"Only if I win," I point out. "If I don't, this whole thing could come back to bite me."

I don't spell it out, but Eric knows as well as I do that *The Rampal Guide to the Gastronomic Gems of Provence* can make or break a business.

He wipes the counter. "Your two recipes for the competition are terrific. You've got this."

I'll be making a rosemary and honey Camargue red rice pudding for the first round and an Arborio rice and almond milk flan for the second. Eric and I spent the last week perfecting the recipes. We also had everyone in our entourage taste the successive iterations and give us feedback. If my execution is flawless, I believe I do have a chance. But if my nerves get the better of me...

"You have nothing to worry about, Chef," Eric insists.

I chew on my lip. "Are the potential rewards really worth the risk? Am I right to put my business, and our livelihoods, on the line?"

"If you win, it'll be a game changer for us," he says. "Julie's Gluten-Free Delights in the *Rampal Guide* with a glowing review and five lavender sprigs? Imagine the sales boost! We'll have people lining up outside the shop."

"But what if I fail? One bad review from Seraphin Rampal could ruin us."

Eric dismisses my fears with a casual wave of his hand. "You're overthinking it, Chef."

"Remember Ugo Drugeon and his fancy restaurant in Cavaillon? It went from always full to half empty overnight, and all because Rampal stripped him of two lavender sprigs in one go!"

Eric rolls his eyes. "It's a temporary effect, I'm sure. If Chef Drugeon lowers his prices, his customers will return. He just needs to ride out the storm."

"Maybe you're right," I say. "Gabriel and I actually like the food he makes."

He casts a look at the door. "Let's taste the flan again while we're alone to remind you why you're going to win."

We each take a spoonful.

I let the creamy texture and delicate flavors melt in my mouth. "It's pretty good."

He scoffs. "It's *incredible*. Trust me, Rampal will be blown away."

I set a dreamy gaze on the wall. "If your prediction comes true, we could hang the certificate right here next to the window, fire Flo, and hire a motivated full-time shop assistant."

"A full-time salesperson would be gre— Did you just say, 'fire Flo'?"

"I should've fired her months ago."

He knits his eyebrows. "But she's your little sister, and she's fun, and she needs this part-time job."

"What she needs is to work up the courage to tell her boss at the gallery to give her a full-time contract."

"Then why don't you wait until she does that, and only fire her if the gallery says yes?"

"Because, if she asks and they say yes, I won't get to tell her 'You're fired!'," I explain. "She'll text me 'I quit!' the second she signs her full-time contract."

He shakes his head. "Nah, she'll call you. It's a matter of courtesy."

"This is Florence Cavallo we're talking about," I remind him, "the woman who most of the time acts like I work for her, and not the other way around."

He considers my words. "True. Anyway, I've been meaning to ask: Was Gabriel able to ID the gardian from the Fête du Riz?"

I groan. "He's working on it."

"Do you have a theory yet? Would you like to bounce some ideas off FERJ?"

I shake my head. FERJ is what we call our little detective group, including Flo, Eric, my grandmother Rose and yours truly, Julie—hence the acronym. All of us are amateurs. Well, except for Rose, who can be considered a semipro, as she's been taking an online PI course and hopes to get her license soon.

Right on cue, Rose sails into the shop with her spaniel, Lady, trotting beside her. She gives me a barrage of happy licks. I'm talking about Lady, of course.

Rose blows an air-kiss to Eric and me. "Julie, you need to come with me right now!"

"What's wrong?" I ask, alarmed.

"It's Victor," she replies. "I'm mobilizing everyone I can to attend the municipal council meeting."

Lady yips in support.

Eric gives me a reassuring nod. "Go ahead, Chef. I've got things under control, and Flo should be here any minute now."

"All right." I untie my apron.

Rose is already halfway out the door.

I hurry to catch up, nearly tripping over Lady. "Will you tell me what exactly is going on?"

"Our dear mayor is planning to ruin the rice festival in Beldoc!" Rose practically spits with rage.

"What? How?"

"That fool wants to radically change the way we celebrate it! You see, Provençal traditions aren't good enough for him." Grandma purses her lips.

Here we go again, I think to myself.

Every now and then, the mayor of Beldoc, Victor Jacquet, tries to force-feed his idea of modernity to our small town. It often backfires. His Christmas tree ban was a total fiasco. The public urinal in front of Magda's shop resulted in a catfight at the council meeting, and the subsequent removal of said urinal. The refractory denizens of Beldoc push back every time, and Victor caves in, loath to risk his seat in the next election.

Fun fact: the younger, bra-burning hippie version of Rose would've applauded Victor's efforts. But like many, Grandma has grown more conservative with age—and more appreciative of all the unnecessary things that give a place a soul.

That's partly why she entered the traditional Queens of Provence pageant, and why she ran as Victor's challenger for mayor of Beldoc—the main reason being that she needed the money. Rose was elected Queen of Beldoc. Victor managed to stay on as mayor. And so, Rose became the leader of the opposition. True to her title, she makes it a point to oppose Victor at every turn.

"Hasn't our mayor learned anything from his previous debacles?" I wonder aloud as we join Igor and Magda waiting outside.

Igor sighs. "Apparently not."

Rose shakes her fist in the direction of the town hall. "And he chose this special month of September, the Camargue rice month, to annoy us again!"

"This protest better be quick," Magda says. "I've left Leslie in charge."

Leslie moved to Beldoc two months ago in early July. Magda hired her less than two weeks ago at the end of August.

"Weren't you satisfied with her performance?" I ask Magda, lowering my voice.

"I am," she confirms. "Her prior experience shows. But minding two shops at once is hard. Even for me it was a challenge, and I'm the best salesperson in the universe."

"Our protest will take as long as it needs," Rose declares, adopting her Gran Boss tone. "The people of Beldoc deserve our best effort."

Magda checks her watch. "*My* protest will take forty-five minutes. After that, the people of Beldoc are on their own."

CHAPTER 3

Our protest group snowballs as we march toward the town hall. Rose's cronies join us, looking like they're ready to storm the Bastille. Shop owners who have skin in the game, a young reporter from *Beldoc Live* with a camera dangling from her neck, and a bunch of concerned citizens all flock to our cause. By the time we reach the council room, we're a full-fledged mob.

We burst in with a cacophony of excited voices and waving hands. Victor looks up from the notes in front of him. When he spots Rose among the protesters, he narrows his eyes. Chantal, his unfazed secretary, ushers us to the vacant seats.

"Rose and uh... everyone," Victor says, "I'm glad you could join us."

"No, you're not," Rose snaps. "You scheduled this meeting last night, hoping I wouldn't see the email in time to make it."

She hands Lady to her bestie Sarah, strides to the front, and stands with her hands akimbo. "Let's hear your latest bright idea."

"I thought it was time to modernize the rice festival," Victor says.

Magda stands up. "You mean ruin it?"

"How do you propose to modernize our festival, Mayor?" Igor asks politely.

Victor adjusts his glasses. "For example, instead of the boat parade, we'll host an international seminar on decolonizing rice production around the world as part of the intersectional struggle against imperialism."

"Indeed, nothing says 'festival' like a PowerPoint with graphs," Igor teases him gently.

The room erupts in laughter.

Victor, desperate to regain control, gestures to a man sitting by his side. "This is our consultant from Paris, Romain Chauvet. He plans events."

Chauvet nods to us with an air of self-importance that makes Victoria Beckham appear humble. He's tall, thin as a reed, and impeccably dressed. His hair is faux disheveled. Trendy eyeglasses complete the look of a man who spends more time in art galleries than at country fairs. He's styled himself so that no one would think he grew up anywhere near a rice field.

"Thank you, Victor," Chauvet says to the mayor, before turning back to the room. "Distinguished fellow humans, I'm thrilled to be here today!"

What's wrong with ladies and gentlemen? I itch to ask.

Next to me, Magda whispers something to Igor, but all I can make out is "Parisian snob."

"It is time to bring your Camargue rice festival into the modern era!" Chauvet enthuses. "Your mayor and I see this year's celebrations as an opportunity to replace the narrow-minded local stereotypes with the broad-minded global ones."

Igor whispers to Magda and me, "Is it me, or does he

want the Camargue rice festival without the Camargue in it?"

"The events we've planned include the antihegemonic seminar that Victor mentioned," Chauvet goes on, "but also exhibitions on the ecofeminism of Afghanistan's poppy fields, the toxic masculinity of Europe's weekend barbecues, and so much more!"

The crowd remains silent, processing his buzzwords.

"We've budgeted two evenings of musical activism," Chauvet adds.

Since no one cheers, Victor fills the awkward lull. "It's time to look beyond the local and embrace the global!"

The room boos.

Igor leans over to me. "Could this be a prank?"

"I'm afraid they're serious," I say.

Believing he's on a roll, Chauvet continues. "There will be interactive installations where visitors can immerse themselves in the history of rice through the prism of class, race, and gender."

"Boring!" Magda shouts.

People laugh.

"I think I speak for everyone here," Rose chimes in, "when I say that we prefer our usual ways of celebrating rice month."

"Well, then you all need to be educated," Chauvet says.

I stare at him, impressed. He's so unshaken in his belief that he knows better than us how we should celebrate Camargue rice it's almost endearing.

"And to kick off the Ritzy Rice culinary competition," he says, "we'll have an expert who'll deconstruct the reactionary narratives and open our minds to new global perspectives."

Rose clears her throat. "Let's put this proposed lecture to a vote. I know how much Victor values democracy, so I'm sure he's totally fine with it."

Chauvet sends Victor a *Mayday!* look.

Victor shifts uncomfortably in his seat but doesn't dare to object.

Rose turns to the room. "All in favor of this educational experience?"

Not a single hand goes up.

Chauvet looks around, visibly thrown. His smugness shrinks while Rose's expands in beautifully inverse proportion.

She grins. "And all opposed?"

Every hand in the room shoots up. Even Victor's loyal secretary, Chantal, lifts her hand. His deputy, Clothilde, has both hands in the air.

"Motion carried!" Rose declares triumphantly. "The lecture is off the agenda of Ritzy Rice."

"Here in the South," Magda says to the consultant. "We don't deconstruct our rice. We eat it."

Laughter ripples through the room. Rose sits down.

"Well, that was unfortunate," Chauvet says. "I'll have to find another slot in the festival program for the lecture. We might have to cancel the farandole."

The room erupts again. Canceling the favorite folk dance of Provence isn't something the Beldocians can be strong-armed into accepting. Loud voices overlap, all speaking at once. Once again, Rose leads the charge. Victor is fuming. Chauvet adjusts his glasses, looking more and more like a lost boy. Clothilde tries to defuse the situation but fails.

Maybe I can do it.

I stand up to command attention. "Did you know that the Ritzy Rice contestants will be making sushi, pilaf, chili con carne, and all sorts of international dishes? Global perspectives guaranteed!"

Chauvet lifts his eyes skyward as if he's losing patience

with us hicks. "You can't cook your way out of bourgeois small-mindedness, madame!"

"What a load of—" I clamp a hand over my mouth.

Zip it, Julie! Better not to rattle our mayor's cage any more than Rose has already done.

"We don't want this year's rice month to be another boring ode to the glorious past," Victor jumps in. "I want Beldoc to drink the tonic of disruption!"

"More like Kool-Aid," I mutter.

Chauvet points a finger at me. "That, right there, is exactly the reactionary attitude we need to move away from!"

"What did I do?" I flash my palms in a show of innocence.

Curling his lip, the consultant turns to Victor. "Monsieur Jacquet, you commissioned a plan, and I delivered one. But your townsfolk aren't ideologically ripe for it."

"Then help them ripen!" Victor pleads.

"I'll do what I can, but I don't deal in miracles."

Victor's shoulders slump in defeat as he looks from Rose to me and then to the rest of the room. "We'll keep the farandole, the boat parade, and the food market, but we'll also host most of Monsieur Chauvet's events. Deal?"

I know an olive branch when I see one. "That sounds great," I say quickly, before Rose can intervene. "Thanks for being so democratic, *Monsieur le Maire!*"

He responds with a weary smile.

Chantal claps. "The meeting is adjourned! Thank you, everyone!"

As we leave the town hall, Igor turns to Rose. "You think Victor will keep his word?"

"Yes," Grandma replies. "He has many flaws, but underhandedness isn't one of them."

CHAPTER 4

The emcee, a local radio personality, takes center stage and announces in the mic, "Ladies and Gentlemen, please welcome our next chef, the incomparable Loïc Parion!"

Loïc struts down the red carpet like he's on a fashion runway. The crowd bursts into applause.

The small Roman amphitheater where the event is set provides a picturesque backdrop to the scene. Olive trees surround the ancient stone walls. Colorful banners flutter in the breeze that carries the scent of ripe grapes from the vineyards mixed with the herbal notes of rosemary and thyme from the garrigue scrubland.

"Loïc is known for his risottos that can make a grown man cry," the emcee informs the audience. "He once turned down an offer from a five-star hotel in Paris to stay in Provence."

Loïc reaches his workstation on the left side of the stage, where the savory chefs will be making rice-based dishes. He gives a bow and busies himself rearranging his ingredients.

"Next up," the emcee announces, "please welcome Colette Leclerc, the queen of fish stew!"

Colette waltzes down the carpet.

"Colette can debone a sea bass and a whiting faster than you can say '*bouillabaisse*'," the emcee jokes.

Colette takes her place on the left side, blows kisses to the crowd, and begins to prep her station.

The emcee's voice booms again, "And now, please welcome Julie Cavallo, the goddess of gluten-free pastries!"

I take a deep breath and step onto the red carpet, laser focused on not tripping over my own feet. The crowd claps. I flash a quick smile to Rose and Gabriel, who are cheering me on from the sidelines.

When I reach the right side of the stage, where we sweet chefs will be making desserts, I wave to the audience. Once the attention shifts away from me, I pick up a whisk, just to feel the familiar comfort of a tool in my hand. It doesn't really help.

The announcement of Ugo Drugeon pulls me out of my bubble of anxiety. He walks down the red carpet to the left side of the stage, head held high. Given the vitriol of Rampal's review, you'd think he'd be hiding under a rock. But no, there he is, all smiles and swagger.

The man's got some nerve… or a death wish. It's hard to tell.

Watching Ugo, I realize something. If he can show up after being publicly eviscerated, willing to risk it all, then I have no excuse. All I need to do is stop worrying about the potential fallout of failure. If I can manage that, I'll get in the zone, and do just fine. Worrying won't achieve anything. Focus and confidence will.

The sun beats down on the arena floor as the remaining participants make their way down the red carpet to their workstations.

The emcee's voice booms once again, "Ladies and gentlemen, I give you the esteemed Mayor of Beldoc, Victor Jacquet!"

Victor waddles onto the stage. "Welcome, everyone, to the first edition of Ritzy Rice!"

His statement is met with a polite round of applause.

"I am so proud that this event has attracted so much attention," Victor continues. "We have Provence's top chefs here today and, of course, the country's best food critics among our judges."

The applause that follows is more enthusiastic than the first round.

He gestures grandly, nearly smacking the emcee with his flailing hand. "And among the public, we have guests from all over the country and abroad, such as Monsieur Takeo Nakashima from Japan!"

At this, the crowd perks up. I have no clue who Takeo Nakashima is, and I doubt the others do, either. But the fact that he came all the way from Japan for Ritzy Rice makes us all feel valued and special. It's a nice feeling, I have to say.

Victor carries on. "This competition isn't just a local event; it's an international sensation!"

He pauses again, basking in the reflected glory of Seraphin Rampal's brainchild, and then rambles on. Some people in the semicircle of the terraced stone rows check their watches. Others yawn. I know that Victor's speech is the trade-off for scrapping the political sermon Chauvet had in store for us. Still, I hope Victor didn't take it as a license to speak as long as he likes.

Eventually, he seems to realize that his speech is dragging, and cuts to the closing remarks. "I want to thank Seraphin Rampal, our main star and generous cosponsor!"

Everybody claps. A few cheers and whistles pierce the applause. Rampal, seated at the judges' table, stands and waves regally. With his tailored suit and commanding presence, he is the epitome of gastronomic elitism.

"Thank you, Seraphin, for making this possible," Victor

says. "Your vision of turning Provence into an international fine dining hot spot is inspiring!"

I can't help but agree. Feared as he is by chefs and restaurateurs alike, no one can deny that Seraphin Rampal has become the region's culinary ambassador.

Victor wraps up. "Enjoy the competition, folks, and may the best chef win!"

He leaves the stage. The emcee introduces Nicole Clesse, the main organizer of the event.

A fortysomething in a tailored blazer and pearls with every strand of blond hair in place steps up to the microphone. "Dear guests and contestants, dearest Seraphin!" She gestures to Rampal.

He acknowledges her with a nod and a smile.

"We are immensely honored to have the country's premier food critic as our cosponsor and head judge!" she says.

We clap again.

"I am not afraid to say," Nicole continues, "that *The Rampal Guide to the Gastronomic Gems of Provence* has now surpassed even the *Michelin Guide* in discernment."

Has it? I'd say the jury is still out on that point, but it's beyond question how influential the *Rampal Guide* has become in recent years. Nicole goes on to highlight certain aspects of the Ritzy Rice competition. As Nicole speaks, Rose climbs onto the stage in her elaborate Arlésienne costume as Queen of Beldoc. Grandma looks poised and ready to address the crowd after Nicole.

Nicole's speech is mercifully brief. She steps down.

"Thank you, Nicole," the emcee says. "Now, a few reminders. We have two categories: savory and sweet. There will be two rounds. Today, we'll narrow it down to the finalists, who will compete again tomorrow. The judges will then choose a winner in each category."

The emcee continues with his household

announcements, his eyes gliding right past Rose as if she were invisible. She stands there, seething, her fists clenched at her sides. I can practically see steam coming from her ears.

Did Victor put him up to this?

While the emcee rattles on, a low buzz of confusion spreads across the stage. I look around, trying to catch what's being said.

A fellow pastry chef near me curses under his breath. "The stoves aren't turning on!"

I flip the switch on mine. Nothing happens. I try the mixer. Silence. I check again, fiddling with the controls. Looks like there's no power.

A technician dashes to the emcee, whispering urgently in his ear. The emcee's eyes widen for a split second, but then he regains his composure.

"Ladies and Gentlemen, it seems we're experiencing a small technical issue," he announces. "We'll take a half-hour break to resolve this hiccup. Please, enjoy some refreshments near the stage and mingle!"

Chefs and guests drift toward the refreshment table. Rose stomps off the stage, muttering Victor's name, and some choice epithets.

I better catch up to her, before she tries to scalp him.

CHAPTER 5

I make my way to the refreshment table and sidle up to Rose at the far end. The spread is unimpressive with just water, coffee, and tea.

Nicole Clesse hovers nearby, looking all apologetic as she says to Seraphin Rampal, "We'll have a lovely selection of drinks and food delivered for the lunch break. This was just in case of emergency. "

"And that's exactly what we're having now," he replies. "What worries me is the power outage."

"It's being dealt with as we speak," she assures him.

When I reach Rose, she's gulping down a coffee and scanning the crowd.

"Can you believe that man's gall?" she hisses at me. "Sidelining me like that. I won't stand for it!"

I grab a glass of sparkling water. "It's quite possible Victor had nothing to do with it. Maybe it was the emcee who decided that your part in the event should be purely decorative."

Gabriel joins us. "Maybe there'll be another opportunity for you to address the audience. The important thing is that the hiccup is resolved, and Julie gets a chance to shine."

His reminder that this event isn't about her does wonders for Grandma's mood. She calms down, blushes lightly, and pats my cheek. "You're going to rock it!"

"I wish I had your confidence," I say.

Gabriel takes my hand and gives it a gentle squeeze. "You're the best pastry chef in Provence, Julie. You've got this!"

Everyone in my entourage, including my dad and twin sister in Paris, and my oldest sister and niece in Montreal, has been very supportive of me doing Ritzy Rice. But Gabriel—he's been psyched. He loves that I am putting extra effort into my craft, as opposed to my side hustle. Detective work almost got me killed last fall. Circumstances made it impossible for Gabriel to protect me. Luckily, others did, but the episode left a lasting mark on him.

A well-groomed Asian man, around seventy, with an impeccable posture and a kind twinkle in his eye, approaches us.

"Bonjour," he says with a slight bow. "May I introduce myself? My name is Takeo Nakashima. Please call me Takeo."

His French is accented, but grammatically perfect.

Rose, Gabriel, and I give our names.

Gabriel points his chin at Victor in the distance. "Are you the guest from Japan that our mayor mentioned?"

"It puzzles me why your distinguished mayor singled me out," Takeo says. "I am no celebrity."

"Then who are you?" I ask.

"Just a man from Osaka who has been in love with Provence for many decades, ever since my first visit as a young man," he replies. "Now that I'm retired, I'm looking to open a sushi restaurant here."

Rose's face lights up. "You mean here in Beldoc?"

"Or some other town in the area," Takeo says. "But Beldoc is high on my list."

Rose bats her lashes. "We don't have a sushi restaurant in town. Beldoc would be a very smart choice."

"I'll bear that mind, Rose." He tilts his head, admiring her Arlésienne costume. "Such beautiful attire!"

"Why, thank you, Takeo." She beams. "I wear this to most public events since my election as Queen of Beldoc."

He inclines his head in a sign of respect. "A town that voted you its queen must have impeccable taste."

Rose practically glows under his compliments. I notice the tip of a colorful tattoo peeking out from under his shirt sleeve. It's quite a contrast to his otherwise polished appearance. He pulls the sleeve down and the tattoo is gone.

Interesting.

As Grandma and Takeo continue to trade pleasantries, Gabriel's phone buzzes.

He looks at the screen. "It's my commandant."

With an apologetic smile he steps away to take the call, leaving me to my own devices. I pour myself coffee. *Yuck!* Granted, instant coffee is always underwhelming, but we're at a culinary event for Pete's sake!

While I'm wincing, a hushed, tense exchange in a corner of the refreshment area draws my attention. Rampal is speaking with a slim, busty blonde wearing a chef's jacket and hat. Her expression is tight with annoyance. He doesn't look happy, either.

"You called it 'competent,' Seraphin," the woman hisses. "Competent! Is that really the best you could say?"

Seraphin, huh? Are they friends? Family? If this contestant is related to Rampal, doesn't that give her an unfair advantage?

His face a study in forbearance, Rampal whispers something back. His voice is too low to carry. The only word I can make out is "Armelle." Is that the woman's name?

"Strengths?" she scoffs. "You know what they call what you did? 'Damning with faint praise'!"

I strain in the hopes of catching Rampal's reaction, busybody that I am.

He says something unintelligible, and ends with, "...like I see it, Armelle. My job is not to inflate egos."

She crosses her arms. "You humiliated me. It felt like a personal attack."

"Nonsense!" He looks around as if seeking an escape. "Listen, this is neither the time nor the place for this conversation."

"Except, I won't get another chance," she parries. "Monsieur is so important and busy!"

He lowers his voice to a whisper again. I can't hear a word that follows, but their argument seems to cool off. A couple of minutes later, they part ways—she with a frustrated shake of her head, he with an inscrutable expression.

Gabriel returns, looking harried.

I pour him some of the tasteless brew. "Be forewarned, this drink is only called *coffee* as a courtesy."

"Thanks for the warning." He takes the paper cup.

"Everything all right?"

"There's a small problem at the station. Nothing major." He points to the stage. "What about the hiccup here?"

"No news yet."

Nicole, Victor, and the emcee have now returned to the stage and are talking to one of the technicians. Two others are scurrying around, trying to repair the outage as fast as they can. A few minutes later, a thumbs-up signal from one of the technicians confirms the fix.

The emcee returns to the microphone. "Thank you for your patience! The technical issue has been resolved."

Applause erupts.

He raises his hand to silence the audience. "Chefs, please return to your stations and judges, to your table. Let the first round begin!"

I hurry to my station, my heart pounding with excitement and nerves. With the clang of a gong, the competition begins. The savory chefs get started on their rice dishes in a flurry of steaming, chopping, frying, and stirring. Here on the sweet side, we rinse and cook our rice, mix the dry ingredients, add the liquid ones, whisk.

I'm making my rosemary and honey Camargue red rice pudding. The clock is ticking inexorably. I stir, taste, and adjust the honey in the saucepan. Next, I rub the spiky leaves of fresh rosemary between my fingers, so they release the aromatic oils. Into the pot they go! I fold everything together with care. The tricky part is letting it steep long enough for the herb to be pronounced but not overpowering.

I look around. Some chefs are panicking. Others are cool. Two tables away on my side, Armelle is a whirlwind of activity, her movements sharp and precise.

Watch the clock, Julie!

I stir the rosemary mixture. As it thickens, the sweetly herbaceous aroma fills the air around me, mingling with the scents from the neighboring stations. In the audience, Gabriel catches my eye and waves. I wave back. Time to toast the rice for the topping! My nerves tingle with adrenaline.

"Five minutes to go!" the emcee announces.

Fortunately, my pudding has now thickened to the right consistency. I remove the saucepan from the heat and spoon the pudding into the rustic ramekins I selected earlier. Each one gets a drizzle of honey and some untreated lemon zest. It will do double duty: complement the pudding's piney flavor and add brightness. I sprinkle a few grains of toasted red rice over the top for a bit of crunch. It's all about texture and contrast! Last but not least, I add edible flowers and tiny sprigs of rosemary for a pop of color.

The final minute counts down.

My heart is racing, but my hands are surprisingly steady as I focus on the last touches. Each ramekin must be perfect. A smudge here, a stray sprig there, and it could mean not making it to the finals. I wipe the rims of the ramekins, so that they're pristine.

"Time's up!" The gong sounds again.

I step back, hands up, breathing hard. The other chefs do the same. There's an almost palpable mix of relief and anticipation in the air. The judges, including Rampal, sit at their table and wait.

Nicole walks onto the stage. Her helpers follow with trays to collect our dishes. They place numbered labels next to each one for the blind tasting.

As my pudding joins the parade of desserts on its way to be judged, I wipe my brow. Rose, Gabriel, and Takeo flash encouraging smiles from the audience. The judges begin their tastings, murmuring to themselves and making notes. Rampal's face is inscrutable as he samples dish after dish, and then dessert after dessert. I try to read his expression as he tastes mine, but it's like trying to decipher a stone statue.

The emcee's voice cuts through the murmurs. "Thank you, chefs, for your outstanding efforts! In a few moments, we will excuse you to enjoy a delicious lunch buffet. We request that the audience eat in town and return by three."

I wipe my hands and clap along with the other chefs. They all look like they're ready for a break.

"Before you go," the emcee adds, "Monsieur Seraphin Rampal would like to say a few words to the chefs."

Rampal steps forward. Not too shabby looking to start with; his confidence and air of success give him a compelling appeal. Around fifty, tall, bespoke suit, expensive watch, and glasses, dark hair touched with a hint of silver—a single mom's fantasy made flesh.

"Ladies and Gentlemen," he begins, "I have had the pleasure of sampling some remarkable dishes and desserts today. The creativity you displayed is commendable."

All the chefs beam, hoping to be among the remarkable ones.

"The judges will deliberate this afternoon," he continues. "As for the chefs and guests, we've scheduled an enlightening lecture for you all to enjoy while the judges work."

He squints as he peers at the paper in his hand. "Oh, God, someone really needs to find time to get his eyes rechecked..."

Sycophantic laughter echoes from both sides of the stage.

Rampal adjusts his glasses. "The lecture is titled 'Intersectional Agronomy: Decolonizing Rice Fields from Grain Supremacy, Paddy Privilege, Harvest Cis-Patriarchy, and the Oppressive Structures of Class-Based Crop Inequality.' "

There's a beat of silence before the arena erupts into murmurs. I glance at Rose, who's shaking her fist in Victor's direction. That sneaky bastard and his fancy-pants consultant never canceled the talk, despite our deal. *So much for democracy!*

Rampal clears his throat. "I know it sounds like a mouthful, but I assure you, it will be informative and eye-opening."

His authority works its magic, and the dissatisfied buzz dies down.

"Enjoy your lunch!" Rampal steps back.

The emcee takes over. "Thank you, Monsieur Rampal! Chefs, please proceed to the buffet area."

As we're ushered toward the buffet, my hands are still

shaking from the intensity of it all. Rose and Gabriel catch up with me.

"I'm not coming back after lunch," Grandma declares.

I jerk my head back in surprise. "Why not?"

"Do you want me to physically attack Victor and embarrass you in public?"

"No."

She gives a little shrug. "Thought so."

"Um, I might be late for the afternoon session," Gabriel says. "Got to hop over to the gendarmerie. My colleagues need a hand with their little issue."

I narrow my eyes, first at my boyfriend, then at my grandmother. "This has *nothing* to do with the lecture on intersectional agronomy, right?"

They both go out of their way to assure me it doesn't.

Well, that's just great. Today being Saturday, I need all hands on deck in the shop. Therefore, Flo and Eric can't be here in the afternoon. And so, Comrade Julie Cavallo will be decolonizing rice fields all by her lonesome.

Living the dream.

CHAPTER 6

In the buffet line, I find myself behind two chefs, a curvy woman and a blond man, both about my age. They're chatting animatedly like friends or old acquaintances. When our eyes meet, the woman smiles warmly. The man's shifty gaze slides right over me.

I step closer. "Hi, I'm Julie Cavallo from Beldoc."

"I'm Mylene Nivault from Eau de Provence." The woman gestures to her companion. "And this is Tanguy Eldin from Saint-Rémy."

Tanguy finally acknowledges me. "Pleased to meet you, Julie. So, what's your specialty?"

"Gluten-free pastries. And you two?"

"I'm in the savory category," Mylene says. "Tanguy, too."

"For the first round," Tanguy informs me, "I made a truffle and saffron risotto."

Mylene laughs. "Tanguy is very creative, and he's all about pushing boundaries. Me, I just want my food to feel like a warm hug."

"Both of those things sound wonderful to me," I say.

We move down the buffet line and fill our plates.

"So, Julie," Mylene asks as we sit down at a nearby table, "what got you into pastries?"

"I'm afraid I don't have a cool origin story to entertain you with," I reply. "I've simply always loved baking."

Tanguy agrees, "Baking is fun. Have you done many competitions?"

"This is my first big one," I admit. "What about you guys?"

"I've entered a few regional contests." Mylene bites into her quiche. "Even won one with my *magret de canard aux figues*."

Tanguy puffs out his chest. "I've been in a few. It's all about the experience and the connections you make."

"Have you made any good connections?" I ask.

"Oh yeah," he answers, but doesn't elaborate.

We eat in silence for a few minutes. From the corner of my eye, I see Armelle and Ugo Drugeon huddled together. They're whispering. From time to time Armelle shoots an angry look at Rampal, who's in a group with the organizers and other jury members.

Tanguy flashes me a dazzlingly white smile. "So, what's your secret weapon?"

"Wouldn't you like to know?" I tease, taking a sip of lemonade. "What about you two? Any special tricks up your sleeves?"

"If I told you, I'd have to kill you," Mylene jokes.

"Fair enough," I concede. "But seriously, what made you decide to compete?"

"Credentials and prestige," Tanguy replies. "Winning Ritzy Rice would take my career to the next level."

Mylene nods. "Same here. Plus, it's a chance to highlight what small-town chefs can do."

As I finish my last bite of quiche, the organizers begin to put up a large tent behind the stage, around the Judges' table.

Mylene whispers conspiratorially to Tanguy and me, "Why would they hide the jury during deliberations?"

"In case it comes to blows," Tanguy offers.

The emcee's voice booms over the loudspeakers. "Lunch break is over in ten minutes! If anyone needs to use the restroom or stretch their legs, now's the time."

I spring up from my seat. "Restroom for me. Be right back."

When I get there, I spot Takeo. He's talking to a middle-aged woman, her hair pulled into a severe bun. Takeo's relaxed demeanor from earlier is gone now. He gestures sharply as he says something to the chignon lady. He's tense, agitated—a stark contrast to the charming man who flirted with Rose.

I slow down, pretending to check my phone while trying to catch a few words of their conversation. But it's no use. Their voices are too low, and I can't linger here without looking weird. I put away my phone and enter the restroom, wondering what that was all about.

When I return to the buffet area, the judges have already gathered in the tent. I find Mylene and Tanguy where I left them.

Mylene waves me over. "All good? Ready to be educated about intersectional agronomy?"

I grin in reply and slide back into my seat.

The emcee grabs the mic again. "All right, everyone, please take your seats in the designated section of the arena." He gestures to where we should go. "The lecture will begin shortly."

Except for a dozen retirees, the seats are empty. It's clear that most of the audience had the same idea as Rose and Gabriel and had better things to do with their afternoon. Unfortunately, we contestants don't have the luxury of skipping the lecture. We're stuck here, waiting to hear who made it to the second round.

Grumbling, we shuffle to the designated area. The buzz of conversation dies down. The amphitheater is now eerily quiet but for the distant rustling of leaves and the occasional cough. The lecturer, a man with wild hair and round glasses, begins his presentation in a monotone that matches our enthusiasm.

"Today, we're going to talk about why we need to make the rice fields progressive, equitable, and free from patriarchal soil conditioning," he begins, never looking up from his notes.

Within minutes, the audience falls into two groups: those who fidget and those who sit still and nap. Cell phones emerge from purses. Earbuds are pulled from pockets. Fingers scroll and tap away. Next to me, Ugo Drugeon is practically glued to his phone, texting frantically. Every few seconds, he shoots a side-eye left and right, checking to be sure no one can see what he's typing.

The lecturer drones on with the energy of a sedated sloth. I try to pay attention, but the truth is I'd rather get a root canal right now than listen to this bore.

Mylene excuses herself halfway through the talk, muttering something about being back in a moment. Her moment lasts twenty minutes. When she returns, she slides into her seat, flustered and clutching her bag tightly in her lap.

The speaker goes on and on, oblivious to our slow agony. "And thus, rice can become a symbol of resistance to the hegemonic structures..."

I tune out again. Fifteen minutes later, he finally finishes his talk with a smattering of polite applause. People wake up, yawn, and stretch. All the eyes turn to the judges' tent. Their deliberations must be over soon.

The closer we get to the announcement of the results, the harder it is to keep a lid on my nerves. *Have I made it to the second round?* All I can do is hope that my pudding delighted the jury's discerning palates and earned more than "faint praise" from Seraphin Rampal.

The emcee comes from the tent and addresses the restless crowd. "The judges have decided to wait until tomorrow morning before announcing the results."

The chefs exchange looks of confusion. Frustrated murmurs run through our ranks.

"Why the delay?" someone in the back asks. "Why not tell us now?"

"The judges don't wish to ruin the evening for the unsuccessful contestants and their fans," the emcee explains.

That's cute. Except, I don't think that's the real reason. The tedious lecture drove away not only most of the audience, but also the press. And I bet that a celebrity like Seraphin Rampal would rather not deliver his life-and-death pronouncements without a single news camera in sight.

The emcee forces a smile. "Everyone, have a good time tonight!"

People start to disperse, resigned.

As I start to leave, Tanguy comes over to me. "Hey, Julie, would you like to join a group of us for a drink? Just to take the edge off all this suspense."

I hesitate. The nosy parker in me is all for having drinks with Tanguy's group and soaking up all the gossip. Besides, Mylene will probably be there, and I like her. But something about Tanguy makes me vaguely uncomfortable.

Is it his slickness? Men this smooth tend to rub me the wrong way. It doesn't help that he reminds me of Denis, my former classmate turned persistent suitor, who creeped me out the last time we spoke.

Fortunately, Gabriel is back in the arena and waving to me.

"I'd love to," I say to Tanguy, "but I already have plans for tonight."

"No problem. Have a good time."

"You, too!" I make my way to Gabriel.

He gives me a kiss. "How did it go? Sorry I missed the afternoon session."

No, he's not.

"Did you solve the crisis at the gendarmerie?" I ask.

"Everything's under control." He looks me in the eye. "So? Are you in round two?"

"The judges won't be announcing the results until tomorrow," I reply with an eye roll. "Apparently, they don't want to ruin anyone's evening."

"How considerate of them." Gabriel offers his hand. "Want to get out of here?"

I take it. "More than anything!"

CHAPTER 7

Gabriel and I step out of my building. I'm carrying a tray with some of my ingredients, and he, a backpack with the rest. We'll stop at the pâtisserie first, which is open this Sunday morning, and then head to the arena.

I push my shoulders back and fill my lungs with the balmy air. Sniffing it in a series of quick breaths, à la Lady, I pick up the scents of ripe fruit, dewy grass, and fallen leaves. Without a doubt, it's this unique mix that makes September so special for those of us with unusually sensitive noses.

The colors, textures, and sounds around me blend together as magically as the smells. Summer is bowing out of Provence just as fall is slinking in. They cross paths and hug each other, knowing they won't meet again until next September, and we're in the middle of that embrace.

As Gabriel and I walk to my shop, the remnant of the night's coolness lingers in the air. But not for long. The sun is already peeking over the terracotta roofs, filtering through the trees and dancing on the cobblestone streets. The vineyards around Beldoc are heavy with grapes. The *vendanges*—grape harvest—have already begun.

It's the kind of morning that makes me forget all my worries and just feel thankful. Leaving Paris and returning to my hometown four years ago was arguably the best decision of my life.

Gabriel and I enter the pâtisserie, where the aroma of freshly brewed coffee overpowers everything else. Eric is behind the counter, whistling a cheerful tune as he sips his java and arranges the cold pastries I made last night.

"Morning, Chef," he calls out. "Hey, Gabriel."

"Everything good here?" I ask after we greet him back.

"All under control," Eric reports. "Flo was on her best behavior all afternoon, customers were plentiful, and we sold a shitload of almost every product."

"Music to my ears!"

"Don't worry about a thing," he adds. "Go win that competition!"

Satisfied, Gabriel and I set out to the arena.

"You'll be in round two," he says. "And that flan of yours is going to blow them away."

"I hope so."

"Medz Mama asked me to tell you she's been praying for your success, and you're going to make it."

I smile over my growing anxiety. "Well, who am to question your grandmother's sources?"

We arrive at our destination with a quarter of an hour to spare. I store my ingredients and the tray in my assigned locker and return to Gabriel's side. The arena is already buzzing with anticipation. Contestants and spectators mill about, chatting in small groups. No one dares to speculate aloud about the results, but the nonstop glances toward the stage leave no doubt as to what's on everyone's mind.

I spot my fans near the entrance. Flo waves enthusiastically. Her gallery is closed on Sundays, and I'm proud she chose to spend her free morning here supporting me. Rose is talking to my friend Salman.

Yay, he made it!

He listens to her, his gorgeous long hair blowing in the breeze and perfectly aligned with the Ritzy Rice banner above his head. The fourth person in their circle is none other than Takeo Nakashima, who, judging by his grin, is back in charmer mode.

"Julie, Gabriel, over here!" Flo calls out.

We go to them. "Morning, everyone!"

"Julie, *ma chérie!*" Rose dispenses cheek kisses. "You look ready to conquer."

"I was sending you good vibes from Avignon all day yesterday," Salman informs me.

"I don't doubt it," I say.

More people gather in the arena. Some of the judges take their seats on the stage. The atmosphere thickens with anticipation.

Victor surveys the crowd and waves Gabriel over, avoiding my eyes. Point taken—I'm not included in the invite. Honestly, it's just as well. I'm annoyed with Victor for breaking his word and inflicting that mind-numbing lecture on us yesterday. Besides, I'd rather talk to Salman while we wait for the results or to Mylene, if she finds me, instead of exchanging canned pleasantries with Victor.

But Gabriel pulls me with him as he heads over to our wayward mayor. We approach Victor's group. It includes Nicole, the main organizer of this event, and the woman with the tight chignon who was arguing with Takeo yesterday by the restrooms.

Victor points at Gabriel, his eyes on the chignon woman, "I'd like you to meet Capitaine Gabriel Adinian of the Beldoc Gendarmerie."

Gabriel and I greet everyone.

"This is Camille Terrien, the mayor of Eau de Provence," Victor says to Gabriel.

We shake hands. I praise her town on autopilot, as my thoughts are elsewhere. *Was her spat with Takeo about his sushi shop or something else?* Before my imagination can hatch some convoluted theory, I remember the principle of scientific reasoning that my sister Cat's mathematician fiancé has told me about. It's called *Occam's razor*, and it says that the simplest explanation is usually the right one. Camille Terrien and Takeo must've been arguing about the sushi shop. He must've found suitable premises, and she won't speed up the red tape.

"Ever since Capitaine Adinian has been stationed in Beldoc," Victor says to Nicole and Camille, "he has helped catch many dangerous criminals."

The ladies ooh and aah.

I cock my head at Victor. Will he add in the spirit of fairness, *And here is Madame Julie Cavallo who's helped catch a few murderers*?

Victor pats Gabriel on the shoulder. "He even saved my nephew's life."

More oohs and aahs. Gabriel smiles politely.

As an afterthought, Victor gestures to me, "And this is Julie, Rose Tassy's granddaughter."

I stare at him. *Is that it?*

"Julie is a gluten-free baker," he adds.

Is that the best he can do? No family name, no accolades, no mention of my murder-solving contributions?

I give Gabriel a quick side-eye. Will he say something about my detective work? Disappointingly, he keeps his mouth shut.

Nicole sends me a sympathetic look. "If you don't make it to the second round, tell yourself you were brave enough to try."

Isn't she sweet?

OK, is everyone done putting me down? Can I go back to my friends now?

"And remind yourself that it's not the end of the world," she adds in the same solicitous tone.

Wait—does she know something?

I stare her in the eye. "Have you seen the results of yesterday's deliberations?"

"Of course not!" She bristles. "Why would you ask that?"

"Because you sound like you have."

She squirms, ill at ease. "I have no idea who made the cut and who didn't, I assure you. The judges have been exceptionally tight-lipped."

While Victor and Camille back her up, Nicole receives a text message. Her expression darkens as she reads it.

"It's from one of the judges," she says to Victor. "Seraphin Rampal hasn't arrived yet."

He waves off her concern. "Surely we can start ten minutes late?"

Nicole looks at the judges' table where the panel members are checking their watches. She then calls Rampal several times in a row. He doesn't pick up. Her gestures become more frantic with each unsuccessful attempt.

"*Merde*," she mutters before leaving him a voice message.

For the next quarter of an hour, everyone's eyes dart between their phone screens and the entrance to the arena. With each passing minute, Rampal's absence becomes more glaring—and harder to explain.

Nicole makes another series of phone calls, pacing a short arc near the stage.

"He isn't picking up," she says. "I left another message."

Off to the side, Mylene and Tanguy have their eyes glued to Nicole. Mylene is twisting her neck kerchief into knots.

Tanguy has a muscle twitching in his jaw. He marches up to Nicole. "Everything we've worked for hinges on Seraphin Rampal's presence. If he doesn't show, what then?"

"He'll be here any minute now, I'm sure," Nicole replies.

Mylene, Ugo, Armelle, and a few others join the edges of our group.

"What's going on?" Armelle asks. "Seraphin... I mean, Monsieur Rampal, is never late."

Mylene bites her lip as she turns to Nicole. "Have you tried his hotel?"

"You think I should?" Nicole checks her watch. "He's only twenty minutes late..."

"Yes, you should," Mylene and several others—including me—say.

"I have a lot riding on this," Tanguy adds. "If you won't call the hotel, then I will."

He sounds harsh. The stakes are high for everyone, yet Tanguy seems particularly exasperated with the situation.

Nicole calls the hotel, her face taut. Seeing as there's only one establishment in town that qualifies as a "hotel," as opposed to bed-and-breakfasts, Airbnb and whatever have you, she must be calling Belle d'Oc. I watch her explain her query, then wait, tap her foot, and then listen, looking more and more concerned.

Finally, she turns to us. "They checked his room. He wasn't there."

Gasps ripple through the crowd.

Questions fly.

"What do you mean, not there?"

"Where could he be?"

"Did something happen?"

Nicole purses her lips and strides to the stage, with Victor hurrying to keep up. They huddle with the judges.

41

Their conversation is a flurry of intense whispers, too low for me to make out from where I am.

After a few moments, Nicole moves over to the emcee, her expression resolute.

Her words to him are louder than her exchange with the judges. "We proceed as planned for now. Hopefully, Seraphin will join us soon."

The emcee steps up to the microphone. The crowd settles into their seats and quiets down, all eyes on him. The chefs, rattled, gather near the stage, exchanging anxious looks. I leave Gabriel's side to join the other chefs.

"Ladies and gentlemen," the emcee begins, "we haven't been able to reach Monsieur Rampal, but we'll go ahead and read the results of yesterday's deliberations."

"Without Seraphin Rampal?" one of the chefs asks.

The emcee nods. "The decisions were made collegially, and the rest of the jury would like me to announce the finalists without further delay." He pauses to let his words sink in.

The arena falls silent as everyone grasps what's going on. I hold my breath.

The emcee pulls a piece of paper from his pocket and unfolds it. "We'll do savory before sweet, just like in a restaurant." He stops to collect a few laughs, then shouts, "Mylene Nivault from Eau de Provence!"

Mylene exhales sharply. Her hand trembles as she brushes a curl away from her face.

"Tanguy Eldin from Saint-Rémy!" the emcee continues.

Tanguy flashes his confident smile to the crowd, but his sagging shoulders tell me he wasn't as sure as he's letting on that he'd make the cut.

The emcee announces the remaining four finalists, which don't include Ugo Drugeon. I steal a look at him. He doesn't move or make a sound, but his jaw is clenched.

We move on to the sweet category. My stomach is a knot of nerves as the names are read.

"Julie Cavallo from Beldoc!"

Yesss! I did it!

I wave to the audience, especially to my little fan club consisting of Gabriel, Rose, Flo, and Salman. They cheer loudly. The emcee finishes reading the names. Armelle Pradine didn't make it. When I catch sight of her, her posture is stiff and her face, a stony mask.

Nicole steps forward. "Congratulations to all the finalists! Please gather your ingredients and proceed to your stations. Round two will begin in ten minutes."

As I head over to the lockers to pick up my tray, I force myself to push all the distracting thoughts aside and focus on the competition. Tanguy isn't the only one with a lot riding on winning Ritzy Rice.

The show must go on.

CHAPTER 8

As I open my locker to get my ingredients, my nervous energy makes way for determination.

Today is the day. I'm ready.

Just then, a panicked voice nearby interrupts my mental preparation for the challenge ahead. I look in the direction of the voice. It's Edmond, a fellow Beldoc pastry chef, who took over his father's bakery last year.

He's on the phone, clearly desperate. "God, I'm hopeless! How could I be so stupid? What am I going to do?"

The person on the other end of the line says something that doesn't seem to solve Edmond's quagmire. He hangs up, looking like he's about to cry.

"Psst, Edmond!" I call. "What's going on?"

"You're not going to believe this, but I left my vanilla beans at home." He shakes his head. "I'm such an idiot! If I'd realized it earlier, my mom would've gotten them, but now there's no time."

"Murphy's Law."

"Yeah," he agrees with a bitter smile.

"Are they indispensable for your dessert?"

"I'm making vanilla puffed rice parfait."

I wince. "Ouch."

"You think I should quit now?" His eyes dart as he thinks on his feet. "That would spare my ego and my business a humiliating review in the *Rampal Guide*."

I hesitate for a moment, thinking of my own limited supply of vanilla beans. Besides, if Edmond drops out, that's one less competitor in my category. Self-interest dictates that I agree he should forfeit. I have no claim to sainthood. And, most of all, I really, really want to win this thing!

Oh, fuck that. "I have some high-quality vanilla beans you can use."

His eyes widen. "Julie, that's incredibly generous of you!"

"Happy to help."

He peers at me. "Even if that means I win?"

"My boyfriend's Armenian grandmother has this saying: 'Do a good deed and toss it in the water.'"

"Are you sure?" he presses. "What about your own dessert?"

"It's a flan, and it only needs half of what I have."

I open the glass tube with my precious six Madagascar bourbon pods and hand him three.

"You're a lifesaver," he gushes, placing the pods on his tray. "Thank you!"

We hurry to the stage along with the other chefs.

Passing me, Tanguy raises an eyebrow. "You know this is a competition, right? Helping someone in your category could put you at a disadvantage."

"Or not," I counter. "We'll never know."

He winks at me. "Unless he wins."

True. Oh, well.

We return to our places.

I'm laying out the ingredients on my worktop, when the emcee's voice announces, "At the end of this round, one winner in each category will receive five lavender sprigs, a glowing review, and a feature in the upcoming edition of the *Rampal Guide*."

All the chefs on the stage applaud, hoping to be that lucky person.

"The other finalists will be attributed three or four lavender sprigs and reviewed accordingly in the *Guide*," the emcee adds.

On his signal, we begin. I pour almond milk into a saucepan to cook the rice for my Arborio rice and almond milk flan. While I work, I glimpse Victor and Nicole stepping down from the stage, their expressions serious. They wave Gabriel over. He joins them, and they huddle together, speaking in hushed tones.

Stay focused, Julie!

Easier said than done. I'm whisking the egg yolks and sugar, when Gabriel looks at me briefly and makes a phone call. *To whom?* My hand is stirring the rice in the saucepan, while my mind is churning out theories. Here's the best one: He's calling the gendarmerie. Victor and Nicole asked him to send someone to Rampal's hotel and try to figure out where our head judge can be.

The nutty aroma of the Arborio rice cooking in the saucepan reaches my nose and pulls me back to the task at hand. I stir gently. *Concentrate, Julie!* I need to get this right.

Gabriel hangs up, nods to Victor, and returns to his seat next to Rose, his face unreadable.

The clock ticks loudly in the background as I whisk in the vanilla bean seeds, salt, orange zest, and orange blossom water. There is still no sign of Rampal. It's less and less likely that his absence is due to a trivial matter. The disturbing possibility that something bad happened to him looks more credible by the minute.

The flan mixture is now thick enough to strain and cook it in a bain-marie. The process calms my nerves, but my eyes keep flicking to Gabriel, who appears tense.

When my flan is set but still jiggly, I remove it from the bain-marie and let it cool a bit, while I toast a large handful of slivered almonds. I garnish the flan and place it in the refrigerator to make sure it's properly chilled for the blind tasting.

The clock ticks away. With a minute left until the gong, I remove the flan from the fridge. The timer dings, marking the end of the second round. We step away from our workstations. The organizers move in to prepare the dishes and desserts for the blind tasting.

The judges' table still has an empty chair at the center, a stark reminder that something is awry. The other judges start the tastings. They scribble notes, their faces tight with unease.

"We'll take a lunch break now," the emcee says into the mic. "The chefs can stay here for the buffet. The guests are invited to return by four to watch a dance performance. The panel will deliberate and announce the winners at six."

"Without Seraphin Rampal?" several chefs ask.

He looks at Nicole.

She takes the microphone from him. "I hope he'll join us in the afternoon, so he can announce the winners."

"Bon appétit!" the emcee says with exaggerated levity.

As we disperse, I find Gabriel near the edge of the amphitheater, his phone in his hand. He looks up with a serious expression as I approach. Before I can ask him for an update, Victor and Nicole join us.

Nicole lets out a frustrated sigh. "I've been calling Seraphin every ten minutes, and it keeps going to voicemail."

"What's the news?" Victor asks Gabriel.

My boyfriend pockets his phone. "The hotel's manager checked the CCTV feed for me."

"And?" Victor, Nicole, and I say in unison.

"Seraphin Rampal left the hotel late last night, alone." Gabriel's expression is grim as he adds, "He never returned."

CHAPTER 9

Victor stares at Gabriel. "What do you mean, he never returned?"

"Exactly what I said," Gabriel replies. "Seraphin Rampal never reentered his hotel."

"Any idea where he might be?" I ask.

"None."

Victor rubs his temples. "This is a disaster! If something's happened to Seraphin Rampal, it's going to cast a shadow over my town!"

"I'm worried sick," Nicole says.

Her pasty complexion suggests her sentiment isn't a figure of speech.

"As mayor of Beldoc, I empower Capitaine Adinian to start investigating at once!" Victor exclaims.

Gabriel rubs the back of his neck. "I'm afraid that's out of your jurisdiction, Monsieur le Maire."

"All right then, call your boss," Victor urges him. "Tell Commandant Lambert I'm asking him to order you to open an investigation."

Gabriel pulls out his phone. "I will, but I doubt Commandant Lambert can do what you ask."

"Why on earth not?" Victor frowns.

"Seraphin Rampal is an adult with no disabilities or mental health issues," Gabriel explains. "We must have a good reason to consider his disappearance suspicious and to devote resources to it so quickly."

"What kind of reason would do it?" I ask.

"Signs of violence, for example," he answers. "Or strange behavior before the disappearance, or a missing person report filed by a family member, or a witness who saw something alarming."

"Try, anyway," Victor demands, his displeasure clear as he glares at Gabriel. "This isn't just any adult—it's Seraphin Rampal!"

Gabriel nods. "I'll be sure to relay that to my commandant. And perhaps someone—a relative or partner —has reported Rampal missing in the meantime."

"Seraphin doesn't have a partner," Nicole interjects. "He's been single since he and Armelle broke up."

I do a double take. "Armelle Pradine?"

"Yes," Nicole says.

I process that.

So, the contestant with whom Rampal had a tense and personal exchange yesterday morning was Armelle Pradine.

Interesting.

Gabriel excuses himself to make the call. Victor and Nicole stride off toward the judges. I make my way to Rose, Flo, and Salman, who surround me, buzzing with curiosity. Takeo hovers nearby.

"People want and deserve to know what's going on." Flo points her index finger at my chest. "Talk!"

I quickly sum up the situation. "It looks like Seraphin Rampal hasn't been seen since last night. Victor wants Gabriel to investigate."

"The organizers won't cancel Ritzy Rice over this, darling." Rose pats my arm. "You can still win!"

I look at her in awe. Her friend Sarah sometimes wears a T-shirt that says on the front "I'm no more fucks to give years old." I think Rose was born that way.

Gabriel ends the call and returns to Victor's side. Try as I might, it's impossible to hear a word of what he's saying to Victor from this distance.

Flo gives me a nudge. "Come to town with us. The emcee didn't say you *have to* eat here, did he?"

"No, he didn't."

I survey the underwhelming buffet for the participants. It's just sandwiches and wraps—much less appetizing than yesterday's menu. Besides, I haven't seen Salman in a while.

He flips his hair back. "We have weeks of gossip to catch up on, my friend. Just saying."

"We do," I agree, before pointing to Gabriel who's still engaged in conversation with Victor. "As soon as he's back, we'll head out."

While we wait, a shadow moves slowly over us. I lift my eyes to the sky. The blue expanse is now dotted with big fluffy clouds that drift across it. It doesn't look like it might rain. When I look down, a familiar figure coming our way catches my attention. His signature shades are firmly in place despite the clouds blocking the sun.

"*Messieurs-dames,*" Capitaine Charles-Antoine Shen greets us before zeroing in on me. "Madame Cavallo. Long time no see."

I nod in greeting. "Capitaine Shen. What brings you here?"

"Got wind of the competition," he replies. "Thought I'd come see what all the fuss is about."

Yeah, right. Four years back, Shen was the lead investigator on what he thought was an open-and-shut case with my sous chef as his prime suspect. Eventually, he saw the error of his ways. But our relationship hasn't been, shall we say, cordial since then.

"How's Eric?" Shen asks.

"Great."

"Good, good..." He looks around. "How's the competition treating you?"

I offer a wry smile. "We're almost done, but the star of the event is missing."

"Yes, I heard about Rampal." He tilts his head to one side. "Tricky situation, huh?"

"You tell me, Capitaine." I stare at him.

He stares back at me without answering.

"Do you guys have a history?" Salman asks, looking from me to Shen.

"They do," Flo replies. "But not like you think."

Gabriel comes over and exchanges greetings with Shen.

"Commandant Lambert won't sanction a full investigation yet," he informs our group, "but he dispatched Capitaine Shen here to poke around a bit."

"Why him and not you?" Flo asks Gabriel. "You're already here, no?"

Gabriel smiles. "I'm here in a personal capacity on my day off. Charles-Antoine—I mean, Capitaine Shen—is on duty today."

"Capitaine Shen!" someone cries out, running toward us.

I turn around. It's Victor with Nicole hot on his heels.

"So glad you're here!" Victor shakes Shen's hand. "I need you to find Seraphin Rampal, but without disrupting the event or causing a panic."

"Or having the media descend on us," Nicole adds.

"Don't worry," Shen assures her. "It'll be informal and low-key. Hopefully, Rampal will turn up before I'm done."

He moves away to start his "informal" inquiries. Victor and Nicole head to the buffet area.

Rose claps her hands for attention. "Well then, let's go

eat downtown! I found a lovely new place not far from here."

A heavy drop lands on her face. Another splashes on mine. And then another one, and many more. The next thing I know, it's pouring down.

CHAPTER 10

The rain catches everyone by surprise. Rose swiftly opens her bright floral umbrella.

"Dibs!" Flo shouts, ducking underneath.

The crowd begins to flee the exposed arena. As a chaotic swarm of people rushes out to find refuge in the surrounding eateries, the organizers spring into action. They herd the finalist chefs and judges, along with Victor, Camille, the emcee, and Shen into the covered area where the lockers and restrooms are located. The caterers scramble to save the buffet, carrying sandwiches, wraps, and water bottles to safety.

My gang and I are making our way to the exit, when Shen runs up to us.

He takes his wet shades off and fixes his sharp eyes on me. "Madame Cavallo, can you stay with the rest of the chefs, please? I'd like to ask you some questions."

I glance at Salman.

"When a cop says 'please,' it isn't really a request," he stage-whispers. "Go. We'll catch up on the phone."

Gabriel gives me a small nod.

I follow Shen to the covered area while Gabriel, Flo,

Salman, and Rose hurry from the arena. He leads me to a spot near the wall, away from where the caterers are handing out food and drink to the drenched crowd.

Is he hoping to pick my brain? Of course, it could just be a coincidence that I am the first person he interviews. But I don't think so.

He pulls out a small notebook. "Did you notice anything suspicious yesterday?"

"Not really," I say. "The only thing that comes close was a tense exchange between Seraphin Rampal and Armelle Pradine before the competition kicked off."

"What were they talking about?"

Should I share my speculation?

"Armelle seemed really upset," I begin cautiously. "As far as I could tell, they were arguing about the lukewarm review he gave her."

Shen jots that down. "Anything else stand out?"

For a moment I consider telling him about Ugo's financial troubles caused by Rampal's removal of two lavender sprigs. Then I decide against it. While Armelle's discontent was something I personally witnessed, Ugo's story is hearsay. As much as I love to hear juicy gossip, it doesn't feel right to spread it.

I shake my head. "No, nothing."

"How well do you know Seraphin Rampal?"

"Until yesterday, only by name."

He closes his notebook. "Thank you, Madame Cavallo. I may have more questions for you after I talk to the others, so don't leave the covered area."

I almost ask if I'm a suspect, but I resist the temptation. Shen has no sense of humor. Annoying him will only aggravate the strain between us.

A caterer hands me a sandwich and a bottle of water. Thanking her, I scan my surroundings and spot Mylene and Tanguy in a corner. They wave me over. Earlier, when I was talking with Shen, I caught them watching, their faces tinged with curiosity.

"Hey," Tanguy says as I stand by his side. "Any news? Seems like you're in the loop."

I take a bite of my sandwich and chew before answering, "The man with black hair and shades is Capitaine Shen of our local gendarmerie. He's trying to piece together what happened last night."

Mylene's gaze travels to Shen. "Is he investigating? Do the gendarmes have any reason to believe something... bad happened to Seraphin?"

Ha! Another one calling Rampal by his first name!

What's Mylene's connection to him? Or am I overthinking it? Is it because I only returned to Provence four years ago and never really had a chance to hang out with these people? I shouldn't read too much into the first-name thing.

"All they've found so far," I say, "is that no one has seen him since he left his hotel late last night."

Mylene's hand flies to her collarbone. Tanguy eyes me keenly.

Did I say too much? Was that the kind of detail the police refuse to divulge, citing an ongoing investigation?

Then again, I've been told there's no investigation yet. *So, I'm good.*

Despite my rationalizations, I know deep down I should've kept my mouth shut about Rampal's last sighting. But what's done is done. All I can do is hope that Mylene and Tanguy will share something in return.

"Yesterday morning," I begin, "I caught Armelle Pradine laying into him. Do you guys know what her beef was?"

"Armelle thought his review didn't do her justice," Mylene replies.

"There's more to it, though, right?" Tanguy shifts his gaze from Mylene to me. "They used to date."

I already know that, but I do my best to look surprised. "Really?"

"Yeah," Tanguy says. "Rampal dumped Armelle out of the blue. Broke her heart. And then he had the nerve to trash her latest creations for that chic hotel in Pont-de-Pré."

I glance at Mylene, expecting a contribution, but none is forthcoming. She's not even looking at me. She's fidgeting and has barely touched her food. Her eyes are glued to Shen who's talking to one of the finalists.

"If I were in Armelle's shoes, I'd be furious," I say to Tanguy.

"Anyone would," he agrees. "To Armelle, the review was Rampal's extra cruel way of saying he was really done with her."

"She was wrong about that," Mylene mutters.

I turn to her. "Why?"

"Just a feeling." She looks away again.

"And what about Ugo?" I ask Tanguy, eager to glean as much as I can while he's in the mood to share. "Rampal's review hit him hard too, didn't it?"

"It nearly sank his restaurant," Tanguy replies.

That bad? "Did he tell you as much?"

"No, but I went to eat there last week, and it was almost empty. If you factor in what it costs to run an upscale place like that, Ugo must be struggling to stay afloat."

Mylene doesn't disagree this time. She offers no opinion at all. But her body language speaks of distress. Her hands tremble as she sips her water, and her eyes follow Shen as if her life depended on him.

"Mylene, are you all right?" I ask gently.

She doesn't react at first, then blinks, and looks at me. "Sorry?"

"Are you OK?" Tanguy repeats. "You're acting weird."

"I'm fine. I'm just... worried about Se—Monsieur Rampal."

I touch her arm. "Maybe he fell and hit his head last night. A concussion can cause temporary memory loss."

"Maybe," she echoes, biting her lip.

I search her face. "If there's something you know that could help the gendarmes find him, you should speak up."

"No, I don't know anything." Her voice cracks.

We eat the rest of our sandwiches in silence. I listen to the rain pounding on the flimsy roof above us and think about Mylene. My gut tells me she knows something she chose not to reveal. Whatever she's hiding could be as harmless as carrying a torch for Rampal—or as sinister as killing him.

CHAPTER 11

I t's half past three, and the rain has finally stopped. The audience is trickling back into the arena. Their hushed conversations fill the air as they wait for the local amateur dance troupe to arrive and begin the entertainment.

Salman had to return to Avignon after lunch, so it's just the four of us now if I don't count Takeo who has taken a seat next to Rose. The judges are sequestered in their tent, deliberating. I watch their silhouettes through the canvas and keep an eye on Shen as he weaves through the arena and talks to the chefs. Suddenly, he whips out his phone. He listens for a moment, barely interrupting. Then, without a word to anyone, he takes off.

What was that call about? What did they tell him?

Apparently, I'm not the only one dying to know. Many others seem to have noticed and are whispering among themselves. The entire arena is on edge. Victor starts to pace. He makes several phone calls that I assume are to Shen or Commandant Lambert. His frustrated expression suggests no one is answering. At his side is Nicole biting her nails.

I turn to Gabriel. "Will you call the brigade?"

Before he can respond, Victor storms over, with Nicole in tow.

"Capitaine," Victor demands, "what's going on?"

"I know as much as you do, Monsieur le Maire," Gabriel replies.

"Then make some calls," Victor urges him.

With a nod, Gabriel steps aside to call his colleagues at the brigade.

Victor turns to us, gesturing wildly. "This is unprecedented! If Seraphin Rampal has met with foul play—"

"Now, Victor," Rose cuts in, "let's not spin out of control. For all we know, Capitaine Shen left to deal with a private matter."

"Or Rampal was found in a ditch, plastered," Flo suggests.

Meanwhile, I keep my mouth shut. If I open it, I'll have to side with Victor. Whatever was said on that phone call was dramatic enough for Shen to rush out like he did.

Gabriel ends the call and returns to our side. Everyone turns to him.

"They found something," he says. "Shen's on his way to a location outside of town."

Victor blanches. Nicole grips his arm.

"What exactly did they find?" I ask.

"Um... They think it might be related to Seraphin Rampal," Gabriel replies evasively.

I stare him in the eye. "So, what do we do now?"

"Now, we wait," he says.

SHEN HAS BEEN GONE for almost two hours. The judges are still inside the tent. I can see their silhouettes moving around and gesturing animatedly. They seem to be struggling to come to an agreement. If Rampal were here, his opinion would've been decisive. But in his absence, the panel flounders, trying to reach a consensus without their leader.

Fortunately, Beldoc's amateur dance company is entertaining the audience. Their show is a unique take on *Prelude to the Afternoon of a Faun*. The dancers are going for a bold fusion of Debussy's classic with trendy TikTok routines. They're all over the place. The faun is moonwalking, prancing, and breakdancing with such enthusiastic dissonance that even the most stoic faces in the crowd break into smiles.

I watch, amused, despite the apprehension. Just as the faun attempts an ambitious spin that nearly sends him into the front row, Shen reappears. With a hard-set jaw and the absence of his aviator shades, he looks particularly somber. Two uniformed gendarmes accompany him. The three of them halt. The gendarmes listen to Shen's instructions and hurry back to the exit.

Something's wrong.

Shen heads straight for Gabriel. Victor, Nicole, and I quickly gather around him, forming a tight circle. Rose, Flo, and even Takeo join us, drawn by the obvious gravity of Shen's return.

"What is it, Capitaine Shen?" Victor asks, his voice tense.

"Seraphin Rampal," Shen begins, "washed up on the banks of the Rhône, just outside Beldoc."

I gasp. Rose clutches her chest. Flo's eyes widen in shock. Victor's face loses the last of its color. Nicole sways on her feet as she processes the news.

Rose demands, "What happened to him?"

"We don't know yet," Shen replies.

"Do you think it was an accident or...?" Victor voices the question on everyone's mind.

"We're treating it as a suspicious death, which might change after the ME examines the body," Shen says.

"So, you aren't ruling out... murder?" Nicole chokes out. "Who would do such a thing?"

"The most likely cause of death, Madame Clesse, is accidental drowning," Shen says to her.

I narrow my eyes. "You mean he went out for a walk late last night, lost his balance, and tumbled into the river?"

"It's possible," Shen confirms. "Especially, if the autopsy shows a severe alcohol intoxication."

"Could it be suicide?" Rose asks.

Shen casts her a weary look. "We aren't ruling anything out at this point, Madame Tassy."

"Are you certain it's him?" Nicole inquires.

"Unless he had a twin or a doppelgänger, then I'm afraid it's him, Madame Clesse," Shen says.

Gabriel steps forward. "Anything I can help with?"

"I had the exits secured," Shen informs him. "No one leaves until I've talked to them."

"Need a hand with the statements?" Gabriel offers.

Shen opens his notebook, flips through it, and points to what looks like a list. "From this name down?"

"Got it."

Gabriel snaps a photo of the page and heads off to gather statements from those on his half of the list.

Is there something I can help you with, Capitaine Shen?

Knowing him, I don't bother asking. To keep myself occupied, I look around. The atmosphere in the arena has shifted. People are starting to notice Shen's return and the increased police presence. A rumble of concern spreads through the crowd like wildfire.

Shen turns to Victor and Nicole and motions for them

to come closer. "Would you mind answering a few questions, one at a time?"

Nicole nods.

"Of course, anything to help!" Victor exclaims.

He goes first. Nicole waits her turn. My gaze drifts back to Shen as questions swirl in my mind. Will he interview me again? Should I work up the nerve to offer help? Should I ask FERJ, my amateur detective crew composed of Flo, Eric, Rose, and me, if we should investigate this on our side? The itch to jump into the fray is hard to resist.

But there are also good reasons for sitting this one out. Hopefully, Shen has learned from his past mistakes and will be aware of his tunnel vision. There are signs he's on the right track already. Even though he thinks Rampal's death was accidental, he's taken measures to keep the Ritzy Rice organizers and participants in the area so he can interview everyone.

I should stay in my lane, shouldn't I?

No doubt. On the other hand, if I'd done that four years ago, when Shen was in charge of Eric's father's case, justice would've been derailed. It was FERJ's involvement that corrected the course.

Flo leans toward me. "What's your gut telling you?"

"Any *snapshots* yet?" Rose asks.

"No," I admit. "I got nothing."

Around us, more and more people realize that something serious has happened. The faun is still moonwalking about the stage, oblivious to the turmoil in the audience, but the laughs are few and far between. The lighthearted performance feels increasingly out of place as the news of Rampal's death spreads in the wake of Shen's and Gabriel's interviews.

The emcee enters the panel's tent. One by one, the judges come out, looking shocked. Which reminds me. Now that Seraphin Rampal is gone, there will be no one to attribute lavender sprigs or write a feature in the *Rampal Guide*. There will be no winners.

Ritzy Rice is over.

CHAPTER 12

The wind whips through my hair as I pedal down the smooth, flat trail, buoyed by the rush of cool air against my skin. My bike is in zero-assist mode, which means I'm getting some exercise. *Well done, me!*

The sun is warm on my back, but the morning freshness still lingers in the air, invigorating my senses. The temperature is perfect—not too hot, not too cold—the kind you savor because you know how rare it is. The weather forecast promises rain and wind, and then, inevitably, colder days. The picnic I'm riding to may be the last of the season.

I turn and continue along the Rhône. With gravity on my side, my legs move on their own accord, propelling me forward with ease.

Up ahead, a purely functional bridge spans the sparkling river. Founded by the Romans, Beldoc has never really embraced the Rhône the way Avignon and Arles have. Or the way Paris cherishes the Seine. Many think that the Rhône's cold waters amplify the formidable mistral wind, especially in winter. Even if true, nothing keeps my town from loving the river in the warmer months. After all, we sit on this majestic watercourse that flows all the way from the Swiss Alps to the Mediterranean Sea!

Beldocians will eventually stop snubbing their river, I'm sure of it. But that day hasn't come yet.

On the bridge, I lean on the pedals, refusing to engage the motor. Instead, I use my body weight to push on.

This should count as an advanced workout! Rose would be proud of me.

When I reach the descent, I let gravity assist me again. Once on the other side of the bridge, I follow the path of the riverbank, small pebbles scattering beneath my tires.

As I round the bend, the picnic spot we've been favoring this year comes into view. Rose, Flo, and Eric are already there, lounging on a brightly colored blanket spread out on the grass under a tree. Lady, Rose's King Charles spaniel, roams around the group, sniffing everything in sight and wagging her tail high and fast. In dog language, it means "I'm happy" but also "I'm the boss of you all."

"Hey, you're late!" Flo calls with a grin.

"Only five minutes!" I shout.

Eric greets me with his favorite split-fingered *Star Trek* salute. "Live long and prosper, Chef!"

I hop off my bike, wheel it over to the tree, and lean it against the trunk. Grinning with anticipation, I kick off my shoes and let my toes sink into the soft, cool grass.

Ah, the simple pleasures!

Rose raises her wine glass. "I'm so relieved to see you smiling, *ma chérie!* I was afraid you'd be depressed after that irresponsible man robbed you of your victory."

It takes me a moment to realize she's talking about Rampal. If the group picnicking nearby could hear her, it would never occur to them that my victory was more than uncertain, and the man in question "robbed" me by dying a premature death.

With a tut-tut to Grandma to let her know I disapprove of her reading of the events, I walk the few steps to the blanket. In its center, Rose has laid out an assortment of quiches, which is the only hot dish she knows how to make. I spot a white wine and two big bottles of water. Simple and nice. The perfect break from the bookkeeping, which is what I do every Monday, alone in the shop behind the Closed sign.

Lady bounces over to me, her big brown eyes full of hope. I kneel, give her a scratch behind the ears, and then plop down on the blanket.

"Any news?" Flo asks.

I reach for a slice of quiche. "According to Gabriel, Shen is analyzing the statements they took yesterday while waiting on the postmortem results."

"Is he leaning toward accidental death?" Eric inquires.

I bite into the quiche. "Likely due to inebriation."

"Was he known to drink a lot?" Flo asks.

I chew before answering, "I don't think so, but apparently, there were no wounds on the body, and no visible signs of violence."

"That's not enough to preclude foul play," Rose declares.

Her authoritative tone is due to the fact that she's been working hard over the last two years to get her PI license. Last year, she got overwhelmed and took a break. She resumed her online program recently, confident she'll manage this time.

"Shen isn't ruling anything out," I say.

"What about you, Chef?" Eric asks. "Which are you leaning?"

"Honestly, I don't know."

Flo rolls her eyes. "Oh, come on! You always have some theory, even if it's wild."

"Well, I don't have any at the moment." After a

hesitation, I add, "The only thing that doesn't sit right with me is that some people were acting weird."

Rose's eyebrows shoot up. "Like who?"

"Armelle, for one," I say.

"Armelle Pradine?" Eric stares at me. "I know her! I did my internship in her restaurant, under her sous chef's supervision."

I tilt my head to the side. "Did you know that Rampal dumped her and then trashed her work in his review?"

"No, I didn't." He massages his neck. "That's a twist."

"And a suspicious one at that," I add.

Flo blows her cheeks out. "Oh, please. Will everyone stop pussyfooting? It isn't a twist—it's a *motive*."

"Hell hath no fury like a woman scorned," Rose recites. "Homer."

"Homer Simpson?" Eric asks, a twinkle in his eye.

Grandma's lips curl into a smug smile. "No, dear boy! There's a world beyond *Star Trek* and *The Simpsons*, you know? It's the Greek Homer."

"Most people think it's Shakespeare," Flo says. "But it's actually another English playwright whose name escapes me."

Rose looks peeved but doesn't argue. My youngest sister has a degree in art history and a part-time job in a gallery in Arles. That makes her FERJ's undisputed expert in all things art and literature.

Eric turns to me. "You said that some people were acting weird. Who did you have in mind?"

"Ugo constantly checked his phone and glanced over his shoulder," I begin, ticking off on my fingers.

"Ugo Drugeon?" Eric cuts in. "The chef and owner of Chez Ugo in Cavaillon?"

I nod. "The very same. Apparently, Rampal's latest review did a number on his bottom line."

"Aaand—motive!" Flo exclaims, pointing finger guns at Eric. "Desperate people do desperate things."

"Anyone else with a possible motive?" Eric asks me.

"Not that I know of, but..." I hesitate before mentioning the little things I observed.

"Spit it out." Rose holds her wine glass aloft as permission to gossip. "It's not like you're talking to the cops."

"During the lecture on decolonizing rice, Mylene Nivault left for a good twenty minutes. And when she came back, she was clutching her purse like it held the crown jewels," I say quickly. "And Takeo Nakashima had a tense conversation with Camille Terrien, the mayor of Eau de Provence. He looked very agitated."

Rose waves her hand dismissively. "Come off it about Takeo! He's just looking to buy a place for his sushi shop. I'm sure that's what the conversation was about."

"Possible," I admit. "But did you see his tattoos?"

Rose shrugs. "Pff, millions of people have tattoos. I do, too. Doesn't make me a gangster."

Flo and I stare at her, dumbfounded.

"Where's your tattoo, Grandma?" Flo asks. "Can we see it?"

She flips her silver hair back. "I can't, not in front of Eric. Besides, it's none of your business."

"Fair enough," I say. "But Takeo also seemed a bit too interested in what Gabriel and Shen were talking about."

Rose huffs. "Nonsense. He was interested in me, not in their conversation."

Lady barks, sensing the confrontational vibe, and trots over to Rose. Halting beside Grandma, she gives me a low growl and threatening wag.

Rose strokes Lady's head. "Easy, baby. Don't bite your sister just yet. Wait for my signal."

"Please, have mercy!" I beg, feigning panic. "I take back everything I said about Takeo!"

Lady couldn't bite me even if she wanted to, given her truncated snout and weak jaws that can't chew through even the thinnest of rawhide sticks. She also happens to be the sweetest and least aggressive dog in the world. She's never bitten anyone, let alone her "sister."

Rose sticks her chin out. "I suggest everyone calm down and wait for the autopsy."

"So, what's our plan?" Eric asks me. "Can we trust Shen to do it right this time around?"

I lean back on my elbows. "You know what? We don't have to decide right now. Rose is right. We better wait for the autopsy."

Flo raises her hand. "I second that."

"Agreed, then." Rose finishes her glass. "Let's not look for trouble where there probably isn't any."

"Uh-huh," I say.

My gut goes, *uh-uh*, but I ignore it. The weather is uplifting, the setting is serene, and I'm determined to enjoy the last days of summer with my loved ones.

Trouble can wait.

CHAPTER 13

My eyes open to the gray light of dawn filtering through the curtains. Beside me, Gabriel's breathing is still deep and steady. He showed up very late last night instead of crashing at the barracks like he usually does when he finishes work after midnight. I was half asleep, and we didn't get a chance to talk.

I glance at the nightstand, where his gun rests. Gabriel and I have been together for almost two years, but after all this time, the sight of his weapon in my cozy bedroom still freaks me out. It's not so much the gun itself as the fact that these days an officer of the law can't afford to let his guard down, even in his sleep.

Many cops changed their habits after the horror story that unfolded in a sleepy Paris suburb, Magnanville, where an Islamist ambushed and killed a police officer outside his home. He then went inside and murdered the officer's wife in front of the couple's three-year-old. Unsure what to do with the toddler, he live-streamed on Facebook, pledging allegiance to ISIS. Special Forces stormed the house. Thankfully, the child survived.

In Gabriel's case, the concern for his own safety is

compounded by constant worry about mine. He gets all worked up every time I investigate. When I tell him to stop fretting, he reminds me about Lena Morillot, murdered by the Mafia. Her death was a warning for her gendarme husband to drop the case he was investigating, or else they'd kill his child, too. It worked. Raphael Morillot resigned from the gendarmerie, took his son, and moved to the Dordogne.

Gabriel claims he sleeps better knowing he can reach over and grab his gun at any time. He's trained to shoot with the lights off. Still in the dark, he's able to empty the clip, insert another magazine and shoot again.

When he sleeps at the barracks, or when he travels for work, he never fails to remind me to check that the door and windows are locked, and that my self-defense gear is accessible. Sure, he's overreacting, but I get it. I also understand why he's refusing to start a family. That is, my brain understands it.

The rest of me? Not so much.

Quietly, I slip out of bed and grab some clean clothes as I tiptoe into the bathroom. A quick shower helps me shake off the lingering sleep. Once I'm dressed, I make my way to the kitchen.

The pâtisserie is closed this morning due to some emergency work on the section of the street in front of my shop. Since I'm in no hurry, I decide to make some donuts. It's funny—I used to despise them, but after my memorable stay at Villa Grare last fall, I've developed a bit of a soft spot for those treats. When done well, they're delightful. Besides, kneading, shaping, and frying the dough is the closest I can get to meditation.

As I finish up, the smell of fresh donuts fills the kitchen, warm and sweet. I'm dusting the last batch with sugar when I hear Gabriel's footsteps. He appears in the doorway, freshly showered and dressed, his hair still damp. He's holding a manila folder in his hands.

"Morning," he greets me.

I pluck a donut from the plate and walk over to him. "Morning!"

He gives me a quizzical look. I hold the donut up like a magnifying glass and squint at his folder through the hole. The folder's cover is blank. There's no title, no abbreviation, no marking of any kind.

"Hmm," I go. "This is highly suspicious."

A smile tugs at the corners of his mouth. "What is, Detective Donut?"

"Your file doesn't have a name, Capitaine."

"Am I in trouble?"

I lower the donut. "It depends."

"What's your professional opinion?"

"You've been working too hard," I say. "You need a break."

He sets the folder down on the counter. "I'll take that under advisement."

"Good. Now have a donut."

He moves to pick one up from the plate but stops halfway and kisses me first. "Thanks for making these."

"My pleasure."

He cups my cheek, and I lean into his touch. The kitchen clock provides a beat for the distant hum of the morning outside. I stand still, savoring the peaceful moment.

"I'd like to offer you a deal," Gabriel says.

"What kind of deal?"

"Will you stay out of Shen's hair?"

I feel a flicker of annoyance rise up, but I keep it in check. "What do I get in return?"

"I'll help you track down your 'ghost' rider—the gardian from the Arles parade."

I pull away and peer at him. "Weren't you going to help me anyway?"

"I was. I am." He leans on the counter. "But if you let Shen handle things without interference, I'll put in the hours, and I promise we'll find the scumbag who caused your mother's death."

I pour us both coffees. "Remember the Dol case?"

"How could I forget?" He picks up a donut. "But this time, none of your friends or family are suspects. You don't have a dog in this fight, Julie."

I cross my arms. "So, am I just supposed to ignore my instincts? Shen botched that case back then. Who's to say he won't do it again?"

"I'm not telling you to disregard your instincts." He runs a hand through his hair. "I just... You almost died on your last case! And the one before that, too."

The old frustration bubbles up. "But I didn't, did I? What happened to your friend Raphael's wife is the exception, not the rule."

"The way things have been going since Lena's murder," he argues, "it may become the rule."

I set my cup down. "I can't go on like this, honey. I don't want to give up on my dream because of fear."

"What dream?" He frowns. "What are you talking about?"

Oops. I didn't mean to go there. Not now, anyway. But I'm tired of walking on eggshells.

More words spill out of me. "I want more from life. I want to have kids."

His expression hardens. "We've been over this, Julie."

"Yes, we have," I say. "But my biological clock has picked up speed since then. I'm thirty-four. Next year, my fertility will plummet. I feel like I have a ticking bomb in my head."

"Sorry, love, but my mind is made up."

The finality in his tone cuts so deep I gasp. "And I'm supposed to just accept that?"

"I wish we could see eye to eye on this…"

Tears of anger and hurt well up. *This*, I'm itching to say, *is a deal-breaker*. But I chicken out. If I say that, and he still doesn't change his mind, I'll have to break up with him.

Oh, God.

"Julie, I—" he begins.

But I don't wait for him to finish. The kitchen suddenly feels too stifling. I storm out the door and into the bedroom, heart pounding in my chest. Taking deep breaths, I shut the door and try to calm the storm raging inside me.

This day had started out so light-hearted!

And now I'm standing barefoot, with pieces of eggshell stuck between my toes.

CHAPTER 14

I sit on the edge of the bed, my head in my hands, trying to pull myself together. The argument with Gabriel echoes in my mind. The air feels thick with the words we said, and the ones we didn't. My heartbeat is still chaotic with a mix of hurt, yearning, and a bunch of other emotions. I exhale slowly.

A soft knock on the door breaks the silence. "Julie?"

"Come in, it's open," I say.

Gabriel steps inside. The bright morning light frames him in silhouette. I look down at my hands clasped together in my lap.

"I'm sorry if I upset you," he says, his voice low and sincere. "I love you."

"I love you, too."

He sits down next to me. "Last night, I uncovered something that might help us locate your ghost rider."

I look up. "Really?"

"Yes. I got some surveillance footage from the Fête du Riz parade in Arles. I stayed late to view it."

"Why didn't you say so earlier?"

"I was going to tell you when I got home, but you were already asleep. And this morning..."

"We had a row."

He hangs his head.

A flicker of hope ignites in me, chasing away everything else. "You think you found him?"

"Come with me."

He offers his hand. I take it, and he leads me back to the kitchen. There, he opens the unmarked folder sitting on the counter and pulls out a photo.

"Look." He puts it in front of me. "This is a still from the parade."

I lean over and examine the grainy image of a man in the crowd. He's walking now. His face is only partially visible, but the height, build, and general appearance match the building contractor I've been chasing—or the Ghost Rider, as Gabriel calls him.

"It could be him," I say.

Gabriel smiles, visibly relieved. "Fantastic! Now, we have more than Flo's sketch to work with."

"Yes." I trace the outline of the Ghost Rider's form with my finger.

"Julie," Gabriel says, "I'm going to track him down. I'm going to serve you his identity on a silver platter."

"Do your terms still apply?" I ask. "About me staying out of the Rampal case?"

He rests his hand on my shoulder. "It's a recommendation, not a condition. I just want you to be safe, *mon amour*. But I'll help you, no matter what."

"Thank you, that means a lot."

We finish breakfast together. The comfort of routine, of sharing a meal, and talking about the day ahead grounds us both. By the time we're heading out, the residual tension is gone. *At least, for now.*

The warmth of the midmorning sun brushes against my face as Gabriel and I exchange a quick kiss by the door.

"Need a ride to the shop?" he asks, eyes lingering on mine.

"Thanks, but I'm walking today."

"No bike?"

"We're not allowed to open for another hour, assuming the power and water come back on as scheduled," I explain. "I can afford a leisurely stroll."

"Sounds nice." He smiles. "I'd walk with you, but I need to be in Arles in thirty minutes."

With a final wave, he drives off, and I start down the cobblestone street. Halfway to the shop it hits me—the hotel Belle d'Oc isn't far, just a small detour through the municipal garden. Given that I have time to kill, I could stretch my legs a bit longer, admire the lovely little park, and... scratch an itch.

Should I?

Before I know it, my feet have already made the decision.

For the record, I'm not investigating.

I'm just going to check out Beldoc's only hotel, which I've never seen from the inside. That's all.

I cross the garden not really noticing its colors or smells. My attention sharpens as soon as the stone façade of Belle d'Oc comes into view. Its ochre walls glow against the faded blue shutters that frame each window. Overflowing floral planters add a splash of life to the tiny balconies. Climbing vines wrap around the exterior, infusing this quintessentially Southern building with an extra dose of charm.

I step inside. The lobby is an homage to the same Provençal style as the front—terracotta tiles underfoot, rustic wooden beams overhead, and walls adorned with watercolors of lavender fields and vineyards.

As I wander through the lobby, taking in the decor, I glimpse a woman talking quietly to a bellhop near the front desk, both stooped in a confidential huddle. I halt by the water dispenser, even though I'm not thirsty. There are already two people waiting ahead of me. *Excellent!* I've never been happier to stand in a line.

As unobtrusively as I can, I take a closer look at the woman. She's wearing dark glasses and a cap pulled down low over her face. Her hair is completely hidden. But something about her thin yet busty figure, about the way she holds herself, pulls on the threads of recognition in my mind...

Holy cow, it's Armelle Pradine—Rampal's ex!

The conversation between her and the bellhop is too hushed for me to make out, but their body language tells a story. Armelle is leaning in, head tilted to the side, like she's pleading with him. I can't see her face from where I'm standing, but her hand is moving in a very interesting way. I'd say she's trying to push something—money?—toward the bellhop. He shoves his hands into his pockets.

If it was money, did he take it?

I can't be sure of what I'm looking at, but a tingle of unease runs up my spine.

Suddenly, Armelle straightens up and rushes to the exit. I panic and pretend to rummage through my purse. From the corner of my eye, I catch sight of her exiting the hotel. She slips into a remastered Mini Cooper parked just outside the entrance. The engine revs softly and then she's gone.

What exactly did I just witness?

As I make my way from the hotel, I mull over the question. It feels like I've stumbled onto something significant. Was Armelle trying to bribe the bellboy for information? Or, worse, to help her cover something up?

It's Tuesday. Seraphin Rampal's body was found on Sunday afternoon. Even if Capitaine Shen is leaning toward accidental death, I bet he had Rampal's hotel room searched already. Shen may not be the gendarmerie's finest, but he's no fool.

So, assuming Armelle is guilty, why show up at Rampal's hotel now? If she was hoping to destroy evidence linking her to her ex's death, why wait two days before trying to do that? Why not attempt to sneak into the room before the cops searched it—for instance, on Sunday at dawn?

Perhaps she did but was spooked and didn't get a chance to finish the job. Or maybe she didn't come here looking for evidence, but for information.

The question is, what information?

When I get to the shop, Eric is already there, and he's already opened it. Rare thing, the roadwork took shorter than planned!

He greets me and frowns. "Everything all right, Chef? You look like you've seen a ghost."

"In a way, I have."

He raises an eyebrow.

"Your former supervisor, Armelle Pradine..." I begin.

"What about her?"

"I think she was at Belle d'Oc this morning. You know, Rampal's hotel? I saw her talking to—"

"Hang on." He flashes a palm. "What were *you* doing at Belle d'Oc?"

"Nosing around, of course. What else?"

"Right. Of course." He drops his hand. "Please go on."

"I saw a woman in shades and a cap talking to a bellhop."

"What makes you think it was Armelle?"

"Same height and pinup body shape," I reply.

His smirks. "She isn't the only slender D-cup in Beldoc, you know?"

80

"True, but how many of those slim D-cups drive a powder-blue remastered Mini?"

"Hmm..." He rubs his chin. "She may be the only one."

I lift my chin. "I think she was trying to bribe the bellhop to gain access to Rampal's room."

"It's a valid theory," Eric concedes.

We decide that the rest of FERJ needs to hear about this, even if we aren't officially, or unofficially, investigating the Rampal case.

Friends don't keep this kind of news from friends, do they?

CHAPTER 15

Business is slow, so I leave Eric in charge and pop into Magda's shop next door.

The days of all-out war with her are over, but let's not kid ourselves—we're not friends. Sure, she no longer actively wishes for my bankruptcy. There was even a moment, right after she bought her second store, adjoining Igor's bookshop, when I thought, perhaps we might bond. But nope, we didn't. What we have now isn't camaraderie. I wouldn't call it lasting peace, either. It's more like a prolonged truce.

Which explains why I prefer to shop for gifts at Lavender Dream 1, manned by hired hands, rather than at Lavender Dream 2, run by Magda herself.

The bell above the door jingles with enthusiasm as I step in. The shop, charmingly cluttered, is a treasure trove of all things pretty and fragrant. Right now, it's as quiet as my gluten-free kingdom next door. Classical music plays in the background. The sun is streaming in, adding a fairy tale-like glow to the items on display. The only snag is the overpowering scent of lavender that makes my sensitive nose twitch.

Magda's new sales assistant greets me from behind the counter. "Julie! How lovely to see you here!"

"Hi, Leslie. I'm looking for something special for Flo's birthday."

"Of course," the blonde chirps. "You've come to the right place. We just got in a new shipment of the most beautiful silver jewelry designed by a local artisan."

"The guy Magda is always raving about?"

"He's the best," Leslie says. "Let me show you."

She goes over to a display case and pulls out a bracelet. The craftsmanship is stunning, on par with Flo's refined tastes.

"It's perfect," I say.

Leslie carefully places the bracelet into a velvet-lined box. "You've made an excellent choice, Julie! This will look amazing on her."

Part of me knows that Leslie is just a good salesperson, and that she may not mean a word of what she said. Still, I smile, flattered, and hand her the money. Normally, I'd swipe my card for anything over twenty euros. But Eric and I catered a wedding in the Heights two weeks ago, and the tips were *very* good.

Leslie takes my handful of fivers and tenners, and rings the sum up, her movements quick and professional. I survey her while she works. Her petite frame, short haircut, and round face with a button nose make it difficult to guess her age. She could be anywhere between thirty-five and fifty.

Leslie returns sixty cents. "Here's your change."

I take the coins, disconcerted. The thing is, I had quickly counted out the money I gave her. It's a habit ingrained from years of running my own shop.

"Um, Leslie," I begin, keeping my tone light. "It should've been two sixty."

She blinks at me, surprised. "Oh dear! Really?"

"Yes, really."

She counts the money out again, this time slowly, and slaps a hand to her forehead. "Unbelievable! Let me fix that for you."

I smile awkwardly as she hands me the correct change. "There you go! All good. I've never made a mistake like this before."

"Don't worry about it. We all have our off days."

Her frown doesn't go away. "Are you going to tell Magda?"

"No."

She beams, visibly relieved. "You're very kind. Have a wonderful day! And give Flo my best wishes."

"Will do. Take care, Leslie."

I tuck the velvet box into my bag and head back to my shop.

The wrong change? No biggie.

Leslie's way too friendly to short a customer on purpose. She looked so genuinely shocked when I pointed out the mistake; I felt like I'd accused a puppy of tax fraud. Plus, with that childlike face, button nose, and doe eyes, she's more likely to steal hearts than cash.

And who am I to judge?

For all I know, I've shorted a customer myself, and the only reason I'm blissfully unaware of my misdeed is that no one caught it. And now I'm strutting around like I'm the retail's moral compass, when I actually have a history of low-key criminal enterprise. *Imagine that!*

I'm in the middle of piping cream onto the éclairs when Eric pokes his head into the lab. "Chef, you might want to step out here for a sec."

"What is it?"

"A delivery."

My eyebrows shoot up. Eric doesn't need my presence to receive something we've ordered, even if it requires a signature.

"It's a personal delivery," he adds enigmatically.

Could it be Gabriel? But if he were in the neighborhood and wanted to say hi, he'd just walk into the kitchen without bothering Eric to announce him.

The more likely scenario? It's yet another bouquet from Denis Noble, aka Denis the Insistent. He's playing the long game, convinced my relationship with Gabriel is on borrowed time. To remind me he's on standby for my inevitable heartbreak, Denis sends me monthly floral reminders. I stick them in a pretty ceramic vase and leave them in the shop.

I wipe my hands on my apron and step out front.

An acned teenager stands by the counter, clutching an envelope.

"Can I help you?" I ask.

"Are you Julie Cavallo?"

"I am."

He looks down at his phone. "Yeah, that's you."

He's comparing me to a photograph on the screen. I recognize the picture instantly—it's the profile shot I submitted to the Ritzy Rice competition.

"Where did you get that?" I ask.

The boy shrugs and hands over the envelope. "I'm supposed to give you this."

"And what's that?"

"No clue. Some lady outside gave it to me along with ten euros. She told me to bring it to you."

"What lady?" I step closer, eyes narrow. "What did she look like?"

"She had sunglasses and a hoodie." He shrugs again. "I couldn't really see her face."

"Did you ask her name?" *I'd be surprised.*

He inches toward the door. "Nope."

I bolt right after him and scan the street for the mysterious woman. Unfortunately, none of the passersby match his description, minimalistic as it was.

Could it be Armelle?

I go back inside. Eric gives me a quizzical look from behind the counter. I'm about to open the envelope in front of him, but a customer comes in, followed by another. They'll keep Eric busy for the next ten minutes, if not more.

No way I can wait that long.

I slip into the bistro corner of the shop, pull out a chair and sit down with the envelope in front of me. My heart beats a little faster as I tear it open. Inside, there are half a dozen typewritten letters, unsigned. I skim them. Sharp, accusatory, threatening words jump out at me from every page.

As far as I can tell, they're all addressed to Seraphin Rampal.

CHAPTER 16

I flip through the pages and spread the letters out on the table. There are seven of them. It's clear that someone was furious with Rampal, and they wanted him to know it by trashing every aspect of his character. Certain passages are dripping with venom. One of the letters contains thinly veiled threats. It demands that he discontinue his guide, quit his job, and leave Provence—or else.

The more I read, the more questions I have. Who wrote this stuff? When? Who was the woman in the hoodie? Why did she want me to have these letters? If I go out on a limb and assume she'd heard about my detective skills, why didn't she deliver the envelope personally? Alternatively, an explanatory note would've been really nice.

Eric joins me as soon as the shop is empty again. He surveys the letters on the table.

After he's scanned them, I comment, "They're all addressed to Seraphin Rampal."

"Yes," he concurs, looking up. "Do you think Armelle wrote them? Is that why she went to the hotel this morning?"

"Maybe she was trying to bribe that bellhop to check if the letters were still in Rampal's room."

He points at them. "But if she managed to get them back, wouldn't she want to destroy them?"

"Logically, yes."

"I don't understand," he says, frowning. "Forensics could find her fingerprints on these letters. Why leave such incriminating evidence around?"

"It makes even less sense for her to have the letters delivered to me."

Eric nods slowly, deep in thought. "Unless she wasn't the one who wrote them."

"Or the one that had them dropped off here."

"Or neither."

I lean forward. "But if she did write them, then whoever had them brought here is trying to implicate her, don't you think?"

"Which raises the question: why hand the letters to you, and not to the gendarmes?"

"Good question." I tap my fingers on the table. "One thing's for sure. Armelle can't be both the author of these letters and the person who paid that boy to get them to me."

"Unless she's schizophrenic."

I let out a short laugh. "You worked with her. Is she?"

"No."

The front door rings, and someone walks into the shop. On impulse, I slip the letters into the envelope. Looking up, I see Leslie.

She shifts her gaze from me to Eric. "Hi, guys! What are you up to?"

"The usual," I reply.

"Was that a courier earlier?" She glances at the envelope. "News from Ritzy Rice?"

"Nope."

"Well, that's a shame," she says. "I was rooting for you. Is there a chance you can still win?"

I shake my head. "Seraphin Rampal sponsored the competition and structured it around his guide. The final results depended on his judgment. It all fell apart with his death."

"I'm sorry to hear that." She shifts from one foot to the other. "Anyway, I, um... I just wanted to apologize again for what happened earlier."

Eric looks from her to me. "What's that?"

"You didn't tell him?" Leslie asks, raising an eyebrow.

"No," I say. "And I'm not going to."

"Now I really want to know." Eric turns to me. "What happened, Chef?"

Leslie smiles. "I made a mistake and shorted Julie two euros, something that's never happened before and will never happen again."

"Ah." Eric grimaces with disappointment. "I was expecting something juicier."

The doorbell jingles again. Several customers troop in. Eric and I rush to our stations. Leslie retreats to hers next door.

"Welcome to Julie's Gluten-Free Delights!" Eric greets the first person in line.

I tuck the envelope under the counter and put on my sweetest customer service face. "How can I help you today?"

My thoughts keep wandering off as I roll out dough for a new batch of gluten-free croissants. I replay the scene with Armelle and the bellhop over and over again. Then I mull over the anonymous letters before my mind circles back to Armelle.

It's pretty unusual to come across two intriguing clues in the space of one morning. *This* morning! No wonder they're now wedged like splinters in my brain, refusing to be ignored.

I check the clock. There's still half an hour left before Flo arrives but I'm already counting down the seconds. The sooner I get these letters into Shen's hands, the better. Maybe then I'll be able to concentrate on my work.

Eric peeks into the lab. "You OK, Chef?"

"Yes, why?"

"You've been awfully quiet since we read those letters."

"I can't stop thinking about them," I confess.

He leans against the doorframe. "Are you going to hand them over to Shen?"

"Yes."

"Why not to Gabriel?"

"Shen is the lead investigator on the case," I remind Eric. "Look, I know he screwed up your father's case, but we have to give him the benefit of the doubt."

Eric lets out a sigh. "It's not like we have a choice, do we?"

"No, we don't," I confirm. "As soon as Flo gets here, I'm going to the gendarmerie."

With a curt nod, he returns to his post behind the counter.

Flo arrives a little earlier than usual, brimming with energy.

"Hey, what's up?" she asks after donning her uniform.

"Quite a bit, actually," I say.

Her eyebrows crawl upward. "Is it about the Rampal case?"

"Yes." I take my apron off. "Eric will tell you."

Before leaving, I scan all seven letters, using an app on my phone just in case I lose them on the way to the gendarmerie or the gendarmes lose them later. It's not that

FERJ is gearing up to investigate in parallel with Shen. *Really, we have no such plans.*

I email the scanned letters to Eric, Flo, and myself, and slide the originals back into the envelope.

Eric winks at Flo. "I'll explain everything if you make me a coffee."

My sister scurries to the coffee machine.

"I'll be back soon," I say to both, grabbing my helmet.

Five minutes later, I park my bike in front of the gendarmerie, a modern building surrounded by typically Provençal houses. I push the button next to the controlled entry door and wait to be told to step into the tiny brand-new security vestibule. It's part of the ever-increasing safety precautions the police and gendarmes have taken in recent years. Other public administrations such as museums and schools, but also shopping malls have them. Street after street in the affluent Heights has been gated off after a series of violent burglaries. *Beldoc Live* used to cover them. But they stopped after Victor issued his decree making it illegal to hurt the criminals' feelings.

I wait in the "airlock" while a gendarme screens me for guns, knives, axes, machetes, and whatnot. *Good thing I left my self-defense knife in the shop!*

The door in front of me opens. I cross the reception area to the tall counter, where a rookie in a crisp uniform nods at me. After he checks my ID, I ask for Shen. Anticlimactically, he's out and won't be back until late afternoon. I leave the envelope with the young gendarme along with a note explaining how I got the letters.

On my way back, the wind in my face combined with the physical exertion clears my head, and I have an aha moment. It's been several months since my last lunch with Yoona, the artist who has a small gallery in Pont-de-Pré, a village near Beldoc. FERJ helped her and her now husband out of a serious bind two years back. Yoona and I have been in touch since then, infrequently but regularly.

Should I pop by and say hello?

Why not? Eric and Flo are both in the shop, and I could use a distraction. The fact that Armelle's restaurant is in Pont-de-Pré is immaterial. Just a coincidence. Honestly, it's so tangential that I don't even know why it crossed my mind.

CHAPTER 17

I text Eric that I won't be back for another hour and steer my bike toward Pont-de-Pré.

It's a pleasant ride, made even more so by the electric motor that helps me uphill. The sun, though still warm, hangs lower in the sky. The air is just as fragrant with flowers and harvests as it was a week ago, but it already carries the first notes of decay. The landscape on both sides of the road is also in transition. The trees are still green, but their tops are veering yellow. The vineyards are reddening, and the distant hills are a mesh of green and gold.

A short time later, I get off the bike in the heart of the village. It's after six. Pont-de-Pré is smaller than Beldoc, so everything closes earlier here. The day's activities are winding down, but Yoona's art studio is still open. I peek in through the glass door. There she is, a delicate Korean princess surrounded by her unexpectedly vivid art.

Yoona spots me and hurries over, beaming. She's happy to see me, but her shoulders are a little tense. The way she glances back at the well-dressed elderly couple standing by her largest canvas tells me this may not be a good time.

The couple sends me a canned smile that telegraphs, "We're waiting; make it quick."

Ooh, this smells like a potential sale! As a business owner, I know better than to give a customer ready to part with some hard-earned cash time to change their mind.

I shoo Yoona away. "I'll come by another time. Looks like you're in the middle of something."

"Julie, wait!" she calls as I'm turning to the door. "Can you hang around until seven? I'd love to catch up afterward."

"Sure, I can do that."

She flashes me a grateful smile before returning to her prospective buyers.

Quietly, I close the door behind me and step back out into the golden afternoon. The best use of this half hour that I suddenly have on my hands would be to find a bench and check my emails. But my feet betray me. They take me straight to Armelle's restaurant in a hotel that's a mere fifty meters down the street from Yoona's studio. My brain protests with every step. Alas, that old frenemy of mine—curiosity—urges me on.

I step into the lobby. You don't need to see the rooms to place this hotel in a category above Belle d'Oc. The abundance of natural light, space, and muted opulence send the message. It strikes me that Gabriel and I can't afford to stay in a place like this when we go on vacation. Then again, if staying in five-star hotels and dining in five-sprig restaurants were my priority, I would've picked creepy Denis over the man I love.

Yuck!

That salutary reminder puts the bounce back in my step. Head held high, I stride through the lobby, bypassing the front desk. I ignore the raised eyebrows of the concierge, and head straight for the restaurant tucked away in the back.

With still an hour until the dinner service begins, the place is as empty as it is pristine. I take in the sleek, modern decor bathed in natural light. Designer tables are set with crisp, white linen. Matching chairs are arranged perfectly, inviting diners to settle in for an evening of gastronomic bliss. Pretty bouquets in cute little jars brighten each table. Soft jazz music plays in the background.

My timing is perfect.

Silencing the voice of reason that screams at me to leave, I march across the room toward the faint smell of fresh herbs and truffle oil. It grows stronger the closer I get to the kitchen. I push through the swinging doors. *Ta-da!* There she is, Armelle, whisking something in a large bowl. By the stove, her sous chef is adding spices to a gorgeous copper pot. Two young *cuistos* at their stations chop and peel under the sous chef's supervision.

It's uncommon for a pastry chef to be the top dog in a restaurant where a savory chef is in charge of the rest. Unless, of course, the pastry chef is well established or famous enough to be the main draw for customers, or if the focus of the restaurant is on desserts.

Armelle spots me and sets the bowl down. "Julie Cavallo?"

"Hi, Armelle!"

"Hello. What brings you to my kitchen?"

My initial impulse is to go with *I was in the neighborhood*, but then I realize it could be a dead end. She could say she's too busy right now, and since my visit is purposeless, I'd have to reply with some banality and get out.

So, I throw caution and good manners to the wind and step closer. "We need to talk."

One of her cuistos shoots me an intrigued look.

Armelle scowls at him before turning to me. "This isn't a good time, Julie. Is it about Ritzy Rice?"

"I just need a minute," I dodge. "It's important."

She nods to her sous chef before turning back to me. "OK. Let's step into my office."

Her movements deliberate, she takes her apron off and hangs it over the back of a nearby chair. Then she motions me to the revolving door. I follow her from the kitchen and in through a door a few meters away. It's a tiny room that's barely big enough for a desk and shelves cluttered with cookbooks, recipe journals, and culinary awards.

When the door closes behind us, Armelle leans against her desk, arms crossed. "What's so important that it couldn't wait?"

"I received some letters today," I begin, watching her closely.

Her expression flickers just for a second. "What letters?"

"Letters addressed to your dead ex, Seraphin Rampal."

Panic flickers on her face before she suppresses it quickly and schools her features into a mask of polite interest. "Oh, wow."

"I believe you know something about them."

"I'm afraid I don't."

"Really?"

"Yes, really." She meets my gaze. "And, if you don't mind me asking, has Capitaine Shen delegated his investigation to you?"

"No, he hasn't."

"Then why are you questioning me?"

"I'm in no position to question anybody," I say. "I'm merely asking you some questions."

She curls her lip. "Ah, well that changes everything!"

"Look, Armelle," I try again, "you've been too busy with your restaurant to listen to the local grapevine, so you haven't heard."

"Heard what?"

"Two years back, I helped the gendarmerie crack a murder case here in Pont-de-Pré. My friends and I have solved other cases elsewhere."

Her mouth twists even more. "Oh my God, am I speaking to the local Sherlock?"

I ignore her sarcasm. "We're amateur sleuths. And we're not too bad at it."

She laughs in my face. "You're out of your depth, girrrl. Why don't you scoot back to your cutesy little shop and let me get on with my work?"

All right then, Madame Pradine, I'm done playing nice.

"I will," I say, "after you tell me what you were doing in the lobby of Belle d'Oc early this morning."

That wipes the smile off her face.

"Nothing," she replies quickly. "I mean, I wasn't there."

"Yes, you were, girrrl," I ape her. "I saw you talking to the bellhop and offering him money."

"Don't be ridiculous! It wasn't me. And why would I do such a thing?"

I shrug. "Dunno. Maybe you were hoping Shen hadn't found your threatening letters during the search, and the bellhop would retrieve them from Rampal's room for you."

"You're talking absolute nonsense."

"Am I, though?" I tilt my head. "That theory did seem far-fetched at the time, but then someone couriered me an envelope with those letters."

The look of genuine surprise on her face is all the confirmation I need that the woman in the hoodie wasn't her. Which makes total sense.

I speak again, my tone softer, "Will you tell me about those letters?"

"I have nothing to tell you, but I do have a theory of my own. You were bored, so you went to the hotel, saw some random woman talking to the bellhop, and then made the rest up."

"Why would I do that?"

"How would I know?" She arches her eyebrow. "Maybe you're a mythomaniac."

Seriously, Armelle? "That woman was you."

She points her index finger at her temple and makes a circular motion, mouthing "You're crazy."

I put my hand on my hip. "What do you think will happen if I tip off Capitaine Shen to watch the hotel lobby's CCTV? I'm sure he'll find an angle that shows your face."

Her jaw clenches. For a moment, I think she's going to deny it again and call me crazy again.

But then her shoulders slump, and she exhales. "Fine. I was there. But it wasn't what you think."

"Then what was it?"

She looks away, her fists clenching and unclenching. When she turns back to me, there's determination in her eyes.

"That bellhop," she says, "I know him. He's the son of a dear friend of mine. A good boy but keeps bad company... um... drugs and stuff. His mom has given up trying to reason with him. So, I thought I'd give it a try."

I tip off an imaginary hat. "Bravo, what a story! And how do you explain the money you put into his hand?"

"It was to help him pay the rent he owes to his landlord," she deadpans.

"I'm not buying any of it."

She squares her shoulders. "I need to get back to my kitchen. Goodbye, Julie."

As I walk out of her office, I can feel her eyes on my back. She didn't tell me the truth, and she's hiding something. That much is clear. The less obvious part is what to do with it... since I'm not investigating this case.

CHAPTER 18

I t's after nine when I finally make it back to the shop. The streets are quiet, and the night air is cool against my skin. I secure my bike before punching in the code to open the metal curtain. Eric and Flo locked up at eight and went home. I feel a little guilty that Eric had to work overtime while I questioned—ahem—*interviewed* Armelle and then had a drink with Yoona. So, I'm going to make up for it now while I wait for Gabriel to finish his shift.

The place is dark, save for the faint glow of the streetlights filtering through the window displays. I push through to the lab, and the familiar scent of baked goods greets me like a comforting embrace. I flip on the lights, put the apron on, and roll up my sleeves. After a quick inspection, I identify the shortfall caused by my absence and set to work on the dough for tomorrow's gluten-free croissants. The tension in my shoulders eases with each press and fold. The soft give of the dough under my palms as I knead is the best thing I could possibly do to take my mind off my dilemma to investigate or not to investigate.

Gabriel arrives.

I let him in and return to my dough. "Give me fifteen minutes, and we can go home."

"You know," he says, a warm smile spreading across his tired face, "I've been thinking."

"About Ghost Rider, I hope? Any progress?"

"No, but I'm working on it."

I nod. "So, what were you thinking about?"

"Maybe I should start a TV show."

I give him an amused side-eye.

He traces an imaginary TV title in the air with his right hand. "*Baking in Blue.*"

"You can't bake," I remark. "But hey, don't let that stop you!"

He shrugs off my quibble. "You'll give me a crash course."

"Hmm."

He tilts his head, so I'll look at him. "Do I have your blessing?"

"Only if I can have a regular appearance as the Pastry Police."

He laughs, walks over to where I'm working and slides a hand around my waist. "Deal."

I rest my head against his chest, loving his playful mood, the warmth and the strength of him, the low rumble of his deep voice...

He kisses the top of my head and watches me knead.

When I'm done, I turn around to face him. "I have a confession to make."

"Listening."

As I stow everything in the fridge and pantry, I recount the events of the day. I start with spotting Armelle at Rampal's hotel. Then, I go over the anonymous letters that ended up in my hands. Finally, I tell him about my conversation with Armelle in Pont-de-Pré.

The longer I talk, the more Gabriel's expression hardens.

"Did you get the letters to Shen?" he asks.

"I left them for him at the gendarmerie," I reply. "But I scanned them first."

"Of course you did."

There's an odd mixture of pride and annoyance in his tone.

I grab my phone and pull up the images. "Here, take a look."

He scrolls through the letters, then hands the phone back to me. "You suspect Armelle, don't you?"

"Yes. She had motive."

"Payback for getting dumped?" He knits his eyebrows together. "But that was a long time ago, wasn't it?"

"Not that long, actually. And revenge is a dish best served cold."

"Didn't he also bad-mouth her pastries?"

"Yes, in the latest edition of the *Rampal Guide*," I confirm. "And culled her before the second round of Ritzy Rice."

Gabriel wrinkles his nose skeptically. "Except, she couldn't have known that, could she? The results of the first round were announced after he was already dead."

"She could have cornered him late in the evening when he was drunk. Maybe he fessed up," I postulate. "And that was the last straw for her."

"You're jumping to conclusions."

"Am I?"

"Yes, you are."

I put my hands on my hips. "You know something I don't, is that it? So, please, enlighten me."

"I was going to tell you in the morning, because I had more romantic things in mind for tonight, but..."

Billions of blue blistering barnacles! If only I'd known

he had "romantic things" in mind, I would've stuck my report in the fridge together with my gluten-free croissant dough.

"I might as well tell you now," Gabriel says. "The preliminary autopsy results came in, and it looks like an accidental death."

"Define *accidental death*."

"The ME didn't find any signs of struggle or defensive wounds, anything to suggest Seraphin Rampal had been attacked or killed prior to falling into the Rhône."

"I get the part about the absence of wounds," I say. "But is that enough to rule it an accident?"

"We don't have the tox report yet, so these conclusions are preliminary," he reminds me. "But everything points to a drowning."

"For example?"

"Water in his lungs," he replies. "But also, microscopic algae. The fact that Rampal could breathe them in suggests he fell into the river alive."

"So, that's what the ME believes? He drowned?"

"It's not about belief," he says gently. "It's about physical evidence. And right now, it paints a picture where Rampal went out for a late-night walk. He was alone. It was pitch dark. Maybe he was drunk—"

"But we don't know that, do we?"

"Not until the toxicology results come in."

I wipe the counters. "What about the exact time of death? Was it in the preliminary report?"

He shakes his head. "Determining the exact time after the body had been submerged in cold water for hours is tricky."

"Why?"

"Cold water slows down rigor mortis and decomposition," he explains. "Basically, it preserves the body but also causes bloating, both of which complicate the usual indicators of time of death."

"Does that mean we might never know the exact time of Rampal's death?"

"Nah, I think we will."

I rinse the dishrag and look up at Gabriel. "What makes you so optimistic?"

"A specialized forensic pathologist with experience in aquatic deaths arrived from Marseilles today and examined the body. She'll wait until the toxicology is in, so she can consolidate her findings and give us a relatively accurate time of death."

My lips form an impressed O. "How very thorough of Shen!"

"He learned from his mistakes." Gabriel winks. "As did I from mine. When we first met, I was so damn sure Maurice Sauve's death was accidental that I didn't listen to you."

I narrow my eyes. "And you do now?"

"I do and not only because of your psychic visions." He takes a step toward me. "Your detective work is solid, too. And your amateur gang is pretty good at getting to the bottom of things."

"We are, aren't we?" I stand a little taller, my chest expanding with pride.

It's no secret that despite my knack for solving crime, Gabriel would rather I focused on my core trade—baking—and left the murders to professionals. And that is why every begrudging compliment he gives and every acknowledgment of how good FERJ is at our noncore work means the world to me.

He steps closer still. "Did you have a vision about Seraphin Rampal? Is that why you keep pushing?"

"I wish!" Frustration deflates my expanded chest. "But no."

He puts his hands on my shoulder. "Then why don't you just let go?"

His question gives me pause. *Why, indeed?*

"But the letters!" I exclaim.

"Typed on a computer and unsigned," he counters. "We don't even know if they were ever sent to Rampal. The hoodie woman could've written them to frame Armelle. Can you rule that out?"

No, I can't.

"But I saw Armelle talking to the bellhop at Belle d'Oc," I counter. "And the explanation she gave me was pure BS. She's hiding something, Gabriel. I'll bet my best rolling pin on it."

"Shen will run the letters for prints," he says. "But even if Armelle's come up, it won't necessarily mean she killed her ex. Chances are, whatever she's hiding isn't murder."

"Then why didn't she open up about it?"

"Are you friends?"

"No."

He sighs. "Good investigators follow where the evidence leads, not the other way around."

"Point taken, but they listen to their instincts, too."

"True." He pauses, choosing his next words. "I get that you want to make sense of Rampal's death. Believe me, I do, too. But not every suspicious death is a murder, love. Accidents and heart attacks are much more common."

I chew on the bitter pill of reason he's served, desperately racking my brain for counterarguments, and coming up empty.

Ugh, I hate it when he's right!

CHAPTER 19

T he tires of my bike hum against the asphalt as I
pedal through the quiet Sunday streets of Beldoc.
The town is almost deserted this afternoon with
only the occasional cat napping in the sun or an elderly
couple strolling hand in hand.

In the basket tied to the front of my bike is a box of
Rose's favorite macarons and a thermos of soup that wobble
with each bump in the road. Grandma is not a huge fan of
consommé, but she's going to drink it. It'll do her good after
the nasty bout of gastroenteritis that kept her in the
bathroom all day yesterday. It wasn't just the vomiting and
diarrhea—she had severe stomach pain, too. Flo, Sarah, and
I wanted to put her in Sarah's car and drive to the ER, but
she refused. Grandma is even more afraid of hospitals than
she is of dying.

Fortunately, her family doctor was able to come by. He
diagnosed her, gave her pills, and assured us she was going
to be fine.

I realize something as I leave Beldoc's center and glide
through the quieter residential streets. It's been four days
since I decided to heed Gabriel's advice and step back from

the Rampal investigation. Four whole days of biting my tongue, ignoring the sour taste of unfinished business, and resisting the urge to follow up on the suspicions that won't go away.

It's been hard.

To be fair, Gabriel's been doing everything in his power to make it easier. As a reward for my good behavior, he's been spending every spare minute working on the Ghost Rider case. He put the bulk of his effort into trying to identify the man in the grainy CCTV image from the Fête du Riz in Arles. This morning while I was in the shop, he called me and dropped a tantalizing "I might have something."

And that was it. No details, just a promise to fill me in when he meets me at Rose's later.

The suspense is killing me!

My heartbeat ratchets up, not from the gentle incline I'm pedaling with the motor assist, but from the anticipation. What does he have? Is it a lead? A name? Could we finally be getting closer to the truth about the elusive criminal who's haunted me for so long?

I get off the bike in front of Rose's house. Lady greets me with a welcome bark from the other side of the fence. Another dog joins her. Baxter, by the sound of it. It doesn't take a detective to deduce that Rose is out on the patio deck, and Sarah is with her.

I unlock the gate, let myself in, and lean the bike against the fence. I untie the basket from my bike, steeling myself for the sight of my unwell grandma. She'll be tired and cranky. Rose hates being sick.

The familiar scents of her garden accompany me as I pick my way to the patio surrounded by old olive trees and vines that lace the wall behind it and the pergola above. Grandma comes into view, reclining on her sunbed. Sarah's here, all right, plus a whole bunch of other people. I'll bet

Rose made sure to tell as many people as she could that she's sick. And I'm sure they've been coming in all day to check up on her, bearing edible gifts, though probably none as good as my macarons.

I survey the retinue currently in attendance. Representing the Cavallo clan are Flo and Lady. In the cronies' corner, we have Sarah, her pug Baxter, and Rose's doga student Marie-Jo Barral, editor in chief of *Beldoc Live.*

"It's killing me that I missed that exam," Rose vents to Marie-Jo.

The reporter comforts her. "You'll take the makeup exam."

"And I had to cancel doga today," Grandma keeps lamenting.

"I can squeeze in an extra hour next week, if you're up for it," Marie-Jo offers.

"I'm always up for it, darling, but I'll have to check with the rest of the class. Not all my students are as motivated as you are."

Marie-Jo responds with a pleased chuckle.

Lady sprints toward me. I hunker down. She reaches up with her front paws and licks me wherever I let her.

Rose resumes her litany. "And the worst crime of this damned bug is that I had to cancel the meeting with Takeo."

Takeo? For a moment, I draw a blank on the name. Then it comes back to me. She's talking about the senior charmer with the flamboyantly tattooed arms.

"Is that the handsome Japanese entrepreneur you met at Ritzy Rice?" Marie-Jo asks.

"He still hasn't decided on the best location for his sushi shop," Grandma says. "I was going to give him the lowdown on Beldoc, Arles, Beaucaire, Les-Beaux-de-Provence, Eau de Provence, and a few other towns in the area."

With Lady's welcoming ceremony complete, I finally get on the deck. After a kiss on Rose's forehead—pale but not feverish—and greetings to everyone, including Baxter, I present my offerings. And then I finally settle into a chair beside Rose.

"You're a doll for making these macarons!" She reaches for one.

I swat her hand away. "First, consommé, then macarons. No consommé, no macarons."

She pulls a face.

But I remain firm. "Just gulp it down, and then you can have your reward."

She sinks back into the sunbed, muttering, "Cruel child."

"I'll get your mug!" Flo dashes into the house.

"You're going to drink that soup, OK, hon?" Sarah picks up the thermos and unscrews the lid. "You need nourishment and hydration."

Rose pouts. "I know, I know."

Flo returns with a mug, and Sarah pours some warm soup into it from the thermos. The aroma of chicken broth, vegetables and herbs tickles my nose. Rose seems to like it, too, because she sits up in her sunbed, takes the mug, and begins to sip the consommé.

I turn to Marie-Jo, who's been quiet until now. "How are you doing? I haven't seen you in a while."

"Swamped," she says. "Absolutely swamped. And now, I'm fuming."

I raise an eyebrow. "Why? What happened?"

"It's Noam."

Rose rolls her eyes. "Threatening to quit again?"

Marie-Jo hangs her head.

Noam Toche is Beldoc's best—and only—investigative journalist. He tells anyone who'll listen that a provincial town like ours stifles his talent, and he's going to quit *Beldoc Live* and move to a big city where said talent can blossom.

To be fair, his frustration isn't entirely unwarranted.

Noam covered the high-profile Dol case while Shen was investigating it. Like Shen, he followed a false lead. It was FERJ that found the culprit. Then the Ponsard case came along, and FERJ solved it before Noam had a chance to make any headway. During the Bray-Rapp case, which I'd asked him to help me with, he wrote a bombshell story about the pharmaceutical company involved. But *Beldoc Live's* owner pressured Marie-Jo to kill that story.

Despite all those setbacks, Noam hasn't left yet, which makes me think he won't because deep down he loves Beldoc.

"I can't blame him," Marie-Jo says. "He wrote an inspired, well-argued story, raising good questions about Seraphin Rampal's death."

My ears prick up. *What questions?*

"But we have a problem," she continues. "Noam's article is pointing the finger at someone. And that person will no doubt sue us."

Please don't tell me she's killing the story! I need it. It would quench my curiosity while keeping my conscience clean, since reading about a case in the paper doesn't count as investigating.

"Let him sue," I say to Marie-Jo. "It doesn't mean he'll win. Journalists are supposed to inform the public, aren't they? Isn't that the whole point of the profession?"

She gives me a sad little smile. "It was."

"What do you mean?"

"Don't quote me on this, but the press is no longer independent," she replies. "The Internet has put a huge dent in our sales. We're all on life support now."

"What do you mean by that?" Flo inquires.

"We depend on the government subsidies and the businessmen who own controlling stakes."

"Even the big national titles?" I ask.

"Even them. We all have overlords now, and they tend to see us as their personal megaphones."

I frown. "Come on, you can still decide what gets published in your paper, can't you?"

"In theory, yes," Marie-Jo says. "In reality, I toe the party line much like an editor under a communist regime. But with better coffee."

"Can you opt out?" I ask. "We're not a communist regime last I checked."

"You'd be surprised," Rose mutters.

Marie-Jo turns to Sarah. "You Brits have a saying about the piper..."

"He who pays the piper calls the tune," Sarah prompts.

Marie-Jo nods. "Yup. And don't get me started on Victor's new decree!"

Rose tut-tuts. "Beldoc should've elected me as mayor!"

"What is Victor going to do if you don't comply?" I ask Marie-Jo. "Don't tell me he'll have you arrested."

"Let me remind you that Durov, the Telegram CEO, was arrested in France, not Russia," Marie-Jo points out.

"My country recently jailed people for rude memes," Sarah chimes in. "Can you believe it?"

"These days, I can believe anything." Marie-Jo turns to me. "Now do you see why Noam's story is giving me such a headache?"

"What if you leave the suspect's name out?" I suggest.

"We might dodge a libel lawsuit that way, but I'm sure he'll recognize himself and take offense," she replies. "And then he'll sue us under Victor's decree."

Wait, what? He? Not she?

I scoot to the edge of my chair. "Does Noam suspect Ugo Drugeon? Does he have any evidence, even circumstantial? Motive alone won't cut it."

"For the reasons we just discussed, I can't answer that," Marie-Jo replies.

Flo clears her throat. "Hear me out. Isn't it a good thing that the press can't smear someone who may be innocent?"

"You're thinking of what we did to Eric, aren't you?" Marie-Jo skews a tight smile. "We were wrong, but we published a retraction and an apology."

Flo shrugs. "Well, now you won't have to apologize to anyone."

Is she for real? Sometimes I think Gen Zers are an alien species.

"Want to know who never gets anything wrong?" I ask Flo.

"Who?"

"Useless do-nothings," I reply pointedly. "From the moment you take action, there's a risk you can make a mistake. But censorship, even when it's well meant, is a cure that's worse than the disease."

"It's like muzzling your guard dog because it might bark mistakenly at a squirrel," Rose offers.

My sister ponders our words. "I see your point."

Phew. There's still hope for her.

Rose sets her eyes on Marie-Jo. "What are you going to do about that article?"

"Either strip it of anything that anyone might find objectionable or axe it," she says.

"RIP, investigative journalism!" Grandma exclaims with flair. "You had a good run. Now you can spin vinyl discs in heaven, and boogie with the long-dead common sense!"

CHAPTER 20

The conversation around the table lulls for a long moment. We just sit there—well, except for Rose and the two dogs, who are recumbent—and absorb the golden sunlight through the vines of the pergola.

"I've been meaning to ask you about a friend of yours," Marie-Jo says to me.

I nod my permission. "Which one?"

"Karl. I haven't seen him and his dog in two, maybe three months? The town isn't the same without the pair of them around. Is he all right?"

Her assumption that I'd know what Karl is up to isn't wrong. Rose, Flo, and I have been looking out for him and his mutt Harley ever since he saved my life two years ago.

"They're fine," I reply. "They went on an adventure."

Marie-Jo raises an eyebrow. "What kind of adventure?"

Flo fills in the details, "Back in July, Marlene bought them tickets to visit her and her son Alex in Tours."

"Marlene...?" Marie-Jo narrows her eyes, lost.

"Victor's formerly estranged sister," Rose prompts.

"Riiight," Marie-Jo lifts her chin slowly, recalling. "The

kid was a drifter for a while, wasn't he? That's how he met Karl."

I nod. "So, Karl went to Tours, and then Marlene persuaded him to make the Camino de Santiago pilgrimage with her and Alex."

"Karl the Tramp went on a pilgrimage?" Marie-Jo echoes in surprise.

"Yep," Rose confirms. "An ex-punk, a former nun, a hobo, and a dog went on a spiritual hike to Santiago."

Sarah giggles. "Sounds like a pitch for a Mark Wahlberg film."

"According to Marlene, Harley became a mascot for the other pilgrims," I say. "They all loved him."

"Are they back now?" Marie-Jo asks.

"Back in Provence, but not in Beldoc," I reply. "Karl is doing seasonal work in the vineyards. Harley is 'employed' as a campsite guard."

The conversation shifts to other topics before it winds down.

"I must be going." Marie-Jo pushes her chair back and stands. "Take care of yourself, Rose. I'll call you tomorrow."

Just as the gate clicks shut behind her, Rose's phone lights up. It's Gabriel's grandmother, Annie, video calling from Cassis. Last winter, Annie became obsessed with some tragic events in her life that happened sixty years ago. She persuaded Rose to help her uncover the truth. Despite a rocky start, the adventure brought them closer together.

Rose puts Annie on speakerphone, and we all exchange warm greetings.

Annie settles her gaze on Rose. "How are you feeling?"

"Better now, but yesterday was a field trip to hell," Grandma replies.

Annie shakes her head in sympathy. "Sorry to hear that."

"The pain, the vomiting!" Rose touches the back of her

hand to her forehead. "I thought it was the end of me, I swear! When my doctor assured me it wasn't, I didn't believe him."

Unexpectedly, Annie grins. "Here's something to cheer you up. You're out of the woods now."

"That's what I just told you," Rose peers at her screen, confused.

"I didn't mean your stomach bug; I meant your health in general."

"Um..." Rose squints, even more perplexed.

"I read somewhere that the decade between sixty-five to seventy-five is the most dangerous time in terms of health," Annie explains. "Statistically, if you survive it, you'll keep going for at least another decade."

Sarah claps her hands. "Cool! I'm out of the danger zone!"

"And I just entered it, Annie," Rose lies through her teeth. "You know that."

"Of course, dear, of course." Annie averts her gaze. "My mistake."

Everyone, including Annie, knows that Rose is seventy-seven and not sixty-five as she claims. Grandma knows that we know it. But she wants us to play along, anyway.

Annie changes the topic. "Come visit me in Cassis when you're back on your feet."

"Maybe next weekend after I've taken my makeup exam," Rose says. "I already suspended my program once. I'm getting that PI license this year; come rain or shine!"

After another round of wishes and promises to visit, Rose ends the call.

Sarah stands up, whistles to Baxter and gives Rose a big smile. "Talk to you later!"

Grandma blows her and then Baxter a kiss.

Mere minutes after the gate clicks shut behind them,

Gabriel saunters in. *Ah, finally!* I can't wait to hear what he's dug up.

Concern flickers in his eyes as he approaches Rose. "How are you doing?"

"Better than yesterday, that's for sure," she replies.

While they chat, I dart to the kitchen, grab a plate and a glass for him, and return to the patio deck.

"Don't mind Rose," I say to Gabriel as I hand him the plate. "I'm dying here."

He grins. "Remember the advanced facial recognition software I mentioned a while ago?"

"Honestly? I don't. What about it?"

He drinks some water. "It came up with a positive match."

"For the Ghost Rider?" I ask, my heart speeding.

He nods. "An individual named Patrice Hivon."

Flo moves her chair closer. "For real? Are you saying that after all these years, we have a name?"

"It may be an alias like the one he used back then," Gabriel cautions. "It's also possible he's not our guy, considering the poor quality of the photo we have. But I'm hopeful."

Dare I hope, too?

"Can you show me a photo of Patrice Hivon?" I ask him.

"Sure." Gabriel pulls out his phone and swipes a few times before turning the screen toward me.

The face staring back at me is both new and familiar. The man in the picture looks more weathered than the Ghost Rider. He also has more gray hair than at the Ponsard soirée, but that was three years ago. His eyes are darker and duller than I remember. But his jawline, the shape of his nose and the set of his mouth send a shiver down my spine.

Could Patrice Hivon really be him?

The first time I "saw" him wasn't in flesh and blood. It

was a snapshot, a vivid vision, of him as a building contractor talking to another man. That conversation had taken place shortly before the explosion at the beach house that took my mother's life. It was thanks to that vision that I was able to recognize him later in real life. First, three years back, at a party I was catering. He showed up late and left quickly before I had a chance to talk to him. Then I spotted him again at the Arles parade, dressed as a gardian.

"Julie?" Gabriel's voice pulls me back. "What do you think?"

"It could be him," I say.

Rose leans forward. "What do we know about this Patrice Hivon?"

"He lives in Saintes-Maries-de-la-Mer, where he runs an electronics repair shop," Gabriel says.

I squint, thinking fast. "If your facial recognition software found a match, it means he was already in the system for something, right?"

"His reckless driving caused a major traffic accident two years back," Gabriel replies. "Luckily for him, no one got seriously injured."

Flo perks up. "A history of bad behavior! Very good!" She flashes a crooked smile. "In the context."

"Has he lived abroad for a while?" I ask.

That's how he avoided arrest after Mom died—he fled Europe.

Gabriel sets his plate down on the table. "Yes. He left France nineteen years ago and lived in Lebanon for six years."

Flo and I share a look of triumph.

Rose gasps. "The timing fits!"

Her words hang in the air for a moment. As the significance of what we just learned sinks in, a flood of emotions washes over me. Thrill, hope, impatience, but also a gravitas from the realization that my poor mom may finally get justice.

Flo bounces in her seat, overexcited. "So, what's the plan? When are you going to nab him?"

"I doubt he can do that just yet," I say.

"That's right," Gabriel confirms. "But while I can't apprehend him at this time, Julie and I can pay him a visit."

I nod. "When?"

"Tomorrow morning, if you can.

A mixture of gratitude and determination bubbles up inside me. "Damn right I can!"

Gabriel reaches out and squeezes my hand. "Just let's not get ahead of ourselves, OK?"

"OK," I say as calmly as possible.

But my thoughts are in a whirlwind. Tomorrow, I'm going to face Patrice Hivon.

Is he the Ghost Rider?

Will my sisters, Grandma, Dad, and I finally get some answers?

CHAPTER 21

The road to Saintes-Maries-de-la-Mer winds through the heart of the Camargue. The landscape stretches out before us like something from a dream. I've been here many times, yet this windswept sandy wonderland will never cease to amaze me. We're still in Provence, but it feels like another continent, if not a different planet.

Gabriel drives slowly with one hand on the wheel. His other hand rests on the gear shift, eyes fixed on the road ahead. I stare out the window at the exotic landscape—marshes, brine lagoons, rice paddies, and reedy grasses that rustle in the morning breeze. The air smells faintly of salt, a reminder of how close the sea is.

"We're in the largest river delta in all of Europe," Gabriel says. "Did you know that?"

"There!" I point, starry-eyed, instead of answering his question.

He looks at the flock of flamingos standing in the shallow brine. Resolutely pink against the azure blue of the sky, they seem delightfully out of place in this part of the world. As if to enhance the surreal effect, their reflections in a paler shade of pink ripple in the shimmery water amid the reeds.

"Psychedelic," I comment.

Gabriel shifts gears as the road bends.

The flamingos aren't the only wondrous creatures that catch the eye around here. A little farther along, I spot a *manade*. It's the local word for a small herd of *Camarguaise* horses. Their coats as white as the clouds in the sky, they amble lazily as if they have all the time in the world. Suddenly, they take off and it's a sight to behold. These aren't your sleek, polished, ultrathin stallions that inhabit racetracks and commercials for men's aftershave. They're sturdy semiferal things, built to withstand the harsh mistral. They can survive on their own in the wild.

"Beautiful, aren't they?" Gabriel comments, following my gaze.

I nod, unable to tear my eyes away. The strangeness and beauty of this region is a blessing, I find myself thinking. Not only in its own right, but also because it takes my mind off the reason we're on this road, driving to Saintes-Maries.

As we drive deeper into the Camargue, the open landscape gives way to sprawling ranches. Many of them breed bulls. Soon enough, I see their rugged silhouettes all around. Then a rustic cabin comes into view, followed by another one nearby. Both have steep roofs, thatched with reeds from the surrounding marshes. This is where the gardians live, close to the bulls and horses.

Speaking of which, I notice a group of men on horseback. They wear their signature black hats and Camargue cowboy boots with rounded toes. Moving with an ease that comes from years of experience, they guide the bulls with subtle shifts of their reins, like it's no effort at all.

Gabriel bobs his head up and down in admiration. "Them skills!"

"It's in their blood," I say.

Most gardians are local ranchers and farmhands, born and raised in these marshlands. The skills in question are learned at a very young age and passed down through generations.

The road dips and the sea appears on the horizon. Saintes-Maries isn't far away now. My heart beats faster with every kilometer we leave behind.

Is this really happening? Am I about to get closure?

When we drive into the town, it feels like we've landed inside a tourist poster. Bathed in sunlight, the whitewashed houses gleam against the backdrop of the blue sky. The red-tiled roofs ooze endless charm. The streets are buzzing with activity. It's because this isn't just a regular Monday morning—it's a Monday morning during the rice fest.

As we look for a place to park the car, I take in the locals in traditional costumes, the gardians on horseback and the cattle breeders proudly showcasing their finest livestock. Everywhere I look I see market stalls, street artists, and music bands.

Gabriel smiles. "This place is even more serious about its rice month than Beldoc."

"This place is more passionate about celebrations than any other town in Provence," I point out, thinking back to the OTT birthday party, a baptism, and a wedding I've attended here with Flo and Tino.

"Tino is from Saintes-Maries, isn't he?" Gabriel asks, as if reading my mind.

"He grew up mostly in Arles with his dad, but he was born here."

Tino's mom is a *Gitan* Gypsy. Some of her family is still nomadic, but most are now sedentary and live in or around Saintes-Maries.

After some circling around, Gabriel finds a vacant spot, and we get out of the car. The sound of distant music fills the narrow streets as we walk to Patrice's shop downtown.

Along the way, the iconic Notre-Dame-de-la-Mer church looms overhead like a beacon. When we reach it, we stop for a moment to admire its thick honey-colored stone walls that give the edifice a fortresslike look.

I turn to Gabriel. "You know about the secret they keep down there, right?"

"What secret?"

"The crypt." I gesture toward the church. "It's where they keep the statue of Sara la Kali, the Gypsy patron saint."

"You're talking about the Black Madonna, queen of the Romani, right?"

I nod. "They worship her because she was a servant to The Three Marys."

"That's not the version I've heard," he counters. "I was told she was a Gypsy queen, smuggled out of Egypt."

"It's part of the same story, silly!"

Happy for the opportunity to educate my boyfriend on something—usually it's the other way around—I recount what I've been told at the events I attended here with Flo and Tino. The Alexandria Romans persecuted The Three Marys, namely, Jesus' aunts Mary Jacobe and Mary Salome, plus Mary Magdalene after the Crucifixion. They put the women, together with their Egyptian servant girl Sara, in a boat with no oars and cast it off. Miraculously, the four women survived and washed up on the Camargue shore.

"Have you been to Saintes-Maries during the Gypsy pilgrimage?" Gabriel asks. "Sara's ritual purification in the sea is a huge event around here."

"It's in May, right?"

He nods. "When I was a rookie gendarme, I was sent here to give the local brigade a hand. Tens of thousands of Gypsies from all over Europe were here for the celebrations. Gitans, *Manouches*, *Tsiganes*, Rom, you name it!"

"I saw some of the festival once, long ago, before..." As

always, I have trouble saying, "Mom's passing," so I say my usual substitute, "Before we moved to Paris."

"I'm an agnostic, but I think it's scandalous that the pompous Vatican still hasn't canonized Sara la Kali," he says. "There are few Catholic saints venerated with such fervor."

"I agree."

We continue forward. As we approach Patrice's electronics store, my nerves begin to tighten again.

At the door, Gabriel glances over at me. "You ready?"

"As ready as I'll ever be." I take a deep breath. "Let's do this."

Gabriel swings the door to the shop open, and we step into what can only be described as organized chaos. The place is crammed with appliances and gadgets of every kind. The shelves are lined with various screens, radios, cameras, cell phones, and other, less easily identifiable, objects. There are two or three half-disassembled devices on the table in the back on this side of stacked motherboards. On the other side, a young man with greasy hair is working on what looks like an ancient transistor radio. He's wearing headphones and nodding to a beat only he can hear.

The poorly ventilated air smells of solder and burnt plastic. That killer combo is so repugnant to my sensitive olfactory organs that my stomach threatens to send its contents up north.

There's no one at the counter.

Gabriel and I call loudly, "Bonjour!"

The young employee takes off his headphones. "Bonjour!" He wipes his hands on a rag and steps toward the counter. "How can I help you?"

"We're looking for Monsieur Patrice Hivon," I say quickly, before I'll have to run out due to the smell. "Is he in?"

The employee shakes his head. "Ah, no, he stepped out."

"Do you know where he went?" Gabriel asks.

"To the rice tasting pavilion," he answers. "You see, my boss worships paella. And he's a real sucker for swag."

Thrown by the mismatch between the lightness of his reply and the gravity of the reason we're here, I give a nervous little laugh.

The employee adds, "He likes to say that the rice fest is his annual preview of paradise."

"Sounds like he's living the dream," Gabriel comments with a low whistle.

The young man nods. "Oh yeah."

"Shall we go and see if we can locate him in that pavilion?" I ask Gabriel.

The sooner I escape the gut-wrenching aromas of this place, the better.

"He won't be long now," the employee says. "If you come back in half an hour, he'll be here."

Gabriel's stomach rumbles just as he opens his mouth.

He gives an apologetic. "It's already noon, and all this talk of paella is making me hungry."

"Come, I'm buying you lunch!" I bolt to the door, fling it open, and gulp in the sweet, sweet air of freedom.

CHAPTER 22

Gabriel and I are sitting at a terrace table overlooking the Amphores Beach, only a five-minute walk from Patrice's shop. The waiter has just served a plate of local clams for me, and a steak for Gabriel, both accompanied with Camargue rice. My clams are packed with flavor. Gabriel's steak is perfectly seared just the way he likes it. The rice is cooked just so and knowing that it was grown in the marshlands right behind this town gives it a special oomph.

The setting here isn't as picturesque as in Cassis or other old fishing harbors. But there's something undeniably charming about it. The golden strip of sand stretches out before us, meeting the calm, deep-blue of the Mediterranean. A lively Gypsy tune played by a brass band we passed on the way carries on the breeze.

Gabriel looks up from his plate. "By the way, I have some news about the Rampal case."

I pause, fork halfway to my mouth. "And you're telling me this now?"

"I wanted to wait until after we saw Patrice Hivon." He

shrugs. "But if you want to hear it without delay, I can tell you."

"Tell me."

"The toxicology report came in early this morning before I left the gendarmerie to pick you up."

I set my fork down. "And how exactly did you get access to it since you're not part of the investigation team?"

He doesn't reply right away.

I stroke his hand with feigned concern. "Oh, *mon chéri*, is the explanation embarrassing? Did you have to beg Shen?"

"No begging was necessary. Charles-Antoine showed me the results of his own accord. He said I could share them with you."

I stare at him. "Did he?"

"Yes, to put your suspicions to rest."

"OK," I say. "So, what did the results show? Do we have the exact time of Rampal's death?"

"Not yet."

I knit my eyebrows. "I thought you had the results..."

"From the lab, yes. But the specialized forensic pathologist is still double-checking everything against the toxicology report. It shouldn't take long now."

"Cool." I fold my arms over my chest. "What did the toxicology peeps find?"

"No traces of poison—and they tested for everything they could think of."

"But?" I prompt, sensing more.

"You know what they *did* find?"

"What?"

"Alcohol," he says.

I feel my mouth curve downward. "Just like Shen expected."

"What's more, the level of it in Rampal's blood was very high."

"So, he fell into the river and then found himself unable to swim to the shore?" I stare Gabriel in the eye. "Is that what you think happened?"

"That's what it sure looks like," he confirms. "Coupled with the autopsy that found no defensive wounds, Shen has concluded, and I believe rightfully so, that there was no foul play, no perp, no murder. Just the victim's bad choices and bad luck."

Frustration swirls inside me at those words. I'm ashamed to admit it, even to myself, but the idea that it was just a tragic accident feels like a letdown.

"No one likes to be proven wrong, love," Gabriel coos, "especially someone with a track record like yours. I totally get it."

Sounds like my disappointment was written all over my face.

I gaze out at the sea sparkling in the sun. Some residual doubt lingers at the back of my mind. Something that doesn't quite fit...

But what? What is it that doesn't add up?

I know—the letters!

I turn back to Gabriel. "What about the threatening letters I passed over to Shen?"

"He had them checked for fingerprints," Gabriel replies. "The only ones the forensics could match were Seraphin Rampal's."

"Aha!" I exclaim in triumph.

"It only proves he'd held those letters in his hands at some point, nothing else."

"But we can't rule out that Armelle wrote them, can we?" I press.

"No, we can't," Gabriel concedes. "However, angry letters are no proof of murder."

"What about Armelle's weird behavior? And her motive? Oh, and Ugo Drugeon also had a motive!"

Gabriel's lips twitch with a hint of amusement. "Good for him."

"Please, I'm serious! Noam Toche seems to have reasons to suspect Ugo."

"Did he tell you that?"

"No, but he covered it in a story he wrote," I say defiantly.

Gabriel tilts his head to one side. "I must've missed it."

"It wasn't published."

"Why not?"

I pout. "Marie-Jo shelved it because of Victor's new decree."

"Ah, yes, the one that would have me arresting folks for mean words."

I squint at him. "You'll have to, won't you?"

"Sure, if those words fall under the French Penal Code."

"And if they don't?"

"Then I won't." He meets my gaze. "Does the decree define what's offensive? Does it set out any objective criteria?"

I pause, thinking it over. "Well, I'm assuming that insults or incitement to violence—"

"Those are already covered by the Penal Code," he cuts in.

"Then what's left for Victor's decree?"

"Beats me." Gabriel shrugs. "Tell you what, Victor can shove his decree as far as I'm concerned."

I burst out laughing. "Have you told him as much?"

"Not in those exact words, obviously, or he might take offense and ask my commandant to arrest me."

My laughter fades. *He was joking, wasn't he?* Commandant Lambert wouldn't arrest my boyfriend just for being rude to Victor... would he?

"Anyway," Gabriel says, "back to the Rampal case. It

doesn't matter how many people had a motive to kill him, because there's no proof whatsoever that he was killed. All the physical evidence points to an accidental drowning."

We finish our meal in silence and head back to Patrice Hivon's electronics shop. Gabriel opens the door. The nauseating scent fills my nostrils again, but I forget all about it when I notice there's now someone behind the counter.

The moment I lay eyes on the man, I know. He looks a lot like the Ghost Rider—same height, very similar facial features. But the slant of his shoulders, the way he holds himself, and the way he moves are all wrong. This isn't our guy.

I turn to Gabriel, shaking my head.

"Not him?" he whispers, disappointment in his eyes.

"No."

Patrice Hivon smiles, oblivious to my turmoil. "Bonjour! Can I help you with anything?"

All I manage to do is force a tight smile.

"No, sorry to bother you," Gabriel says.

Without another word, we turn around and leave. The fresh air outside is a godsend after the stench of the shop. I take a few deep breaths, and then we trudge back to the parking lot.

Gabriel unlocks the car with the press of a button. "Damn it, I thought we had him!"

"We tried our best." I plonk myself into the front passenger seat.

"We'll find him, Julie." He starts the engine. "I have a few more tricks up my sleeve."

I want to hold on to hope, I really do. As we get back on the scenic road, I gaze out the window at the unique nature and wildlife of the region. But even the gaggle of pink flamingos strutting across a salt flat like it's a catwalk does nothing to lift the weight of this dead end off my chest.

CHAPTER 23

The imperturbable Rhône flows beneath us as Eric and I push the serving carts over the uneven pavement of the bridge. Dressed in double-breasted emblazoned jackets and chef's hats, we're on our way to a birthday party we're catering on the other side of the river. Without Eric's minivan, which broke down yesterday, as it often does, it's a twenty-minute walk.

Not ideal, but doable.

I breathe in the sweet, buttery aroma wafting from my three-tiered cart, loaded with boxes of pastries. We're also hauling some utensils, but they're light. It's all paper plates and cups, cornstarch drinking straws and disposable wooden cutlery.

My chest swells with pride. Julie's Gluten-free Delights could be the most health-conscious and eco-friendly pastry shop in town. Without compromising taste or texture, I've managed to cut the sugar in all my recipes by 50 percent. The remaining half is replaced with my unique combination of natural substitutes whenever the recipe allows it.

And I gave up plastic!

I won't lie; natural substitutes and compostable utensils are more expensive to buy than sugar and plastic. But knowing that I'm not causing diabetes, polluting the oceans, and poisoning marine animals is worth the financial outlay. Incidentally, I've raised my prices, so it's the customer that covers the extra cost.

Like I said, totally worth it.

Eric's cart is heavier than mine. In addition to the pastry boxes, he has the cake in a cooler. We move slowly, to accommodate the fragility of our load and the bumpiness of the bridge. All the trays are lined with contact grip sheets to keep the pastry boxes from slipping, but you can never be too careful.

The air is a tad colder than in the previous days, but still mild, without even a hint of wind. On an afternoon like this, it's hard to believe how much havoc the mistral can wreak when it blows for days on end. But we're still in September —the mistral is uncommon at this time of year.

Eric adjusts his grip on the cart handle. "Almost there."

"I'll never complain about your van being too beat up or reeking of gas again," I vow. "Just make sure it's fixed by tomorrow."

He winks. "You might miss the exercise, though."

"Why would I? I ride my bike to and from work every day."

"Ten minutes each way on even ground." He sneers. "I call that a warm-up, not a workout."

Snob! "You can call it whatever you want; it's still cardio."

We're nearing the middle of the bridge, when I feel a gust of wind against my face. Bizarrely, it doesn't flap the napkins or anything else on the carts. I frown, puzzled, and then another highly localized gust hits me harder than the first. The air shifts in that familiar way, both frightening and exhilarating. The world around me starts to flicker like a broken film reel. My physical surroundings gradually melt away. My hands on the handles of the cart disappear, and so does the cart itself.

Suddenly, I'm small, but not microscopic like in some previous visions. I'm large enough to have *parts*. My perspective is low, close to the ground. I'm in motion. It's dark, but I can make out the narrow sidewalk in front of me. To my left, I distinguish a loafer on a man's foot. Above me is the hem of a pant leg. To my right, I catch the occasional glimpse of a railing.

Are we crossing a bridge?

I'm attached to something smooth and brown, made of leather, like myself... The other loafer! My "head" is fixed to it, and my tentacle-like parts swing and bob with each step.

Am I a tassel?

Looks like I am. The shoe I adorn is shuffling across the bridge. I jolt with each unsteady step and rattle with each awkward tilt of the foot.

Is this man drunk?

The steps slow down. I sway gently as the foot pauses mid stride. There's a hesitation in this stance, as if the man wasn't sure where he was going, or if he should be going there at all.

Is it because it's so dark?

The feet walk on, still unsteadily, to the center of the bridge. We stop by the railing, facing the river. I hover right over the edge of the bridge, between two balusters. Below, the waters of the Rhône flow deep and dark. We remain like this for a while. Then the feet shift and turn ninety degrees, pointing back to the bank that they came from.

Overhead, a voice breaks the silence. "Do I really need to jump?"

I know that voice... *It's Seraphin Rampal's! Oh my God, it's him!*

With hindsight, I should've guessed. But I was too

wrapped up figuring out what exactly I was in this snapshot to consider the identity of the person wearing me.

The stillness that follows Rampal's question is suffocating. I peer in the direction his feet are pointing, but I can't see squat. I do hear something, though. At least, I think so. A faint whisper, carried by the breeze. "Yes." It's the slightest brush of sound, so soft I can't be sure if it's real or if it's just my imagination.

"All right, then," Rampal mutters, resigned.

The loafers turn to face the river. The other foot lifts off, trembles. "My" foot stands on tiptoe while the other one swings over the handrail. Rampal straddles it, balancing precariously, one foot still touching the pavement. And then he pushes off. I plummet in a swoosh of air—

Static noise. An invisible faulty light bulb glimmers. The falling sensation ceases. The darkness dissipates. The sun snaps back into place above me and illuminates everything. I'm me again, standing on the bridge, gripping the cart handles so tightly my knuckles are white.

"Chef? You all right?" Eric is looking at me, his brow furrowed in concern. "You spaced out for a second there."

I gasp. "I know, I just... I had one of my visions."

His eyes widen. "About who? Your mother? Seraphin Rampal?"

"Rampal," I reply. "Let's move on."

He begins to protest. "Come on, you have to tell me—"

"I'll tell you after work," I say firmly.

He doesn't insist, no doubt aware that if we start talking about it now, we'll never make it on time. We start walking again. The wheels of the cart clatter over the paving stones. The sound helps me recover from my psychic experience. I focus on the task at hand and refuse to think about the implications of what my snapshot revealed.

CHAPTER 24

The last customer waved goodbye forty minutes ago, after which we flipped the Open sign to Closed. Eric cleaned up the kitchen, and Flo the front shop. I counted the cash in the register, stashed it in the safe box, and dimmed the lights. Rose, now fully recovered from her stomach bug, made tea for everyone.

In the quiet of the shop, we sat down in the bistro corner, and I spilled all the details of the snapshot that had hit me earlier that afternoon. Rose, Eric, and Flo heard how Seraphin Rampal had stopped in the middle of the bridge to ask if he really had to jump, and how a whispered "yes" sent him over the edge.

"It was a remote-controlled murder," I conclude solemnly. "The person in the shadows forced him to jump. That person counted on the cold water, darkness, alcohol, and Rampal's poor eyesight to do the rest."

Rose leans back in her chair, arms crossed, face skeptical. Flo's expression is tentative. I can tell she's on the fence. So is Eric, a half-eaten flute in his hand. I stand up and start pacing to let out some of the nervous energy simmering inside.

"He was drunk, darling," Rose says. "We know that from the toxicology report. He could've been hallucinating."

"He could but he wasn't."

Flo cocks her head. "How do you figure?"

I stop near her. "For one, I heard a whisper."

"Are you sure?" she asks.

I take a moment to give her question the most honest consideration I'm capable of. There's a 10 maybe 20 percent chance that I misheard or, to put it more bluntly, that I heard what I wanted to hear. I can't deny that Shen's accidental death theory hasn't convinced me, despite the physical evidence.

He was wrong on the Dol case, wasn't he? I didn't buy his conclusions, and I was right. That's a fact. What's less clear is if I'm letting my ego, inflated by my past successes, affect my judgment.

OK, let's stick to the facts.

"Rampal was sober enough to ask his question without slurring or stuttering," I say.

Eric swallows a bite and chimes in, "It sounds to me like he didn't want to jump. The way he phrased his question suggests he was hoping for a *no*."

Exactly! Thank you!

I turn to Rose. "Since he didn't want to jump, why would his imagination conjure up someone telling him to do so?"

"I have a counter-question," she says. "Assuming someone made him jump, how did that person get him to do it without spiking his drink? The toxicology report didn't show any drugs in his system."

Flo raises her hand. "Without resorting to drugs, are there other ways to make a grown man of sound mind, a man who isn't suicidal or depressed, jump off a bridge?"

"I don't know," I admit.

Eric picks up the last crumbs of his flute from the table. "Hypnosis?"

"You can't hypnotize someone against their will," Flo points out. "As far as I know successful hypnosis requires the cooperation of the hypnotized."

Rose adopts her professorial tone. "What Eric has in mind about is a technique often referred to as *mind control*. It's not supported by science."

That's rich, coming from a woman who believes in Karma!

"Reincarnation, on the other hand," I purr with a saccharine smile, "is totally scientific. Everyone knows that."

Grandma gives me the same look of betrayal she does when I accidentally step on her dog's tail. I hold her gaze, even though I feel awful for disparaging her beliefs. *But she was asking for it!*

We glare at each other.

"Ladies, ladies." Eric lifts both hands and does the Vulcan salute. "As Surak would say, let us acknowledge that we have differences, and let us make sure that, together, we become greater than the sum of us!"

"Please, not another *Star Trek* quote," Rose scoffs.

"Quote away, I love it!" Flo fist-bumps Eric. "Especially, anything by Spock."

"Back to Rampal." Rose finally takes her reproachful gaze off me. "I think he was just roaring drunk. People do crazy shit when they're that far gone."

I put my hands on my hips. "He didn't sound like he was that far gone—and I'd know, because I was there, dangling from his loafer."

Eric flattens his hands on the table. "I'm with Julie on this one."

"Because you, too, were there?" Rose asks him meanly. "Or because Julie is your boss?"

That was below the belt, Grandma!

Luckily, he grins, unruffled. "Neither, Madame Tassy. I simply find her arguments convincing."

Flo sets her eyes on him. "What about her theory that Armelle Pradine did it? Do you find that convincing, too?"

"No way!" His voice is firm. "I know Armelle. No matter how pissed off she was at Rampal, she's no killer. I think we should be looking into Ugo Drugeon instead."

Rose strokes the sides of her mug. "Is that the chef in Cavaillon whom Rampal ripped to shreds in his review?"

"Ugo's business took a hit," Eric says.

I drum my fingers on the table. "Armelle's motive seems stronger to me—heartbreak, compounded by public humiliation. And she sent him those letters!"

"We don't know that for sure," Rose interjects.

"I can talk with Armelle," Eric offers. "She treated me well when I was her intern. Maybe she'll be more open with me than she was with you, Chef."

Flo holds her phone up. "I'll look into how one can compel a man to kill himself without drugging him."

"I'll talk to Noam Toche tomorrow morning," I announce. "Seeing as Marie-Jo pulled the plug on his story, I'll try to coax him to share what he's uncovered with me."

Rose gives me a wry smile. "Reporters never share their scoops, whether they're allowed to publish them or not."

"I can be very persuasive," I parry.

She shakes her head. "You never give up, do you?"

"I'm like Lady when she smells a piece of something edible under the cupboard," I say. "She can't see it, but she knows it's there. Does she ever give up until you retrieve it for her?"

Rose laughs softly. "No, she doesn't. Just don't count on me to retrieve anything for you in relation to this case."

"Seriously?" Flo goggles at her. "You're out, Grandma?"

"First off, I don't think it was murder," Rose begins.

"Second, I'm done with pro bono work, which is why I'm trying to get a PI license. To do that, I must pass the makeup exam, and then study for the next one. Not to mention all the other activities and responsibilities that keep me busy."

"And let's not forget the daily episode of *Passions Burn Bright on the Fazenda* in the evening!" Flo teases her.

"I never forget it," Rose deadpans.

"No problem," I say. "We'll go FEJ on this case."

Rose winces. "Ew, FEJ sounds terrible... Anyway, please, keep this investigation low-key."

"Always!" I exclaim.

She fixes her gaze on me. "Haha. Funny."

A short time later, we disperse. I get on my bike and pedal home. Gabriel is already there. We eat dinner and spend the rest of the evening watching *Law and Order: SVU*. Then we go to bed and make love. He leaves early in the morning, without explaining what new approach he's going to try to ID the Ghost Rider. Actually, I don't mind that. This way, I feel less guilty that I neglected to tell him about my snapshot and FEJ taking on the Rampal case.

CHAPTER 25

The crowd crackles with silly excitement as rubber ducks bob and weave down the Rhône, each one carrying the hopes and dreams of its supporters. A loudspeaker blares updates on the race's progress. A brass band plays a martial tune, entirely too serious for the occasion.

I scan the crowd for Noam. I was told by his colleagues at *Beldoc Live* that he will be here this morning to cover the event for the paper.

There he is!

Noam is standing at the edge of the riverbank, hands on his hips, his professional camera neglected, his eyes riveted on the little yellow ducks floating by. He looks genuinely invested in the race. It's hard to believe that this is the same man who writes long op-eds on national and international politics, world affairs, and how the agro-pharmaceutical industry undermines public health for profit.

Yet here he is, gesticulating and cheering, as if the fate of the world depended on the right duck crossing the finish line.

I weave my way through the crowd toward him. "Hey, Noam!"

He glances in my direction, but his focus is still on the river.

When I'm close enough, I ask, "Got a minute? I have a theory I wanted to run by you."

"As much as I love your theories, this isn't a good time," he says without looking at me. "I'm in the middle of something."

I raise an eyebrow. "Is that something to do with rubber ducks?"

"Duck 14," he specifies, his tone grave. "It's losing ground, and I have twenty bucks riding on it."

"You're betting? I thought you were here to cover the event..."

"I was. And I did. But I got bored." He gives me a quick wink. "And voilà, I'm not bored anymore."

Haha. We're only human, after all—even Noam.

"Can we talk after the race?" I ask. "It's about Seraphin Rampal."

That gets his attention. "What about him?"

"I don't think his death was an accident."

The ducks float farther downstream, and Noam inches along the riverbank, along with the other fans.

I follow, jostling to stay close. "Marie-Jo told me you don't believe it was accidental, either."

"Did she?" he mutters, never taking his eyes off the ducks. "You should ask her why she won't publish the piece I wrote about it."

"I have. Apparently, you name names in it, and she's afraid of the consequences under Victor's new decree."

He scoffs. "She asked me to redact all the details, but I won't do it. That kind of rewrite would make my article as investigative as this piece about the duck race."

"I respect your decision, Noam." I hesitate before adding, "Will you tell me who your prime suspect is?"

"Why should I give you that information?"

"Um... Because it's the right thing to do? You know, so that the murderer could be brought to justice."

The crowd moves farther down the bank, and I scramble once again to avoid being separated from Noam.

Did I convince him?

He curses under his breath. My first thought is that my request annoyed the hell out of him. But then I follow his gaze and realize he's pissed because Duck 14 is now so far behind that its chances of coming in first are close to nil. Which makes it unlikely Noam will recover his twenty euros.

I try another tactic. "How about a trade? You show me your suspect, and I'll show you mine."

"Another wild theory of yours?" he snickers.

"I have something factual, I assure you! And it's, um... juicy."

He shoots me a look. "How juicy?"

"Very." I wiggle my eyebrows. "Come on, Noam! You know you want it."

"Is your suspect Ugo Drugeon?"

"No."

He sighs in defeat. "Fine. Let's hear it."

"Armelle Pradine," I say, watching his reaction. "She had every reason to hate Rampal. He ditched her, bad-mouthed her desserts, and booted her from Ritzy Rice before round two."

"I knew all that."

"Did you also know that she went to Belle d'Oc two days after Rampal's death, and tried to bribe a bellhop there?"

He peers at the ducks. "That's a serious allegation. Are you sure?"

"I saw her doing it, so yeah, pretty sure."

"Hmm..." He turns to me. "Did you hear their conversation?"

"No."

"It could've been related to her work. Maybe she was bribing the bellhop to tell the Belle d'Oc guests that the food is better at her hotel?"

"That's a valid theory, but it's at odds with the threatening letters."

His eyebrows shoot up. "What?"

"I can show them to you, if you want, after you tell me about your suspect."

He nods, too intrigued to resist. "Ugo Drugeon. Rampal's review didn't just hurt his business, Julie. He's toast. Drugeon is filing for bankruptcy."

"And you know that how?"

"I have my sources," Noam dodges. "Ritzy Rice was Drugeon's last-ditch attempt to restore his image and save his restaurant."

"And Rampal got in his way again, crushing his hopes to rebound!"

"Exactly." He peels his gaze off his duck and fixes it on me. "Did you know that the contestants eliminated after the first round were getting a brutal review and a single lavender sprig in the next Rampal's guide?"

Holy cow! A retrospective panic attack makes my forehead break into a cold sweat. Had I known how high the cost of failure was, I would've never signed up.

"I had no idea," I murmur.

"It wasn't something the organizers advertised, so as not to discourage chefs from participating."

"No shit." I squint at him. "How did you find out about those terms?"

"I have my sources," he repeats himself. "Which, it goes without saying, I can't divulge. But I can tell you that

141

two judges I interviewed separately corroborated that intel."

I wipe my brow with the back of my hand, still shaken. "So, let's recap. After killing Ugo's business, Rampal was about to end his entire career as a chef."

Noam nods. "The one-star review in the Guide would've been the final nail in Drugeon's professional coffin."

"But Armelle was in the same boat, wasn't she?"

"True," he agrees. "Both were facing career-ending reviews."

"Then what makes Ugo, and not Armelle, your prime suspect?"

"What he did on Saturday evening, after the first round." His attention wanders back to the rubber ducks.

"What?" I ask.

"He canceled his bed-and-breakfast in Beldoc."

"Where did he sleep then?" I think on my feet. "We're talking about the night of Rampal's murder... If Ugo canceled his accommodation, what did he do instead of sleeping?"

"Plotting and then murdering Seraphin Rampal is one possibility."

Hmm... This doesn't sit right with me. Ugo canceling his B and B on the night of Rampal's murder is almost too self-incriminating to be incriminating.

"Say, one of the judges leaked the results of round one to Ugo on Saturday evening, before the official announcement," I continue thinking aloud. "Say, he decided to kill Rampal, either in retaliation, or to avoid the one-star review—"

"Or both," Noam cuts in.

"Or both," I echo. "It's just... If that's what he had in mind, then canceling his B and B was a really dumb thing to do. Wouldn't he want to arouse as little suspicion as possible?"

"He would, if he was thinking straight," Noam points out. "But he was livid. And don't forget, he's broke. Maybe he told himself, 'Why pay for the bed if I'm going to stay out all night, killing Rampal?' "

I stare at him from under my brow. "Are you being serious?"

"Absolutely. Rage makes people act in irrational ways."

While I process his argument, he focuses on the race again, like he's still hoping his duck will make a comeback.

When that becomes indisputably impossible, he turns to me, his face sour. "I should've bet on Duck 7! Dammit!"

"It's only twenty bucks."

"Have you seen what *Beldoc Live* is paying me?" He waves his hand. "Never mind. The bottom line is, Ugo Drugeon doesn't have an alibi for the night of Seraphin Rampal's death."

"That doesn't mean he's guilty," I insist. "My sources in the gendarmerie tell me the autopsy found no signs of struggle, and the toxicology report was clean. I mean, no drugs, just alcohol."

Noam smirks. "Your sources are your boyfriend, huh?"

"I can't divulge them."

He laughs. "Anyway, you told me you didn't think Rampal's death was accidental. May I ask why?"

Because I had a vision.

"A gut feeling," I say instead, before tilting my head to one side. "What's your excuse?"

"You're not the only one with a source in the gendarmerie," he begins. "When I learned about the alcohol in Rampal's blood, I talked to his mother and sister, his friends, and his employees at Rampal Guide."

"OK," I say, unsure where he's going with that.

"No one has ever seen him drunk. And you know why?" Noam answers before I get a chance to ask why. "He could hold his liquor, Julie! The man was famous for that."

"Is that why you don't believe that he got plastered and fell into the Rhône?"

He nods. "Yes."

"But how do you explain the absence of defensive wounds?"

"I don't have an explanation," Noam admits. "Do you?"

I shake my head. "Shen is convinced it was an accident."

"Have you told him about Armelle?"

"Yes," I say. "Have you told him about everything you uncovered?"

"He said he'd look into it."

We fall silent. Duck 7 crosses the finish line, followed by Duck 2 and 8. Noam's duck arrives last.

He moans in frustration. "Great. Just great. The story I worked on all week won't be published, and now I lost twenty hard-earned bucks in the Rubber Duck Race!"

To comfort him, I launch into a detailed account of Armelle's letters to Rampal. I even forward him the scanned copies I'd made.

Meanwhile, the organizers of the race pull the rubber ducks from the water for the awards ceremony. Noam remembers his camera and snaps pictures of the podium with Ducks 7, 2, and 8. After that, we move away from the crowd, shake hands, and part ways on a promise to keep each other updated.

Why can't I just let this go? I ask myself as I trudge back to the pâtisserie.

It feels like I've doubled my weight. Every death I investigate takes a toll. I wish I could just walk away from them, from this case, from my insatiable hunger for justice!

Life would be infinitely easier if I didn't care about the murders of people who weren't my family or friends. It's what Gabriel wants. And Rose. And Dad.

Why can't I do that for them, or for myself?

What is wrong with me?

CHAPTER 26

I'm doing my best to hide my impatience as Madame Portelli slowly makes her way toward me, leaning on her walker. Under normal circumstances, her snaillike pace wouldn't be an issue. In the absence of other customers —like now—we'd chitchat. I'd get the full scoop on her kids, grandkids, and great-grandkids before she reaches the counter, and that would be totally fine.

But this morning, my patience has gone AWOL. I'm *dying* to hear the rest of Eric's story. I'd just updated him on Noam's discoveries concerning Ugo Drugeon, when a large group of tourists came in. We served them. After they left, Eric said he'd gone to see Armelle after work yesterday. And that was when Madame Portelli decided to burst in.

Well, metaphorically speaking.

Judging by the size of Eric's smile, he did see Armelle, and perhaps even learned something new. But I won't know until we've sent Madame Portelli on her way.

She asks for a box of vanilla and pistachio macarons for her next visit with her daughter. I begin gift wrapping it, while she unwraps the latest on her most troublesome grandson. Eric rings her purchase up. We wish her a wonderful day, and she embarks on her return journey to the door.

The moment she's finally outside, Eric picks up where he left off. "Armelle was cagey at first, didn't want to talk about it at all."

"And then?"

"And then your brilliant sous chef got her to open up, after some coaxing."

"Well done!" I rub my hands together. "What did she say?"

He lowers his voice conspiratorially, "She admitted writing six nasty letters to Rampal in the months after he dumped her."

"Oh my God, that's huge! I wish she'd tell that to the gendarmes!"

"She already has."

I blink in surprise. "She went to see the gendarmes?"

"No, Shen came to talk to her after you shared your suspicions with him, and she came clean to him about the letters."

Wow. "He did follow up, huh?"

"I'm just as surprised as you are."

Something Eric said before jumps out at me. "Wait, you mentioned six letters. Didn't you mean seven? Because there are seven of them."

"No, I meant six." He goes to the cash register as another customer comes in.

The interruption is brief this time, but it's enough to make me want to pull my hair out.

Eric turns to me the instant the customer is out the door with his muffins. "Armelle claims the seventh letter wasn't from her."

"Who wrote it, then?"

"She doesn't know."

"Or," I say, "she just forgot she wrote seven letters."

"Unlikely—her memory is phenomenal."

I rub my chin. "OK, what about the hoodie woman who brought us the letters? Did you get a chance to ask Armelle about her?"

"Armelle has no idea who that could be or how she obtained the letters," he replies.

"Our mystery woman must've gotten to Rampal's room before the bellhop and even before the gendarmes."

"Or maybe Rampal gave her the letters while he was still alive." Eric leans against the counter. "Anyhow, Armelle regrets writing them bitterly. She was in a dark place at the time, and it was a misguided way to vent her anger."

"Why didn't she vent to Rampal's face? Why send anonymous letters?"

"He was avoiding her. He traveled a lot, never set foot in Pont-de-Pré again, blocked her number..." Eric spreads his hands. "And she didn't see herself stalking him."

"OK, then why didn't she simply email him her thoughts?"

"Because emails can be traced back to the sender." He flicks a crumb off the counter. "She didn't want to hand him a stick with which to beat her, what with all the verbal abuse in her letters."

"I see. So, she made sure they were typed and unsigned." I press my lips together, thinking. "Was she certain he knew they were from her?"

"One hundred percent."

The bell jingles again. A man walks in, eyeing the display case. He buys an apple pie.

After he leaves, I ask Eric, "Did she say anything about where she was on the night Rampal died?"

"She told me she was with someone."

"Ooh, an alibi! How convenient!" I raise an eyebrow. "Who was she with?"

"She didn't say."

I wipe down the counter, pondering this.

Eric grabs a new apple pie from the fridge and slides it into the display case. "When I was leaving, Edmond showed up," he says. "From the way he greeted her, he and Armelle seemed close."

"Edmond? As in Edmond the baker?"

"The very same."

"How close would you say they seemed?" I narrow my eyes. "Friends? More than friends? Do you think he's the one she was with on the night of Rampal's death?"

"No idea."

Before I can respond, a group of teenagers come in looking for cookies. Eric and I fall into step behind the counter. He tells them something that makes them laugh. But my mind is elsewhere, replaying everything I've learned today and trying to make sense of it. Unsuccessfully.

Perhaps the best thing to do now is to let the puzzle rest, like the dough. I'll consider it again in the afternoon, when I recount everything to Flo, and then again in the evening, when I recap it for Gabriel. I better tell him about my snapshot, too...

The bell chimes again, and Capitaine Shen steps into the shop.

He greets us without taking off his aviator shades, before fixing me with a stare. "Can I have a word?"

I glance at Eric.

"I got this, Chef," my second-in-command says.

Nodding thank you, I turn to Shen. "Shall we take a walk?"

We stroll down rue de l'Andouillette, past Magda's Lavender Dream 1 shop, from where her new sales assistant Leslie waves at me. I wave back. Leslie has been exceedingly affable ever since she shorted me on the change. Across the street, Magda glares at me from the counter in Lavender Dream 2. I wave a bonjour. She looks away, pretending she didn't see me.

Shen breaks the silence, "I wanted to give you an update on the Rampal case."

"Why, thank you!" I say, genuinely surprised.

"You've been sharing your findings with my team, so I thought I'd return the courtesy."

I smile tightly. "By the way, thank you for checking those letters for prints, and for talking to Armelle."

"I also followed up on Noam's tip about Ugo Drugeon."

"Already? Wow."

He gives me a funny look.

"Isn't it odd," I say, "that Ugo canceled his B and B reservation for the night of Rampal's death?"

"Monsieur Drugeon claims that he checked his bank account on Friday before the competition," Shen begins. "He discovered he was in the red. So, he canceled the reservation, and then biked all the way back to his home in Cavaillon."

I frown. "That's a good two hours, if not more, by bike."

"Correct. And the only person who can verify his whereabouts is his wife."

"Sounds like a weak alibi to me..." Letting my voice trail off, I slant a look at Shen.

"We call that a spousal alibi," he says. "Hardly bulletproof."

"It follows."

He nods. "Motivated familiar others are the least reliable source of alibis."

"So, are you going to dig deeper into Ugo? Is he your prime suspect now?"

"No," he says. "I know you want there to be more to this story, but none of the evidence suggests Rampal's death was a murder."

"You mean the autopsy and the toxicology?"

"I'm just waiting on the exact time of death, and then I'm done."

Ah, if only I could tell him about my snapshot without losing my credibility!

It took me three years to come clean about my visions to Gabriel, and I consider myself fortunate that he believes me. But he's my boyfriend, so he has a strong positive bias toward me. Shen will simply write me off as another nutcase, and that will be that.

We reach the end of the street. My gaze drifts to the toddlers squealing in the playground.

"Do you really have to close that case so quickly?" I ask Shen. "Can't you wait?"

"For what?" He stops and turns to me. "Madame Cavallo, I respect your instincts, but I'm a facts man. And the facts say it was an accident."

We head back to the pâtisserie.

"What if the facts change their tune?" I probe. "Will you reconsider?"

He chuckles dryly. "If that happens, then sure, I'm open to new evidence. But it better turn up before the forensic expert's report lands on my desk."

"What time frame are we talking about?"

"Twenty-four hours?" He wrinkles his nose. "Forty-eight, tops."

We arrive at the shop's door.

"Thanks for the update, Capitaine Shen," I say.

He gives me a faint smile. "Madame Cavallo, take my advice—move on."

"Perhaps in twenty-four hours."

"Just don't go looking for trouble, will you, Julie?" His tone and use of my first name startle me.

"Gabriel will blame me if anything happens to you during this investigation."

I stare at him. "Did he ask you to make sure I stayed out of it?"

"No. But I believe he asked you to let me do my job, didn't he?"

"Yes."

I'm tempted to add, "And, annoyingly, you seem to be doing it," but I bite my tongue.

He curves his lips into a smile. "So, then."

"Wait, why should anything happen to me, if you're so convinced Rampal's death was an accident?"

He responds with a resigned sigh.

Is that it? He won't even acknowledge my gotcha?

He inclines his head. "It was nice talking to you, Madame Cavallo. Be safe!"

"Good day to you, Capitaine," I call after him and step into the shop.

CHAPTER 27

It's three-thirty. As often, the pâtisserie is quiet during this slice of the afternoon, between the lunch rush and the after-work crowd. Eric is in the kitchen, baking. I'm stacking boxes of supplies in the front shop. The door swings open. I know it's Gabriel, before I see him. His aftershave and the familiar sound of his footsteps give him away.

We exchange a quick kiss.

"Busy?" he asks, eyeing the empty front room.

"Not at the moment. What's up?"

"Remember I told you I had another lead for the Ghost Rider?"

"How could I forget?"

"It may amount to nothing," he warns, "but I managed to lay my hands on the list of everyone registered as a gardian for the Fête du Riz parade."

"That's not nothing, Capitaine Adinian! That's fantastic!"

He pulls out a folded-up sheet of paper from his pocket and opens it out it with a flick of his fingers. "I looked up every name on this list. Most are legit."

"Meaning?"

"I was able to match them to real people," he replies. "Unfortunately, none of them could be our guy. There was always some detail, most often age or physical appearance that didn't fit."

His expression is so sad at this point I feel the urge to hug and kiss him. Which I do, since we're alone. My efforts seem to cheer him up.

"Hey, you tried," I say. "I appreciate you taking the time to check out all those people."

He points out three names highlighted in yellow. "These are the outliers."

"You mean, they don't correspond to any real person?"

"Two of them have no digital footprint. Nothing in the police databases, either."

I feign shock. "Oh my God, we're dealing with ghosts!"

"Or with perfectly corporeal individuals that registered for the parade under an alias, since there was no ID verification."

"What about the third one?" I inquire.

"That's where it gets complicated."

I fold my arms over my chest. "Complicated how?"

"His name is Julien Martin."

"Sounds uncomplicated so far."

"Precisely," he agrees. "That name's as common as mud. I found thirteen Julien Martins in the area who could potentially be the Ghost Rider."

"You think it's an alias, too?"

"If this is our guy, then it wasn't a randomly chosen alias," Gabriel says. "He must've known how ridiculously common that name is."

"It makes sense."

He rubs the back of his neck. "I haven't had time to dig into those three outliers yet."

"You've done plenty." I take the paper from him. "We'll take it from here. This is perfect FERJ territory."

"You're going to sic Flo on them?"

"You bet! She's a wizard at finding people on social media, forums, and other places on the Internet that I didn't even know existed. The platoon of Julien Martins is right up her alley."

"True, but I don't see what she can do about the two names with no digital print."

"We'll use other methods on them," I retort confidently, even though I have no clue right now what those methods might be.

"Just be sure to stay within the confines of the law, all right? No trespassing on private property to snoop around or any other illegal activity, please."

I widen my eyes in feigned affront. "I'd never!"

He responds with a sarcastic, "Uh-huh."

Is this a good time to tell him about my snapshot?

"I have an update of my own for you," I say.

"About the Rampal case?"

"Yep."

Just as I open my mouth to begin, Gabriel's phone buzzes.

He pulls it out for a quick look. "I have to head back to the station. Sorry!"

"No problem, do what you have to do."

"You'll update me tonight?"

I smile sweetly. "Of course."

With a final nod, he beelines for the door, stopping to look over his shoulder. "Just... stay safe, OK? And keep me posted."

I perform a salute. "*Oui, mon Capitaine!*"

∼

THE STREETS ARE quiet except for the rhythmic patter of Lady's paws on the pavement and the occasional passing car. After fifteen years in Paris, it took me a while to reaccustom myself to how calm a provincial town gets after nine on a weeknight. But I'm used to it now, and I don't find the quiet in the evening eerie anymore.

Woot, woot! Julie Cavallo is a small-town girl once again.

Gabriel's still at work, caught up in some raid with the uniforms. I got roped into dog sitting Lady until tomorrow morning. Normally, Sarah handles this gig, but tonight, both she and Rose are off living it up on some yacht, courtesy of one of Sarah's book club members. They don't expect to be back until midmorning.

Sarah's chill about Baxter. She fed him, walked him, and knows he'll snore happily through the night until she's back. But Rose? She can't bear the idea of Lady spending the night alone. So, with just an hour's notice, she dumped her on my doorstep.

Smart play! She knew I'd never let Lady down.

I reel in the leash and tug lightly on it. "Come on, sweetie, let's head back."

Lady gives me a look that's equal parts defiance and plea—a human's "Just five more minutes!" I extend the leash again. She trots on down the street and pauses by one of those little free libraries set up all over the town. I know it was Clothilde's initiative but, of course, Victor took the credit.

Lady's nose is glued to the wooden post as she reads the latest canine news in the pee mail. While she's sniffing every square centimeter of the library's pedestal with businesslike efficiency, I tap my foot, waiting. The streetlight is weak here, so I pull out my phone and use the flashlight to see what books people have left in the free library.

There's the usual selection—classics with boring covers, worn-out romances with bent spines, paperback mysteries, and a bunch of children's books. One cover, sandwiched between a battered copy of *Madame Bovary* and some paperback thriller, catches my eye. It's *The Rampal Guide to the Gastronomic Gems of Provence*.

I pull it out and flip through the pages.

The cover design looks different. The volume itself is faded and creased with dog-eared corners. I check the publication date. It's an old edition, from twelve years ago. I'm putting it back on the shelf, when a twinge of guilt makes me hesitate. This guide is Seraphin Rampal's life's work. For many years, it was hugely popular and so influential it rivaled the *Michelin Guide* here in Provence. But now that the man is dead, someone discarded it like it's worth nothing.

On a rational level, I know that giving away an old, outdated edition of a restaurant guide is just a practical decision that has nothing to do with the author's death. But my heart is pinching for him. Now that he's gone—murdered—taking this opus home seems like a small way to honor his love of gastronomy and to keep his legacy alive.

I tuck the guide under my arm. Lady finishes perusing her news bulletin and moves on.

"All done, girl?" I ask, patting her head.

She wags her tail, and we make a U-turn. When we get home, Lady's energy switches from leisurely to a full-on riot mode. She zooms straight into the kitchen and starts barking like a drill sergeant.

"Coming!" I toss my keys onto the counter and put the *Rampal Guide* down. "I'm a terrible servant, I know."

Lady continues to yap until I run into the kitchen and open the pantry. I grab the tub with her food and scoop a portion into her bowl. She doesn't even wait for me to set it down before she dives in, her little butt wiggling with excitement. The ruckus stops. Phew.

You're lucky you're so cute!

Funny thing is, she's very well-behaved when Rose eats out. If you haven't seen Lady at home, you'd think she doesn't really care about food. She settles at Rose's feet, makes herself comfortable and falls asleep within seconds. Grandma can order meat, fish, chicken—*chicken,* folks!— and Lady won't give a woof. She'll snore peacefully through the longest four-course dinner without as much as a sniff of interest or a bark of protest.

If you think Lady can turn off her sense of smell at will, think again.

Back when she was a puppy, she realized she never gets any food outside of home, which also includes Sarah's house and my apartment. No matter what. She tried pulling the sad puppy face, barking, whining, standing on her hind legs, and clinging to the human in desperation. Nothing doing. And so, she gave up, the pragmatic little thing that she is.

Why waste energy on pointless things?

At home, it's a different story. She growls and barks at mealtime because she's noticed she always gets her meal, without discussion. It doesn't matter if she was good or naughty, if she behaved herself or got into a pooch melee during Grandma's Doga class. It changes nothing. Three walks a day, a healthy meal after the walk, unlimited water, and unrestricted cuddles are hers by birthright.

She knows it, she tolerates no delays, and she doesn't bother to express her gratitude afterward.

Her approach to optional goodies is radically different. Lady knows that the treats and scraps aren't guaranteed by the Universal Declaration of Canine Rights. She understands that the factory setting for these favors is randomness, and so she never demands them. She appeals. She doesn't bark; she whines patiently in a low, nasal tone.

And if she gets the treat, she'll wag her tail or give you a lick to say thank you.

After Lady has finished her supper, we go to the main room. I find a place on my bookshelf for the *Rampal Guide*, and then plonk myself down on the couch. Lady settles at my side. I select a playlist, and we listen to my favorite songs, waiting for Gabriel to come home.

As I pet Lady, it occurs to me that we humans are just as quick as our dogs to distinguish what we consider a right from what we know to be a favor, and to act accordingly.

CHAPTER 28

Flo breezes into the shop at four, wet from the rain, but full of energy. Given that she's come from her morning job in Arles, I can't help but feel a twinge of envy. It's crazy how much zing we lose in one short decade between our mid-twenties and mid-thirties!

Eric wipes his hands on his apron and nods at her. "You're up, Flo. I'm off."

"Can you stay ten more minutes?" My sister strides to the counter. "Then you'll hear my progress report firsthand!"

Eric nods. "Yes, sure."

"Then go ahead," I say to Flo. "Talk, while there are no customers."

Flo looks from me to Eric. "You have no idea what a productive weekend I had!"

I hope she isn't setting the scene for one of her cruel jokes where she inflates my expectations like a helium balloon, and then punctures it by delivering a singularly underwhelming piece of info.

She dumps her purse on a stool. "Tino and I went to a wedding."

"When you described your weekend as 'productive,' " Eric interjects, "did you mean you caught the bride's bouquet?"

She rolls her eyes. "No, that's not what I meant, ye of little faith! I'll have you know I worked while we partied. Multitasking is my middle name."

"Get on with it already," I say.

She flips her hair. "So, on Saturday, Tino's youngest cousin, Indra—she's seventeen—was getting married to her sweetheart, nineteen."

"Seventeen?" Eric lets out a whistle. "Isn't that against the law?"

"The Gitans live by an adapted version of the law," Flo points out. "Anyway, they were having this massive wedding in a humongous tent on a gigantic RV parking lot."

"I'm sure the local authorities were thrilled," I say without hiding my sarcasm.

She turns to me. "Did you know every town with a population over five thousand has to have an area where nomadic Gypsies can park? It's the law!"

I arch an eyebrow. "Gitan law?"

"Nope, French law, you ignorant fool."

Holding my palms together in remorse, I urge her, "Please, go on. Eric is eager to get home. Can you finish your story?"

"I will, if you stop interrupting me," she quips. "So. It was a great wedding. I'm talking flamenco music, mountains of food, over-the-top decorations—"

"We get the picture," I say.

"Every single Gitan in the area was there," she continues. "It was wild."

"Sounds like fun, but quit stalling," I warn her.

"Fine, fine." She glances at Eric. "Remember Gabriel's shortlist of possible Ghost Riders?"

He nods.

She goes on, "One of the two names without a digital footprint stuck out to me: Pepito Gil. I thought it could be a Gitan name, so I did some asking around at the wedding."

"And?" Eric and I ask simultaneously.

"Aaand ta-da! I have an address."

She pulls out a crumpled piece of paper from her pocket and flattens it on the table. It's a rough map of the Camargue drawn in Biro with a circle around an area not too far from Beldoc.

"Well, not really an address but an approximate location," Flo corrects herself. "Pepito is seminomadic, you see. But since he's currently employed as a gardian at a bull breeding farm near Saliers, he'll be based in the area within that circle."

I put a hand on her shoulder. "Great job, detective!"

Eric claps his hands.

She bows. "Thank you, thank you!"

"Do you have a phone number, or any other way to get in touch with him?" I ask.

"Pepito is a traditionalist," she says. "And by that, I mean he rejects everything modern that has corrupted the Gitan way of life, including stationary homes and moving phones. We'll have to travel to that area and ask around."

"I can drive you," Eric offers.

"Tino has already volunteered to take us there tonight, but thanks!" Flo flashes me a smug smile. "Oh, and before I forget, my productivity didn't end with the wedding. On Sunday, I spent hours at my laptop, scouring the Internet for the thirteen Julien Martins."

"Did you find anything?" I ask.

"I've ruled out five so far," she replies. "They're either too young, or too old, or look nothing like the Ghost Rider. I'll tackle the others after our field trip."

"You amaze me, baby sis!" I bob my head, genuinely impressed.

She puts her hands on her hips. "What have *you* been doing since last Friday, aside from bookkeeping?"

"My focus has been on the Rampal case, seeing how little time we have before Shen closes it," I admit. "I dug deeper into Ugo and Armelle but found nothing beyond what we already know."

"What about their alibis?" Flo asks. "Ugo's was flimsy, wasn't it?"

"Armelle spending that night with a secret new boyfriend is equally unconvincing, if you ask me." I shrug. "I was looking for something incriminating, but I've found nothing so far."

"Does Shen have the exact time of death yet?" Eric asks.

"Not to my knowledge," I reply.

He nods. "By the way, I spent some time poking around the Rampal case myself."

"Really?" I look up at him, hopeful. "Why didn't you mention it before?"

"Because I went down a deep, deep rabbit hole, and came up empty."

"Damn!" I exclaim.

He pulls out his phone. "Well, since we're all giving progress reports—successful or otherwise—I guess I should update you on mine."

"You should," Flo says smugly. "There is no shame in failure, for the owl asks not why it hoots."

"Fair point," Eric agrees.

I stare at her. "What does that even mean?"

She shrugs. "How should I know?"

"Right," Eric jumps in. "So, I've been researching drugs that can mess with someone's head enough to make them jump off a bridge if told to."

Flo and I inch closer, intrigued, even though we already know he got nowhere.

"Here's what I've found so far." He reads from his

phone, "Scopolamine, aka Devil's Breath, Pentothal aka truth serum, Rohypnol, aka roofie, aka date-rape drug, GHB, sodium thiopental, some exotic nootropics, and certain barbiturates."

Flo's eyes bulge out. "All that could make a grown man kill himself on command?"

"Theoretically and under very specific circumstances," Eric moderates. "Thing is, all those would show up on a tox screen, so we can rule them out."

Flo stage-whispers, "What if it was a new top-secret mind-control method developed by the CIA?"

Eric grins. "If we're taking this investigation into spy-thriller territory, I'm going to need some gadgets."

"Like what?" I ask him.

"Do you think you can get me an Aston Martin DB5, and a cool gun like a Walther PPK? Oh, and a jetpack, too?"

I pinch my chin. "Hmm... You can have my old bike, Flo's water pistol, and Rose's leaf blower. How's that?"

"Pfft!" With a flippant wave of his hand, he heads out the door.

A customer walks in. Flo takes Eric's place behind the counter. I go to the kitchen and spend the rest of the afternoon baking and counting the minutes until we drive to the Camargue to look for Pepito Gil.

CHAPTER 29

Tino's van bumps along the narrow dirt road. Outside, the grassy wetlands of the Camargue stretch on both sides. The sun is low in the sky. Birds are skimming the surface of the water. Three white horses are grazing by the roadside. The landscape is so beautiful it's easy to forget that we didn't come here just to soak it up.

We've been driving around for at least an hour, searching for Pepito Gil's wagon. When we spoke to Monsieur Duval, the bull breeder who currently employs Pepito, he told us that Pepito lives in an old-fashioned wooden wagon tucked away in the southwest corner of the ranch amid the marshes. Duval described the wagon and gave us its approximate location. He assured us it'd be easy to find.

What he probably had in mind was that it would be easy for someone like himself—someone who knows the area like the back of his hand.

Flo sits beside Tino in the front passenger seat and is uncharacteristically quiet. No jokes, no random commentary, but a whole lot of tension in her shoulders.

Suddenly, she squeals and points ahead to a clearing in the marsh, just beyond the turn in the road.

"Pepito's wagon!" Tino translates for me.

I squint through the windshield until I make out a delightfully vintage wagon parked in the middle of the meadow. Its celadon-blue paint has peeled off in places, revealing a muted red underneath. Small and rounded, it looks like a relic or a history book illustration come to life. The wagon is towed by a van. It's even more battered than either Eric's or Tino's, and almost as antique as the wagon itself.

Tino pulls over. The three of us get out and head across the meadow. The tall grasses brushing against my legs as I walk are soothing, but I'm too anxious to calm down. Flo must be feeling the same pins and needles, because she grabs my hand nervously.

"What if it's him?" she whispers.

I exhale slowly. "Only one way to find out."

We approach the wagon and knock on the door. For a while, nothing happens, but then the door creaks open—and there he is. Pepito Gil.

The man standing before us is on the short side. His gaunt face is wrinkled, not by age, but by a hard life under too much sun. He has dark, deep-set eyes. His long, wavy hair, streaked with gray, falls past his shoulders.

Pepito is not the Ghost Rider. The mismatch is obvious even to Flo and Tino, both of whom only know the man from my description and the blurry pic from the Fête du Riz.

"Bonsoir," Pepito says. "How can I help you?"

"Sorry to bother you, monsieur," I begin, my voice raspy with the awkwardness of the situation. "We were looking for someone and... well, you're not him."

I expect Pepito to shut the door on us, but instead he peers at Tino. "Wait a minute, aren't you Maria's boy?"

"Um, yes," Tino replies.

Pepito grins, showing a missing tooth. "I knew it!" He swings the door open wider. "You can't just turn up here and leave. Come in for a cup of tea or coffee. I haven't seen any of Maria's kin in quite some time."

I glance at Tino, wondering if it would be too rude to refuse.

"A coffee would be great, thank you," Tino says to Pepito.

Well, there's my answer.

The older man steps aside, motioning us to enter and sit around a small table. Flo and I opt for tea.

I look around. The wagon's interior is just as colorfully old-world as the exterior. There's a kerosene stove in the corner where Pepito busies himself brewing and infusing. A guitar leans against one wall in another corner. The wall above the bed is wallpapered with pinned photos. In the fading light, I discern family reunions, portraits, and snapshots of nature and animals.

Pepito lights a candle and sets four steaming mugs on the table before joining us.

"You're both *gadje*," he says, his eyes flicking between Flo and me.

"*Gadje* means 'non-Gypsy,' " Tino explains to us.

Flo and I nod.

A mischievous smile on her lips, Flo adds, "But I have a mitigating circumstance. Tino and I have been together for almost five years."

"His mother married a gadjo," Pepito adds, nodding toward Tino. "It ended in a divorce."

Flo blinks, taken aback.

Subtle, dude, I nearly blurt. *Real subtle. Great pep talk for the young lovebirds.*

Tino smirks. "It's not like there's no divorce among the *Gitans*."

"I wish I could deny that!" Pepito exclaims, "But family isn't as sacred for us as it used to be. The new generation has lost its way."

"How?" I inquire.

"They're too eager for the comforts of the gadje," he explains. "Consider this: the Nazis interned the Gypsies in camps all over Europe, including one here at Saliers. They tortured us so we'd quit the traveling lifestyle. They failed. But now their dream is coming true."

Tino laughs. "I'll tell my cousins they must move out of their nice houses and quit their good jobs or else the Nazis won."

"But you, Monsieur Gil—" I begin.

"Please, call me Pepito."

"But you, Pepito, you've literally joined the maquis!" I sweep a hand around the wagon. "No electricity, no indoor plumbing..."

He smiles. "It's a small price to pay. I refuse to trade our traditions for a flat-screen TV."

"By the way, Flo and I don't own a TV," Tino jumps in.

Pepito cocks his head. "Do you live in a caravan?"

"No," Tino admits. "We live in an apartment inside a building. But I do own a van!"

Pepito waves dismissively. "It's not the same. The gadjes' artificial world cuts you from the elements. If you don't stick your head out the window, you won't know if it's cold or warm, dry or rainy, dark or light. That's no way to live."

"I'd rather not freeze my ass off in winter than feel the elements," Tino retorts.

"Unfortunately, you're not the only one." Pepito sips on his tea. "Too many Gitans have settled down. One by one, camps turn into villages, the kids go to school—"

"You're upset that the Gitan kids go to school?" Flo interrupts him. "Seriously?"

He gives her a sad smile. "Yes, seriously. When they finish middle school and sometimes even high school, they get jobs in the city, marry a gadje, and forget who they are."

I consider arguing that it may not be such a bad thing, at least not for those less enchanted with the nomadic life than he is. But I bite my tongue. I do see why he feels the way he does. For centuries, his people kept their uniqueness by rejecting all things modern, refusing to take root, and only marrying within the community. To Pepito, the sacrifice was worth it, and seeing how he lives, he probably doesn't even see it as a sacrifice.

Tino clears his throat. "Um, on a different subject, I hear you took part in the Fête du Riz parade this year?"

"Yes," Pepito replies. "For my grandkids' sake."

He has grandkids? He's, what, forty-five? Merely a decade older than me...

"You look too young to have grandchildren," I remark.

"We Gitans marry young," he says. "Anyway, the little ones wanted me to ride through Arles with other gardians."

"They must've been very proud of you," Flo offers.

"They were," Pepito confirms. "Who knows, maybe seeing me cheered by the crowd would make them want to be like me rather than like their parents."

Before he can launch into another tirade about how the younger generation is drifting away from the Gypsy ways, I pull out my phone and find the photo of the Ghost Rider.

"Pepito, may I ask you something?" I hold the phone up. "Did you see this man at the parade?"

He takes the phone and studies the image. For a moment, I worry it's too blurry, but then Pepito's face lights up with recognition.

"Yes! I saw him. He was there, all right." He hands the phone back.

My pulse quickens. "Did you notice anything about him that stood out?"

Pepito stares upward, thinking. "The way he rode," he says finally. "It was off."

"Off how?" I ask.

Pepito mimics someone sitting upright on a horse. "Too graceful, too studied for a real gardian. It was like he was role-playing."

Holy cow!

That's exactly what I told myself when I saw him for the first time, in my vision. Dressed in coveralls, he was talking to the owner of that cursed beach house. There was something off, something performative about him, like he was *playing* a building contractor not actually *being* one.

Flo leans forward. "Can you recall anything else? Even the tiniest detail could be helpful."

Pepito closes his eyes. His face relaxes as if he's mentally rewinding the parade. It's eerily quiet except for the cries of the night birds outside.

He opens his eyes. "Yes, perhaps there was something else. During the parade, various local officials came by to say hello to the gardians. Mostly, they just wanted photo ops for their newsletters."

I chuckle diligently, trying to hide my impatience.

"The man in your photo," Pepito continues, "he seemed to know some of them well."

"What makes you say that?" I ask.

"I saw him whispering something to one of the officials, a lady. They leaned in close, conspiratorial-like." Pepito rubs his chin. "Then your guy made a dumb joke, and lady boss laughed. But it was a forced laugh, like she had to. Your guy gave her a small envelope. And another one to another official, a man."

Tino perks up, intrigued. "Did you recognize any of those officials?"

"Nah, son," Pepito says. "I've made it my business to

keep as far from the authorities as possible. I don't know who they were, and frankly, I don't want to know."

Pepito's words hang in the air while the three of us exchange looks. This visit with Pepito turned out to be surprisingly informative. Even if he couldn't name any names, his memories from the parade have added some important brushstrokes to the Ghost Rider's portrait. We know now that he's a disguise-loving chameleon with possible ties to several local officials.

What kind of ties?

Does he work for them, or do they work for him? Is that how he's been able to hide in plain sight all these years?

Who the hell is he?

CHAPTER 30

With the deposit slip safely tucked into my purse, I leave the bank. On my way back to the pâtisserie, I pass Edmond's bakery again. Only this time, something makes me stop. I remember what Eric said about seeing Edmond enter Armelle's restaurant and greet her in a way that suggested they were close.

Friends? Lovers? Was Armelle with him on the night Rampal died?

Before I know it, my feet steer me straight to Edmond's door. His shop smells of yeasty, glutenous, comforting bread, the kind I haven't baked in years. I can't deny that I miss it.

Edmond spots me and waves. "Julie! What a nice surprise."

"Thought I'd pop in and see how things are going." I smile. "Business good?"

"Busy as ever."

OK, how do I get to the question I want to ask from here?

"Listen, Edmond..." I look over my shoulder to make sure we're alone. "I have to ask. Are you seeing Armelle?"

His eyes widen a little. "You mean, are we dating?"

"Yes."

He snorts with laughter. "No. We're just friends. We've known each other since culinary school. There's nothing romantic between us."

The gears in my head start turning. If Edmond isn't her new boyfriend, then who is? Does she have one or did she lie to give herself an alibi?

"Is she currently seeing anyone?" I press.

Edmond shifts uncomfortably. "Armelle's love life is none of your business, Julie."

Correct. But I'm not giving up. "She told me she was with someone on the night Rampal died," I begin. "You see, I caught her doing something suspicious, and I need to know if she was telling the truth."

Edmond casts a look toward a closed door behind him. Judging by the clatter of trays and the low hum of conversation coming from there, it's his kitchen.

"Your staff can't hear us," I assure him.

"Julie..." He lowers his voice. "I'm only telling you this because you helped me out during the competition, so I owe you. After this, we're square, OK?"

"OK."

"Armelle does have a new boyfriend, but it's complicated," he whispers.

"Complicated how? Is he married?"

"No."

I curl my lip. "Are you sure he exists?"

"He does. Armelle told you the truth."

"Did she?" I sneer harder. "Because to me, this 'complicated' new relationship sounds like a convenient alibi to me."

He lets out a frustrated breath. "She was with Tanguy. He's her new boyfriend."

My mind flashes back to Mylene Nivault's sidekick Tanguy Eldin and his too-smooth charm.

I narrow my eyes. "You're telling me Tanguy and Armelle are together?"

"Yes. But you didn't hear it from me, OK?"

I search his face. "I thought Tanguy was with Mylene. They were inseparable during Ritzy Rice."

"Nah, they're just good friends like me and Armelle."

I keep peering at him, trying to wrap my head around his scoop. "Are you sure?"

"Yes, Julie, I am. But, please, don't tell anyone. They're keeping it under wraps."

"Why the secrecy?" I ask. "They're both single as far as I know."

"Armelle is divorced. She's older than Tanguy. Her family—especially her teenage daughter—wouldn't approve."

I digest this. "Tanguy's, what? Thirty?"

"Yeah, and Armelle's forty. Not a huge gap, but you know how people can be."

He must see it on my face that I'm not convinced, because he adds, "There's another reason."

"Shoot."

"Tanguy is in talks to be the star chef of some culinary show, and the producers want him to be officially single for the first season. It's part of his image—young, handsome, and unattached."

Reluctantly, I begin to envisage that I've been barking up the wrong tree. Is Armelle really innocent, despite her obvious motive and angry letters?

"So, she'd risk weakening her alibi to protect Tanguy's TV deal?" I ask, grasping at straws.

"Yeah, she would. She's that kind of girl," Edmond confirms. "That said, she didn't hide Tanguy's identity from the gendarme who came to talk to her."

"Capitaine Shen?"

"I believe that was his name, yes."

"Thank you, Edmond, I appreciate it."

He lets out a sigh. "I hate myself right now. We're even, right?"

"We are. See you around."

I leave the bakery almost at a run, then plod back to the pâtisserie, my heart heavy. Pushing a good guy to spread gossip about his friend makes me feel anything but proud of myself. The rest of the weight pressing down on my chest comes from the realization that I was wrong about Armelle. Her letters, whether she wrote all seven or only six, as she claims, are no proof of murder. And her alibi is stronger than I thought.

Shen is going to close this case as soon as the forensic expert has determined the exact time of death. Ugo Drugeon, my other suspect, doesn't seem to interest the gendarmes despite his motive and the weakness of his "spousal" alibi. Does Shen know something I don't? Does he have evidence exonerating Ugo that he forgot to share with me? I should ask Gabriel.

What if there really was no murderer in this case?

Maybe I misinterpreted my snapshot. Maybe the voice that told Rampal to jump wasn't real. It could've been a fantasy, something he heard in his head while hallucinating —and, somehow, I heard it too.

As I approach my shop, I spot Karl and Harley hanging out near the entrance. Harley trots over to me, his tongue lolling out in a goofy grin.

I crouch down. "Look who's here!"

An energetic scratch behind his ears earns me a happy wag from the mutt.

I look up at Karl. "Hey, you! Done at the vineyards?"

"*Salut*, Julie! It's my day off, so I thought I'd come say hi."

I straighten up and take a step toward him. Something's off with Karl, but I can't put my finger on it right away.

Then it hits me. I'm picking up no body odor and no stale sweat from his clothes. Even more unusual, there's a faint whiff of soap coming off him. His white hair is pulled back into a low ponytail, as always. But there's a silky sheen to it, like he washed it this morning as opposed to last month.

"You look shocked," he says with a chuckle.

"You look good."

"The campsite has showers for the workers, and a laundry service too. So, I've been washing daily."

I laugh. "That's a bit of a change."

"Don't get used to it, though," he warns. "I'll be back on the streets in two weeks."

Must you?

I don't ask that aloud. Karl and I have had this conversation before. He lives on the streets by choice. I can't fathom why, and his whimsical, ever-changing explanations make no sense to me.

He opens his arms. "Meanwhile, you can take advantage of my pristine state and give me a hug."

Before I second-guess myself, I step forward and embrace him. His eyes widen in surprise, as if he didn't expect me to rise to the challenge. But he hugs me back gently and a little awkwardly. As we step away, the door to Magda's shop opens. Leslie comes out and freezes in the doorway, staring at Karl.

He turns around and locks eyes with her.

She breaks the silence, her voice shaky, "W-what's your name?"

"Um, Karl. What's yours?"

There's more intense staring.

Her eyes flicker. "I'm Leslie. You... you remind me of someone I knew a long time ago. But you can't be him. You're *not* him."

"Funny you should say that." Karl skews a feeble smile. "Your voice reminds me of someone, too, from way back.

But you can't be her, either. Besides, you don't look like her at all."

Leslie's shoulders relax. "I'm sorry, I didn't mean to stare."

"Me neither."

"I better get back inside," she says. "Nice meeting you, Karl." She turns on her heel and walks back into the shop.

After the door clicks shut behind her, I turn to Karl, who's scratching Harley under the chin, like nothing happened.

He looks up at me. "I better hurry or I'll miss my ride back to the vineyard. See you around, Julie! Say hi to Rose."

"I will. Take care, Karl!"

He gives Harley a low whistle, and they wander off down the street.

CHAPTER 31

Now that my business is in its third year of turning a small but steady profit, I can afford to close the shop on Sunday afternoons. That's what I typically do, except for Easter, Christmastime, Valentine's, and Mother's Day. Which explains why I'm at home this afternoon, baking for pleasure.

I'm smoothing the frosting over the chocolate cake when I hear familiar footsteps behind me. I can see Gabriel tiptoeing into the kitchen like a cartoon burglar, but I keep my focus on the cake.

Only when he attempts to dip a finger into the bowl do I spin around. "Caught red-handed!"

He throws both hands up. "I plead guilty."

"Where's the remorse?"

"I'm feeling terribly repentant right now." He pulls a silly face. "Doesn't it show?"

"Repentant, my ass."

I wish there was more bite in my rebuke! But the truth is, a bit of tomfoolery is exactly what I need at this moment. Since my conversation with Edmond, a cloud of self-doubt has been hanging over me, dimming my usual spark. Gabriel's antics made my world a little brighter.

After our row over having kids, I've steered clear of the subject. Things have been great between us. The issue hasn't gone away, but we put it in a box, locked it, and shoved it in a closet—and made a point of pretending it's not there.

Except, of course, it is.

It's the proverbial elephant in the room. We can be in denial. We can restrain and subdue it. But we can't escape it. And right now, it's raising its trunk and demanding to be heard.

"We need to talk about the kids thing," I blurt out.

Gabriel's face hardens as if he's bracing for impact. While I'm choosing my words, he stares me in the eye.

And then, instead of shutting down, he speaks, "All right, let's talk about it. But I want you to imagine something first."

"What?"

"Imagine we go ahead and start a family."

I blink, thrown off. *Did he just say those words?* Has he been warming up to the idea? It seems too wild to be true.

My eyes fixed on his, I say, "OK."

"You'd have to move into the barracks with me."

Ah.

He nods. "You'd have to do that for your safety and for the baby's. You can't stay here, exposed, while I'm out there doing what I do with a target painted on my back."

"You exaggerate."

"No, I don't."

I wave him off. "Are you seriously telling me that the only safe place for a gendarme's family is the barracks?"

"Yes," he deadpans. "Our families face the same threats as we do, except they're unarmed and untrained."

"Threats from who?"

"Gangsters, drug dealers, muggers and thugs, political and religious terrorists, violent junkies and nutjobs the system won't lock up... The list goes on."

"You're painting a deliberately bleak picture," I say. "The vast majority of the people around me are good."

"Walk in my shoes, and you'll see how many aren't."

Hang on... He has a target painted on his back? That sounds more specific than the laundry list he just gave me.

I narrow my eyes. "Have you been investigating the Morillot case?"

"My commandant tells me I can't."

Interesting. He didn't say he wasn't looking into the murder of his friend's wife. He said his commandant was *telling* him not to.

"Is that why you're so obsessed with my safety?" I search his face. "Because Lena Morillot's murder involves the Mafia—and the Mafia is ruthless?"

He looks away. "The bottom line is that you and the baby would have to live in secure housing."

I look around my cozy kitchen. "Oh well, if that's what it takes... I guess I can do it."

"When I'm transferred out of Beldoc," he continues, "will you follow me?"

I panic. "Are they transferring you?"

"No, but they won't keep me here forever." He smiles. "I'm a gendarme, not a municipal policeman."

"I'm aware of that."

He presses on, "So, are you prepared to move away from Rose, Flo, and your friends? Are you prepared to quit FERJ and your sleuthing hobby?"

"What are you trying to tell me, Gabriel?" I ask through the lump in my throat. "Are you saying that if I want a family, I have to give up everything else?"

"I'm saying you can't have your cake and eat it, too, Julie."

I flinch. This hypothetical scenario of his wasn't a sign that he's opening up to the possibility of having kids. It was just a sterile thought experiment. Actually, it was worse than that. Asking a price he knows to be too high for me was his new and creative way of saying no.

Gabriel's expression softens. "Remember our first kiss?"

I nod. "It was in Paris, two years ago. Why?"

"I'd been crazy about you for over a year before that, but I held out. Do you know why?"

This is obviously a rhetorical question, so I let him answer it.

"Because I knew we wouldn't be just a hookup or causal friends with benefits," he says. "I also knew you weren't the type of woman to be content tucked away in the barracks."

"You can't handle worrying about me, is that it?"

He hangs his head. The silence between us stretches, heavy. I turn my back to him and continue frosting the cake.

He wraps his arms around my waist. "You know I love you, don't you?"

"Yes," I say, leaning back into his embrace. "I love you, too."

He holds me as I finish with the cake.

When I'm done, I bottle up my heartache and turn around to face him. "Would you happen to know if the time of Rampal's death has come in yet?"

"They narrowed it down to a two-hour window."

"Between when and when?"

"Between one and three in the morning." He watches me carefully, like he's gauging how this will land.

I stare back at him.

"Now that Shen has the exact time of death," he says, "Ugo Drugeon's alibi checks out."

"How does the time of Rampal's death give more weight to Ugo's wife's word?"

He smiles. "It doesn't. But guess what does? CCTV."

Huh? "Explain."

"Drugeon was caught on camera at a gas station on the way to Cavaillon," Gabriel begins. "He parked his bike there at one-fifty a.m., used the bathroom, and bought a bottle of water. That station is at least an hour and a half away from Beldoc by bike, riding fast."

"So, he really was on his way home, just like he told Shen?"

Gabriel nods. "It appears so, yes."

"Is his bike electric?"

"No."

I do some mental math. "He couldn't have killed Rampal between one and three because he must've left town at around twenty past midnight."

"Correct," he agrees. "Now, let's say he changed his mind at the gas station and decided to pedal back to Beldoc, just in case there was an opportunity to kill Rampal."

I calculate in my head again. "He couldn't have made it back to Beldoc before three a.m."

"That's right, Detective Cavallo!" He points a finger at me in a *You!* gesture. "Rampal drowned between one and three in the morning, and Drugeon was demonstrably *not* in Beldoc during that lapse of time."

I let the implications sink in. "Well, that's the second suspect down."

"You're disappointed."

"No."

But, of course, I am—and he knows it.

He pulls me back into his embrace. "I have some news that might cheer you up."

"Hit me with it."

"There were two gardians on my list with no digital footprint, right?"

"Right," I say. "Pepito Gil and..." I shut my eyes, trying to recall the other name.

"Jean-Jacques Tillier," he prompts. "I checked property records in the area, just in case, and found something."

My ears perk up at that. "What? Don't keep me in suspense!"

"Jean-Jacques Tillier owns a farm," he declares. "I have an address near a village called Coulbon."

"That's huge! Where's Coulbon? Can you take me there?"

Gabriel raises an eyebrow, amused by my eagerness. "Now?"

"Why not? Is it too far?"

"No, it's in Camargue." He bows ceremoniously. "Your wish is my command, madame!"

CHAPTER 32

Forty minutes later, we pull up to a microfarm, nestled in the marshlands. The first thing I see is a tiny house, complete with a well-kept little orchard, a compact fruit garden, and a small barn. Two cows graze lazily in the front pasture. A pair of chickens peck at the dirt on one side of the house.

We exit the car and make our way around the property.

"I know what's going on here," I say to Gabriel. "Monsieur Tillier saw an Internet ad for a complete Noah's Ark. It was ninety percent off, so he ordered it. And this came in the mail."

"Yeah, well, he won't be restarting life on earth with it, come the next Flood."

"Why?" I ask without thinking.

Gabriel points to the cows and hens. "Because it's an all-female crew, silly."

Annoyed at my lapse in observation, I pout. "You shouldn't assume their gender."

He looks at me over the rim of his shades but says nothing. We continue our inspection. There's not much more to see, really, other than a rundown tractor and an assortment of agricultural tools leaning against the barn.

I walk over to the house and knock on the door. No answer. No dog barking, no muted TV sounds, no footsteps, nothing.

Gabriel joins me. "I don't think he's home."

"Or maybe he heard us circling around the farm and ran outside to hide."

Gabriel sweeps his hand around the diminutive farm. "Where?"

"Hmm."

I knock again, louder and more insistently this time, but the house remains eerily quiet. We give up and head over to Tillier's nearest neighbor, farther down the dirt road. After some shouting from the front gate, an elderly woman in a floral apron comes out and gives us the once-over.

"Bonjour, madame." Gabriel puts on his most charming smile. "We're looking for Jean-Jacques Tillier. Is he around?"

She points somewhere behind us. "He's probably in Coulbon, selling his eggs and cream. It's market day, so he'll be there until five or six."

I check my watch. It's barely three-thirty. Plenty of time.

Gabriel thanks her, and we hurry to the car.

"To Coulbon, Capitaine!" I call, sliding into the passenger seat. "We've come this far; let's check out that market."

Gabriel starts the engine. "You don't expect Tillier to be the Ghost Rider, do you?"

"No."

"Because of what Pepito Gil told you? That the Ghost Rider was friendly with various officials?"

"Yes." I look back at the miniature farm as we drive away. "I just don't see Tillier as that guy."

No more words are exchanged between us during the seven minutes it takes to get to Coulbon.

~

THE VILLAGE TURNS out to be a life-size Provençal postcard, frozen in the nineteenth century if it weren't for the cars. Honey-colored stone bastides hug the hillside. Paved streets wind through clusters of smaller houses with red-tiled roofs and vines draped over the walls. Leaves tinged with warm hues add a touch of nostalgia to Coulbon's picturesque charm.

Gabriel parks the car near the square where the market is held. It consists of just a handful of stalls selling fresh produce, cheeses, and other local goods. Judging by the familiar way the vendors greet market goers, everyone here knows everyone else.

It's almost too cozy for comfort.

I much prefer the size of Beldoc. That said, I think I could live here. Flo, too. But if our big-city sisters—my Parisian twin and our oldest in Montreal—had to move to Coulbon, they'd go crazy in less than a month.

Gabriel points his chin toward a man behind one of the stalls. "There he is."

To my surprise, the guy isn't as clearly and unequivocally *not* the Ghost Rider as Pepito was. The only possible match in this tiny farmers' market, he's about the same height and build as the man I've seen three times now —once in a vision and twice in real life. Tillier is wearing sunglasses and a faded cap to shield his eyes from the sun. He's lankier than the Ghost Rider, but weight isn't a permanent characteristic.

I study him as inconspicuously as I can.

There's something missing from Tillier compared to the

Ghost Rider. I don't know how to describe it... An imposing aura, maybe? A certain charisma, for sure.

Then again, people can look different in different circumstances and clothes. A man in a well-cut suit or a romantic cowboy outfit will seem more attractive than if he shows up in baggy jeans, a linty old sweater, and a grimy cap.

Appearances do matter, unfortunately.

"Could be him," I whisper to Gabriel, albeit without conviction.

We stroll over, pretending to browse the stalls. When we approach Tillier, we feign interest in his cheese. He offers a small piece to sample, which we happily accept. It's surprisingly good, so I ask him to pack three hundred grams. The transaction provides me with an opportunity to make small talk.

"Nice day for a market," I say, handing him a tenner. "Do you come here often?"

He starts counting the change. "Every Sunday. I sell the surplus from my farm."

"Sounds like a dream life."

He hands me the change. "Depends on your dreams. I grew up in a prepper family, so self-sufficiency was the ideal. But if you asked me twenty years ago what my dreams were, I had no plans to live on a farm."

"What were your dreams back then?"

"Anything but hoarding for doomsday!" He chortles. "At eighteen, I rebelled, moved to Avignon and got a job."

"What job, if I may ask?"

A part of me hopes, against all odds, that he'll say, *"A building contractor."*

"A fishmonger. I did my best to adapt to city life but..."

"The marshes called to you," Gabriel finishes for him.

"Something like that." Tillier shrugs. "I'm just better off here in the Camargue, growing my own food."

Can this man be the scumbag responsible for my mother's death?

Honestly, I doubt it.

"Do you ever work as a gardian?" I ask, just to be thorough.

"Yeah, I do some seasonal work for breeders," he replies. "I don't own a horse, so that's how I get to ride. It's something I love."

"Do you ride in the Fête du Riz parade?" Gabriel asks.

"My boss at the bull ranch makes me."

I arch an eyebrow. "*Makes* you?"

"He's big on local traditions," Tillier says with a smile.

I pull out my phone and show him the photo of the Ghost Rider. "Did you see this man during the parade?"

Tillier studies the image for a moment.

"I don't think so," he says after a beat. "Lots of faces that day, though. Hard to remember everyone unless they stood out."

"Of course." I slip the phone back into my purse.

He cocks his head. "That dude, who is he?"

"It's what we're trying to find out," I say.

He squints at me, then at Gabriel. "And who are you two?"

"My name's Julie Cavallo," I point at Gabriel. "And this is my boyfriend, Gabriel Adinian."

"Jean-Jacques Tillier," he introduces himself. "Call me Jean-Jacques."

"I'm a pastry chef in Beldoc," I add.

"Cute town."

"Oh, you know it?" I smile. "Have you ever been to Julie's Gluten-free Delights on rue de l'Andouillette?"

"*Oui, madame!*" His eyes light up with recognition. "As recently as two weeks ago. I bought a box of macarons in that shop for my ex, Candice. She's from Beldoc."

I wrinkle my nose. "I hope she didn't become your ex because she hated my macarons."

"No, she loved them. We broke up for a more substantial reason."

"What reason?" I ask.

I'm totally prying, but I can't help myself.

To my surprise, he humors me. "She was OK with my low-tech lifestyle in the beginning. But last week she decided she won't live on a farm and broke up with me just before our one-year anniversary."

"I'm so sorry to hear that!" I exclaim.

And I mean it. The reason for his breakup hits depressingly close to home. And I'm not talking about the living arrangements. Gabriel and I love each other too much to split over that. We'll work something out, find a compromise. But there's no meeting each other halfway about having a baby. It's an either-or situation.

A customer stops by, and we wait while Jean-Jacques sells her a carton of eggs.

When she's gone, he turns his attention back to me. "Since you're a pastry chef, did you take part in that ill-fated cooking competition... Ritzy Rice?"

"Yes, I did. And *ill-fated* sums it up nicely."

"Candice told me all about it. How the head judge fell into the Rhône and drowned before the final round."

"He was a celebrity in the culinary world," I say.

"Tragic business." He looks at me from behind his shades. "You know, we saw him that night."

"Who?" I double-check, startled.

"Your celebrity chef—what was his name, already?"

"Seraphin Rampal," I prompt.

Jean-Jacques nods. "Right. He was with a woman, strolling along the river."

I find myself uncharacteristically at a loss for words.

Fortunately, Gabriel jumps in. "What time was that?"

"After midnight for sure." Jean-Jacques scratches his chin, thinking. "Maybe half past or closer to one. I took Candice out to dinner, and we strolled by the river afterward."

I recover my tongue. "Did you get a good look at the woman?"

"No, it was too dark, and honestly, I wasn't paying much attention until we passed them, and Candice told me who he was."

"Did he seem drunk to you?" I press.

"Yeah. He had that telltale unsteady gait." Jean-Jacques shakes his head. "If I'd known what was going to happen to him later that night, I would've made sure he was safely in bed, before I dropped Candice off and went home."

"Could we get Candice's last name?" Gabriel asks, the cop kicking in.

Jean-Jacques raises his eyebrows. "What for?"

"I'm a gendarme," Gabriel says. "You and Candice were probably the last people to see Seraphin Rampal alive. My colleagues might want to ask her some questions."

Jean-Jacques's eyes widen. "I see. Her name's Candice Ferrero. She's a warehouse clerk."

Gabriel types Candice's name into his phone. "Why didn't you come forward, you and Candice, when you heard Rampal was found dead?"

"Are you aware that most people would rather stay away from the police if they can help it?" Jean-Jacques parries.

That makes me an outlier, I realize.

"Not to mention that I was raised by conspiracy-loving preppers," he adds. "Distrust of authority is second nature to me."

"Fair enough," I interject before Gabriel can tell him off.

Jean-Jacques looks from me to Gabriel. "Do you suspect foul play?"

"No, but we like to be thorough." Gabriel sticks his phone in his pocket. "Thank you for your help."

I thank him, too, my mind still processing the implications of what he told us. Gabriel takes the cheese. We wave goodbye to Jean-Jacques and head back to the parking lot.

In the car, I turn to Gabriel. "What are you going to do with this new info?"

He turns the key in the ignition. "I'll pass it along to Charles-Antoine."

"I bet he's closed the case by now."

"That decision is up to the investigative judge," Gabriel reminds me. "It's possible the case hasn't been officially closed yet."

"And if it has, do you think they'll reopen it?"

"Not for this," he replies. "But Shen might want to talk to Candice, anyway."

"You think he will?"

He shrugs.

My chest tightens with regret. I should've told Gabriel about my vision on the bridge, as inconclusive as it was. If I'd done it sooner, then Jean-Jacques' testimony would've lent it extra credibility. But that ship has sailed. If I bring up the snapshot now, it's going to sound like I'm just trying to tie things together after the fact.

Dammit, Julie!

CHAPTER 33

Flo puts a bottle of wine on the coffee table. "For the record, I don't think we should be calling this guy *Ghost Rider*. Sounds overdramatic to me."

"What do you want to call him, then?" Rose slices into the quiche she brought. "Unidentified gardian? It lacks punch."

"He'll be Ghost Rider for now," I declare.

Lady, curled up at Rose's feet, wags her tail.

"See?" I point at her. "She agrees."

I set down the platter with the pastries that I made for this family gathering. Usually, we get together at Rose's, but tonight I invited FERJ to my place. I was too tired after a day of negotiating with my suppliers and baking to ride my bike to Grandma's.

Gabriel is still at work. Eric will join us from his place via video call. So, for now, it's just Rose, Flo, and me.

Flo pours everyone some wine. "Fine, Ghost Rider it is, then." She turns to me. "Now, tell us about this Jean-Jacques Tillier. What do you make of him?"

"He's not the Ghost Rider," I reply. "He looks different and doesn't fit the profile."

Rose fixes me. "Are we back to square one?"

"Not yet," Flo interjects. "We still have the Julien Martin lead. I've now screened out eight of them. Five more to go."

Rose pats her hand. "Well done! And, in case anyone cares, I passed my exam."

We cheer.

Flo raises her glass. "To Grandma and to perseverance!"

We all clink glasses.

"All right, back to the Ghost Rider," I say. "If he has local officials on his payroll, as Pepito's testimony suggests, that would explain why he signed up for the parade."

Flo raises an eyebrow. "I'm not sure I follow."

"Think about it," I urge her. "What better way to corrupt a bunch of officials than to do it in public? No need for secret meetings."

"Disguised as a gardian," Rose picks up, "he could shake hands with them, exchange pleasantries, and conduct his affairs right under everyone's noses."

Flo nods. "And no one suspected a thing. Genius!"

Rose turns to me. "Do you think he's more than a common thug? Could he be some kind of criminal mastermind?"

"It's possible," I say.

"Or maybe itsh another falsh lead," Flo mumbles through a mouthful of quiche.

We wait for her to finish chewing.

She continues, "What if he works for the authorities, and not the other way around?"

"In what role?" I ask.

She puckers her mouth. "As a snitch?"

I scoff.

"I wouldn't rule that out," Rose says. "And, please, don't call informants *snitches*. They help keep our streets safe."

"For a fee," Flo points out.

Rose lifts her chin. "They value their time, unlike you and your sister."

Unwilling to go down that road, I point at the clock on the wall. "We better call Eric to discuss the Rampal case. He said he'd be home about now."

Flo hits the call button on her phone, and soon Eric's face, framed by shelves of comic books and video games, pops up on her screen. He's in his home office.

"Evening, team!" he salutes.

We greet him. I position the phone against a pitcher in the middle of the table so that we can all see each other.

Flo points at me. "Julie has some news."

"Ugo Drugeon's alibi checked out," I say. "He was caught on CCTV at a gas station an hour and a half away from Beldoc."

"So, he's in the clear?" Eric asks.

"Yes," I confirm. "The investigative judge will close the case, unless Shen finds Candice Ferrero, and she makes it worth his while."

"Who's Candice Ferrero?"

"A Beldoc warehouse worker who may or may not have seen something on the night Rampal died," I answer.

"Assuming Shen talks to her," Flo jumps in, "do you think it's likely she can describe the woman Rampal was with?"

Eric's eyebrows shoot up. "He was with a woman?"

"Apparently, yes," I say, doing my best to not look smug.

Flo covers her ears. "Will you stop mentally screaming 'I told you so'? My head is exploding."

"Sorry."

"Your sister has a right to gloat," Rose interjects. "Her vision on the bridge has just been vindicated."

"Thank you, Grandma!"

"I still don't think you should be investigating this case," she says, "but what's fair is fair."

I turn back to Eric. "So, Candice and her ex saw Rampal strolling down the riverfront with a woman. Candice's ex, who Gabriel and I talked to yesterday, didn't get a good look at her, but we're hoping Candice did."

"How close was it to the time of Rampal's death?" Eric asks.

"Very close," I reply. "Sometime between twelve-thirty and one in the morning."

"Unless Candice was wearing night vision goggles," Flo points out, "it's hard to imagine she can provide enough detail for Shen to ID the woman."

Everyone agrees with that observation. We fall silent, deflated.

Rose finishes her wine. "Which one of you has been looking into substances that might've made Rampal compliant? Any breakthroughs?"

"Everything I've researched so far," Eric says, "would've been flagged in his toxicology report."

"What if it wasn't a drug?" I begin.

Flo rolls her eyes. "Are you thinking hypnosis? Please, not again! We already dismissed that as unrealistic."

"It's just..." I hesitate, searching for the right words. "Rampal wasn't suicidal. He wasn't completely zonked out, either."

"Right," Eric agrees. "He had the presence of mind to ask his mystery companion if he should really jump."

I nod. "So, if there was no chemical or hypnotic compulsion involved, why *did* he jump?"

"Maybe you misheard him in your vision," Rose says gently. "Sometimes our minds play tricks on us when we're too invested."

Eric's voice crackles from the phone, "I know you trust your gut, Chef. And believe me, I'm the last person to defend Shen, but he did everything by the book this time."

"He went all out," Flo chimes in. "I'd say he's learned his lesson after the botched job with Eric's dad."

"I have to admit there was no tunnel vision and no cutting corners." Eric's image pixelates as he shifts. "He insisted on a detailed tox screen, brought in an expert on drownings, checked all the alibis, ran Armelle's letters for fingerprints—the works!"

I cross my arms. "I know he did his job, but—"

"But maybe this time," Eric interrupts, "it really was an accident."

We fall silent again.

"Then, what?" I look from Flo to Rose to Eric. "We quit? We don't try to talk to Candice Ferrero in case Shen won't?"

Rose picks Lady up for a cuddle. "It does sound like Shen meticulously followed up on every lead. Maybe it's time to trust the process, Julie."

"You're telling me to trust the system?" I snort. "You, the self-proclaimed nonconformist?"

She scratches Lady behind her ears. "Even a broken clock is right twice a day, wouldn't you agree? My advice is to take a step back from this case."

I glance at Eric's face on the screen. He adjusts his glasses and smiles uncomfortably. I look at Flo. She's sipping her wine, eyes on my bookshelf. All three of them feel bad about ganging up on me, but the fact is they agree that FERJ should drop this case.

Flo's eyes fall on the *Rampal Guide* that Lady and I found the other day. "Is that the latest edition?"

"No, it's an old one." I take it off the shelf and put it on the coffee table in front of her. "I found it in a free library down the street."

"Ah." She gives me a polite half smile but doesn't pick up the guide, as I'd expected.

Is it to convey that she's done with Rampal?

I should listen to my gang, shouldn't I? They've made some excellent points.

Then why is it so hard to let go of this case?

Could it be because, like most people, I have a tough time admitting I was wrong? Am I confusing my vanity with my intuition?

"All right," I say quietly. "I'll take a step back."

Rose smiles. "Good."

"That way we can focus our energy on the Ghost Rider," Flo says.

"Wise decision, Chef," Eric agrees. "All the evidence points to an accidental death. The rest is speculation. And, to quote Spock, 'Insufficient facts always invite danger.' "

He wishes us a good night, and we end the call.

Flo stands up. "I have five more Julien Martins to go through. Otherwise, all we have is speculation just like with the Rampal case."

"Wasn't speculation the whole point of this confab?" I tease, getting up from the couch.

"Was it?" Rose sets Lady down on the floor. "I thought you just needed a pretext to spend time with me, considering how busy I've been lately."

If I didn't know her as well as I do, I'd assume she was being ironic. But she wasn't. She was 100 percent earnest.

"Oops." I bite my finger. "I was hoping you wouldn't notice the ruse."

"You can't fool me, child." She turns to Flo. "Come on, I'll give you a lift."

"You're the best, Grandma!"

Rose shoots me a reproachful look. "There's no need for ploys, ma chérie. You know you can come to the house any time I'm home and in the mood." She nudges Flo. "Both of you."

My sister and I nod solemnly, our faces as straight as we can manage. We love our grandmother to smithereens. We worship her.

But wow.

How does she do it? How can she coast through life never doubting that the universe revolves around her?

CHAPTER 34

I sit back down on the couch, balancing a plate with the last slice of Rose's onion quiche on my knees. Gabriel's message is still glowing on the screen of my phone next to me. He doesn't expect to finish work until one in the morning and will be crashing at the barracks.

Nothing unusual, but still... My cushy little apartment feels colder in the evenings when he's not around.

Absentmindedly, I pick up the *Rampal Guide* from the table and start flipping through its dog-eared pages. I skim past the restaurants I can't afford and the wine cellars with reservations booked years in advance. Most of them have four or five lavender sprigs. But there are also places with three, two, and even one. I doubt the latter are still in business.

When I get to the last page, I leaf backward—until I spy something that makes me stop and take a closer look.

Nicole Clesse.

The name is right there on the title page. It isn't hidden away in the fine print of the acknowledgments as one might expect for a minor contributor. Instead, it's printed in big, bold letters right at the top, with Seraphin Rampal's name.

Above it, as it happens.

I stare at the page, my brain pulling up what little I know about the woman. While Rampal was the sponsor and the star of Ritzy Rice, Nicole Clesse was the one who made it happen. Her name makes me think of the logistics of the event—not the art of culinary critique. I don't know what her day job is, but it never occurred to me she could be Rampal's associate. People would treat her differently if she were.

So, why is her name printed above his? Did she coauthor this edition with him? Or, rather, he with her?

I rub my eyes, just in case fatigue and Flo's wine are playing a trick on me. But Nicole's name is still there on the title page. I flip to the front cover. Sure enough, there it is again, printed at the top as if Nicole and Rampal were equals.

How come I didn't notice it before?

Tunnel vision.

I was watching Shen for it, but this time it was me who fell into the trap! I saw what I expected to see. That night, when I shined my phone's flashlight on the cover and took a quick look, all I registered below the familiar title was Seraphin Rampal.

OK, but how come I've never heard of their partnership?

It's like the entire food scene in Provence has memory-holed Nicole's past as culinary critic and only thinks of her as an event organizer. No one ever mentions her in connection with the *Rampal Guide*. In everyone's mind, Seraphin Rampal is the lone genius behind it.

Now, it's true that my fifteen years in Paris have distanced me from the local currents. But this goes beyond my knowledge gap. It feels like a deliberate erasure.

It's confusing, not to say disturbing.

I look down at the quiche. My appetite is gone, replaced by a slow-burning sense of unease. Why did Nicole leave

Rampal Guide? Or was she pushed out? Could this be related to Rampal's death? Could Nicole's disappearance from Rampal Guide be a motive for murder?

Woah, Julie, hold your horses!

I pledged to table this case barely an hour ago. Am I this eager to keep investigating it? No, not eager. I must be *desperate*, given how quickly I went from noticing Nicole's name in an old edition of the *Rampal Guide* to suspecting her of murder.

Chastising myself, I clean up the remnants of the evening and grab my laptop. Back on the couch, I fire it up. My intention is to see what the *Guide's* official website has to say about Nicole Clesse.

I navigate to the "Who We Are" page, which is the most logical place to begin. It contains not a single mention of her name. No bio, no trace of her on the team roster, no acknowledgment of her past contributions, nothing at all.

That's odd.

All right, moving on. I open the page dedicated to Seraphin Rampal. It goes on and on glorifying his accomplishments. Photos, accolades, a timeline of his career, links to the various TV shows he took part in, and so on.

Still no mention of Nicole. Not even in a footnote.

Frustrated, I lean back and stare at the screen. Why would a publication—and the company producing it—so blatantly snub someone who coauthored at least one of its early issues?

Maybe she did something terrible or remarkably stupid that nearly ruined them? That might explain her brutal eviction and erasure. Except... there's a hole in that theory. Two, even. First, Rampal let her organize Ritzy Rice for him and, second, the pair of them were very cordial with each other during the competition. Watching them interact, I thought they were good friends.

Hmm, then what gives?

I pull up the archives page, which proudly displays every single cover of the Guide since its inception. I zoom in, and there it is—her name on the covers of the first three editions, above Rampal's. The font size is the same. The placement, if alphabetical, suggests equal involvement. If it's not, then it means she contributed more to these early editions than he did.

I comb through the rest of the page. Aside from her name on the covers, there's no explanation, no story behind her role, nothing else to go on.

This doesn't add up.

Determined to be thorough, I revisit each page of the website and use Command-F to search for "Nicole Clesse." Page after page, my queries produce the same result: No matches found.

What's going on here?

An early coauthor, still friends with the other coauthor, has been wiped from the history of their famous culinary guide.

Why?

And, more importantly, how come no one's noticed this glaring omission?

After checking and rechecking the entire website, I go back to the browser's search box and look up Nicole Clesse once again. In addition to organizing culinary events, she has a regular job as a realtor with A Provence Home for You. I've seen that agency! It's in the modern part of Beldoc on the other side of the Rhône.

I stare at the screen some more until my eyes begin to blur. It's almost midnight. I shut the laptop, stretch out, and head to the bathroom. The best thing I can do at this point, the only sensible thing, is to sleep it.

The buzzing of my phone on the counter interrupts my bedtime routine. It's a text message from Flo.

If you're still up, call me. I may have found
something.

I rinse out my mouth, dry my hands, and hit Call.

Flo answers on the first ring. "Julie?"

"What's going on?"

She exhales loudly. "OK, I have a confession to make. I felt guilty about something I said tonight."

"If you feel you were too hard on me—"

"I'd never feel guilty about that," she cuts in. "No, it was when Grandma asked about our research on the mind-bending drugs. Eric said he'd found none that fit the bill, and I kept my mouth shut."

"Did you have something to say?"

"Maybe." There's a pause before she continues. "I'd done some research of my own, just out of curiosity, and there was one drug that I thought deserved a closer look."

"Why didn't you mention it?"

"Because I agreed with Grandma that it was time to call it quits." She sighs. "Anyway, when I got home, I went down that rabbit hole instead of digging into the remaining Julien Martins."

"What did you find?"

Flo's voice drops. "Some disturbing facts about scopolamine, an odorless and tasteless drug also known as Devil's Breath."

"What facts?"

"Its effects are almost instantaneous," she says. "As in, it can rob you of your free will within seconds of being administered. And, once it's out of your system, you won't remember what you did during your chemical submission."

I shudder. "How frighteningly convenient!"

"Plus, it leaves no trace in the body after just two or three hours, which means that tox screenings can detect it only for a limited time after exposure."

My mind races to fit this new piece into our messy puzzle. "So, the killer—"

"Assuming there was a killer," Flo interrupts me.

"Yes, of course. So, the *alleged* killer could've drugged Rampal with scopolamine without it showing up on the tox screen."

"Theoretically, it's possible."

I continue to piece it together. "The killer would've had to time it perfectly. She would've needed to get Rampal to the bridge two hours after giving him the drug."

"She? Because of the mystery woman Rampal was seen with after midnight? Or because poison is a typically female MO?"

"Both, and more," I reply. "I'll explain tomorrow with Eric present and my mind fresh."

She huffs. "Fine, whatever. But I disagree that the killer had to wait two hours. Devil's Breath peaks about an hour after it's ingested or inhaled."

"Think about it. If Rampal had died only an hour after ingesting the drug, there would still be traces of it in his system."

"Because once you're dead, your metabolism stops!" Flo exclaims, her voice sharp with realization. "The body stops eliminating the drug."

I bite my lip, my mind spinning. "The killer had to be extremely precise about when she drugged him, took him to the bridge, and made him jump."

"That sounds way too risky to me."

"To me, too," I admit.

Is my theory too whimsical? Maybe.

Does my discovery about Nicole change that? Not really.

Flo and I fall silent. I run through the scenario again in my head. The precision required would take an OCD level of meticulousness. And even then, it'd be a huge gamble.

"It's best to sleep on this," I finally say. "We'll discuss it in the shop tomorrow. And thanks for telling me about Devil's Breath!"

"You're welcome."

We hang up. I rub my temples and stare at my reflection in the bathroom mirror.

Did we just find the missing pieces?

Is this the unhoped-for break in the Rampal case?

Or am I still chasing shadows?

CHAPTER 35

The sun is barely up as I make my way through the sleepy streets to the farmer's market. No matter how hard I try to focus on the day ahead, my mind keeps spinning back to the Rampal case. I stop at a corner, let go of my wicker shopping cart, and pull out my phone. Before I know it, I'm dialing the gendarmerie.

A few rings later, someone picks up. "Gendarmerie de Beldoc, how may I help you?"

"Julie Cavallo for Capitaine Shen, please."

"One moment."

I tap my foot, watching the flower shop across the street to pass the time. It's still closed. The flowers and potted plants behind the perforated security curtain are a big, blurry splash of color.

Shen comes on the line, "Madame Cavallo. What can I do for you?" He sounds tired.

"I wanted to talk to you about Nicole Clesse. I think she might be connected to—"

He cuts me off, "No. The case is closed."

"I beg your pardon?"

"The investigative judge closed it this morning based on my recommendation."

"But—"

"Listen, I get it," he cuts in. "You were deep into this, and I appreciate your efforts. But there are other cases that need my attention."

"I didn't mean to—"

"That's all right, Madame Cavallo," he interrupts again. "I just hope you realize I've done more than what was required on this case, even though it's been obvious from the beginning that Rampal's death was an accident. Every step of the investigation supports that conclusion."

I grip my phone a little tighter. "But what about Candice Ferrero? She could have seen something that night."

"We won't be pursuing that." His tone is so final there's no wiggle room at all. "The gendarmerie isn't spending any more time or resources on this."

"Despite these new elements? Nicole Clesse might have a motive, and Candice Ferrero could be a material witness."

"I have a massive caseload, all of it urgent," he says. "One case involves a child in a dangerous situation."

Disappointment builds in my chest as I mumble, "Of course."

"Madame Cavallo—Julie—ask Gabriel; he'll confirm I did my best," Shen urges me in a gentler tone. "I can't keep spinning my wheels on a tragic drowning that doesn't have a shred of evidence pointing to foul play."

I bite my lip and stare at a pigeon pecking under a café table. Shen is right about the total lack of evidence. That's what makes this case so frustrating.

"I understand, Capitaine," I say. "Thanks for everything."

"Have a nice day, Madame Cavallo."

The line goes dead.

I shove the phone back into my pocket. Unlike the Dol case, I don't blame Shen. His job is to follow the evidence, which he did with the utmost diligence this time without cutting any corners.

A passerby bumps into me, almost knocking me off my feet. With a heartfelt apology, he hurries away. The collision shifts my focus to the present, to my own life, and my main job—the one that pays the rent and puts butter not only on my tartines, but also on Eric's and Flo's.

I better get going.

The smells and sounds of Beldoc's market get closer with every step. A few minutes later, I immerse myself in a joyful chaos where vendors shout out their deals, buyers haggle over prices, and sunlight dances off the colorful stalls.

I find my go-to stand for peaches and apricots.

The vendor smiles warmly. "Good morning to my favorite gluten-free chef! Are you back for some more of the best peaches on this market?"

"Two kilos, please," I ask after greeting him back.

"Take more! These might be the last of the season."

His argument works, and I ask for an extra kilogram. As he weighs the peaches, my mind drifts again, wondering who could answer my questions about Nicole.

Armelle Pradine would know more about her past than I do, that's for sure. But I resent the idea of calling her. Our last conversation didn't go well.

People get very upset when you accuse them of murder, especially if they're innocent.

Who knew?

Yeah, it wasn't my finest moment...

Now that Armelle has an ironclad alibi, the nasty letters she'd sent Rampal appear to be exactly what they were—the angry outburst of a scorned woman. I get why she tried to recover them. It's less obvious to me why she'd claim she wrote only six out of the seven. But I'm not going down that road anymore.

With the peaches in my cart, I thank the vendor and move on. A stall piled high with figs catches my eye. They're dark, plump and ripe, but not overripe. I reach out and pick one up. Its velvety skin delights the nerve endings in my fingertips. It smells delicious, too. These will be just perfect for the fig tart recipe Eric and I wanted to try out this week.

"Two kilos of figs, please," I say to the woman behind the table.

While she's weighing and bagging them, my mind conjures up an image of Mylene Nivault, the curvy chef from Eau de Provence, who said that her duck magret with figs won a regional contest. Mylene was friendly and nice to me during the Ritzy Rice competition. And she seemed genuinely shaken by Rampal's death.

Maybe she could help me with this Nicole Clesse angle? She's local, well-connected, friends with Tanguy and other chefs...

I pay for the figs and step aside to let another customer take my place. As I head toward the next stall, I chew on the idea of reaching out to Mylene. It feels like the right move.

After I finish loading the last of my finds into my wicker cart, I leave the bustling market behind and head to the shop. The urge to call Mylene gnaws at me, too strong to fend off. When I reach a green area near a fountain, I decide this is as good a place as any to make that phone call.

I dig out my phone and scroll through my contacts until I find Mylene's number. She'll probably be too busy to answer at this time of day. I'll leave a message.

The phone rings three or four times, but instead of going to voicemail, a familiar voice says, *"Oui, allô?"*

Surprised, I almost drop the phone. "Hi Mylene, it's Julie... Cavallo from Ritzy Rice?"

"Oh, Julie!" Her tone changes from neutral to—dare I say—excited? "How nice to hear from you! How are you?"

"I'm good, thanks. Just left the market. You?"

"Having my second coffee," she replies. "My sous chef went to the market today. You caught me at the perfect time."

She *does* sound excited. Have I made such a good impression on her or is this her norm?

I sit on the edge of the fountain's basin. "Listen, I came across something interesting and thought you might shed some light."

"Go on."

"Did you know that Nicole Clesse was the coauthor of the first three editions of the *Rampal Guide*?"

"Yes," she says. "Nicole and Seraphin were business partners when they started the *Guide* sixteen years ago."

"Really? What happened?"

"Well," she begins, "the *Guide* didn't do so well at first. Sales were dismal, and no one cared about their reviews or the lavender sprig ratings. Two years in, Seraphin offered to buy out Nicole's shares."

"And she agreed?"

"She did," Mylene says. "And wouldn't you know it, the very next year the *Guide* took off!"

"What was Nicole's reaction?"

"Naturally, she wasn't thrilled." I can hear Mylene snicker. "The following year the *Guide* was a hit again. Its popularity kept growing until it became the fine dining bible we all know."

"What a coincidence," I say, not hiding my sarcasm.

"Nicole didn't think so either. She accused Seraphin of holding back during their partnership. She blamed him for putting zero effort into their joint venture until it became *the Rampal Guide*."

"How did he take her accusations?"

"About as well as you can imagine. They had a major falling out."

I watch the water ripple in the fountain. "But they seemed to get along very well during the competition."

"I was wondering the same thing," Mylene says. "When I heard Nicole was organizing Ritzy Rice and wanted Seraphin to be the head judge, I thought he'd say no. But he accepted."

"He must've seen her invitation as an olive branch."

"That's right," Mylene agrees. "I watched them discuss the event several times. Nicole was very gracious. I remember thinking she really has put the past behind her."

"Maybe she's the forgiving type."

"Maybe. I was going to ask Seraphin about his reconciliation with Nicole, but then..." Her voice trails off as if she can't bring herself to say it.

"Were you and Seraphin close?" I ask.

There's a pause, then, "We'd become friends, perhaps headed for something more. But we didn't want to rush it."

"Do you think his death was an accident?" I blurt.

"Funny you should ask." Her voice drops. "Do *you* think it was an accidental drowning?"

I choose my words carefully. "I have my doubts. Something doesn't add up."

"Thank goodness," she breathes out. "I also have doubts, huge doubts! Seraphin wasn't the type to get drunk and fall into a river. He was always in control."

My pulse quickens, "Have you told Capitaine Shen about your doubts? Has he talked to you?"

"Yes, and yes." She sounds disheartened. "But I hear he's closing the case."

"It's done. He's moved on."

"Merde!"

I grip the phone tighter. "My friends and I have been looking into Seraphin Rampal's death, too. I haven't given up yet."

"I knew you wouldn't."

Huh? Why would she say that?

As if sensing my confusion, she quickly adds, "I've heard about your amateur detective talents from Caroline Poyac."

There's a split second where my mind goes blank. Then I realize she's talking about the woman who used a stage name when we met—Malvina. It's still the name I associate with her. Caroline is from Eau de Provence like Mylene. FERJ helped her get justice for her brother.

"It's a small world," I say.

"It is," Mylene agrees. "Caroline's house is next to mine."

"That explains it."

"Promise you'll call me if you discover anything?" she asks, her voice laced with emotion. "Please?"

Sounds like she really cared for Rampal.

"I promise I'll let you know if I unearth anything new," I say. "And be sure to call me if you remember any detail that might help, even if it seems insignificant."

"You bet I will!"

As we end the call, a million questions swirl in my head. What if Nicole Clesse isn't such a forgiving person after all? Is it possible that she never let go of her old grudge?

That's the motive right there! All that time and effort she put into Ritzy Rice—was it to lure Rampal in and get revenge? Was the whole competition an opportunity she engineered to give herself the means to succeed?

How far am I willing to go to find out?

CHAPTER 36

Perched in the bistro corner of the shop, I'm drinking my third coffee of this eventful morning. The pâtisserie is empty but for Eric and me. It's ten-thirty, and I don't expect an influx of customers for another hour. Over my second coffee, I brought Eric up to speed about Nicole Clesse. I also recapped for him my conversations with Shen, who's thrown in the towel, and with Mylene, who told me about the falling out between Nicole and Rampal.

Eric agrees with me that Nicole sounds suspicious. He thinks the best way forward is to persuade Gabriel to convince Shen that my findings, though circumstantial, warrant reopening the case. It's a sensible course of action.

My coffee is already lukewarm when I take another sip and type "Candice Ferrero Beldoc" in the browser on my phone.

My spontaneous search is so fruitful I almost spit out my next sip of coffee. There she is, right at the top of the results. It's got to be the right Candice. The age matches, and—drumroll, please—she works at a warehouse! According to her social media posts, it's the La Redoute warehouse across the river. Ten minutes by bike from here, tops.

I check my watch. Eric is behind the counter, humming to himself as he listens to something through his earphones.

I stand up and grab my bike helmet. "Is it OK if I run an errand?"

"Of course, Chef," he replies.

Out the door I go. Helmet on, bike unlocked, and I'm off to the nearest bridge. There isn't much traffic. In no time, I'm crossing the Rhône, my brain working as hard as my legs.

How should I introduce myself? What would be the best approach to get Candice to talk to me? Should I be fully transparent or find a roundabout way to get to the part that interests me?

I pull up to the massive La Redoute warehouse. After chaining my bike by the main entrance, I go inside and beeline to the reception desk. The receptionist directs me to the back. I fumble my way through the endless rows of shelves until I spot a woman who resembles Candice's pictures on the Internet. She's slim, bespectacled, and completely engrossed in checking the inventory on her clipboard.

I clear my throat. "Excuse me, Candice Ferrero?"

She glances up. "Yes, can I help you?"

"I'm Julie Cavallo," I say. "I was wondering if I could have a few minutes of your time. It's about Séraphin Rampal."

"What about him?" I can see it in her eyes that she's intrigued.

"Can we talk outside?"

She looks down at her clipboard, then back at me. For a second, I fear she's going to tell me to get lost.

But curiosity wins out.

"I'm due for a break in a few minutes," she says. "Wait for me outside by the loading dock."

"Thank you!" I turn on my heel and exhale in relief as I scurry to the exit.

Five minutes later, Candice emerges from the warehouse, shading her eyes against the midday sun.

She doesn't return my smile when she spots me on the bench. "So, what's this about Seraphin Rampal?"

"I believe you might be the last person to see him alive," I explain. "You and Jean-Jacques."

Her brow furrows. "I doubt it."

"Why?"

"Because Monsieur Rampal wasn't alone, that's why! He was with a woman."

There's a silent "dumbass" at the end, judging by the twist of her mouth.

I choose to ignore it. "What woman?"

"How should I know?"

The look in her eyes tells me that this time the unspoken word is stronger than "dumbass."

With a sigh and an eye roll, she explains, "That woman was still with Rampal after Jean-Jacques and I passed them, so she must be the last person to see him before the accident."

"It's possible his death wasn't accidental."

"What?" She stares at me. "I thought he drank too much and fell in the river. That's what I read in *Beldoc Live*."

Poor Noam! He'd written a story that raised some good questions about Rampal's death. Granted, his theory about Ugo Drugeon turned out to be as wrong as mine about Armelle Pradine. But Noam was right to suspect foul play! I already knew that his investigative story was scrapped because of Victor's stupid new law. But now it sounds like they forced him to copy and paste the gendarmerie's press release under the guise of an article.

Noam must be so frustrated!

"*Beldoc Live's* original story, before they axed it, was more nuanced," I say. "My own investigation also found some unresolved issues with the accident theory."

She crosses her arms. "Isn't it the job of the police to investigate?"

"It is. But sometimes they give up and decide that their limited resources are better spent elsewhere."

"Is that why no one has come to talk to me?"

"Yes," I confirm.

She sizes me up. I'll bet she's trying to decide whether I'm a serious person or some wacko playing detective.

"How did you find me?" she asks.

"Thanks to Jean-Jacques."

I say nothing more and let her assume that I know her ex. There's no need to go into the long and convoluted story of how he was a suspect in my *other* investigation.

"OK," she finally says. "Ask your questions."

"Can you tell me everything you remember about that night? Especially the woman you saw with Seraphin Rampal."

Candice rubs her neck. "We were walking by the river. It was dark. We were near the bridge when we saw them."

"Did you recognize Rampal at once?"

"Yes." She smiles. "I'm a sucker for any show like *Top Chef*, and he's often a judge on them. I mean, he was. Such a handsome, charismatic man! Such a damn shame!"

"Indeed," I say, trying not to seem impatient.

"Jean-Jacques had no clue who Rampal was! Can you believe it?"

"I can."

She snorts with laughter. "It figures. He lives in the

Stone Age, with a tin foil hat on his head! Now that we've broken up, I don't understand how I dated him for a whole year."

"You don't seem like a good match."

"He's great in bed, so there's that..."

Candice, for Pete's sake, focus! My silent plea must be written all over my face because her expression changes.

"Right," she says. "You were asking about Rampal."

"Did he look drunk to you?"

"Yes," she replies without hesitation. "Not wasted, but tipsy."

"Can you describe the woman he was with? Did you get a good look at her?"

"She was blonde, well-groomed." Candice thinks for a moment. "I couldn't see her face in the dark, but there was something about her general appearance... She looked preppy."

"Preppy how?"

"She had this neat air about her," Candice replies. "I remember a clean-cut blazer and tailored pants. And a very precise haircut."

My mind screams, *It* was *Nicole!*

"I guess that's what struck me," Candice continues. "She didn't look like someone you'd expect to see out with a man in the middle of the night."

I smile inwardly. *Trust a woman to notice something like that!*

Men can be very observant, but in a different way. They'll register the location of exits, tracks, possible hiding places, and even the sex of the domestic animals. But details like personal style can go over a man's head—especially a man like Jean-Jacques Tillier.

A shiver runs down my spine. Everything Candice has said so far about Rampal's companion fits Nicole Clesse perfectly. I take out my phone. A quick online search brings up a picture of Nicole, the one from Ritzy Rice.

"Could this be the woman you saw?" I hold the phone up.

She squints at the screen. "Yes... Yes, it looks like her."

"Are you sure?"

"As sure as I can be, considering how dark it was," she replies. "But that's her vibe. Blonde, clean-cut, put together."

I put the phone back in my pocket. "Thanks! You have no idea how helpful you've been."

"If Seraphin Rampal was murdered, then I hope you catch the person who did it."

"I'm working on it."

"That woman..." She peers at me. "You think she did something to him?"

How much should I reveal, I wonder?

"I don't know yet," I say.

She glances back at the warehouse. "I have to get back. Is there anything else you need?"

"Just one more thing: Did you notice anything unusual about the interaction between her and Rampal? Were they arguing? Talking? Holding hands?"

She ponders this. "There was a space between them. They didn't look like a couple, if that's what you're asking."

"Did you hear them talking? Any words exchanged?"

"No." She shoots another look at the warehouse.

"Thank you, Candice! I'll let you get back to your work."

Her jaw hardens. "Killing an eligible bachelor, given the dearth of them in the forty-plus age group, is despicable!"

Mylene Nivault might agree with that, I think to myself.

Candice's mouth becomes a thin line. "Catch the bitch who did it, and I'll start a petition to reinstate the death penalty."

"Um, I'll see what I can do."

She walks away, grumbling, "If such a heinous crime against single women doesn't deserve the lethal shot, then I don't know what does."

CHAPTER 37

As Candice disappears back into the warehouse, I dial Mylene's number. I promised to update her if something new came up, and Candice's account is it. Besides, given the lack of enthusiasm this case has generated within FERJ, it's nice to speak with someone who wants to find Rampal's killer as much as I do.

Mylene answers just when I expect the voicemail to kick in. "Julie! What's up?"

"I just talked to a witness who saw Rampal with a woman by the river shortly before he died."

"Who..." She draws an audible breath. "Who was that woman?"

"The description matches Nicole Clesse."

There's a pause, then, "Are you calling from your shop?"

"No, I'm near the La Redoute warehouse in the modern part of Beldoc. Do you know where it is?"

"No. Can you give me an address?"

"Hang on."

I open the map app on my phone. To pull up the exact street name and number for Mylene, I type in "Redoute warehouse Beldoc" and wait for the map to zoom in on the location. A few seconds later, it does.

And what do I notice near the warehouse? The real estate agency where Nicole works, A Provence Home for You!

I share this bit of trivia with Mylene.

"You've got to be kidding me," she says.

"Nope."

"Listen, I can get in the car and be there in an hour," she says. "Unless you must go back to your shop, in which case I can meet you there."

"I'll wait here. I'm too antsy right now to stand behind the counter."

"I'll call you as soon as I get there."

But it's almost noon... "Can you just leave the restaurant like that, before the lunch service?"

"My sous chef will have to make do," she replies. "This is more important."

I suggest we talk over lunch, but she says she's committed to her new diet, which involves skipping the midday meal. We hang up. All this talk of lunch reminds me I'm getting hungry. I walk down the street until I see a Mexican joint that looks like a great place for a quick and satisfying meal. It also happens to be right across the street from Nicole's agency.

Pure coincidence.

I step inside. The spicy aromas wrap around me like a warm hug. I order a burrito and a bottle of water at the counter, pay, and settle at a table by the window.

I'm halfway through my lunch when I see her. *Nicole.*

Her pantsuit flutters in the breeze as she steps out of the agency. She's with a colleague. They're deep in conversation, but then Nicole looks my way.

Our eyes meet.

I freeze.

She says something to her colleague, who gives a quick nod and continues down the sidewalk. To my horror, Nicole starts crossing the street. She appears to be headed straight for the Mexican place.

Petrified, I watch her walk inside. My heart is hammering in my chest. The burrito feels like cement in my mouth. For a second, I consider ducking under the table, which is ridiculous because she's already seen me. And, anyway, it's too late. She's marching my way.

"Julie Cavallo, right?" She offers a bright smile. "What a pleasant surprise!"

I swallow the food stuck in my throat. "Bonjour, Nicole. Nice to see you again."

"I noticed you through the window. Mind if I join you?" Without waiting for an answer, she slides into the seat across from me and hangs her purse on the back of her chair.

I squirm, eyes downcast.

She signals to the waitress hovering nearby, "The usual, please," then turns her attention back to me. "So, what brings you to this part of town?"

"Just running some errands."

She tilts her head to one side. "Really?"

"Yes."

Her gaze sharpens. "Is there something you want to tell me, Julie?"

"No," I mutter. "Why?"

She doesn't answer.

My mind races. Does she know I've been poking around her past? Or worse, that I suspect her of killing Rampal?

But how can she possibly know that?

Nicole wasn't even on my radar until last night, when I saw her name in that old edition of the *Rampal Guide*. There only three people I discussed it with this morning: Mylene, Candice, and Eric. There's no way Eric would stab me in the back. As for Candice, she'd had no idea who Nicole was until I showed her a picture. Why would she reach out to Nicole and warn her about me? It doesn't make any sense.

Which leaves Mylene.

Have I completely misread her? I've been wrong about people before, but I can't remember being this wrong. I really liked her and didn't doubt her sincerity for a second.

Nicole and I stare at each other. The cheerful din of the restaurant fades into the background. The air feels sticky.

She breaks the silence. "How have you been, Julie?"

"Good," I say. "You know, work, life, the usual."

"The usual, huh?" Her eyes narrow ever so slightly. "Well, I hope you're not overworking yourself. You've been very active lately."

She knows. It's got to be Mylene.

"Just trying to keep busy," I say.

"You should've stuck to baking." A rueful smile touches her lips. "Why don't people just mind their own business? Why?"

Something snaps inside me. Adrenaline surges. Panic fades, replaced by a devil-may-care defiance that pushes me to go all out.

I scoot forward. "Can you account for your whereabouts between one and three in the morning on the night Seraphin Rampal died?"

"What a bizarre thing to ask!" She arches her eyebrow. "But I'll humor you. I was at home, asleep in my bed. It's my routine. Early to bed, early to rise."

"Do you live alone? Can anyone corroborate your story?"

"Yes." She leans in so close I can see the shimmer of her lipstick.

"Yes to which question?"

She pulls a small notebook from her purse. "Let me show you."

Her eyes never leaving mine, she flips the notebook open. Suspicion hits me and I jerk back. But it's too late. Nicole blows some white powder from the notebook straight into my face. I inhale quite a bit involuntarily. I cough, disoriented.

Must call for help! I open my mouth to scream.

"Shut up," Nicole hisses. "Don't talk. Eat the rest of your burrito."

I obey. The desire to scream, and push table over, and run is there, but my body betrays me. Instead of helping me survive, it chooses to do exactly what Nicole ordered me to do. Horrified, I watch myself pick up the burrito and take a bite. The taste is like cardboard in my mouth, yet I keep eating, powerless to stop. She said I should eat the rest of it.

Nicole sits back. "Good girl. Keep eating."

I finish my burrito. My mouth is dry. My vision begins to blur. A headache pounds at my temples.

"Smile," she murmurs.

My lips curl into a forced grin. My body feels sluggish, detached, like I'm watching everything from afar. The waitress arrives with a plate of chili con carne and puts it on the table.

"Thank you." Nicole hands her a twenty-euro bill. "Keep the change."

The waitress beams. "Enjoy your meal!"

After she leaves, Nicole turns back to me. "Get up. We're leaving."

I rise from my seat. My head is throbbing. My legs move without my permission as Nicole leads me to the door.

We step out onto the street.

She slips her arm through mine, her grip firm. "Keep smiling. We're just two friends out for a walk."

I try to focus on my surroundings as we move down the

sidewalk, but everything is hazy. The buildings sway. The sounds of the street are muffled. I can't do anything that Nicole hasn't expressly authorized. I know it's dangerous for me to go with her but feel I must.

Does a puppet on strings have a choice?

The fog around me thickens. My head is spinning. A wave of nausea hits me hard. The world tilts as my legs wobble beneath me. I grip her arm to steady myself. We keep walking. My cheeks hurt from the fake grin plastered on my face. But I can't stop smiling.

It's the stuff of nightmares.

In the distance, tires screech as a car brakes suddenly.

A familiar voice cuts through the haze. "Julie!"

It's Mylene. Relief washes over me but suspicion follows close behind. *She's the one who tipped Nicole off.*

"Julie!" she calls again.

I slow down.

"Don't stop," Nicole orders.

I keep walking. Mylene jumps out of her car, leaving the door wide open. She sprints toward us. People pause and turn. Conversations hush. Eyes focus on the unfolding scene.

As soon as she's close enough, Mylene grabs my arm. "Come with me."

I glance at Nicole who pulls me toward her. "Don't listen to her, Julie. Come with me."

Disoriented, I stand between them, pulled in both directions.

"She's kidnapping my friend!" Mylene shouts to the onlookers.

"No, she's the one trying to kidnap my friend!" Nicole counters, glaring at her.

A small crowd gathers around us. Faces blur together. My head throbs.

A tall, muscular man steps forward. "Hey, what's going on here? Who's trying to take you, madame?"

My head is swimming. The words I need to say bounce around in my skull. I concentrate as hard as I can to get them out.

Nicole tightens her grip. "Tell him Mylene wants to hurt you, tell him!"

"Mylene wants to hurt me," I hear myself say.

Shock flashes across Mylene's face. "What? Julie, no! That's not true!"

The man shoots her a stern look. "Back off."

More people press in. Their murmurs grow louder. I see phones recording. My skin is slick with sweat. My legs are trembling.

Nicole attempts to drag me away, yelling to the crowd, "Can't you see she's unwell? I need to get her to the hospital!"

"Don't go with her!" Mylene, still gripping my other arm, yells. "Julie, tell them she's lying!"

I comply. "She's lying."

The muscle man looks between us, visibly lost.

Mylene's voice rises above the commotion, desperate, "Somebody call the cops! Now!"

The bystanders start dialing. The noise around me swells. Voices overlap. Everyone's shouting over everyone else. The cacophony makes my head feel like it's splitting open. The sun blazes down on me, too bright, too hot. My knees buckle. The only reason I'm still upright is because Nicole and Mylene are holding me.

But after a few seconds, that's no longer enough. I feel the ground tilt and slip from under my feet.

"Please," I whisper.

I'm not sure who I'm pleading with or if I said that out loud.

And then everything goes black.

CHAPTER 38

I wake up to an unpleasant, sterile smell. *Disinfectant.* Slowly, I peel my eyes open. The first thing I see is the ceiling. It's too white, and the light in the middle of it is way too bright. It stings my eyes. A beeping sound pierces the silence, then stops. I'm in a single bed with stiffly starched sheets.

My head feels heavy and soggy, like an overfilled éclair. I turn it a little to the side. Gabriel is sitting next to the bed. His arms are crossed, his jaw clenched. Rose and Flo hover nearby, both looking worried.

Gabriel's eyes meet mine and his eyes open wide. His expression brightens.

"She's awake!" he calls out to the others.

Flo leaps closer and takes my hand.

Rose leans over me, eyes filled with relief. "How are you feeling?"

"Like I've been hit by a truck," I mumble, my mouth dry as a desert. "Water, please?"

Rose hands me a glass, and Gabriel helps me sit up. I drink hungrily.

"What happened?" I ask when I've finished the glass.

Gabriel leans forward. "What's the last thing you remember?"

I sift through the fog in my mind. "I was at the Mexican place. Nicole came over to my table. Nicole Clesse." I pause, trying to grasp the slippery memories. "That's it."

Rose squeezes my hand. "You've had quite an adventure."

Why can't I remember it? "Someone want to fill me in?"

"I was hoping you'd fill us in." Gabriel runs a hand through his hair. "Anyway, Nicole Clesse is under arrest. She's being charged with attempted kidnapping, and there may be more charges coming."

My eyes widen. "Kidnapping? Of who?"

"Of you, genius," Flo quips, but there's an uncharacteristic kindness in her voice.

I stare at her, flummoxed.

"You fainted on the street, while Nicole was trying to drag you away," Rose explains gently.

"Mylene saved you," Flo adds. "She saw you and Nicole walking down the street together, arm in arm, and she knew something was wrong."

Gabriel picks up, "She was following her GPS to the address you'd given her. When she spotted you with Nicole, she ran over, grabbed your arm, and started shouting for help."

"Why can't I remember any of it?"

"Because you were very likely drugged," he says.

An image of Nicole leaning in across the table and something powdery hitting my face flashes in my mind.

"Oh God," I whisper. "She blew something at me."

"My money is on the scopolamine left over after she drugged and killed Rampal," Flo declares.

No wonder I feel like a zombie.

Suddenly, panic rises in my chest. "Scopolamine leaves

the body super quickly. What if it's already gone? How will we prove she did it?"

"Don't worry." Gabriel places a hand on my shoulder. "A nurse will take your blood and urine samples in a moment. We'll send them to a specialized lab to test for everything, including scopolamine."

I begin to calm down.

"Let me go get her." Gabriel strides out the door.

Flo gives me a reassuring smile. "Based on my research, even if Devil's Breath is out of your blood by now, it should still show up in your urine."

"Oh, good," I say, relief washing over me.

Gabriel returns with a nurse carrying vials and syringes.

She nods at me. "Good to see you're awake! Ready for some tests?"

"Let's do this!"

"It's nice to see a patient excited about a blood test." Smiling, she draws my blood and hands me a cup for the urine sample.

After the not-so-glamorous parts are over, she leaves us alone again.

I settle back into the medical bed and close my eyes. More memories flicker and flash, like in that experimental movie Flo took me to last month.

Nicole telling me to eat, smile, and do as I'm told.

The waitress bringing her chili.

Nicole paying, and then both of us leaving the Mexican joint...

"Where is Mylene now?" I ask, opening my eyes.

"She had to get back to her restaurant," Flo says. "But she asked to be informed when you woke up."

"I'd like to talk to her," I blurt to Gabriel.

He gets my purse from the locker in the corner of the room and places it in my lap. I fish out my phone and dial Mylene's number.

She sounds ecstatic when she picks up. "Julie! You're awake!"

"Hi there."

"Thank goodness! How are you feeling?"

"Groggy, but OK. Thank you for coming to my rescue! If you hadn't shown up—"

"Don't mention it," she interrupts. "It was pure luck. I hit no traffic and got to Beldoc in just forty minutes. And there you were, all chummy with Nicole."

I let out a laugh. "She drugged me."

"Figures."

"Do you have any idea how she knew I was investigating her?"

"No clue," she replies. "That eyewitness you'd talked to before you called me, could she have ratted you out?"

"Nicole was a complete stranger to her. I don't see why she'd go to the trouble of tipping her off."

"Well, it for sure wasn't me, in case you had any doubts."

"I did," I confess, "but not anymore, not after you saved my ass. Thank you again, Mylene! I owe you one."

"Just get better," she says warmly. "We'll talk soon."

We hang up.

Gabriel sits down on the edge of the bed. "You'll be pleased to hear that, in light of everything, the investigative judge is reopening the Rampal case."

"That's the best news I've heard all day!"

"Charles-Antoine will be coming by to talk to you as soon as you're up for it," he assures me.

"You can tell him I'm ready."

He pulls his phone from his pocket. "Texting him as we speak."

"He should also interview Mylene Nivault and Candice Ferrero, the eyewitness. And he needs to check Nicole's alibi for the time of Rampal's death."

"He's already on it," Gabriel says.

I study his face. He's being sweet and attentive, but there's a tightness around his eyes.

"You're mad at me," I state.

He looks away briefly before meeting my gaze. "I'm just glad you're OK."

"I swear I didn't plan on getting drugged," I joke to lighten his mood.

"Exactly, you didn't plan." He averts his gaze.

Not only is he not smiling, but his expression has hardened. He's seething, it's obvious. I'd be getting an earful right now if it weren't for Flo and Rose.

As if on cue, my sister clears her throat. "Maybe Grandma and I should give you lovebirds some space."

"Stay," I almost beg. "It's fine."

Rose shifts. "Actually, I need to check on something anyway. And I need coffee. Flo and I will go down to the café in the lobby and come back with a cup for each of you."

"Traitors," I mutter as they make a hasty exit.

Gabriel stands at the foot of my bed with his arms crossed. "Why didn't you talk to me first, before you went looking for the woman you suspected of murder?"

His voice is low and controlled, but I know him well enough to hear the anger simmering beneath the surface.

I take a fortifying breath. "You've been working night shifts and crashing at the barracks these last couple of days."

"Why didn't you take your discoveries to Charles-Antoine?"

"I tried, but he said the case was closed, and he had other priorities now."

Gabriel's eyes narrow. "Are you sure you told him you'd found an eyewitness who saw a woman with Rampal shortly before his death, and that she matched Nicole Clesse's description?"

I shift under the sheets. "I believe I did."

"Did you tell him about Nicole's possible motive?"

"I didn't get a chance," I reply. "Then again, neither of those things counts as evidence, does it? I wanted to give him something foolproof—"

He cuts me off, "And to obtain that foolproof thing you recklessly served yourself up as bait to the suspected killer, as you often do."

"Not often," I argue, sitting up straighter. "I've done that only once or twice before."

"You were attacked on six separate occasions, Julie."

"Half of them were through no fault of my own," I say in my defense. "I just happened to be in the wrong place at the wrong time. I didn't think the baddie would attack me."

"That's the problem," he snaps. "You didn't think."

I bristle. "I was focused on seeing that justice was done. On finding the truth!"

He doesn't respond. His jaw clenches tighter, and there's that hard look in his eyes that doesn't bode well for the rest of the day. Or the rest of the week, for that matter.

I fold my arms over my chest, mirroring his stance. "Three bad decisions over four years doesn't qualify as often. You can't say I'm reckless."

"That's exactly what you are—a danger to yourself."

"You'd rather I sat on my hands while Nicole got away with murder?"

He shakes his head, the muscles in his jaw flexing. "You don't get it, do you?"

"What?"

"Watching you risk your life, knowing I might lose you —" He cuts himself off. "It's driving me insane."

His words give me a sense of déjà vu. We've had this conversation before. More than once.

He speaks again, "You can't handle the frustration of a crime going unpunished, and so you keep digging, even when you know you shouldn't. You—"

"What about you?" I cut in. "Are you any better at handling that kind of frustration?"

"What do you mean?"

A part of me knows the sucker punch I'm about to deliver could damage our relationship. But I'm too far gone.

"Look me in the eye and tell me you've followed Commandant Lambert's order," I say. "Tell me you've turned the page on your friend's case. Can you do that?"

He shuts his mouth.

"I knew it!" I cry out. "You've been secretly investigating Lena Morillot's murder."

He looks away.

I murmur, "We're not so different underneath it all, my love."

"No, we're not," he agrees. "And that's the problem."

The door opens, and the nurse pokes her head in. "Doctor says you can be discharged later today."

"Music to my ears," I reply.

She gives Gabriel and me a thumbs-up and goes away.

The door opens again.

This time it's Flo. "Is it safe to come in?"

"Yes," I reply. "Gabriel's done schooling me."

Flo hands him a steaming paper cup. He thanks her. Rose saunters in and passes me a cup that smells like surprisingly decent coffee.

I sniff at it. "You're a lifesaver!"

"That was meant for the coffee," Flo says to Gabriel. "But I'm sure Julie appreciates Grandma delivering it."

He struggles for a second to keep up his upset-tough-guy attitude, but then he gives up and smiles.

CHAPTER 39

Beldoc's main square is alive with colors, sounds, and smells. The closing banquet of rice month is in full swing. Beneath the garden lights hanging from the old plane trees of the *place de la mairie*, long communal tables line the perimeter. They're decked with checkered tablecloths and flickering candles. The smells of grilled meats, aromatic herbs, and fried garlic fill the air. The paella platters are a feast for the eyes. Complete with shrimp, chorizo, chicken and veg, they make my mouth water as I wait for my turn to dig in.

Off to one side, a dessert spread composed of pastries from two local bakeries—but not mine, sniff—looks better than I'd hoped.

I sit between my friend Salman, who came over from Avignon, and an empty seat that I'm holding for Gabriel, who's still at work. He's not mad at me anymore. As usual, it took about a week of extra special care to thaw him out.

I wish he'd learn from me to worry less! But he equates optimism with recklessness, so that's not going to happen.

Across the table, Flo and Tino are listening to something Eric is telling them. Rose is sipping wine and murmuring something to Takeo, who seems entertained by her story. Earlier this week, she surprised everyone by announcing that she was forfeiting her right to co-preside this banquet as Queen of Beldoc. I thought it was an odd move for someone who thrives on attention.

Not so odd, after all, I realize as I watch her having a good time and flirting with Takeo.

"The guy has some gorgeous tattoos," Salman whispers in my year.

I follow his gaze to Takeo's wrist where his shirt sleeve has ridden up a little.

"Did you see that?" Salman murmurs. "I bet the rest of him isn't too shabby, either."

"First, he's too old for you," I whisper back. "Second, he's straight."

Salman scrunches up his face and swats my arm. "You don't know that."

Actually, he's right—I don't.

Would this be the first time a gay man charmed a dewy-eyed woman just for sport? Nope. It's happened before. At least once. Fourteen years ago, during the summer trip to Cannes taken by a group of Cordon Bleu students.

And that's all I'll say about that.

Up on the makeshift stage, Mayor Victor Jacquet drones on about the success of rice month. His voice is monotone and peppered with pauses. Sometimes he breaks off intentionally and waits for applause that never comes. I'm annoyed with Victor that I didn't get the nod for the dessert catering. Still, I'm willing to cheer him on just for sparing us that sanctimonious consultant he'd brought in for Ritzy Rice.

I won't clap alone, though. Everybody has tuned him out. People are talking over his speech, passing plates, and enjoying the feast. My gaze shifts to the paella.

OK, I'm going in!

Tino turns to me. "Flo has news."

I tear my eyes from the paella. "Sorry, what was that?"

"I've now officially eliminated all but one Julien Martin," my sister announces.

"Really?" I perk up. "Tell me more!"

"The last one has very little online presence," she begins. "An egghead profile, barely any posts, and no photos. It's like he's hiding on purpose."

"He could be a tech hater, like Jean-Jacques Tillier," I say.

Flo stabs a lettuce leaf on her plate. "Or he could be our slippery Ghost Rider."

"Julien Martin could be one of the aliases he uses," Eric says.

Gabriel arrives and takes the seat I'd kept for him. "I'll try to find out more about this Julien Martin."

Over on the podium, Victor says something that makes a bunch of people around the table cringe.

"He didn't just say 'rice-tastic,' did he?" Salman stage-whispers, eyes wide in disbelief.

"It's worse than that," Rose jumps in. "He said, 'The rice-tastic grains of fraternity in the savage salad of life.'"

"Your mayor is great," Takeo offers, poker-faced. "I had a good meeting with him yesterday, and I think I'll be setting up my sushi bar here in Beldoc."

Rose's face lightens up. "Oh? That's awesome! And, yes, Victor is, um, great."

Flo and I exchange an amused look. She deserves a medal for the feat of abnegation she carried out by calling her political arch-rival "great."

She really likes Takeo, doesn't she?

Gabriel sees an opening and dishes out a portion of paella for me, before serving himself.

Did I mention I love him?

Salman puts his glass down. "Any update on your kidnapper? Did she change her story about the attack?"

"Nope. She still claims she wasn't trying to kill me."

"What was she trying to do then?" he asks.

"Take me to her amazing hypnotherapist, the one who helped her quit smoking after everything else failed."

Gabriel lifts his eyes skyward. "That's a load of BS."

"According to Nicole," I continue, "she was going to ask him to hypnotize me into leaving her alone and getting on with my life."

"Sounds like a bulletproof defense to me," Takeo mutters.

This time, there's clear sarcasm in his tone.

"Did Shen check out that therapist, by the way, just in case?" Rose inquires.

I nod. "Nicole gave him a name, Laurent Richard, and an address. But Shen found no such person at that address. The place is an empty apartment, whose owner has been dead for a year."

"A dead end," Rose concludes.

"Literally," Takeo adds.

She giggles.

"Do you believe that story?" Salman asks me.

I gaze up at the lantern swaying gently above. "I honestly don't know. Maybe? Why make up a hypnotherapist with a name and an address?"

Gabriel snorts. "Oh, please! She's lying, Julie. She's trying to frame her murderous plan as something much less violent, hoping for lenience."

"Do you think she has a chance?" Eric asks him.

Gabriel shrugs. "Nothing surprises me anymore. But she won't weasel out of standing trial for the murder of Seraphin Rampal."

"So, what's the latest on that murder case?" Salman asks. "I'm out of the loop."

"Nicole hasn't confessed," I reply. "There's little doubt, however, that the jury will convict her."

Rose looks up from her plate. "Does Shen have enough proof? Aside from Candice's testimony, I mean."

"Nicole's alibi collapsed," Gabriel says, keeping his voice low. "She claimed she was home between one and three in the morning, but her phone pinged along the riverbank."

Salman's mouth forms an O. "Betrayed by her phone!"

"Yes," I confirm. "Its location data places her near the bridge at the time of Rampal's death. Plus, a neighbor saw her leaving her building with a man who matches Rampal's description."

"Not bad!" He smiles.

"Is there more?" Rose asks. "Something new that I haven't heard?"

Gabriel lifts a single eyebrow. "Don't they teach discretion about ongoing investigations in your PI class?"

Grandma squirms and focuses on her mushroom risotto. I understand why my boyfriend is reluctant to show his colleagues' hand, but I wish he would. There's plenty more. Toxicology tests on my urine sample confirmed the presence of scopolamine. The gendarmes even found traces of the powder on the table at the Mexican place.

Nicole's apartment was searched. Tiny fibers from the clothes Rampal wore that night were found on her sofa and carpet. Her laptop history showed she spent days reading up on how to bend someone's will. She'd researched scopolamine and looked for where to buy it.

Unfortunately, the investigators have no proof she went ahead and bought it. She must've moved her research to the dark web and concluded her transaction there. She probably paid in cash. But even without proof of purchase, Shen has enough to convince a jury of her guilt. Especially, after she drugged me with what was left of her scopolamine.

"I think we can tell Salman and Rose a little more, without revealing the prosecution's strategy," I begin. "On the first night of Ritzy Rice, Nicole lured Rampal to her apartment so they could talk and mend fences over a drink."

Salman nods. "And he fell for that."

"Unfortunately, he did," Flo picks up. "She got him tipsy. Then, she slipped Devil's Breath into his drink. By the time she walked him to the river, he was under her complete control."

Eric jumps in. "Once she had him at the bridge, she ordered him to jump."

It hit's me: that's exactly the part I saw in my snapshot.

"The drug," he continues, "combined with the alcohol, made sure he wouldn't be able to swim properly. Plus, it was dark, the Rhône is cold at night, and he had poor eyesight..."

"Dude didn't stand a chance," Tino sums up.

Salman frowns. "And no one saw this? No cameras?"

"None that picked it up," Flo replies. "Nicole was careful. Avoided the CCTV. That bridge was the perfect spot."

"Her timing was perfect, too," I say. "She had to wait until the drug wasn't at its peak anymore, but still effective. Because if Rampal had died too soon, there would've been traces of it in his system."

Eric finishes the story, "While Rampal struggled in the water, still alive, his body kept metabolizing and eliminating the scopolamine. And by the time he drowned, there was nothing left for the tox screen to pick up."

Salman whistles softly. "That's brutal."

"Calculated," I add. "It wasn't some spur-of-the-moment crime. Nicole plotted every detail, and it all worked as planned."

Of course, her well-plotted murder could've gone awry. Devil's Breath peaks at about an hour after ingestion or

239

inhalation. Rampal's system might've gotten rid of it by the time he and Nicole got to the bridge. He would've recovered his free will and refused to jump.

Heck, he might've chucked the wicked witch into the Rhône instead!

Or, if his metabolism was slower than average, he might have died before his body had a chance to fully clear his system of the drug. In that case, the forensics would've found traces of scopolamine in Rampal's blood or tissue samples. Nicole took a big risk, driven by her long-festering resentment and desire for revenge.

And that's what bothers me. It seems out of character. None of the information I've pieced together so far suggests she's the gambling type.

There are other things that bother me about this case.

Who was the woman in a hoody who delivered Armelle's mean letters to me?

How did Nicole find out that I was onto her?

She says someone on the street overheard my call with Shen on my way to the market. That anonymous whistleblower then tipped Nicole off. Her phone records do show a call she received from a burner phone, but the story sounds too contrived.

And, more importantly, why, after so many years, would Nicole's grudge against Rampal flare up so badly she'd decide to kill him? Shen's and Gabriel's explanation is that she was patiently waiting all this time to exact revenge, which is a dish that's best served cold.

Sure, it's possible. But my gut tells me something else was at play here. And Mylene, the hero who pulled me from Nicole's clutches, agrees.

Across the square, Victor wraps up his speech, "May Beldoc always stay united, like the sticky rice in sushi!" He motions toward Takeo. "Incidentally, I hope our town will soon be able to enjoy Japanese food, made with sushi rice grown here in the Camargue!"

The announcement finally gets the public's attention and earns Victor hearty applause.

"I dig your mayor," Takeo says. "Such a warm, welcoming man!"

Rose attempts to make her snarl look like a smile. "Yes, our Victor is... smooth."

Salman's elbow nudges my side. "Takeo is gay."

"Doubtful," I murmur. "You'll need stronger evidence."

Finally, our smooth Victor climbs off the stage. My work neighbors Magda and Igor take his place. Magda remains standing, while Igor sits down with an old accordion in his lap. I've seen him play the guitar many times, enlivening gatherings with his mix of French and Russian ballads. But I didn't know he could play the accordion. He must've been practicing in secret.

Igor starts off with Edith Piaf's waltz, "Padam, Padam."

Salman extends his hand to me. "Will Beldoc's best amateur sleuth honor her queer friend with this dance?"

Oh, I see what he did there! It was a rather elegant yet unambiguous way to show his colors in case Takeo is into men. Mind you, regardless of who he's into, it looks like the tattooed gentleman is going to leave this table with more than one stolen heart.

"The honor is mine," I say to Salman, dropping a curtsy theatrical enough to match his invitation.

I take his hand, and we make our way to the open area where others are already swaying to the familiar tune. Salman leads like a pro. As we dance, I catch Gabriel watching me from his seat, a softness in his gaze that's as rare as it is precious. Magda's husky voice joins Igor's accordion. She's no Piaf, but she can sing.

I glide across the cobblestones, lost in the magic of the evening and in the joy of being with people I love.

AFTERWORD

Dear Reader,

I hope you enjoyed this Julie Cavallo mystery set in the Camargue. The next one in the series, **The Fatal Farandole**, will bring you more of that unique French region—along with some edge-of-your-seat fun.

A young chef's tragic death unravels a sprawling conspiracy

—and more secrets than the townsfolk know what to do with...

The Fatal Farandole will be hitting the shelves in Fall 2025.

Preorder The Fatal Farandole now!

If you're all caught up on my books (see **"Also By Ana T. Drew"**), here's a non-exhaustive list of ways you might boost both your happiness and mine:

1. Leave a review for *The Ruthless Rice on Amazon.*

Even a short one makes a big difference. If you can also cross-post to Goodreads or BookBub, that would be fantastic! It's the best thing you can do to support an author and encourage them to keep writing.

Plus, reviews help readers discover new books. Everyone wins!

2. Enjoy the bonus content at ana-drew.com/bonus-content.

My not-so-secret stash of goodies includes a short story from Gabriel's point of view, a juicy issue of *Beldoc Live*, a deleted scene, video trailers, an interactive game, and more!

3. Sign up for my occasional newsletter at ana-drew.com/free-books.

You'll be the first to hear when I add new goodies or release a new book. As a welcome gift, I'll email you a **hilarious novella** titled *The Canceled Christmas* and a **gluten-free recipe book**.

Warmly,
Ana

ALSO BY ANA T. DREW

The JULIE CAVALLO INVESTIGATES series
(PROVENCE COZY MYSTERIES)

The Murderous Macaron

Pastry chef Julie Cavallo has her freedom, her shop, and a corpse growing cold on her floor.

The Killer Karma

Julie unmasked a killer. Life is good once again... until her sous chef becomes a murder suspect.

The Sinister Superyacht

When a luxury cruise turns deadly, the caterer and her breezy gran must figure out which guest is the killer.

The Shady Chateau

Three unlikely culprits plead guilty for a baron's death at a Napoleonic re-enactment. Who's lying? And why? And who really killed the baron?

The Perils of Paris

When someone tries to kill her sister, it's time for Julie Cavallo to don her sleuthing cap.

The Bloodthirsty Bee

It's springtime in Provence! Trees are in bloom and critters are abuzz — including a murderer or two.

The Deadly Donut

As bodies pile up at the secluded hotel Villa Grare, Julie has precious little time to find the killer!

The Ruthless Rice

When an influential food critic turns up face down in the Rhône River, the gendarmes call it an accident. But Julie disagrees.

The Fatal Farandole

A young chef's tragic death unravels a sprawling conspiracy—and more secrets than even Julie can handle.

CHRISTMAS SPECIALS

The Canceled Christmas (novella, free with signup)

Mayor Victor Jacquet receives a mystifying note. And then his small town mounts a rebellion...

An (un)Orthodox Christmas (novella)

While in Cassis with Gabriel's rowdy relatives, Julie and Gabriel investigate a thorny family situation—and a murder!

The Twelve Suspects of Christmas (full-length novel)

A cold case meets new mayhem in two quirky grandmas' rollicking journey from Provence to Picardie.

The Snow Globe Affair

As Christmas cheer spreads across Paris, a psychic and a mathematician compete in a scavenger hunt — and get entangled in the heist of the century!

Printed in Great Britain
by Amazon

DEANE'S SERIE
General Editor ...ge W. Bishop

THE YOUNG IN HEART

A COMEDY IN THREE ACTS

By DEREK BENFIELD

(Author of " The Way the Wind Blows ")

Y·B·P

PRICE 5s. NET

London :
H. F. W. DEANE & SONS LTD.
31 MUSEUM STREET, W.C.1

BOSTON, MASS., U.S.A.: THE WALTER H. BAKER COMPANY

MADE IN ENGLAND

30130 145981659

ACTING FEES FOR PERFORMANCES OVERSEAS

Apply—South Africa: Darter & Sons, Cape Town. Australia: Doreen Rayment, 19 Chapman Avenue, Beecroft, Sydney. New Zealand: Play Bureau, 7 Disraeli Street, Hawera. Canada and U.S.A.: Walter H. Baker Company, Boston.

This play was first produced by Reginald Salberg's Preston Repertory Company at the Royal Hippodrome, Preston, with the following cast of characters :—

Arthur Purvis	Derek Benfield.
Edna	Greta Whiteley.
Mary Williamson	Joan Humphries.
Margaret Purvis	Peggy Mount.
Roger Purvis	John Randall.
Freda Purvis	Doreen Andrew.
Helen Purvis	Joan Peart.
Nigel Grahame	Charles Mardel.
Albert Foster	Frederick Jaeger.
Major Todd	Anthony Sager.

Production by John Barron.

Decor by David Curtis.

CHARACTERS :—

(in order of appearance)

ARTHUR PURVIS

EDNA

MARY WILLIAMSON

MARGARET PURVIS

ROGER PURVIS

FREDA PURVIS

HELEN PURVIS

NIGEL GRAHAME

ALBERT FOSTER

MAJOR TODD

Time : The present.

SCENE. The Sitting-room of the Purvis's country home in Surrey.

ACT I.

Early evening on a Friday—one day in late summer.

ACT II.

SCENE 1. Saturday evening.

SCENE 2. A few hours later.

ACT III.

Sunday evening.

THE YOUNG IN HEART

A Comedy in Three Acts

By DEREK BENFIELD

ACT I.

The Scene throughout is the comfortably furnished sitting-room of the Purvis's country home in Surrey.

There is a large window-seat in an alcove slightly left of C. *A door in the* C. *of the* L. *wall leads into the hallway and the rest of the house. The dining-room we presume to be immediately across the hall, and the front door downstage in the* PROMPT *corner. Another door* U.R. *in the* R. *wall leads to Arthur's private study. The fireplace is* D.R. *with an arm chair below it facing slightly* U.S., *and a sofa facing slightly towards the fire. A low divan is against the wall below the door* L. *A drinks' table* U.R., *and a small table against the* L. *end of the sofa with the telephone and directory on it. A radiogram* U.C. *Bookshelves* U.R. *and above the divan* D.L. *Table lamp on a shelf above the divan. Standard lamp* U.R.C. *There are two main light switches below the door* L. *A table below the window-seat with a chair set* L. *and* R. *of it. See Stage Plan p. 63.*

The room must be tastefully furnished and decorated in the modern manner, but there is a lived-in homely atmosphere.

L. *or* R. *refers throughout to the actors'* L. *or* R.

Early evening on a Friday—one midsummer day.

When the curtain rises, ARTHUR PURVIS *is sitting on the sofa, smoking his usual pipe and doing a crossword puzzle in the evening paper. He is oblivious of the telephone bell which is ringing violently. Arthur is a quiet, unaffected man in his early fifties.*

(EDNA, *the maid, and* MARY WILLIAMSON, MRS. PURVIS'S *sister, appear from* L. *carrying a mattress between them. They cross and go off* R.)

(MARGARET, ARTHUR'S *wife, appears from* L. *carrying two sheets and two pillows. She crosses and goes off* R.)

(*The 'phone bell continues to ring.*)

(EDNA *crosses back from* R. *and goes off* L.)

(MARY *crosses back from* R. *and goes off* L.)

(ARTHUR *rises, moves as if to the 'phone, but merely picks up a box of matches and returns to his seat.*)

(MARGARET *appears from* R. *at great speed as* EDNA *returns from* L. *with two blankets. They meet* C. *and collide. They right themselves and exit in their appropriate directions.*)

(MARGARET *returns.*)

MARGARET. Arthur!
ARTHUR. What is it?
MARGARET. The 'phone, dear.

ARTHUR.   What about it ?
MARGARET.   It's ringing.
ARTHUR.   What ?
MARGARET.   I said the 'phone's ringing!
ARTHUR.   Oh—so it is. Alright, Margaret, I'll answer it.

(MARGARET *goes off* L. *leaving the door open.*)

(*At 'phone.*) Hullo. Arthur Purvis here.
MARGARET (*off* L.).   Where did you put the pillowcases, Mary ?
MARY (*off* L.).   I didn't have them, dear.
MARGARET (*off* L.).   But I gave them to you just now!
ARTHUR.   Who ?
MARY (*off* L.).   You didn't, darling.   Perhaps they're with the eiderdowns in the small back room!
ARTHUR.   I can't hear a word you say.
MARGARET. (*off* L.).   Go and ask Edna, will you dear ?
MARY (*off* L.).   Alright!
ARTHUR.   No, No! *This* is Arthur Purvis! I want to know who *you* are!
MARY (*at door* L.).   Edna!
MARGARET (*off* L.).   I expect she's put them in a safe place.   She always does.
EDNA (*at door* R.).   What is it, Miss Williamson ?
MARY.   Have you seen the pillowcases ?
EDNA.   No, I thought you had them last.
MARY.   Alright, Edna.
ARTHUR.   Who is that speaking, please ?

(*Exit* MARY L., *and* EDNA R.)

MARY (*off* L.).   No, she hasn't seen them!
MARGARET (*off* L.).   But that's too stupid for words. If we can't find them, whatever shall we do ?
ARTHUR.   Just a minute.

(*He crosses to door* L. *to shut it.*)

MARY (*off* L.).   Do you think that mattress will be quite comfortable, dear ? It's a bit hard!
MARGARET (*off* L.).   Why not ?   I've slept on it many a time when we've had a house full.

(*Door shuts.*)

ARTHUR.   That's better. (*At 'phone.*) Now, who is that ? . . . What ? . . . No, I am not the Victoria and Albert Museum ! . . . No. I am Arthur Purvis . . . Not at all. Don't mention it . . . Just a minute. Perhaps you can help me. (*Refers to crossword.*) What's an eleven-letter word beginning and ending in " s " meaning " a kind of stone used for Egyptian coffins "? . . . What ? . . . Yes, S . . . S, S, S . . . What ? . . . Oh, thanks very much. (*Hangs up and resumes his seat.*) Now, how the hell do you spell that ?

(MARGARET *comes in from* L. *She is warm-hearted, charming and forty-eight. She carries a list and a pencil, to which she continually refers.*)

MARGARET.   Who was it, Arthur ?

ARTHUR. Who was what, dear ?

MARGARET. The person on the 'phone.

ARTHUR. I don't know.

MARGARET. Really, Arthur ! Didn't you answer it ?

ARTHUR. Of course I did. Someone was wanting the Victoria and Albert. I told them that the only useless antique we had here was your sister Mary.

MARGARET. I do wish you'd try to be polite to my relations, Arthur.

ARTHUR. Why ? They're never polite to me. I sometimes have nightmares about them. It's awful.

MARGARET. Mary is being very helpful. I don't know how I'd manage all the preparations without her.

ARTHUR. Thank Heaven we don't have a Silver Wedding every year ! Is there anything I can do ?

MARGARET. Arthur, how is it you always manage to ask that question when all the work is done ?

ARTHUR. Through years of practice, my dear.

MARGARET. I'm having to put Nigel in your study, I'm afraid.

ARTHUR. Oh, so that's what all the procession was about.

MARGARET. Yes. Edna's just making the bed up.

ARTHUR. Will he be quite comfortable there ?

MARGARET. Well, there's nowhere else unless we move out of our room.

ARTHUR. Oh, well, it'll have to do, then. I expect he slept in much worse places when he was in the Army.

MARGARET. Well, it was your idea to invite him.

ARTHUR. Does Helen know he's coming?.

MARGARET. No. I've pledged everyone to secrecy.

ARTHUR. That's good.

(*Pause.*)

MARGARET. Do you think it's wise, Arthur ?

ARTHUR. Wise ?

MARGARET. Inviting Nigel here. After all, they broke off their engagement pretty finally, didn't they ?

ARTHUR. Yes, I know. But, my dear, they were so—so right for each other. I can't really believe that it's all over.

MARGARET. How did Nigel react when you mentioned it ?

ARTHUR. As I hoped he would. Just for a moment I saw the old look in his eyes, then he said very firmly that he couldn't come. But I soon talked him round.

MARGARET. We're a couple of matchmakers, you and I !

ARTHUR. No, we're not. Matchmenders, if you like.

(*Enter* EDNA *from* R. *A gloomy pessimistic maid.*)

EDNA. I've made up the bed, Mum. I've had to close the window again, though, because the rubbish pit in the garden is smelling something terrible. Is there anything we can do ?

ARTHUR. Pray for the wind to change.

EDNA. It's liable to get in all the back rooms, sir, and I can't think of anything worse than the smell of rubbish in a bedroom.

MARGARET. Arthur, why did you have to pick to-day to start burning things?

ARTHUR. Well, you don't want the garden looking like a wilderness when people come, do you?

EDNA. Everything's going wrong to-day, Mum. I knew it would. I dreamt about an earthquake last night—that's always a bad sign. Then my corn was giving me twinges this morning. It'll probably rain. It's looking black already.

ARTHUR. Nonsense. The sun's shining.

EDNA. It won't be for long, sir. Mark my words. It's going to be a bad day. The rubbish pit was the beginning.

(*Exit* EDNA L.)

ARTHUR. We have such nice, cheerful servants ! What's a six-letter word meaning a sacred temple found in the East?

MARGARET. Pagoda. (*Crossing to window.*) What time did Nigel say he'd arrive?

ARTHUR. Should be here in about half an hour.

MARGARET. I do hope Helen gets here first. She's rather late coming from work.

('*Phone bell rings.*)

ARTHUR. Now who on earth can that be?

MARGARET. I don't know.

ARTHUR. Well, aren't you going to answer it?

MARGARET. Oh, yes. (*At 'phone.*) Mrs. Purvis speaking . . . Who do you want? . . . Yes, he's here. It's for you, dear.

ARTHUR. Well, ask who it is.

MARGARET. Who is that speaking, please? . . . She won't say.

ARTHUR (*taking 'phone from her*). Purvis here . . . Who is that? . . . No, no, this is Arthur Purvis. Yes, he's in. Just a moment. ('*Phone down.*) It's for Roger. (*At door* L.) Roger ! Roger !

ROGER (*off* L.). Coming, Dad !

MARGARET. Who is it, Arthur?

ARTHUR (*crossing* D.S. *to* R.). Can't make it out. Sounds like Tallulah Bankhead.

MARGARET. Didn't she say?

ARTHUR. No. She didn't say. (*Sits armchair* D.R.)

(*Enter* ROGER *from* L. *He is a pale, handsome young man of twenty-three. He is never quite relaxed and is something of an introvert.*)

ROGER. (*entering*). Did you call me?

ARTHUR. Yes, Roger. Somebody on the 'phone for you.

ROGER Oh. (*Slight pause.*) Oh, thanks. (*At 'phone.*) Hallo, Roger Purvis here . . . What? . . . (*Glances at his parents.*) Well, I can't really, no . . . I said on Wednesday. I can't make it before . . . What? . . . Oh, alright, I'll be there. So long. (*Hangs up.*)

ARTHUR. A date, Roger?

ROGER. Er—yes. A girl I met at the Club the other night. She's got some sort of a party on and wants me to go along.

ARTHUR. Is she pretty?

ROGER. Sort of.

ARTHUR. You're a dark horse, Roger. Keeping it to yourself like that ! Better bring her in to tea one day. Let's have a look at her.

ROGER. Yes, I'd like to. Well, I'd better be getting ready. (*Moving to door* L.)

MARGARET. You'll have time for tea first, won't you, dear?

ROGER. Oh yes. I don't have to go for an hour or so.

MARGARET. Will you be very late coming back?

ROGER. Yes, I expect so. But don't wait up.

MARGARET. Alright, dear.

(*Roger goes out* L.)

ARTHUR (*lightly*). I must say his girl friend has got the most attractive bass voice I've ever heard !

(*Pause.*)

MARGARET. Arthur . . .

ARTHUR. H'm?

MARGARET. I'm worried about Roger.

ARTHUR. Now, then, my dear. I thought we decided not to worry about him any more.

MARGARET. Yes, but he seems so—unsettled.

ARTHUR. Yes. (*Pause.*) Yes, I know . . .

(*Enter* MARY *from* L. *with two pillowcases. She is an angular lady in the middle forties, with a brittle speech and a dry humour but warm-hearted for all that. She is* MARGARET'S *sister and a spinster.*)

MARY. The pillowcases were upstairs all the time.

MARGARET. Good. I knew we'd put them somewhere safe.

ARTHUR. I hear you're making yourself useful, Mary.

MARY (*Going* R.). Yes. Margaret needs someone to help her with an idle husband like you on her hands.

ARTHUR. Did I ever tell you that you are my favourite relation?

MARY (*up* R.). No, you didn't. But I guessed !

ARTHUR. I don't know how I'd get on without you, but I'd like to try.

MARY (*going*). Very funny, and quite original ! (*Exit* U.R.)

MARGARET. Now then, you two !

(*Enter* HELEN *from* L. *She is a charming, vivacious young lady of twenty-four, dressed as for the office.*)

HELEN (*entering*). Hello, everyone !

MARGARET. Had a good day at the office, dear?

(ARTHUR *rises as* HELEN *reaches him.*)

HELEN (*kissing* MARGARET U.C.). Ghastly. I sat there all day ready and willing to take some letters, but no—nobody calls. (*Kisses* ARTHUR. D.R.) Then at five-thirty when I'm all set to leave, my boss sends for me and dictates solidly until six.

ARTHUR.   Don't you get overtime ?

HELEN.   No fear. If anyone asked for overtime in our place the boss would have blood pressure. I think I shall go on strike very shortly. Anyhow, I left the typing to do in the morning. The trouble is that I shan't be able to decipher my shorthand by to-morrow.

(*And she goes out* L.)

MARGARET   (*calling*). Tea won't be long, dear !

HELEN   (*off* L.). Okay !

(*Enter* EDNA *from* L.)

EDNA.   Excuse me, sir, but there's a very peculiar man at the door who says that the Time has come, and that if I don't repent now I shall be condemned to the Everlasting Bonfire. What ought I to do ?

ARTHUR.   Well, you'd better repent.

MARGARET.   Give him a cup of tea and tell him to be on his way.

EDNA.   What if he says that's no answer ?

MARGARET.   Don't be silly, Edna. A cup of tea is always an answer.

EDNA.   Very good, Mum. (*Starts to go.*)

(*Re-enter* MARY *from* R.)

MARY   (*moving* C.).   Are you pickling your peanuts as usual this year, Edna ?

ARTHUR.   Pickling her what ?

MARY.   Peanuts ! She always pickles peanuts every year.

ARTHUR.   But you don't pickle peanuts.

MARGARET.   Edna does. They're her speciality.

EDNA.   Oh, thank you, Mum.

ARTHUR.   Did you smile, then, Edna ?

EDNA.   Er—yes, sir, I think I did.

ARTHUR.   Well, don't do it again. It frightens me.

EDNA.   Very good, sir. What shall I do if this man won't go away, sir ?

ARTHUR.   Put on a brave face and tell him to prepare the stake.

EDNA.   Very good, sir. (*She goes* L.)

ARTHUR.   She doesn't look a peanut pickling person to me.

MARGARET.   By the way, Arthur, the Vicar wants us to do the prize-giving at the Ball to-morrow night. (*Sits* L. *end of sofa.*)

ARTHUR.   Oh, Lord !

MARGARET.   We *are* the guests of honour, after all, dear.

ARTHUR.   I shall hate it.

MARY.   He also said that someone put a button in the plate at Church last Sunday.

ARTHUR (*guiltily*). Huh ?

MARGARET.   Oh, really, Arthur !

ARTHUR.   I did no such thing ! (*Moves to fireplace* R.)

(FREDA *runs into the room at full speed. She is a bright young girl of seventeen although at times she appears to be considerably younger. Outwardly a little precocious, but with a heart of gold. When she stops behaving naturally—which is often—she tries to be much older than her years.*)

FREDA.   Anyone seen my hat?
MARGARET.   It's on the table.
FREDA.   Thanks. (*Picks it up and rushes off.*) G'bye!
MARGARET.   Freda!
FREDA.   (*re-appearing at the door* L.).   What?
MARGARET.   Where are you going?
FREDA.   To help Mabel Corner fix her dress for to-morrow night. Won't be a sec! (*She goes again.*)
MARGARET (*rising* C.).   Freda!
FREDA (*re-appearing once more*).   What?
MARGARET.   What if Albert calls?   He said he'd probably pop in later on this evening.
FREDA (*gaily*).   Let him wait!   It'll do him good! (*She goes.*)
MARY (*sitting on sofa beside* MARGARET).   And who is Albert?
ARTHUR (*in front of fire*).   Albert Foster.   A young lad who lives down the street.   He's an orphan, comes from Yorkshire—and he was adopted by Major Todd, one of our neighbours.   Nice boy, but not a glamour type, if you know what I mean.   He's quite a character.
MARGARET.   He's sweet.
ARTHUR.   Anyhow, he seems to have taken a fancy to our Freda.
MARY.   And she hasn't taken a fancy to him, is that it?
ARTHUR.   So she says.   Calls him gormless.
MARY.   Gormless?
ARTHUR.   Yes, you know—a bit loose up here.
MARY.   And is he?
ARTHUR.   Well, he's no Romeo.   Falls over the furniture a bit and has five thumbs on each hand, but he's alright underneath.
MARGARET.   He's sweet.
ARTHUR.   You just said that.
MARGARET.   Well—he is.
ARTHUR.   Well, don't try to convince *me*.   He doesn't want to take me to the dance!
MARY.   I should think not.
ARTHUR.   Or you!
MARY (*rising and moving* L.).   Your husband is becoming unpleasant once more so I shall get on with some work.
ARTHUR.   Don't let me keep you from that.

(MARY *goes out* L.)

(ARTHUR *returns to his crossword. There is a pause.*)

MARGARET.   We haven't done so well for ourselves, have we?
ARTHUR.   What do you mean?
MARGARET.   Our children.

ARTHUR. There's nothing wrong with them, and you know it.

MARGARET. Not fundamentally. But—well—they seem to be all mixed up inside. They don't seem settled, somehow.

ARTHUR (*joining her on sofa*). Were you settled between the ages of seventeen and twenty-three. They are very tender years, you know.

MARGARET. Don't sidetrack, dear. Anyhow, I married you when I was twenty-three.

ARTHUR. Nineteen you always tell the children.

MARGARET. I do no such thing !

ARTHUR. Well, perhaps they'll all be settled at that age, too. How many f's in " effervescence " ?

MARGARET. Two, aren't there ?

ARTHUR. That's what I thought. It doesn't fit.

MARGARET. I don't think Roger will *ever* be settled.

ARTHUR. He'll be alright. Don't worry about him.

MARGARET. Do *you* know what's troubling him ?

ARTHUR. No. He never talks to me about such things.

MARGARET. I wish he would. We are his parents, after all.

ARTHUR. That's a strange thing about parents, isn't it ? One always tends to take other people's advice rather than ask father, when he's really the only person who can be expected to understand completely.

MARGARET. Like in the Victorian days, when father really was rather a frightening person.

ARTHUR. Well, perhaps, *I* am.

MARGARET (*smiling*). Yes, dear.

ARTHUR. Don't you think I am ?

MARGARET. Er—no, dear.

ARTHUR. You're biased. Perhaps I've got the wrong approach or something. I should hate to think he was too afraid of me to come and talk to me about things.

MARGARET. Silly darling ! You couldn't frighten a day-old chick !

(*Enter* FREDA *from* L. *in a hurry.*)

You've been quick.

FREDA. She isn't in. Tea ready ?

MARGARET. It will be in a second. We've all been very busy to-day so it's rather late.

FREDA. By the way, is Nigel coming ?

MARGARET (*with a glance at* ARTHUR). Nigel ? (*Rises to fire.*)

FREDA. Yes. You see, I saw such a smashing-looking man in a red sports car in the village about half an hour ago. I thought it was Nigel at first, but *he* wouldn't be around here, would he ?

ARTHUR. No. No—er—he wouldn't be around here. (*Busies himself with his crossword and pipe.*)

FREDA. Pity. I liked Nigel. He was wizard ! Albert been ?

MARGARET. No.. Not yet.

FREDA (*moving* L.). Well, I'm off for my ablutions, now.

ARTHUR. Your what ?

FREDA. I'm going to wash my neck, silly ! (*She goes out* L.)

MARGARET (*calling, and crossing* C.). Don't be long. That's what comes of her going about with that awful Peter Goodacre. I do wish she wouldn't.

ARTHUR. Isn't she a bit young for all that sort of thing ?

MARGARET. What sort of thing ?

ARTHUR. Well—boy friends and all that.

MARGARET. She's seventeen.

ARTHUR. She's only a baby! He's twice her age.

MARGARET. He's twenty-one, darling.

ARTHUR. I don't care. I don't like him. Certainly wouldn't like him in the family! (*Pause.*) That " lovely looking man in the red sports car " should be here any minute.

MARGARET. You think it was Nigel, then ?

ARTHUR. Of course it was. Taking him a long time to get here from the village.

MARGARET. I suppose we'd better tell Helen about him, hadn't we ?

ARTHUR. Yes.

MARGARET. I'll leave it to you. (*Moves to door* L. *quickly.*)

ARTHUR (*rising*). No, you won't ! It's more in your line.

MARGARET (*returning* C.). I shouldn't know what to say.

ARTHUR. You know you're wonderful in cases like this.

MARGARET. I really think it would be better if it came from you.

ARTHUR. I don't see why. You're her mother.

MARGARET. Well, you're her father, aren't you ?

ARTHUR. So I've always been led to believe !

MARGARET. Please, darling—you.

ARTHUR. No, dearest—you !

(*Enter* HELEN *from* L. *She has changed into an afternoon frock.*)

HELEN. You two have a mysterious look. I think you're up to something.

MARGARET. Up to something ? What do you mean ?

HELEN. I don't know, but when I came into this room just now there was an atmosphere.

MARGARET (*to* ARTHUR). Are we " up to anything," dear ?

ARTHUR (*airily*). No. No, of course not. (*Moves to tap out pipe.*)

(*A pause.* HELEN *looks from one to another.* MARGARET *makes a dive for the door.*)

ARTHUR. Where are *you* going ?

MARGARET. I thought I'd go and see how Edna is getting on with the tea.

ARTHUR. Edna is perfectly capable of managing on her own so come and sit down.

MARGARET. I thought you'd like to be alone.

ARTHUR. Why should I want to be alone ?

MARGARET. Well, you know——

(*A pause. They look guilty.*)

HELEN. I thought so ! You *are* up to something ! Come on, out with it. (*She is between them* C. *now.*)

MARGARET. Go on, Arthur, tell her.

ARTHUR. No, no—you !

MARGARET. You're head of the house.

ARTHUR. You only say that on occasions like this ! Besides, you're in charge of matrimonial affairs.

MARGARET. Well, I——

HELEN. Matrimonial ? (*Pause.*) Come on. What is it ?

MARGARET. Well . . . it's—it's about Nigel.

HELEN. Nigel ?

MARGARET. Yes.

HELEN. What about him ?

ARTHUR. He's coming here to-day.

HELEN. What ? !

MARGARET. Your father invited him.

ARTHUR. We both invited him !

HELEN. I see . . .

(Pause.)

MARGARET. Then—you don't mind ?

HELEN (*sarcastically*). Mind ? Why should I mind your inviting my ex-fiancé to the house ? I'm overjoyed, naturally ! (*She turns away* D.L., *past* MARGARET.)

MARGARET (*in a whisper to* ARTHUR R.C. *below sofa*). I told you we shouldn't do it.

ARTHUR (*also a whisper*). You told me no such thing. You thought it was a wonderful idea!

HELEN (*without turning*). When's he coming ?

MARGARET. Any minute now. (*Pause.*) He was to have stayed a couple of days.

HELEN (*turning to face them*). A couple of days !

MARGARET. But if you'd rather he didn't we'll ask him to go away to-morrow.

HELEN (*smiling, after a pause*). That won't be necessary. If it gets beyond what I can stand I'll send out an S.O.S. (*Moves between them and takes both of them by the arm.*) You *are* a couple of naughty children, aren't you ?

MARGARET. We hoped you wouldn't mind.

HELEN. What about my tea ? I need it all the more after that !

MARGARET (*moving to door* L.). I'll go and see what's happened to Edna. (*Door-knock off* L.) Come on, father.

ARTHUR (*vaguely*). What do you need me for ? Can't you manage in the kitchen ?

MARGARET (*pointedly*). I think the bathroom tap needs looking at.

ARTHUR. We'll get a plumber first thing . . . What ? Oh, I see !

(*Exit* MARGARET *to* L. ARTHUR *follows her, she remonstrating with him ad lib.*)

(HELEN *stands for a moment, then turns on the radio, and sits on the sofa facing the fire. The radio warms up and a dance band is playing " It's a Small World " or some slow sentimental popular melody.*)

(*Enter* NIGEL GRAHAME. *He is a tall, good-looking man of thirty with a charming manner and a sense of humour. He stands for a moment in the doorway.*)

NIGEL. Hello, there !

(HELEN *gets up and faces him.*)

HELEN. Hello . . .

(*There is a pause.*)

NIGEL. The door was ajar so I came straight in.

HELEN. I'm—I'm glad you got here.

NIGEL. So am I. I would have been here earlier only my car broke down and I had to walk from the village.

HELEN. The town.

NIGEL. Oh yes, of course. The town.

(*Pause.*)

HELEN (*turning to face the fire*). It wasn't very thoughtful of Daddy to invite you, was it ?

NIGEL. It wasn't very thoughtful of me to accept. (*With a smile.*) But I didn't anticipate such a wonderful reception ! You shouldn't have sent the band to meet me. It was far too expensive.

HELEN (*moving slightly* D.R.C.). I'm sorry. I suppose I was pretty rude, but it seems so strange seeing you again after all this time. Although you haven't changed a bit, you know.

NIGEL (D.C.). Oh yes, I have. I now have three grey hairs.

HELEN. I don't believe it !

NIGEL. Look.

HELEN. Why don't you pluck them ?

NIGEL. I'm proud of them. Make me look distinguished. You haven't changed much either. More colour on your lips, perhaps.

HELEN. It's a new shade. Called " Enchantment."

NIGEL. Very appropriate. You look a lot younger, too. Your eyes are brighter.

HELEN. Are they ?

NIGEL (*slight pause*). Much brighter.

HELEN. That's because I've been out in the open air. Getting rid of my night-club tan.

NIGEL. I see.

(*Pause.*)

HELEN (*sitting on sofa*). What have you been doing since I last saw you ?

NIGEL (*moving to above* L. *end of sofa*). Well, I should like to say that I've been living in an igloo fretting my heart out, or dashing madly around the world in a chariot ; but I haven't really done either. You see, I've had rather a lot of work to do.

HELEN. Did you get your promotion ?

NIGEL. Yes, thank you. Not much difference, really, except that I get an extra ten shillings a week which just puts me into the higher Income Tax group. Oh! And the office boy has started calling me "Sir."

(*Enter* FREDA *from* L. *at full speed to* C. *She sees* NIGEL.)

FREDA. Oh ! Excuse me !

(*And she giggles and sidles out, gazing at him.*)

HELEN. My sister.

NIGEL (*moving* R.C.). Oh, is that what it was ! She's grown.

(*There is a pause.* HELEN *moves about the room, and turns off the radio.*)

HELEN (U.R.C. *back to him*). *Why* did you come to-day ?

NIGEL. Perhaps I wanted to see you again.

HELEN (*turning*). Did you ?

NIGEL. I don't completely abhor the sight of you, you know.

HELEN. You *seemed* to when you last saw me.

NIGEL. We were both a bit bad-tempered that day ! (*Sits* L. *arm of sofa.*)

HELEN (*moving* D.S. *past* R. *end of sofa*). We certainly used to quarrel a lot.

NIGEL. Is that why you broke it off ?

HELEN. I didn't really break it off, Nigel. We decided between us. We just disagreed about too many things. Life would have been dreadful.

NIGEL. I should probably have beaten you at regular intervals. It would have done you the world of good.

HELEN. Now you're being flippant.

NIGEL. Why not ? We've had our serious moments, God knows.

HELEN. Do you quarrel with other people the same as you did with me ?

NIGEL (*rises and moves below sofa*). Good heavens, no ! I'm the essence of charm and good temper.

HELEN. The same with me. We obviously brought out the bad in each other. I hope we shall be the best of friends while you are here, anyhow. My mother would hate to see you throwing the piano at me.

NIGEL. I am always polite to you in other people's houses.

HELEN. I don't remember it.

NIGEL. You wouldn't remember the good things about me, naturally.

HELEN. That sounds more like the old you.

(*Gong in hall* L.)

That's tea.

NIGEL. Good. I'm hungry.

(*Enter* MARGARET.)

MARGARET. Why, hello, Nigel ! What a lovely surprise ! Come and have some tea.

(*They go off* L. *chattering, ad lib.*)

(*Stage empty. Door bell* L. *Door off is heard to open.*)

FREDA   (*off* L.). Hello you !
ALBERT   (*off* L.). Hello, Freda. Are you busy ?
FREDA   (*off* L.). I'm having my tea. You'd better wait in there. I won't be long.

(*The door* L. *is flung open, and* ALBERT *is practically thrown into the room by* FREDA. *He regains his balance but only just. Exit* FREDA.)

ALBERT FOSTER *is a quiet, shy young man of nineteen, with untidy hair and wearing horn-rimmed spectacles. He speaks with a slight North Country accent. The comedy of this part must come more from the pathetic than the ridiculous.*

(ALBERT *closes the door and wanders vaguely about the room. He sees a photo of* FREDA *on the mantelpiece and picks it up.*)

FREDA   (*off* L.). Alright, Mother, I'll get it !

(ALBERT *panics, starts to put back the photo and knocks off a jug which breaks into pieces. Frantically he collects the pieces.*)

(*Enter* MARY, *carrying a cup of tea.*)

MARY.   Hello.
ALBERT.   Oh—hello.
MARY.   You're Albert, aren't you ?
ALBERT.   Yes. (*He has concealed the broken jug in his coat pocket.*)
How did you know ?
MARY.   They told me about you. I'm Mrs. Purvis's sister.
ALBERT.   Oh.
MARY.   How do you do.
ALBERT.   What ? Oh—er—how do you do.

(*They shake hands. Slight pause.*)

MARY.   I wasn't very hungry so I left them to it.
ALBERT.   Oh.

(*Pause.*)

MARY.   Are you waiting for Freda ?
ALBERT.   Yes.
MARY.   She won't be long now.
ALBERT.   Good.
MARY.   Won't you sit down ?
ALBERT.   No—thanks very much.
MARY.   Do you mind if I do ?
ALBERT.   No.
MARY.   Thank you. (*She sits on sofa. A pause.*) Would you like an apple ?
ALBERT.   No, thanks very much.
MARY.   Pear ?
ALBERT.   No, thanks very much.

B

MARY.   Do you smoke ?
ALBERT.   No, thanks very much.
MARY.   Aren't you feeling very well ?
ALBERT.   No, thanks very much. I mean——
MARY.   What is it ?
ALBERT.   Nothing. I'm alright—(*pause*)—thanks very much.

(MARY *smiles and relapses into silence.*)

(*After a while*). Mrs.—er ?
MARY.   Williamson.
ALBERT.   Mrs. Williamson, I——
MARY.   I'm afraid it's " miss."
ALBERT (*as if* MARY *had divulged the death of a near relative*). Oh,
I'm sorry. I didn't know.
MARY.   That's alright. (*With a smile.*) Thanks very much.

(*He smiles nervously back at her.*)

ALBERT.   Miss Williamson, if you—well, if you—I don't know how
to put it . . . If you had something you wanted to be rid of . . . what would
you do with it ?
MARY.   What sort of thing, Albert ?
ALBERT.   Well . . . a sort of an —an object ; an object that you
couldn't keep with you because it wasn't yours and which you couldn't
leave behind where it was because it didn't look the same as it used to
look—what would you do ?
MARY.   Well, it's difficult to say. I think I'd probably get someone to
dispose of it for me.
ALBERT.   Oh, I see.

(*A pause.* MARY *rises, puts down tea-cup.*)

MARY.   Albert.
ALBERT.   Yes, Miss Williamson ?
MARY.   Why don't you give the bits to me ? I'll put them in the
dustbin.
ALBERT.   What ?   (*He comes forward sheepishly and gives her the
pieces from his pocket.*) Thanks very much.
MARY.   Don't worry ! I won't tell anyone !

(MARY *goes out* L. *as* ROGER *enters.*)

ROGER.   What are you doing, Mary ? What have you got there ?
MARY.   Nothing that would interest you ! (*Exit.*)
ROGER (*annoyed at finding someone in the room*). Oh, hello, Albert.
I didn't know you were here.
ALBERT (*in front of fire*). Hello.

(ROGER *crosses to 'phone, and picks up 'phone directory. He glances through
it impatiently. A pause.*)

ROGER (*pointedly*). Are you—waiting for somebody ?

ALBERT.   Yes. I came to see Freda.

ROGER.   Oh. (*Puts down directory and sits on sofa, resigned.   Takes cigarette from case and lights it.   Leaves case on table* C.)

(*A long pause.*)

ALBERT.   It's been a lovely day, hasn't it ?
ROGER.   Yes—lovely !

(*Pause.*)

ALBERT.   I like these long summer evenings, don't you ?
ROGER.   Oh yes. I do.

(*Pause.*)

ALBERT.   Much better than the short winter evenings.
ROGER.   Much better.

(*Pause.*)

ALBERT   I'd have long summer evenings all the year round if I had my way !
ROGER.   Yes. So would I.

(*Pause.*)

ALBERT.   That would be better than having short winter evenings some of the time, wouldn't it ?
ROGER.   Yes, I think it would.

(*There is another hideous pause.*)

(*Enter* ARTHUR *from* L.)

ARTHUR.   Hello, Albert !
ALBERT.   Hello, sir.
ARTHUR.   Waiting for Freda ?
ALBERT.   Yes.
ARTHUR.   She won't be long.
ALBERT.   Good.
ROGER   (*rising*). Well, I'd better be off now, Dad.
ARTHUR.   Righto.
ROGER.   I'll try not to be too late.
ARTHUR.   Have a nice time.
ROGER.   Thanks. Goodnight. Goodnight, Albert.
ALBERT.   Goodnight.

(*Exit* ROGER *to* L.)

ARTHUR.   Won't you sit down ?
ALBERT.   No, thanks, sir.
ARTHUR.   Do you mind if I do ?
ALBERT.   Oh, no !

ARTHUR.   Thanks. (*Sits on sofa with evening paper.*)

(*A long pause.*)

ALBERT.   I like these long summer evenings, don't you, sir?
ARTHUR.   No. As a matter of fact I prefer the short winter evenings.
ALBERT (*taken aback*). Oh . . .
ARTHUR.   I say, I suppose *you* don't know a thirteen-letter word meaning " possessed of a dual personality," do you?
ALBERT (*casually*). " Schizophrenic."

(ARTHUR *looks at him.*)

ARTHUR.   Oh. Oh, yes of course. Silly of me. Schizo . . . Now who the devil has removed that Toby jug ! That damn maid, I expect.

(*Enter* MARGARET *from* L. *with* FREDA *and* MARY.)

MARGARET.   Edna won't allow us to help her with the washing-up and insists that we come and sit down.
ARTHUR.   That was kind of her ! What do you think I pay her for?
FREDA (*to* ALBERT.) Hello, you. Still here?
MARGARET.   Hello, Albert. (*Sits beside* ARTHUR.) Freda will be in in a minute.
FREDA.   I'm already here, Mother !
MARGARET.   Oh, so you are. (*To* ARTHUR.) What's new in the paper, dear?
ARTHUR.   Nothing very much.

(MARGARET *takes pencil and crossword from* ARTHUR *leaving him the page of advertisements.* MARY *sits on window-seat.*)

FREDA (D.L.C.).   What do you want, Casanova?
ALBERT (*moving over to her*). I came to see you.
FREDA.   Well, here I am ! *Can* you see with those glasses?
ALBERT.   I wanted to talk to you.
FREDA.   Well? (ALBERT *casts a look at the others.*) It's all right. They won't listen. (*They move* D.L.)
ALBERT.   I just wondered if you were going to the Ball to-morrow night.
FREDA.   Of course I am, silly !
ALBERT.   Well—has anyone asked if they can take you yet?
FREDA.   Yes. Lots of people !
ALBERT.   Oh.
FREDA.   But I haven't said " yes " to anyone yet !
ALBERT.   Oh, good ! Well, could I——
FREDA.   But Peter Goodacre is very persistent.
MARGARET (*suddenly*). Good heavens ! Who's moved the Toby jug!
ARTHUR.   Don't shout in my ear.
MARGARET.   Sorry, dear.
ALBERT.   Well, I'd like to take you, if you've no one else better.
FREDA.   Well, you're not very exciting, are you? Why don't you go to the pictures and watch Michael Wilding?

ALBERT.　Oh, all right, I will. But I shan't have time before to-morrow night.

FREDA.　Well, I'm not promising anything, Albert. I did half say I'd go with Peter. I'll think it over !

ALBERT.　All right. Well, I'd better be getting along. Goodnight, Mrs. Purvis.

MARGARET.　Goodnight, Albert. We'll see you to-morrow.

ARTHUR.　'Night, son !

ALBERT.　Goodnight, sir, Goodnight, Miss Williamson.

MARY (*with a twinkle*). Bye-bye, Albert !

ALBERT (*near the door* L.). Well, goodnight.

FREDA.　Goodnight, you ! (*He starts to go.*) Albert. (*Moving to* R. *of him.*)

ALBERT.　Yes ?

FREDA (*in a whisper*). You can kiss me if you want to.

ALBERT.　Can I ? Can I really ?

FREDA.　Just once. (*He approaches.*) There ! (*Gestures to forehead.*)

(*He closes his eyes and kisses her quickly on the forehead. She closes her eyes.*)

FREDA.　Well ?

ALBERT.　Thanks very much ! (*He rushes out* L.)

(*She goes with him to the front door. A loud crash as he falls over the hall-stand. We hear her telling him not to be clumsy, etc., and then shouting " Goodbye!" Door slams off* L.)

ARTHUR (*reading*). I rather like this : " Gardener wishes to make acquaintance of young lady who owns motor lawn-mower with view to marriage. Please send photograph of motor-lawn-mower." (*He shrugs.*)

(*Re-enter* FREDA.)

MARY.　Why are you so cruel to that boy ?

FREDA (*taking an apple from the table and munching*). Cruel ?

MARY.　Yes.

FREDA.　I'm not cruel.

MARY (*rises and moves* D.S. *to* R. *of* FREDA). You may not do it consciously but every time you speak to him you say something to hurt him.

FREDA.　I don't mean to.

MARGARET.　Why not try being nice to him for a change, dear ?

FREDA.　Well, I . . .

MARGARET.　Don't you like him at all ?

FREDA.　Yes, of course I like him. I like him a lot.

ARTHUR.　Well, for God's sake tell him so and put him out of his misery !

FREDA (*loftily*). I'm too young to marry.

MARGARET.　Nobody mentioned marriage.

FREDA.　Besides, he's not my Ideal.

MARY.　Your what ?

FREDA. My Ideal.

MARY. What on earth is that ?

FREDA. My ideal man. Everybody has one. The person you'd like your husband to be. All the good things rolled into one.

MARY (*glancing at* ARTHUR, *as she moves chair to* D.R. *where she sits*). There must be a lot of shattered ideals in the world !

FREDA. But I must wait until He comes along, mustn't I ?

MARGARET. Darling, the man you marry will take the place of your ideal man, don't you see ? Do you imagine that your father is the sort of man anyone would dream of as an ideal ?

ARTHUR. Hey !

MARGARET (*taking his arm*). But I'm quite satisfied.

MARY. Besides a Perfect Man would be a dreadful thing to have about the house. Now run along—and try to think of something nice to say to Albert next time you see him.

FREDA (*at door* L.). I like him a lot, really, you know. (*She goes out* L.)

MARGARET. They make a nice pair, don't they ?

ARTHUR. Young Albert may not be a Romeo but he's an intelligent boy. He'll be doing well in a few years.

MARY. I liked him at once.

(*Enter* EDNA *from* L. *in a hurry.*)

EDNA. Oh Madam ! Something terrible has happened !

MARGARET. What is it, Edna ?

EDNA. The cakes, Mum——

MARGARET. The cakes ?

EDNA. The ones Miss Williamson was making. Burnt to a cinder ! !

(SHE *rushes out, followed by* MARGARET *and* MARY, *both screeching.*)

(ARTHUR *shakes his head and smiles. Takes out his pipe, and looks for tobacco pouch in pockets. He crosses to fireplace.*)

(*Enter* ROGER, *wearing a raincoat.*)

ARTHUR. Oh, aren't you away yet ?

ROGER. Just going now, Dad. Left my cigarette case here. (*He picks it up off table* C. *and moves to door* L.)

ARTHUR. Oh, Roger.

ROGER. Yes, Dad ?

ARTHUR. Do you *have* to go for a minute ?

ROGER. Why ?

ARTHUR. I just wanted to have a little talk with you, that's all.

ROGER (*lightly*). Oh, alright. (*Sits sofa.*) Fire away ! But don't be too long-winded, will you ?

(*Pause.*)

ARTHUR. Well . . . er . . . I . . .

ROGER. You know, you don't *have* to tell me, if you don't want to. I read a few books !

ARTHUR. Oh, it's not that! Have you seen my tobacco pouch around here ?

Roger (*smiling*). It's in your pocket, Dad.

Arthur. What? Oh—oh, yes, so it is. (*Starts to fill pipe.*) It's a very good brand, you know.

Roger. Is it?

Arthur. Yes. It's called Harvest Mixture. I never smoke any other. You might remember that on my next birthday. That'll save you buying that awful thick stuff you usually give me!

Roger. Well, is that all you wanted to say?

Arthur. No, Roger. That's not all. It's you. You seem a little on edge these days. Something on your mind? (*Pause. Roger does not reply.*) Is it a girl?

Roger. Why do you say that?

Arthur. No reason. (*Pause.*) Is it?

Roger. No.

Arthur. That's alright, then.

Roger. Have you finished cross-examining me?

Arthur. I wasn't doing that, Roger. (*Longish pause.*) If ever you're in any trouble—any sort of trouble at all I mean——

Roger. I'm not.

Arthur. No, but *if* you are, you will come and talk to me about it, won't you? That's what I'm here for, you know.

Roger (*softly, with a smile*). I'm not in any trouble, Dad. Do you mind if I go now?

Arthur. No, you run along. Sorry if I was a little clumsy about it.

(*Roger crosses to door L.*)

Oh, Roger.

Roger (*in doorway*). Yes?

Arthur. Don't forget, will you?

Roger. What?

Arthur (*gestures with tobacco pouch*). Harvest Mixture.

(*Roger goes out L.*)

(*Arthur sits on sofa thoughtfully filling his pipe. 'Phone bell rings throughout the next speeches.*)

Freda (*off L.*). Helen, can I borrow your Chanel?

Helen (*off L.*). No, certainly not! You're too young for Chanel!

Freda (*off L.*). Be a sport, Helen! I want to smell nice!

Helen (*off L.*). Not now. I'll let you to-morrow night for the Ball.

Freda (*off L.*). Oh, gee, thanks!

Helen (*off L.*). And don't go swilling it all over yourself!

Margaret (*off L.*). Arthur!

Arthur. Yes, dear?

Margaret (*off L.*). I think the 'phone's ringing! Will you answer it?

Arthur. Oh. Oh, yes. Alright, Margaret! (*He rises and crosses to 'phone.*)

Arthur. Hello? . . . No, this is not the Victoria and Albert Museum!

Quick Curtain.

ACT II.

SCENE 1.

(*The following Saturday evening. Curtains drawn, etc.*)

(*When curtain rises* MARGARET, *on sofa in evening dress, is assisting* FREDA *in fastening up the back of her evening gown. Enter* ARTHUR *from* L., *half-dressed.*)

ARTHUR. Who's taken my collar stud?
MARGARET. Nobody's taken it, dear. You've just mislaid it.
ARTHUR. It isn't where I put it, anyhow.
MARGARET. And where did you put it?
ARTHUR. In a safe place.
MARGARET. You shouldn't have done that. You know you can never find anything when you put it in one of your " safe places."
ARTHUR. It has been removed.
MARGARET. Why should anyone remove it, you silly darling? Go and look again.
ARTHUR. Alright, but don't blame me if I'm late! (*He goes.*)
MARGARET. There, that's alright, dear.
FREDA (*pirouetting*). Thank you, Mother. How do I look?
MARGARET. Very pretty.
FREDA. I want to look glamorous.
MARGARET. You're not old enough for that, darling.
FREDA. Well, I'm growing up!
MARGARET. Yes, my dear. But don't do it too quickly, will you?
FREDA. Peter says he hates very young girls. He thinks they're silly.
MARGARET. I wonder what the " very young girls " think of Peter.
FREDA. You don't like Peter, do you, Mummie?
MARGARET. Of course I like him, dear. But I shouldn't take anything he says seriously, if I were you. Has he told you *you're* silly?
FREDA. Of course not! He says I'm—mature and sophisticated. (*Poses against mantelpiece, but her foot slips and spoils it.*)
MARGARET. Oh, I see.
FREDA. Do *you* think I am?
MARGARET. Ye-es.
FREDA. You don't sound very certain.
MARGARET. I think you look very pretty.

(*Pause.*)

FREDA. Mummie, do you think Nigel and Helen will get married after all?

MARGARET.   I'm sure I don't know, dear, and you shouldn't ask such things.

FREDA.   But you and Daddy want them to, don't you?

MARGARET.   It's not what we want that matters.   It's what they want (*putting away needle and thread in workbasket*).

FREDA.   But you do, don't you?

MARGARET.   Perhaps.

FREDA.   Well, you wouldn't have invited Nigel here this weekend unless you hoped they'd get together again, would you?

MARGARET.   Never you mind.

FREDA.   Well, I hope they do, too.   I ought really to do my hair on top.

MARGARET.   Did Peter tell you to?

FREDA.   No.   But I know he likes it on top.

MARGARET.   It suits you better as it is.

(ARTHUR *appears again from* L.)

ARTHUR.   I still can't find it!

MARGARET.   Have you looked carefully?

ARTHUR.   Of course I've looked carefully, Margaret.   It isn't there.

MARGARET.   Well, you've got another one, haven't you?

ARTHUR.   Yes, but that's not the point.   This is a special one.   You know I always wear my expensive studs and links for the Annual Ball.

MARGARET.   Well, just for once you'll have to wear the inexpensive ones, dear.

ARTHUR.   I shall do no such thing.   I tell you someone has taken it! Where's Nigel?

(*He goes off, calling* " NIGEL! ")

FREDA.   Don't men fuss?

MARGARET (*pause*).   Who's taking you to the Ball to-night, Freda?

FREDA.   Peter, I expect.   He said he wanted to.

MARGARET.   So did Albert.

FREDA.   He can't dance.

MARGARET.   Can't he?

FREDA.   No.   Besides he's . . .

MARGARET.   He's what?

FREDA.   He's so shy.   He never knows what to say.

MARGARET.   And Peter does?

FREDA.   Yes.   Peter's amusing.

MARGARET.   Yes, dear, but be careful, won't you?   Don't hurt Albert. He's very sensitive, you know.

FREDA.   Alright, Mummie.   Won't be a minute!

(*She runs out* L., *bumping into* NIGEL *who is coming in*.)

FREDA.   Oh, sorry!   (*Exit.*)

NIGEL (*closing door* L.).   Did somebody call me?

MARGARET.   It was Arthur.   He thinks you've stolen his collar stud.

NIGEL. Not guilty. (*Stopping.*) While I remember, you've got me down for a waltz, a fox-trot, and the boomps-a-daisy, haven't you?
MARGARET. I have no such thing.
NIGEL. Then make a note of them, now.
MARGARET. No. You dance with the younger people.
NIGEL. Nonsense. You put them down and don't forget.
MARGARET. Well, alright, but only the waltz. Certainly not the boomps-a-daisy!
NIGEL. I insist.
MARGARET. We'll see!

(*Enter* ARTHUR *from* L.)

ARTHUR. Ah! There you are, Nigel!
NIGEL. Is anything the matter?
ARTHUR (*pointedly*). Someone has taken my front collar stud.
NIGEL. No!
ARTHUR. Can't find it anywhere.
NIGEL (*pointing*). But it's in your shirt, sir.
ARTHUR. What? (*Finds it.*) Oh, so it is.

(MARGARET *laughs.*)

Well, all I can say is, it wasn't there just now! (*Exit* L.)

(HELEN *rushes in from* L. *in a housecoat, colliding with* ARTHUR.)

HELEN. Where's my handbag?
MARGARET. Just where you left it, dear.

(HELEN *picks it up and rushes off* L. *She re-appears immediately.*)

HELEN. Hello, Nigel. You're all dolled up!
NIGEL. What are you doing all this time?
HELEN. Making myself beautiful for you, de-ah! (*Exit.*)
MARGARET. I've never seen this house thrown into such chaos since the time the cistern leaked and came through the roof. Arthur practically floated out through the window still asleep on the sofa!

(MARY *comes in from* L., *in a very colourful, Japanese-ey dress.*)

MARY (*entering*). Don't I look wonderful?
MARGARET. Like something out of Gilbert and Sullivan.
MARY. I've had such trouble with the bathroom. Helen was in there for hours, and when she came out the place smelt like a chemist's shop.
NIGEL. Let us hope that the result is worth it! (*Up to window seat.*)
MARY. And as soon as I got in there, that man—that man!
MARGARET. Do you mean my husband?
MARY. Yes. That man bangs on the door and says " What on earth are you doing in there, Mary—swimming? "
NIGEL. And were you?
MARY. Certainly not. As a matter of fact I was reading last Sunday's " News of the World."

(*Enter* EDNA.)

EDNA. Excuse me, Mum, but do you think I might be allowed to go, now?

MARGARET. Why, Edna?

EDNA. It's my young man. He's got a dreadful cold and I promised to rub his back with wintergreen before to-night.

MARGARET. You mean to say he's coming to the Ball smelling of wintergreen?

EDNA. Oh, no, Mum. I'll rinse him with eau de cologne afterwards.

MARGARET. Alright, Edna, you can go now, but make sure the cake for the party is iced first thing in the morning.

EDNA. Thank you, Mum.

(*She starts to go.*)

NIGEL. How's *your* cold, now Edna?

EDNA. Gone, thank you, sir.

NIGEL. Good!

EDNA. There's a lot of it about, you know.

NIGEL. Is there?

EDNA. Oh, yes. Everyone's getting it. One minute you're feeling fine—bright as a button! A smile on your face!—and the next minute—pouf!—you're down with it. Are you sure you aren't sitting in a draught, sir?

MARGARET. Go and put the cake in a safe place, Edna.

EDNA. Oh yes, Mum. (*At door.*) Come to think of it, sir, you do look pretty green about the gills. (*She goes out* L.)

MARGARET. Don't take any notice of her, Nigel. If we listened to her all day, we'd be in our graves!

NIGEL. Miss Williamson, you look very charming.

MARY. Thank you, Nigel.

NIGEL. But if you are going to the Ball you must hurry up and dress.

MARY. Dress! (*Witheringly.*) I am ready. This is it!

NIGEL. Oh, I beg your pardon! (*Moves to fireplace.*)

(*Enter* ARTHUR, *now fully dressed.*)

ARTHUR. Well, Nigel, how do I look?

MARY. Like a very old Portuguese fisherman.

ARTHUR. Alright, nobody asked *you*, Madame Butterfly!

(MARY *sits on sofa. Door bell rings.*)

MARGARET. See who it is, Arthur.

(ARTHUR *goes* L.)

It's possibly Albert come to see if Freda has made up her mind, yet.

ARTHUR (*off* L.). Hello, George, old man!

TODD (*off* L.). Hello, Arthur! Just wondered if you could loan me a front collar stud. The mice must eat 'em in my house!

MARGARET (*up* C.). It's Major Todd. He's Albert's guardian, you know, and really quite a dear when you get used to his manner.

(Enter ARTHUR.*)*

ARTHUR.   Look who's here!

(Enter MAJOR TODD. *A large, blustery ex-Army major. He is in evening dress, but wears a white scarf in place of collar and tie.)*

TODD.   Good evenin', all!

MARGARET.   Hello, George.   How nice of you to pop in.

TODD *(moving up* C. *to meet* MARGARET*).* I'm on the scrounge, dear lady, on the scrounge! Can't find a blessed collar stud in my house.

MARGARET.   Do you know everyone here?

TODD.   Think so, Mrs. Purvis, think so . . . Your sweet self, of course. And very lovely you look, too, if I may say so. You're a lucky man, Purvis. *(Shakes hands with each in turn.)* Ah, Nigel! You're quite a stranger around here. Nice to see you back on the old stampin' ground!

*(*MARGARET *moves* L.C. *towards* ARTHUR.*)*

NIGEL.   Thank you.

TODD *(to* MARY*).* Now, then, I've often seen you about the place but I've never had the pleasure.

MARGARET.   My sister, Mary Williamson.   Major Todd.

MARY.   How do you do.

TODD *(on her* R.*).* How do you do, Mrs. Williamson.

MARY.   *Miss* Williamson.

TODD.   Oh. Oh, well, can't have everything! You mean you're eligible?

MARY.   I'm redundant, if that's what you mean!

TODD.   What a lovely dress! If I may say so.

ARTHUR.   We were just admiring it, too, George.   *(*MARY *gives him a withering look.)* I'll get you that stud. *(Exit.)*

TODD *(moves* C.*).* Well, I'll string along with you all, if I may. May as well all get there together, eh? Don't like stragglers. Let's go en masse, and baffle 'em, eh? United we stand, and all that!

MARGARET.   Where's Albert?

TODD.   Not quite ready. Having difficulty with his shirt when I left him. Wouldn't let me help. In a bit of a flap, so I said I'd go ahead and do a recce and he could follow up with the rations, as it were. He'll be along in a little while. Told him not to be later than twenty hundred hours. *(To* MARY.*)* Are you booked for all the dances, Madame?

MARY.   Er—no, not all of them.

TODD.   May I book a couple of waltzes, then?

MARY.   Certainly.

TODD.   Thank you. I shall be honoured. Used to shake quite a nifty limb when I was a youngster, y'know.

MARY.   I can imagine.

(Crash off.)

TODD.   What the devil was that?

MARGARET.   I don't know, but I have an awful premonition.

(Doors open slowly. Enter EDNA, *dishevelled.)*

EDNA. You needn't give me notice, Mum. I'll just pack my things and go quietly. I knew it would happen. Me twinges told me that.

MARGARET. Edna, what was it?

EDNA. The cake, Mum.

MARGARET. No! Not *the* cake?

EDNA. Yes, *the* cake, Mum. I tripped over the carpet and fell flat on my face!

MARGARET. But the cake for the Anniversary?

EDNA. All over the 'all floor, Mum!

MARGARET. No!

(MARGARET *and* MARY *rush off, followed by* EDNA. ARTHUR *is pushed aside as he enters with a collar stud which he gives to* TODD.)

ARTHUR. Edna has spoilt the cake for to-morrow, I see. Here's your stud, George. Well, what about a drink everyone. (*General assent.*)

(*Enter* ROGER. *He is not dressed in evening clothes.*)

Roger. You're just in time for a drink.

TODD. Hello, my boy!

ROGER. Hello, sir.

ARTHUR. Whisky good enough for everyone?

TODD. No complaints, sir! (*Crosses to fireplace.*)

(ARTHUR *and* NIGEL *are pouring drinks.* *Enter* FREDA, *with her hair done on top.*)

NIGEL. Great jumping Jehosophat!

FREDA. What's the matter? Don't you like it?

NIGEL. Yes, indeed I like it. You're grown up all of a sudden.

TODD. Charmin', my dear—charmin'.

FREDA. Oh, hello, Major Todd. Do you like it?

TODD. Immensely, immensely!

ARTHUR. Whose idea was that?

FREDA. Mine, of course.

ARTHUR. Was it?

FREDA. Well—Peter Goodacre suggested it, really.

ARTHUR. I thought so. Is he wearing his on top, too? Lord knows it's long enough!

(*Re-enter* MARGARET *and* MARY. *They sit on sofa.*)

MARGARET. After that I think *I* need one of those whiskies.

ARTHUR. You bet! Mary?

MARY. Well, I really don't ——

TODD. Go on, my dear Madame! Must have a bracer before we leave.

MARY. Oh, very well. But I mustn't make a habit of it.

TODD. Why not, eh? Why not? Been a habit of mine for years. Never done me any harm.

NIGEL. That's a matter of opinion.

ARTHUR. Now, has everyone got?

FREDA. I haven't!

MARGARET. You're too young.

FREDA. I'm seventeen, Mother!

NIGEL. Give her a short whisky and a long splash, Mr. Purvis.

ARTHUR. Don't let this create a precedent, now.

(*Enter* HELEN, *now in an evening gown.*)

(NIGEL *gives a wolf whistle, and the others murmur approvingly.*)

NIGEL.   My, my! How beautiful you look to-night!

HELEN.   Thank you, Sir Galahad.

NIGEL.   Well, I shall certainly be the envy of all the men to-night.

HELEN.   What makes you think I shall be with *you* all the time?

TODD.   Hello, my dear.

HELEN.   Are we going to samba together as usual?

TODD.   You bet! You bet! Pretty nifty couple we make, you know, Nigel.

ARTHUR (*handing her a drink*). Here you are, my dear.

HELEN.   Thanks, Pop.

TODD.   I think this calls for a speech, what do you say? Come on, Arthur, old man! Better get some practice in for this evening, y'know.

ALL.   Yes, speech! Come on, Arthur! Speech!

ARTHUR (*reluctantly*). Oh, alright.

(*The rest sit around to listen.*)

What shall I say?

TODD.   Anything, old boy! Anything!

MARGARET.   Come on, darling!

(*A pause.*)

ARTHUR.   Hey, you come and hold my hand!

(*She does so.   Another pause as he considers an opening.*)

Well—er—twenty-five years of married life is nothing out of the ordinary in this modern age of long life and medical science. Everybody does it. Anyhow, Margaret and I have done it.

(*Cheers and applause.*)

Maybe it was because we couldn't afford the divorce but we stuck together. (*Laughs.*) And anyhow she's a pretty good cook, and I should have had to pay a housekeeper, anyway. (*Laughs.*) And she would have had to pay some odd-job man to cut the grass on the lawn and keep the dandelions down. And then there were the children—so we *had* to be Allies against *their* united force. (*Laughs.*) Anyhow, now we look back I can hardly believe it's twenty-five years to-morrow since we married. She hasn't changed a bit. She looks just as lovely now as she did on the day we met.

(*Applause.*)

MARGARET.　Oh, Arthur.

ARTHUR.　Well, you do to me anyhow. (*Pause.*) By the time the next twenty-five years have rolled by there'll be changes in this house. The children—they won't be children then—will be married, and, God willing, Mother and I will be Grandma and Grandpa. That'll date me! (*Laughs.*) Anyway, if we're still here—and we're going to try very hard to be—then I hope *you'll* all be here, too. (*Pause.*) I shall be too old to crack any jokes. Any new ones anyhow. (*Quiet laughter.*) But I shall be able to give you a toast. Just as I can now. (*Raising his glass.*) To the *next* twenty-five years. And may they be as happy for you young people as the past twenty-five years have been to your Mother and me.

ALL.　The next twenty-five years!

(*They all drink.*)

TODD (*amid murmurs of approval for the speech*).　You should have been a politician, Arthur.

(*Door bell rings.*)

NIGEL.　That's the taxi!

(ARTHUR *goes out to door. Exit* L. *Activity from everyone—glasses down, bags up, coats on, etc.* TODD, MARY *and* ARTHUR *retain their glasses.*)

MARGARET.　Oh, dear, and I'm not quite ready yet!

MARY.　Well, let the young people go on now, and we'll follow on the second trip.

MARGARET.　Yes, alright.

NIGEL.　All set, Helen?

HELEN.　Yes, I'm ready.

FREDA.　I can't go yet. Peter said he'd call for me.

NIGEL.　Just the two of us on this trip, then, Helen?

HELEN.　Yes, darling. Aren't you lucky?

MARGARET.　Now, make sure the taxi comes back, won't you?

HELEN.　Don't panic, Mother.

ARTHUR (*off* L.).　Come on, you people!

NIGEL.　Coming!

(*Exit* HELEN *and* NIGEL *amidst good-byes, followed by* ROGER *and* MARGARET.)

(*The* MAJOR *discovers he is alone with* MARY *and reacts.*)

(*A pause. Bus.*)

MARY.　Cheers!

TODD.　Selfridge's!

(*They drink.*)

TODD.　How is it I've never run into you before?

MARY.　I can't think, Major.

TODD.　Makes you wonder, doesn't it?

MARY.　Oh, yes. It does.

TODD.　Might even be sort of—Fate, mightn't it?

MARY. Yes, I suppose it might.

TODD. H'm. Dickins and Jones! (*They drink.*) I'm looking forward to this Ball, y'know. I was a demon at the Tango in my youth.

MARY. Really?

TODD. Yes, rather. Knew about thirty-seven different variations.

MARY. You must show me to-night.

TODD. 'Course, I'm not as agile as I was! Not bad whisky, this, is it?

MARY. I'm afraid I don't drink enough to know.

TODD. Let's drink to our meeting, eh?

MARY. Alright.

TODD. To—Fate.

MARY. Fate!

(*Enter* ARTHUR.)

ARTHUR. Oh! . . .

(*They react to his presence.*)

Will you excuse me? I'd better go and powder my nose. (*He hurries out again.*)

TODD. What did he say?

MARY. Said he was going to powder his nose.

TODD. Huh! Must be this stuff. Probably isn't used to it. Now, when I was out in Africa we drank oodles of this stuff—oodles!

MARY. Really?

TODD. Oodles. Yes. Thought up all sorts of potent brews out there. One of our specialities was the Kilimanjaro Cocktail.

MARY. It sounds *very* potent.

TODD. Cheers!

MARY. Swan and Edgar's! (*He reacts to this.*)

TODD. Look, why don't we pop along to my place now, and have one to set us up for the evening?

MARY. Well, I——

TODD. No excuses, Madame! Come along! We'll meet the rest of 'em at the Ball.

MARY. Oh, very well.

TODD (*at door* L.). We'll see you there, Arthur!

ARTHUR (*off* L.). Alright. (*Pause.*) Who's we?

TODD. Miss Williamson and myself, sir!

ARTHUR (*off* L.). Oh, alright.

MARY. We'll see you there!

TODD. 'Bye!

(*They go. Door slams. A pause.*)

(*Enter* ARTHUR. *He crosses to fireplace and lights his pipe.*)

(*Enter* MARGARET.)

ARTHUR. Did you hear what I heard? (*To* L. *of sofa.*)

MARGARET. I think I did.

ARTHUR. Oh well, perhaps we shall get Mary married off after all!

MARGARET. They were just being friendly. (*Sits* L. *end of sofa.*)

ARTHUR. I don't think so. George had a look in his eyes the like of which I've never seen there before. (*He sits on sofa* R. *of her.*)

MARGARET. You made a nice little speech to-night.

ARTHUR. Thank you.

MARGARET. Made me feel all warm inside.

ARTHUR. Did it?

MARGARET. H'm. (*Pause.*) Do you know something?

ARTHUR. What?

MARGARET. I like being married to you.

ARTHUR. Only about another fifty years to go. (*Takes her hand.*)

MARGARET. Not long enough.

(*Door bell rings off* L.)

That can't be the taxi, already!

FREDA (*off* L.). Alright, Mother, I'll go!

ARTHUR (*sombrely*). Peter Goodacre.

MARGARET. Oh, dear.

ARTHUR. Let's hope she'll get over it in time.

MARGARET. I don't want her to hurt Albert. I'm afraid she will if she goes to the Ball with Peter.

FREDA (*putting her head around the door* L.). It's Peter. Look what he's brought me! (*Brandishes a cellophane box containing orchids.*) Orchids! Isn't it smashing of him? We're off now, then. See you later. Good-bye!

MARGARET. Good-bye, dear.

ARTHUR. Cheerio!

(*Exit* FREDA. *Door slams off* L.)

Poor old Albert. What'll he say when he comes to see if she's ready?

MARGARET. It's quite late. Perhaps he isn't coming after all. I do hope something good has cropped up to stop him coming.

(*A long pause.*)

The house feels suddenly cold.

ARTHUR. It is nice having a crowd in, isn't it?

MARGARET. I don't like it when they go. The place gets so—so empty.

ARTHUR. Sentimental creature! It's got to happen sometime. They'll still pop in and see us occasionally.

MARGARET. Yes, but that's different somehow. It'll be dreadful to think they won't belong here any more.

ARTHUR. They'll always belong here, really.

MARGARET. It'll be so lonely when they don't rush in for meals and things. And none of their clothes about the place.

ARTHUR (*after a pause*). Well, I know it's only small compensation, but—I'll still be here.

MARGARET. Oh, Arthur, I'm sorry. I didn't mean it like that.

ARTHUR. Don't worry. We'll be alright. It'll be like being married all over again. Just the two of us.

c

MARGARET (*kissing the top of his head*). Now who's being sentimental?
(*Door bell rings off* L.) (*They look at each other.*) Oh, dear . . . (MAR-
GARET *goes off* L.) (*Off* L.) Oh, hello, Albert. Come in.

(*Door slams.*)

(*Enter* ALBERT *in evening dress, looking quite presentable.* MARGARET
follows him in and remains L.C. *He is carrying a small bunch of flowers.*)

ALBERT. Good evening, Mr. Purvis.
ARTHUR. Hello, Albert. Did you see the Major?
ALBERT. No. I thought he was here.
ARTHUR. You must have just missed them.
ALBERT. Yes.

(*A pause.* ALBERT *looks around the room,* MARGARET *looks painfully at*
ARTHUR.)

ALBERT. Er—is—is Freda ready?
MARGARET. Well, I—(*gesticulates " You tell him " to* ARTHUR.)
ARTHUR. I'm afraid she's gone, Albert.
ALBERT. Gone?
ARTHUR. Yes.

(*Long pause.* ALBERT *looks from one to the other.*)

ALBERT. Oh. Oh, well, never mind. I didn't really think that . . . It
doesn't matter . . . not really.
ARTHUR (*rising and moving* R.). Like a drink, my boy?
ALBERT. Oh, no, thank you, Mr. Purvis. (ARTHUR *sits* D.R.) Mrs.
Purvis, would you be offended if I gave you some flowers?
MARGARET. Oh, Albert.
ALBERT (*handing her the spray of flowers he has brought in with him*).
I'm sorry that they're—well, sort of second hand.
MARGARET. I don't mind a bit ! Thank you very much. I shall
wear them to-night. (*Takes them.*)
ALBERT. Well, I'll be off, now.
ARTHUR. Aren't you coming to the dance?
ALBERT. No, I—I don't think so. Not now.
MARGARET. But you're all dressed up. It would be a shame not to go.
ALBERT. I don't feel very comfortable in these things.
MARGARET. You look very nice.
ALBERT. Do I?
MARGARET. Very smart.
ALBERT. Thanks very much.
MARGARET. The young ladies at the dance will be missing a treat if
you don't go.

(ARTHUR *covers his face with the newspaper.*)

ALBERT. I'm no ladies' man !
MARGARET. That's surely for the ladies to decide.

ALBERT.   They think I'm daft.

MARGARET.   I'm sure they don't.

ALBERT.   They laugh at me.

MARGARET.   That's because they like you, and you're amusing.   Lots of men try to be amusing, you know.   It's a very enviable accomplishment.

ALBERT.   But I don't have to try to be amusing.   They laugh at me anyway.   You see, I'm not very bright.   I mean, I can't talk about Blue Pacific skies and Love and all that stuff.   I wish I could.   People just find me dull.

MARGARET.   *I* never find you dull.

ALBERT.   That's because you're sorry for me.

MARGARET.   No, I'm not.   Look, why don't you go to the dance ?

ALBERT.   Well, I was hoping to take Freda, but it seems she's otherwise engaged for the evening.

MARGARET.   Freda isn't the only girl in the world.

ALBERT.   She is as far as I'm concerned.   I'm happy with her because I can relax a bit.   When other girls are about I feel self-conscious and can't say a word ;   and all the time I'm racking my brains for some sparkling funny thing to say, and thinking that if I don't say something soon they'll think I'm dense : and as soon as that happens I can never think of anything !

MARGARET.   You try too hard.   It's only in books that the young man speaks to his lady love in poetry.   (*She glances at* ARTHUR *who is apparently dozing beneath his newspaper.*)   Look, fast asleep.   I'll let you into a secret, if you promise not to tell my husband.

ALBERT.   I won't tell.

MARGARET.   When Arthur proposed to me, he hardly said a word !   He stammered and stuttered, and eventually I had to say " Are you asking me to marry you ? " and he said " Yes.   Will you ? " and I said " Yes " and that was that!

ALBERT.   Not very romantic.

ARTHUR (*from beneath his newspaper*).   Don't you believe it.

MARGARET.   I thought you were asleep.

ARTHUR (*removing paper*).   Let that be a lesson to you!

ALBERT.   Do you think Freda knows ?   How I feel about her, I mean.

MARGARET.   Not if you've never told her.

ALBERT.   Well, I did try once.   We'd just come out of the pictures after seeing " Passionate Nights," and we were walking home through the Park.   I held my breath and took her hand, and I was just going to take the plunge when she pulled her hand away and said " Aren't your hands hot ! "

MARGARET.   What a shame !   Did you try again ?

ALBERT.   Oh no.

MARGARET.   Why not ?

ALBERT.   Well, it isn't very nice, is it ?   Having hot hands, I mean.   Is there a cure ?

MARGARET.   Yes.   Self-confidence.   You develop self-confidence and you'll soon forget all about hot hands.

ALBERT. But how can I develop it? I'm frightened whenever I'm near a woman. I've no conversation, I'm not good-looking, I can't dance, I can't play tennis and I'm afraid of water! Couldn't be much worse, could I?

MARGARET. Well, you must learn how to do those things if it'll make you happier. But it isn't necessary.

ALBERT. Learn?

ARTHUR. We've all got to learn sometime. I couldn't swim until I was twenty-one.

ALBERT. I wouldn't know how to start.

MARGARET. Well, I'll start by teaching you how to dance.

ALBERT. I don't want to take up your time.

MARGARET. I shall enjoy it. Make me feel young again. What about your hair, first of all. Got a comb?

ALBERT. Yes. (*He produces one.*)

MARGARET. Now, then—comb! (*He does so.*) Better already. You're not at all bad-looking when you want to be.

ALBERT. You're just saying that.

MARGARET. I'm meaning it, too. Now then, conversation.

ALBERT. I never know what to say.

MARGARET. Once you stop trying to think of something, you'll be alright.

ARTHUR (*rising and moving above sofa*). Only two things to remember. Never talk about yourself. Nobody's interested. But always ask other people about *themselves*. You'll find that they'll talk for hours and then admire *you* for your conversational brilliance. It's infallible. (*He goes to radiogram, turns it on and selects a record.*)

MARGARET. Now, you're going to that dance if I have to drag you there! (*pulling him into the* C. *of room*). Now—the waltz! One long pace and two short ones—alright?

ALBERT. One long pace and two short ones.

MARGARET. Ready? Now! (*They try to dance.*) One-two-three. One-two-three. One-two-three.

(*He trips.*)

ALBERT. Oh, I'll never do it!

MARGARET. Of course you will. Now, come on!

(ARTHUR *drops the needle on the record.*)

ALBERT. Why are you doing this for me, Mrs. Purvis?

MARGARET. Lots of reasons.

ALBERT. What reasons?

MARGARET. Well—because I like you. And perhaps because *I* don't like Peter Goodacre much either! Now, come on—DANCE!

(*With the gramophone playing a waltz tune,* MARGARET *calls out* " One-two-three " *and drags* ALBERT *round the room in a frantic waltz as* ARTHUR *watches them, smiling.*)

QUICK CURTAIN.

Scene 2.

(*When the curtain rises* ROGER, *in a dressing-gown, is lying on the sofa with a book. The radio is on, and a dance orchestra is playing a slow fox-trot. Standard lamp and table lamp on only.*)

(*Door bell rings off* L.)

(ROGER *gets up and goes off* L.)

ROGER (*off*). Hullo, Albert.
ALBERT (*off*). I left my hat here.
ROGER (*off*). Come on in for a bit.

(*They enter.*)
The Ball over ?
ALBERT. Not quite. I left before the end. I hope I'm not interrupting you.
ROGER. Of course not, Albert. (*Turns off radio.*) I was just listening to some dance music before turning in.
ALBERT. Keep the radio on, if you want to, I won't stay.
ROGER. No, it's alright. I wasn't really enjoying it. I—I think I'd rather talk to somebody at the moment. That is, if you don't mind staying and talking for a bit.
ALBERT. I'm not very good at it.
ROGER. Neither am I. Perhaps we can help each other out. Now— tell me about the Ball. Was it any good ? (*Sits on sofa.*)
ALBERT. Quite good, I think. Everyone seemed to be enjoying themselves. I think you would have liked it. (*Sits beside* ROGER.)
ROGER. Oh, I don't know. Did you ?
ALBERT. Yes.
ROGER (*with a smile*). Is that why you left early ?
ALBERT. I'm not very good at that sort of thing. I trod on Freda's toes, I'm afraid. She wouldn't dance with me again after that. She was doing a samba with Peter Goodacre when I left.
ROGER. What a shame. (*Pause.*) Are you very fond of Freda ?
ALBERT. Yes.
ROGER. I thought so.
ALBERT. I don't think I'm very good as a lover.
ROGER. Neither am I !
ALBERT. Have you had much experience of women ?
ROGER (*lightly*). No, not much. I had a crush on a girl in the Fifth Form when I was at school. She had red hair—masses of it !—but she let me down and went off with an awful urchin from the Upper Fourth !
ALBERT. You don't know what it's like, then ?
ROGER (*quietly, looking away*). No. No, I don't know what it's like.

(*During the next few speeches they are not looking at each other.*)

ALBERT. Supposing you loved somebody very much, and knew that you could never live without them, and they went off and married somebody else, what would you do?

ROGER. I don't know. I suppose I'd try to forget about it.

ALBERT. What if you couldn't?

ROGER. I just don't know.

ALBERT. You see, I still have a bit of hope with Freda, but I think I'd die if she said she was going to marry Peter Goodacre.

ROGER. No, you wouldn't. You'd find something to take your mind off it.

ALBERT. It's not easy to explain . . . and I suppose it's hard to understand, when you haven't been in love yourself.

ROGER (*rises and moves to fire, brightly*). Oh, I read about it in a book, though! Be practical, it said. Reduce life to an algebraic formula. It all works out quite easily in the end. Love is the unknown—X—and works out quite simply to three places of decimals !

(*Enter* FREDA, *now wearing the orchids*.)

FREDA. What are *you* doing here?

ROGER. I was talking to Albert.

FREDA. Not you—him !

ALBERT. I was talking to Roger. I came to collect my hat.

FREDA. Oh.

(*Pause.* ROGER *looks between them.*)

ROGER. Have a nice time?

FREDA. Yes, thank you. (*Takes off orchids and puts them on table* L. *of sofa.*)

ROGER. Splendid !

(FREDA *takes off her coat.*)

Is the Ball over?

FREDA. Not yet. Peter brought me back before the rush started.

ALBERT. I thought so. Your lipstick's smudged.

ROGER (*crossing to* L.C.). Do you mean to say you wear lipstick at your age?

FREDA. Why not?

ROGER No reason !

(*Another pause.* FREDA *glares at* ALBERT.)

Well—er—I may as well go to bed. I seem to be rather superfluous down here. Goodnight. (*He waits for a reply. There isn't one. He shrugs and goes off* L.)

ALBERT. Did you have a nice time?

FREDA. Yes, thank you !

ALBERT. So did I. (*Pause.*) Did you see Peter Goodacre during supper?

FREDA. No, I didn't. He went out for a smoke.

ALBERT. I saw him.

FREDA. Did you?

ALBERT. Yes. (*Pause.*) Do you want to know where I saw him ?
FREDA. Not particularly.
ALBERT. He was kissing Sarah Logan.
FREDA. Where ?
ALBERT. Right in the middle of the balcony !
FREDA. I don't believe it !
ALBERT. It's true.
FREDA. You've been drinking !
ALBERT. Only a little—and I feel much better for it !

(*Pause.*)

FREDA (*with a superior air*). Hadn't you better go ?
ALBERT. Can I speak to you for a minute first ?
FREDA. We've got no chaperone.
ALBERT What do you want a chaperone for ?
FREDA. You should know, you—you Fifth Form wolf!
ALBERT. Please . . .
FREDA (*touched by his tone*). Oh, alright, Albert. Go ahead. But if you don't mind I'm going to hold this in case you get carried away!

(*She grabs the poker from the fireplace and holds it between them.*)

ALBERT. I've been wanting to say this for a long time, but I've always lacked the courage at the last minute, or something has cropped up to interrupt me. Now at last we're alone, and—Blast!

(*Voices can be heard off* L.)

FREDA. Somebody's coming! Whatever will they think if they find you here alone with me—and no chaperone ! In there, quickly !

(*She pushes him into the room up* R. *and shuts the door. She starts to go towards the door* L. *but the voices of* NIGEL *and* HELEN *are heard just outside. She switches off lights and then turns and rushes back* R. *and goes off* R. *and shuts the door.*)

(*Enter* NIGEL *and* HELEN. *They are gay, but by no means drunk. She turns on the lights.*)

NIGEL. " But soft! What light through yonder window breaks ? It is the East and Juliet is the sun . . ."
HELEN. You're very poetic to-night.
NIGEL. Why not ? There's a moon as big as a soup plate out there that does things to my senses. And it's shining just for me.
HELEN. How very considerate of the man who holds the lantern !
NIGEL. Not at all. I give him bones for his dog. (*He kisses her lightly.*)
HELEN. Aren't you forgetting something ?
NIGEL. What ?
HELEN. I'm the girl you *aren't* engaged to.
NIGEL. You like it, don't you ?

HELEN. That's not the point.
NIGEL. I'm sorry.
HELEN. You're not a bit sorry.
NIGEL. No, I know, but it's only polite to say so. (*Sits on sofa.*)
HELEN. Like a drink?
NIGEL. Now you're talking sense. A large whisky and soda.
HELEN (*pouring*). One large whisky and soda for the gentleman sitting
by the pink elephant under the table.
NIGEL. What are *you* having?
HELEN. Nothing.
NIGEL. Oh, go on. I can't drink alone.
HELEN. Are you trying to get me tight?
NIGEL. Why not?
HELEN. I know you.
NIGEL. Well, don't say it like that.
HELEN. Like what?
NIGEL. " I know you." Makes me sound like an old wolf.
HELEN. That's right.
NIGEL. Oh, for heaven's sake, have a drink !
HELEN. Alright, but——
NIGEL. Behave myself ! Alright, I know. (*Pause.*) Mind you don't
spill it on your crinoline.

(*She gives him a drink, and has one herself.*)

Thanks!
HELEN (*lifting glass*). Good hunting!
NIGEL. Don't encourage me. Tally-ho! (*They drink.*)

(*She goes as if to sit next to him, thinks better of it and sits on the divan* D.L.)

NIGEL (*pretending to call over a great distance*). Hey, you! . . .
HELEN. Who—me?
NIGEL. Yes.
HELEN. What?
NIGEL. Come over here.
HELEN. Only if you promise to behave yourself.
NIGEL. Scout's honour !

(*She sits beside him. There is a pause.*)

HELEN. Well?
NIGEL. What do you mean—well?
HELEN. Well, what do you want?
NIGEL. You have no soul.
HELEN. I know you.
NIGEL. Don't keep saying " I know you "!

(*Silence. They look at each other, smile.*)

I have a feeling of romance coming over me.
HELEN. I thought I recognised the symptoms.

NIGEL. What symptoms?
HELEN. Your left ear is twitching.
NIGEL. I don't believe it.
HELEN. It is.
NIGEL. My left ear never twitches !
HELEN. Well, it's twitching now.
NIGEL. Not noticeably.
HELEN. Quite enough. It's sending out little danger signals on a high frequency.
NIGEL. You haven't got one ounce of romance in you, do you know that ?
HELEN. I'm glad of it—if it would mean my left ear would twitch. (*Pause.*) Do you know—I feel hungry.
NIGEL. Do you? Good. So do I.
HELEN. What would you like ?
NIGEL. Cold roast duckling and pickled onions.
HELEN. You've got a hope ! I could get you some cold ham.
NIGEL. Cold ham it is ! Can I help?
HELEN. Certainly not. I know you in the kitchen.
NIGEL. You've had my word of honour as a Cub Leader. What more do you want ?
HELEN. I want you to stay here. Play the gramophone or something.
NIGEL. I don't want to play the gramophone or something.
HELEN. I won't be long. (*She goes out* L.)

(NIGEL *rises and puts out the main lights and the table lamp—two cues— and then turns on the radio. He sits on sofa again. An orchestra is playing " Clair de Lune " (Andre Kostelanetz).*)

(*After a moment* HELEN *re-appears, with coffee cups. She stops in the doorway and takes in the lighting change.*)

HELEN. Have the lights failed, de-ar ? (*Cups down on table.*)
NIGEL (*rising*). My God! What a merciful release when I didn't marry you! You've no sensitivity at all! I'd rather be married to a—a boa constrictor!
HELEN (*sweetly*). Well, why don't you propose to one, dear ? (*She goes off again.*)

(NIGEL *puts the lights on again—two cues—and switches off radio. Takes a book from the shelf and stretches out on the sofa, reading.*)

(*Enter* HELEN *with sugar basin and milk jug. She puts them on the small table* D.S. *near the fire. She registers the lighting as she comes in.*)

HELEN. Reading, darling?
NIGEL. Yes. Trying to improve my mind.
HELEN. What's the book called ?
NIGEL (*looks at cover*). " Little Women."

(HELEN *goes round to the lights, deliberately turning them off again. He reacts, but pretends not to notice, and continues reading. She pushes his feet off the sofa. She sits. Pause. She moves up close to him. He looks at her.*)

NIGEL.   Got enough room, darling ?
HELEN (*snuggling up to him*).   Do I look like a boa-constrictor ?
NIGEL.   Yes, you do !   (*Softening.*)   But only in the moonlight.

(*They kiss.*)

HELEN.   Gosh!   The coffee!   (*She rushes out.*)

(*He smiles. Moves back to the radio and turns it on again. After a suitable pause,* HELEN *comes back with two plates of cold ham and potato salad, plus two forks, and a pot of coffee.*)

HELEN.   All ready.
NIGEL.   It looks wonderful.   (*She puts the plates on the table, and they begin to eat, sitting on the window seat.*)   H'm—very nice.

(*Pause. Music. Eating.*)

NIGEL (*quietly, after a pause*).   Do you ever get that feeling that you'd like to do something very much but you don't know if you ought to or not ?
HELEN.   Frequently.   I often see things in shop windows that are really far too expensive for me to afford.
NIGEL.   What do you do about them ?
HELEN.   I usually buy them.
NIGEL.   Well, there's something I'd very much like to do, now.
HELEN.   Is there ?
NIGEL.   Yes.
HELEN.   What is it ?
NIGEL.   I—I'd like very much to kiss you.
HELEN.   Then—I think I would . . .

(*He kisses her gently on the lips.*)

NIGEL.   Can you hear my heart beating ?
HELEN.   Yes.
NIGEL.   Oh, good.   I thought it had stopped !
HELEN.   Beast!
NIGEL.   I want to talk to you.   Look, Helen, I've tried to kid myself about us, but it's no use pretending any more.   I happen to be very much in love with you, and the fact that occasionally we quarrel doesn't alter that one bit.
HELEN (*crossing* D.R.C.).   Nigel, we've been through all this before.   It wouldn't work darling.   We tried before and it didn't work.   (*Pause.*) When I marry I want my home to be happy all the time—*all* the time, Nigel—not spoilt by constant rows.
NIGEL (*following her*).   Look at us—we're not rowing now, are we ?

Helen. That's only because we've had more than a little to drink and we haven't seen each other for a long time. (*With a smile.*) The novelty—and the alcohol—will wear off by the morning.

Nigel (*ruffled*). You won't even try!

Helen. There you are. Even the moonlight doesn't stop us for long.

Nigel. Only because you're being unreasonable!

Helen. Unreasonable! You think it was easy for me to break off our engagement? Do you? Do you think I enjoyed those weeks and months afterwards—never seeing you from one day to the next—missing you like hell!

Nigel. Hey, darling——

Helen (*almost in tears*). And now, just when I thought I was getting over it all, Daddy has to invite you back to the house and start it all over again! (*Tears.*)

(*A pause.*)

Nigel. I'm sorry, Helen. I'm terribly sorry. I should never have come back.

Helen. No, Nigel—it's me—I'm being beastly. Forgive me. I'm just overtired.

(*Long pause.*)

Nigel (*very quietly*). I say . . . we've forgotten the coffee . . .

Helen (*wiping eyes, smiles at him*). So we have.

Nigel. Shall I be father?

Helen. Please.

(*He pours it out.*)

Nigel. Milk?

Helen. No, thank you. (*Sits on sofa.*)

Nigel (*handing it to her*). There you are.

Helen. Thank you. (*He sits beside her again.*)

(*Pause. They sip coffee.*)

Nigel. I'm sorry I upset you and spoilt your evening.

Helen (*touching his arm*). You haven't spoilt my evening. I've had a wonderful time. Really.

Nigel. I'm so glad. So have I.

Helen (*after a slight pause*). But, please, Nigel—please never ask me again—about us. It wouldn't work, not for long. I want to bring my children up in a happy atmosphere, and you know just as I do what tempers we both have. We always say the very things that hurt and upset each other.

Nigel. We don't mean to——

Helen. But we still do it.

Nigel (*gently*). I don't expect my home to be without its little storms. I don't believe any happy home really is. It's a poor marriage that can't weather the rough passages.

Helen. No, Nigel. I've made up my mind.

Nigel. I believe you really mean that.

HELEN.   I do.

NIGEL.   Alright, darling.   I won't mention it again.

HELEN.   Thank you.

NIGEL (*casually*).   But I still love you.

HELEN (*catching his mood*).   Once you get away from here and think of me, weeping like this, you'll thank yourself for a merciful escape.

NIGEL.   I shall have to marry my typewriter, that's all!   (*Pause. Softly.*)   Still friends?

HELEN.   Of course !   Perhaps we'd better get back for the end of the Ball, hadn't we ?   They'll be wondering what's become of us.

NIGEL.   Right.

HELEN.   I'll just put these things away.

(*She collects up the plates, etc., on a tray and takes them off L. NIGEL turns off the radio. Then the lights. HELEN re-appears. He crosses to her. They look at each other for a moment.*)

NIGEL (*quietly*).   Let's go.

(*They go out.   Door slams off.*)

(*FREDA appears from door up R.   She turns on the lights.*)

FREDA.   It's alright, Albert.   They've gone.

(*ALBERT comes out, dishevelled.*)

And wipe that lipstick off your face !

(*He does so, sheepishly.*)

I knew I couldn't trust you.   I'm going to bed.

ALBERT.   Please don't go yet.   I want to talk to you.

FREDA.   Why aren't you more romantic ?   If only you were like Nigel.   Some girls have all the luck !

ALBERT.   Don't go away !

FREDA.   I think I'd better.   You've got a funny look in your eye !

ALBERT.   Please don't.   I must ask you something now.   I shan't get another chance like this.

FREDA.   Well, wait a minute.   Let me get the poker, first.

(*She does so and holds it between them as before.*)

Well ? . . .

ALBERT.   It's just that . . .   Oh, that thing puts me off !

FREDA.   Alright, I'll put it behind my back.   But don't you forget it's there !

(*Pause.*)

Well, get on with it, silly !

ALBERT.   I don't really know how to start . . .   Well, as I told you, I've just got this good job.   It'll mean quite a bit of money coming in, and I shall be able to start to save a bit . . .

FREDA.   Yes?

ALBERT.   Well, after a while I shall be able to think about arranging a mortgage on a little house in the country that I've rather taken a fancy to.

FREDA.   A house?

ALBERT.   Oh, it's not very big ! But there's room for two. (*Pause.*) Or three.

FREDA.   Albert, are you proposing to me?

ALBERT.   I know I'm not much to look at, and I'm not right bright at conversation, but I'm a hard worker, I don't drink—well, not usually —and I don't run after other women . . . and I'd try very hard to make you happy. Oh, and I do love thee, lass.

FREDA.   Oh, Albert . . .

ALBERT.   You don't have to answer right away. I'm not likely to change my mind. Think it over. I'll wait.

FREDA.   Oh, Albert, I—I like you, Albert, I like you a lot. But—but I . . .

ALBERT.   But you don't love me.

FREDA.   No, Albert. I don't think I do. I'm—sorry.

(*He looks at her, smiles, looks away.*)

ALBERT.   Oh, that's alright. I—I didn't really think there'd be much hope . . . but I had to ask. You—you aren't angry, are you?

FREDA (*brightly*). Angry? Oh, Albert, of course not. I'm very flattered. (*She finds herself feeling sorry for him and quickly adds :*) Perhaps you'd better go before anyone else comes back. I'll get your hat! (*She rushes off* L.)

(ALBERT *moves above the sofa. He suddenly catches sight of the orchids on the table. He picks them up and looks at them for a moment, then he sighs, slips both hands into his jacket pockets and moves slowly towards the door.*)

THE CURTAIN FALLS.

ACT III.

(*The following Sunday evening.*)

(*When the curtain rises the stage is empty. The lights are on and the room is decorated with paper trimmings, etc. One sign over the window says "HAPPY SILVER ANNIVERSARY" in bold colourful lettering.*)

(*Voices off* L. *are heard singing the closing few bars of "For He's a jolly Good Fellow." It ends amidst cheers.*)

(*Enter from* L. *amidst a burst of laughter from off* L. MARGARET *and* ARTHUR, *wearing paper hats.* ARTHUR *closes the door. Noises off fade.*)

ARTHUR. I think we were lucky to get out of there alive! Come and sit down for a bit. Do you know I haven't had a moment alone with you all the evening?

MARGARET. Well, you've been alone with me often enough before.

ARTHUR. Yes, I know. But it's a poor look-out if we can't be alone for a moment on our twenty-fifth anniversary.

MARGARET. Romantic old thing!

ARTHUR. Well, why not? Why should the young people have priority over romance?

MARGARET (*sitting*). Well, here I am.

ARTHUR. May I hold your hand? Or should we call a chaperone?

(*He takes her hand. A pause.*)

MARGARET. It's a nice party, isn't it?

ARTHUR. Yes. We seem to have done rather well for presents, don't we?

MARGARET. There are fifteen rose bowls!

ARTHUR. Really?

MARGARET. Yes.

ARTHUR. What ever shall we do with them all?

MARGARET. We *could* give them away to other people next Christmas.

ARTHUR. That's too dangerous. Three years of Christmases and birthdays and they'd be back to the people who gave them to us.

(*The men off* L. *start to sing "If You Were the Only Girl in the World." There is a pause.*)

ARTHUR. Do you mind if I tell you something that I probably haven't told you for years?

MARGARET. What's that, Arthur?

ARTHUR. I love you.

MARGARET (*moved*). Thank you. That was nice of you.

(*There is a gentle knock at the door.*)

ARTHUR.   Blast !

MARGARET.   Arthur !

ARTHUR.   I cannot be alone with you for one moment !   Always somebody in and out !   In and out—all the time!

MARGARET.   Hadn't you better say " Come in " ?

ARTHUR.   What ?   Oh, yes.   Come in !

(*Enter* MARY, *carrying a parcel.*)

MARY.   Am I interrupting anything ?

ARTHUR.   No, of course not, Mary !   I was just saying to Margaret that I wondered how you were getting on in there.   And the moment you tapped on the door I said " How nice!   That'll be Mary."

MARY.   I've been waiting for an opportunity to catch you two alone. I'd just like to offer you both my sincere congratulations.   Yes, you, too, Arthur !

MARGARET.   Thank you, darling.

ARTHUR (*with a smile*).   Thank you.

MARY.   Oh, I got this for you.   (*Hands the parcel to* MARGARET *who starts to open it.*)   Nothing very much.   Just a little token of my—may I say it ?—my very deep affection for you both.

ARTHUR.   That's kind of you, Mary.

MARGARET (*having opened parcel*).   Oh, how nice !   It's absolutely lovely, Mary !   Look, Arthur—a rose bowl.

ARTHUR (*taking it*).   Oh, *very* nice !   Just what we needed.   Thanks most awfully, Mary.   Shall I put it with the others, dear ?   (*As* MARGARET *gives him a glare.*)   Er—the other presents, I mean.   (*Puts rose bowl on table* U.L.C.)

(*Enter* NIGEL *and* HELEN, *talking.*)

NIGEL.   Ah, what's all this ?   Some secret drinking going on in here ?

ARTHUR.   Look—not a glass between us.

NIGEL.   Shame on you, then.   We've run out of whisky in there.

MARY.   Whisky !

ARTHUR.   Yes.   Don't you like it, Mary ?

MARY.   I prefer rum.

ARTHUR.   Well, well, well !

HELEN.   Have we any rum, Daddy ?

ARTHUR.   Oh, yes surely.   (*Looks in drinks cabinet.*)

MARGARET.   If not, there's a small bottle upstairs in my wardrobe.

HELEN.   Mother, you old toper !

MARGARET.   I keep it for medicinal purposes.

NIGEL.   That is the oldest excuse in the world and I don't believe it.

MARGARET.   I keep it for when I feel faint.

ARTHUR.   Which usually coincides with when she feels thirsty ! (*Producing a bottle of rum.*)   Here we are—bottled sunshine.   And un-opened, too.

MARGARET.   Isn't that the bottle we won in a raffle at the Jamieson's last Christmas, dear ?

ARTHUR. No, darling. That was the port substitute.

HELEN. Yes. Mrs. Jamieson made it herself from all sorts of obscure herbs.

ARTHUR. It tasted like senna pods.

NIGEL. It probably *was* senna pods.

ARTHUR. I never thought of that !

MARY (*taking bottle of rum*). May I return to the party with my loot ?

ARTHUR. I think I'd better come and keep an eye on you.

MARY (*at door*). I *am* over twenty-one !

ARTHUR. I never for a moment thought otherwise !

MARGARET. Now then, you two. Let's have a truce for to-night. (*Exit* MARY.) Shall I bring this, Arthur ? (*Picking up rose bowl from table.*)

ARTHUR. Yes, I suppose so. Perhaps we could make some rum-punch in it.

(ARTHUR *and* MARGARET *go out* L. *There is a pause.* NIGEL *moves* D.L.)

NIGEL. I shall be leaving first thing in the morning.

HELEN (*above sofa*). Oh, yes, I—I suppose you will . . .

NIGEL. I have to be up in Town by eight-thirty.

HELEN. Oh.

(*Pause.*)

NIGEL. What time have you got to be in Town in the morning?

HELEN. Not until nine-thirty.

NIGEL. Oh. (*Pause.*) I was going to offer you a lift in my car.

HELEN. That's kind of you, but it would be a little soon. My boss would have a heart attack if I rolled up an hour early instead of ten minutes late.

NIGEL (*quietly*). Why are we talking like strangers ?

HELEN. Are we ?

NIGEL. I think so.

HELEN. I hadn't noticed it.

NIGEL (*moving to her*). We're very nearly discussing the weather !

HELEN. I'm sorry.

(*Pause.*)

NIGEL. I—I suppose we couldn't meet for dinner once in a while ?

HELEN. Good heavens, yes! You're not a leper or something, y'know.

NIGEL. Aren't I ? You make me feel like one, sometimes.

HELEN. I'm sorry. I don't mean to.

(*Pause.*)

NIGEL. You've quite made up your mind, I suppose ? About us, I mean.

HELEN (*avoiding his eyes*). Yes, Nigel. I've—quite made up my mind.

(*He moves away. Turns. Comes back.*)

NIGEL. I'd like you to know something, Helen, before I go to-morrow.

HELEN. Oh. What's that?

NIGEL. I want you to know that when your father invited me here, I accepted because—well, because I knew that I still loved you. I hoped that perhaps you felt the same, and maybe we could get around our silly differences. I see now that I was hoping for the impossible.

HELEN. Oh, Nigel, you make it so difficult for me.

NIGEL. It isn't exactly easy for me, Helen. Believe me, it isn't. (*Pause.*) I've changed a lot during the time we *haven't* been engaged. I love you in a different way now, and I think it's a better way. I want to do things for you! I want to buy you a bunch of flowers occasionally, and take you to the theatre when we can afford it ; and I want to look after you and take care of you, and—and I want so much to have you around. Maybe it's the drink, but if I say any more I shall burst into tears. And that's something I haven't done since I was a very small boy, so let's go back to the party.

(*Moves to door* L.)

HELEN. Nigel ! Wait ! (*He stops.*)

NIGEL. Yes?

HELEN (*she crosses slowly to him*). Nigel . . .

NIGEL. What?

HELEN (*softly*). Nothing. Just—Nigel . . .

(*They look at each other for a moment and then suddenly they are kissing passionately.*)

(*Enter* MARGARET *from* L.)

MARGARET. Well, really !

(NIGEL *and* HELEN *separate.*)

NIGEL. There you are—your mother has seen us kissing ! You'll have to marry me, now !

MARGARET. What's all this about?

HELEN. Nigel and I have decided to get married, after all.

MARGARET. And so I should think !

HELEN. So your little plan succeeded, Mother. Now you and Dad can preen yourselves.

NIGEL. What plan is this, may I ask?

MARGARET. Oh, nothing, Nigel, only . . .

HELEN. She and father only brought you back here to try and bring us together again.

NIGEL. Well, of course, I knew that! And you've done a very good job of work. She's not getting away from me again, I can tell you.

MARGARET. I'm so pleased. May I kiss you, Nigel?

NIGEL. But of course !

(*She does so. Then turns to* HELEN.)

MARGARET. Now get married soon and have a baby.

HELEN. Mother !

D

MARGARET. Well, what's wrong with that? Everyone should have babies. What's the sense in marriage if you don't. Look at *me*—I've got three !

HELEN. And don't you ever regret it, Mother?

MARGARET. Regret it? No fear ! I wish I'd had a dozen !

(*Enter* ARTHUR.)

Arthur, Nigel and Helen are going to get married.

ARTHUR. Well, it's about time ! (*Pats* NIGEL *on the back and then kisses* HELEN.) I'm very pleased. You're doing the right thing, you know. I'm sure you'll be happy.

HELEN. We'll try hard to be, Daddy.

MARGARET. Well, I must go and tell the others.

ARTHUR (*following her to the door*). Now, wait a minute—that's my privilege! Now, really, Margaret, I insist——

(*They exit, talking* ad lib.)

NIGEL. And we will try, won't we, darling?

HELEN. Yes, Nigel. We'll try. (*Kisses him lightly.*) Come on.

(*They go off* L. *into a burst of cheering from the dining-room, which develops into " For He's a Jolly Good Fellow."*)

(*During this,* ALBERT *comes in, carrying a small package. He stands* C., *not quite knowing what to do.*)

(*Enter* ARTHUR *and* MARGARET, *talking.*)

ARTHUR. Oh, hello, Albert. So you've made it at last.

ALBERT (L. *of* MARGARET). Yes. Sorry I'm late. Good evening, Mrs. Purvis.

MARGARET. Hello, Albert.

ALBERT. May I wish you both a very happy anniversary.

MARGARET. Thank you, Albert.

ALBERT. I'm late because I had to go and see a man about a job.

ARTHUR (R. *of* MARGARET). Oh, yes. The Major was telling us about it. How did it go? Any luck?

ALBERT. Yes. I've got it.

ARTHUR. Good show ! That's the stuff !

MARGARET. Congratulations !

ALBERT. Thanks. I don't know how I did it. I was shaking at the knees the whole time.

ARTHUR. How soon do you start?

ALBERT. A week on Monday.

ARTHUR. Fine !

MARGARET. You'd better tell Freda about it. She's through there. I'm sure she'll be pleased.

ALBERT. Do you think so?

MARGARET. Of course.

ALBERT. Well, now that I've got this job I shall be able to save quite a lot, and before very long I shall be in a position to keep someone else as well as myself, if you know what I mean . . .

ARTHUR. I think I do, and it's a good idea.

ALBERT. I'm going to ask her again to-night, if I can pluck up courage. Would that be alright with you? I mean, if she happened to say yes.

MARGARET. We'd be very pleased.

ARTHUR. You have our blessing, my boy. And make sure she accepts you. Use force if necessary. She needs a firm hand.

ALBERT. Thanks very much. I feel better now that I know you're sort of backing me up ! (*Picks up his little parcel.*) Oh, and I brought this along for you. I hope you like it.

MARGARET. Thank you, Albert. That is sweet of you.

ARTHUR. You shouldn't have troubled, really. What is it?

MARGARET. Don't be impatient, dear.

ARTHUR. Well, I can tell by the shape that it isn't a rose bowl, thank heavens ! (*To* ALBERT.) We've hundreds of those !

MARGARET. Oh, it's lovely ! Really lovely ! Look, Arthur. (*She holds up a beautiful little alarm clock.*) Oh, that *is* nice. Albert. Come here and let me kiss you ! (*She does so.*)

ARTHUR (*moving* R.). It's inscribed, too. (*Reading.*) " To Mr. and Mrs. Arthur Purvis. Two of the happiest and the nicest people in the world." That's very kind of you, Albert. We shall treasure it. (*To* MARGARET.) And what are you weeping about?

MARGARET. Arthur, you know very well I always cry when people are kind to me. Thank you, Albert, very much.

(*Enter* FREDA.)

FREDA. Oh, so you've arrived at last!

ALBERT. Yes.

MARGARET. Freda, Albert's got the most wonderful news.

FREDA. Oh? What's he been up to now?

MARGARET. Tell her, Albert.

ALBERT. I got the job, that's all.

FREDA. You did? Oh, that's wonderful! Thank goodness someone finds you useful. When do you start?

ALBERT. Next week.

FREDA. I wonder how long you'll last. About five minutes if you're no better at it than you are at dancing !

MARGARET. Freda !

ALBERT. I know I don't dance very well.

FREDA. You don't dance at all !

ARTHUR. Albert may not have it in his feet, but he's got it in his head. Which is more than can be said for Peter Whatshisname, who is dead from the neck up.

FREDA. Daddy, don't talk like that !

ARTHUR (*aside to* ALBERT). Use force.

MARGARET. Look what Albert has given us, Freda.

FREDA. H'm. Jolly nice. Better than I expected. I thought you'd buy something hideous !

(ROGER *puts his head round the door* L.)

ROGER. Hey, Freda ! You're wanted for charades ! Hello, Albert.

FREDA. We've played charades already.

ROGER. Well, we're playing it again so come on !

FREDA. Alright, I won't be a minute.

ROGER. Hurry ! (*He disappears again.*)

MARGARET. We've saved some chicken for you, if you'd like it, Albert.

ALBERT. Oh, good. I am a bit peckish. I was too nervous to eat before I went for my interview.

MARGARET. Freda will see to it for you. Won't you, Freda ?

FREDA. Oh, well, I suppose you deserve it. Come on. (*She puts one arm around his shoulder and starts to take him off* L.)

ARTHUR. You have a good big meal, my boy. A man can do anything on a full stomach.

ALBERT. What ? Oh—oh, yes.

FREDA. Come on, Gorgeous !

(*They go.*)

MARGARET. I hope she marries him in the end. He's a nice boy.

ARTHUR (*sits* L. *of sofa*). I think they'll be alright. He's got that fighting look in his eye to-night. I shouldn't be surprised at anything that happened.

(*Enter from* L. MAJOR TODD, NIGEL *and* ROGER, *all carrying glasses and wearing paper hats.*)

TODD. Come on, you love birds ! Wakey-wakey ! Billin' and cooin' in a corner like that !

NIGEL. You ought to be ashamed of yourselves—deserting us like that.

ARTHUR. I don't seem to have had one moment alone with my wife the entire evening.

TODD. I should jolly well think not ! You're past all that sort of thing, y'know.

ROGER. We've given up charades in despair. We're lost without Freda.

MARGARET. And why have you all forsaken the womenfolk ?

TODD. My dear Madame, we decided en masse that we needed a few minutes away from charming femininity to prevent our heads from reeling.

MARGARET (*rising and crossing to door* L.). It looks as if your heads already are reeling—and not from femininity, either! I'd better go and see if they're alright. (*Exit* L.)

ARTHUR. I'll come with you, if you gentlemen will forgive me for not joining the Stag Assembly. (*To door* L.)

TODD. Traitor to your sex !

ARTHUR (*turning*). I haven't seen my wife the entire evening !

Todd. Carry on, sir ! (*He salutes.*) Fall out, the ossifers ! (*Exit* Arthur l.) Has anyone got an empty glass ?
All. Yes ! ! !
Todd. That's what I thought. Whisky all round !

(*Todd replenishes each glass in turn. Todd fills his own glass, drinks it, starts to fill again, but puts down the glass and keeps the bottle instead. He puts on the gramophone and plays a record of " Macnamara's Band." They all join in.*)

(*During this* Freda *and* Albert *enter* l., *talking.*)

Freda. But I don't want to be serious to-night, Albert !
Albert. But I simply must talk to you !

(*They react to the singing.*)

Freda. Oh! Come on, silly—let's see what the others are doing.

(*She drags him off* l. Todd *turns off the record, but they continue singing.*)

(*Enter* Mary.)

Mary. Hey ! (*No response.*) Hey ! ! ! (*They stop singing.*) Come on, oh strong and silent sex ! Your company is required within.
Todd. Very good, Madame. Gentlemen—follow me !

(*The men line up behind the* Major, *holding the waist of the man in front. They circle the room and then exit* l. *singing lustily.*)

(*Mary chuckles and crosses to drinks cabinet.*)

(*Todd reappears.*)

Todd. Excuse me—I left my bottle. (*He picks it up.*)
Mary. You're not drunk, are you ?
Todd. Good heavens, no ! (*And he isn't.*) Just trying to be the life and soul of the party, that's all. Not succeeding very well. I suppose ?
Mary. I think you're doing very well indeed. Keeping us all lively. Are you any good at cocktails ?
Todd. You bet your sweet life !
Mary. I mean making them not drinking them. I know you're good at that !
Todd. I was the King of the Cocktails when I was in Africa, y'know. Mixed some snorters in my time. Here, watch this. (*Starts to mix.*) There's a subtle art in this, y'know. The slightest drop too much and you can ruin the whole effect. I remember a concoction I made for a mess party once in Beirut. Used some primitive wines that a Wog had flogged to me after I'd sold him a couple of rubber tyres. Looked like sulphuric acid. The Colonel sampled the mixture and passed out for three days.
Mary (*examining the brew*). This won't explode or anything will it ?
Todd. Hard to say, Madame. Hard to say.
Mary. It won't make me sick, will it ?

TODD. Good lord, no ! Might put you out for a couple of days like the old Colonel, but it won't make you sick. I guarantee no after effects. There we are! Now a good shake! Just wait till you taste this. (*Pours two glassfuls.*) Well, here goes!

MARY. Cheers !

TODD. Marshall and Snelgrove's !

(*They drink.*)

MARY. H'm. (*Drinks again.*) Very nice. Congratulations. What held Albert up, to-night ? He was very late getting here.

TODD. Oh, yes. He had to see a man about a job first.

MARY. A new job ?

TODD. Yes. I think he'll get it alright. He can be quite clever behind a desk, y'know.

MARY. I'm so glad. I hope he gets it alright. He's a nice boy.

TODD. Yes, isn't he ? I'm very fond of the lad. I shall miss him when he goes.

MARY. When he goes ? Is the job abroad ?

TODD. Oh, no ! But I have a sort of a feeling that he'll be wanting to settle down on his own in a year or so. That's if the blighter can pluck up courage to speak to the girl as an equal and not be afraid of her. It'll—it'll be very lonely in the house when he does go. I shan't like that. Can't bear being alone, don't you know.

MARY. I should have thought you were very self-sufficient.

TODD (*suddenly quiet*). Would you really ? I expect I do give that impression, but—well, since I've been retired from the Army I've missed it all terribly. I was very happy in the Army. I miss the comradeship and the discipline and—let's face it, I miss the people. Nobody here talks my language. I'm out of date. Even the Army's run differently, now. People think I'm a bore. (*Pause.*) Yes, I shall miss the boy.

MARY. What about your housekeeper ?

TODD (*brightly again*). She's leaving me next month. Retiring, believe it or not. Don't know how she can manage it on what I pay her ! Have to find a new one.

MARY. Yes, you will.

(*Pause.*)

TODD. I suppose—I suppose—*you* wouldn't—er—well . . .

MARY. I'd be no good as a housekeeper, I'm afraid.

TODD. No, no ! I meant—permanently. As my wife.

MARY. You're—asking me to marry you ?

TODD. If you can put up with me. We get along alright. You seem to understand me. Might work out alright. (*Pause.*) Will you ?

MARY (*casually*). Do you know, I think I will ! Thank you, George. You're probably my Ideal Man.

TODD. Your Ideal Man ?

MARY. Yes. I thought he'd lost his way and wasn't coming !

TODD. Then—then that's settled ?

MARY.   It's alright with me.
TODD.   Well, then—er—I . . .
MARY.   What's the matter?
TODD.   Well, it's customary, to—er—seal the bargain with a kiss, isn't it?
MARY (*retreating*).   Don't be foolish, George!   We're far too old for that!
TODD (*advancing*).   Come on !   It's customary !
MARY.   No, George.   Don't be silly.   We'd better go back in there, I think !
TODD (*following her off* L.).   It's customary . . .

(*A record of the Samba "It's Later Than You Think" is played in the next room, amidst laughs.   This continues softly behind the* ROGER-ARTHUR *scene.*)

(*After a moment,* ROGER *comes in.   He pours out a drink and sits on sofa.*)

(*A pause.   Enter* ARTHUR, *lighting his pipe.*)

ARTHUR.   Oh, so that's where you've got to.
ROGER.   Hello, Dad.   I was just taking five minutes out to get my breath back !
ARTHUR.   It is a bit over-powering in there, isn't it?

(ARTHUR *pours.*)

ROGER.   Well—happy anniversary !
ARTHUR.   Thank you.   (*They drink.*)   That's what I want it to be, you know.
ROGER.   What?
ARTHUR.   A happy anniversary.
ROGER.   And isn't it?
ARTHUR.   No.   Not completely.
ROGER.   Why not?
ARTHUR.   I suppose because everything is not in harmony.   Being a father is a very strange experience, you know.   Can be very satisfactory, sitting back and seeing your children forging ahead, successful, happy.   But if one of them is unhappy, I know about it instinctively.   And that makes *me* unhappy, too.   And frustrated, when I don't know what the trouble is and I can't help.
ROGER.   *Is* one of your children unhappy?
ARTHUR.   Yes, Roger.   I think so.   *Very* unhappy.

(*Pause.*)

ROGER (*rising*).   Hadn't we better go back and join the others?
ARTHUR.   No hurry.   They've plenty of food and drink.   They don't need us for a few minutes.   And besides you've left some of your whisky.   Here.   (*He holds out* ROGER'S *glass and* ROGER, *now at the door* L., *turns.   A pause, then he crosses back and takes the glass.*)

ROGER. Thanks.

ARTHUR (*gently*). Sit down, Roger.

(ROGER *sits. A long pause.* ARTHUR *lights his pipe.*)

Roger, you've been so very far away from us all these last few months. Your mother and I—we want you back again. Won't you let me help ?

ROGER (*after a pause*). I don't know what you're talking about.

ARTHUR. Yes, you do. Is it because of Sheila ?

(*A long pause.*)

ROGER. No.

ARTHUR. Is it ?

ROGER. Of course not. Dad.

ARTHUR. I may be a father, Roger, but I'm also a human being, you know. (*After a suitable pause.*) Do you want to talk about it ?

(*Pause—*ROGER *moves* L.)

ROGER. You didn't know this, but when I met Sheila she had just been very unhappy. Her husband had treated her badly and their marriage had gone on the rocks. She had divorced him, and so she was unhappy and miserable, and I came along, and—well, I suppose she found that I was something to—to cling on to. Something to help take away the pain and make her think that life was perhaps really worth living in spite of what had happened to her. And I suppose because of that she imagined she was in love with me.

ARTHUR. But are you so sure that what you felt for her wasn't just pity and a very deep affection ? Affection is very different from love, you know, and pity is something of which you should beware.

ROGER. I don't know. I *was* sorry for her at first ; that was only natural. But I soon fell really in love. I'm sure of that, now. For a time everything was wonderful. (*Pause.*) She told me—that she was grateful for what I'd done for her and been to her. She said—she said I'd given her very real happiness, and that she'd always cherish the times we'd had together, but that now the old wound had healed up she realised that she never had been in love with me, not properly.

(*Long pause.* ARTHUR *moves up* C. *and then comes down.*)

ARTHUR. Now, I'm going to tell *you* something. Something about me. I remember when I was about your age—I met a young lady. She was older than I was, nearly ten years older, and she was very lovely. I admired her for a long time. I used to go out of my way to pass her in the street, but I never dared to say a word to her. Then one day I *did* pluck up courage, and I spoke. I said " Good morning! " And she smiled and said good morning back. We went on like that for another month, and then she came out for a walk with me. I fell in love with her almost at once. I couldn't tell you why. But it was love. The way she walked, the way she smiled, and things she said—everything about her was what I suppose every young man dreams about. I told her that I loved her, and

she said that she loved me, too. We became engaged, we even planned
the date of the marriage. Then one day she came to me and said it was all
no good. She'd met another man. She was sorry, but of course we could
still be friends. I was brokenhearted. (*Pause.*) But this is the point ;
six months after that, I met your mother. And that made me realise that
I never had been really in love before. It was only infatuation. And that
is not very different from love—not at the time, you know.

(There is a long pause.)

ROGER. Thanks, Dad. I'm—I'm glad you told me that.

ARTHUR (*sits on sofa beside* ROGER). I know it hurts, Roger, but give
yourself time, I assure you, it will be alright, one day.

(Another pause.)

Well, we'd better go back in there before they miss us.

ROGER. Yes, alright. (*At door* L.) Oh, and Dad——

ARTHUR. Yes ?

ROGER. You won't say anything about this to anyone, will you ?

ARTHUR. No, I won't. Not even to your mother. This will be our
little secret.

ROGER. Thanks, Dad.

(ROGER *goes out* L. *as* MARGARET *comes in.*)

MARGARET. There's an atmosphere in here ! What were you two
talking about ?

ARTHUR (*airily*). Oh—just man-to-man stuff—you know.

MARGARET. You weren't telling him the facts of life, were you ?

ARTHUR. Well, not the usual ones.

(*She looks at him, smiles and perches on the arm of the sofa next to him.*)

MARGARET. I see. So he came to father, after all ?

ARTHUR. Yes. Yes, he came to father.

MARGARET. Everything all right ?

ARTHUR. I think so.

MARGARET (*as he looks up at her and smiles*). Hey . . .

ARTHUR. What ?

MARGARET. There's a tear in your eye.

ARTHUR. Is there ? I'm just a silly, sentimental old fool !

MARGARET. They're playing games again in the other room.

ARTHUR. Oh, good. Now perhaps we can have a few quiet moments
together. (*Sits beside him.*)

(*Enter* FREDA *in a rush, followed by* ALBERT. FREDA *to divan* D.L.)

FREDA (*not noticing Ma and Pa who are over* R.). I refuse to listen to
another word!

ALBERT (*following her*). Well, you're going to listen to me whether
you like it or not !

FREDA. What ?

ALBERT. I said you're going to listen to me whether you like it or not. And I mean it ! It's my turn now and——

FREDA. But you can't !

ALBERT. And don't interrupt me while I'm talking ! I've stood all I will stand from you, and now I'm going to give the orders.

FREDA. Albert, I will not——

(*She starts to go but he stops her.*)

ALBERT. And you're staying right here to listen to what I have to say. Now sit down.

FREDA. I will not !

ALBERT. Sit down!!! (*He pushes her on to the divan* D.L.) You've laughed at me for long enough, but now you're going to see me as I really am. I may come from Yorkshire but that doesn't stop me having feelings the same as anybody else. And you've hurt my feelings in every possible way ever since I first met you. I may not be able to dance like Victor Sylvester, or play tennis like your precious Peter Goodacre, but I love you more than Peter Goodacre could ever love anybody ! And I've made up my mind that it's time I stopped being pushed around by you or anybody else. And if any of your glamour-boy beaux start flirting with you again while I'm around I shall punch them on the nose! I'm as good-looking as anybody else ! I can work for you and make you happy better than anyone—and I've got as much sex-appeal as Rudolph Valentino!!!

FREDA. You're drunk !

ALBERT. I've never been more sober in my life ! I've said all, now, Freda. The time is ripe for action. I'm going to kiss thee, lass.

FREDA. Oh, no, you're not !

ALBERT. Oh, yes, I am !

(*She tries to get out but he catches her and plants a big kiss on her mouth.*)

ALBERT. There !

FREDA. Oh, Albert ! (*She kisses him heartily.*)

ALBERT (*taken aback*). But I thought——

FREDA. Why ever didn't you talk to me like that before ? I didn't know you had it in you!

ALBERT. Then—you don't mind ?

FREDA. Mind ? Kiss me again !

(*He does so.*)

(*Suspiciously.*) Have you been practising ?

ALBERT. No, but I've been watching Michael Wilding like you told me to! (*Pause.*) Then—a bit later on, will you wed me, lass ?

FREDA (*imitating his accent*). Aye, I'll wed thee, lad !

ALBERT. Say no more, Freda Purvis—you're mine !

(*He picks her up in a fireman's lift and carries her off* L.)

ARTHUR (*to drinks table*). See what a good helping of roast chicken can do for a man ! I'm going to have a little drink. How about you?

MARGARET.   Just a very small one, dear.

(*He pours in silence, then returns and sits* L. *of her.*)

ARTHUR.   Here.

MARGARET.   Thanks.

ARTHUR.   Let's be selfish, shall we, and keep this toast to ourselves? To—us.

MARGARET.   To us . . .

(*They drink.*)

(ARTHUR *rises, puts his drink on table* L. *of sofa, and puts off lights at door, leaving them only a dim light from the standard lamp and the light from the fire.*)

MARGARET.   What's all that for?

ARTHUR.   Why not? I feel romantic. Besides, it doesn't show up the wrinkles so much. (*He sits beside her on the sofa again.   Pause.*) Happy?

MARGARET.   Very happy. (*Pause.*) So it's a clear blue sky and plain sailing from now on?

ARTHUR.   Well, I wouldn't go so far as to say that exactly. Life never is plain sailing, is it? You and I know that.

(*Pause.*)

MARGARET.   I don't suppose they'll be needing us for very much longer, will they? I shall hate to think they don't rely on us for everything any more.

ARTHUR.   But we've done our share, my dear.   We'd have failed miserably as parents if they never stopped needing us.   We've seen them through the tenderest years, and now it's up to them.   And don't worry. They're going to be alright.

(*A record off* L. *starts to play " Always."   A pause.*)

MARGARET.   Arthur . . .

ARTHUR.   Yes?

MARGARET.   Do you ever feel you'd like to be young again?

ARTHUR.   Yes. I suppose I do, sometimes.

MARGARET.   Would you alter anything? I mean, do anything differently from the way you have done?

ARTHUR.   Only some of the little things.   The big things wouldn't change.   I'd want those to be the same. And there are a lot of things I'd enjoy more if I'd known what was going to happen afterwards.

MARGARET.   What, for instance?

ARTHUR.   Well—courting you, for one! If I'd known you were going to accept me, I wouldn't have gone through such agony thinking you might turn me down !

MARGARET.   Ah, but the uncertainty made you appreciate me more.

(*They laugh quietly.*)

MARGARET. But don't you find that there were lots of wonderful moments that happened to us when we were young that you'd like to live all over again ?

ARTHUR. Oh, but I do live them over again, often—in my mind. And that makes me feel young again.

MARGARET. Does it ?

ARTHUR. Yes. It does. Just sitting here with you, now—forgetting this twenty-fifth anniversary for a moment—I feel very young indeed.

MARGARET. H'm. So do I . . . I don't suppose you ever feel differently, do you ? I mean, however old you get, you still feel the same—inside.

ARTHUR. I'll tell you on my hundredth birthday !

MARGARET. Come to think of it, you look *very* young at the moment.

ARTHUR. That's just the dim light. I said it flattered me.

(*Long pause.*)

MARGARET (*very quietly*). I don't want this moment to stop—ever. I feel closer to you now, than I've felt in the whole of my life. . . .

(*Door* L. *bursts open, throwing a shaft of bright light across the stage.* HELEN, FREDA *and* ROGER *are in the doorway. At the same time the record stops playing.*)

THE CHILDREN. Come on, you two! What are you up to in there ? Come in and join us! The party's breaking up! etc.

(*They withdraw, shutting the door.*)

(MARGARET *and* ARTHUR *look at each other and smile.*)

ARTHUR. Our family seem to want us.

MARGARET. Brings you back to earth, doesn't it ?

ARTHUR. Yes. I feel as old as Methuselah again now !

MARGARET. We'd better go and join them.

ARTHUR. Yes, I suppose we had.

(*They get up. He moves* L.C.)

MARGARET. Arthur. . . .

ARTHUR (*turns*). Yes, my dear ?

MARGARET. I—I wouldn't *really* want to be young again, would you?

ARTHUR (*pauses. He smiles. Shakes his head*). No. No, I don't think I would. Not really.

(*Door flung open again.*)

THE CHILDREN (*off* L.). Come on, you two! etc.

(*Singing starts off stage—" Auld Lang Syne."*)

ARTHUR (*gently*). Come along, my darling . . .

(*She takes his proffered arm.*)

ARTHUR.   All's well?

MARGARET.   Yes, Arthur. All's well . . .

(He kisses the top of her head, and they move off towards the door L. into the shaft of bright light. " Auld Lang Syne " grows louder as they reach the door and go through. The singing continues.)

THE CURTAIN SLOWLY FALLS.

PROPERTIES.

Act I.

Box of matches ('Phone table). Evening paper (Sofa). Mattress (Off L.). 2 sheets (off L.). 2 blankets (off L.). 2 pillowslips (off L.). 2 pillows (off L.). Freda's hat (table). Photo of Freda (mantelpiece). Breakable jug (mantelpiece). Cup of tea and saucer (off L. for MARY). Telephone directory ('Phone table). Telephone ('Phone table). Bowl of fruit (table). Apple (bowl of fruit. For FREDA).

Act II.

Scene 1 : Workbasket with needle and thread, etc. (sofa). Helen's handbag (divan). Collar stud (off L.). Bottle of rum, bottle of whisky, soda syphon, jug of water, glasses, other bottles for dressing (drinks table). Orchid in cellophane (off L. for FREDA). Small bunch of violets (off L. for ALBERT).

Scene 2 : Poker (fireplace). 2 coffee cups and saucers (off L. for HELEN). Sugar basin, milk jug, pot of coffee, 2 plates of ham and potato salad (off L. for HELEN).

Act III.

Paper hats for all (off L.). Rose bowl wrapped in tissue paper (off L. for MARY). Small alarm clock wrapped in brown paper (off L. for ALBERT).

PERSONAL PROPS.

Pipe (ARTHUR). Tobacco pouch (ARTHUR). Spare box of matches (ARTHUR). Pencil (MARGARET). Job list (MARGARET). Spectacles (ALBERT).

MUSIC.

" Always " (before each Act). " It's a Small World " (or other sentimental tune). Old-fashioned waltz tune. " Claire de Lune "—Andre Kostelanetz recording. "Macnamara's Band." "Later Than You Think "—Samba.

PRINTED IN GREAT BRITAIN BY LOWE AND BRYDONE (PRINTERS) LIMITED, LONDON, N.W.10

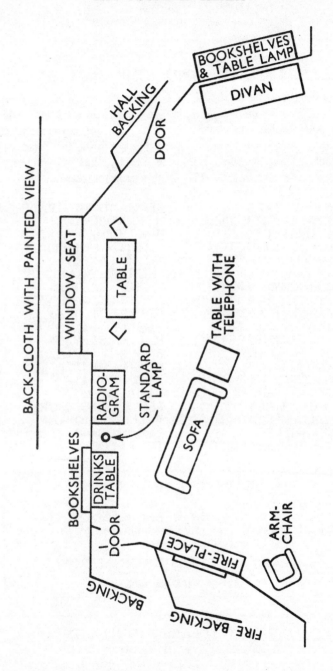